Rev John Todd

The Student's Manual

Anatiposi

Rev John Todd

The Student's Manual

Reprint of the original.

1st Edition 2023 | ISBN: 978-3-38210-591-4

Anatiposi Verlag is an imprint of Outlook Verlagsgesellschaft mbH.

Verlag (Publisher): Outlook Verlag GmbH, Zeilweg 44, 60439 Frankfurt, Deutschland
Vertretungsberechtigt (Authorized to represent): E. Roepke, Zeilweg 44, 60439 Frankfurt, Deutschland
Druck (Print): Books on Demand GmbH, In de Tarpen 42, 22848 Norderstedt, Deutschland

PREFACE TO THE AUTHOR'S EDITION.

During the time since this volume was first issued there has been never less than one edition yearly published in this country. In the Old World I know not how many editions, nor in how many languages it has been printed, sometimes with, and sometimes without, the author's name; sometimes as an imposing, beautiful volume, and sometimes dwarfed down to the dimensions of a good-sized tract. As nearly as I can learn, not less than one hundred thousand copies have been sold across the waters.

But the most gratifying circumstance connected with this book is, that, from all parts of the world, I constantly receive letters from those whom I never expect to see in this world, who, of their own accord, write to the author in terms of gratitude so warm that I am almost afraid to read them.

I have added notes to this new edition, gathered, with more labor than would at first appear, from different sources, which, I hope, will be useful to the reader. They came from so many different quarters that I could not, in all cases, give credit to the pages from which I have drawn them.

When I wrote this volume, I felt a deep interest in students, because I had just passed through their trials and temptations; and now, having children whose feet are just placed upon "the sandy hill of learning," I feel an interest no less deep, even if it seem more selfish.

Most sincerely do I return my thanks to the unknown friends who have so often cheered me with words of approbation and testimonials of usefulness, and most truly do I thank my heavenly Father for having been pleased to own an instrument so unworthy, as a benefactor to minds created in His image.

Pittsfield, Jan. 2, 1854

THE

STUDENT'S MANUAL;

DESIGNED,

BY SPECIFIC DIRECTIONS,

TO AID IN

FORMING AND STRENGTHENING THE INTELLECTUAL AND MORAL CHARACTER AND HABITS

OF

THE STUDENT.

BY REV. JOHN TODD, D. D.,

PASTOR OF THE FIRST CONGREGATIONAL CHURCH, PITTSFIELD, MASS.; AUTHOR OF GREAT CITIES, LECTURES TO CHILDREN, YOUNG MAN, ETC.

NEW REVISED EDITION;

TO WHICH ARE ADDED

NOTES BY THE AUTHOR

NORTHAMPTON:
BRIDGMAN AND CHILDS
PHILADELPHIA: E. H. BUTLER & CO.
ST. LOUIS: J. W. McINTYRE.
1871.

PREFACE

Hardly any class of men are so difficult to be reached as students, and the undertaking is hazardous; but no class of men are so open to conviction, so alive to manly principle, so susceptible of good impressions, when the effort to aid them is judicious and worthy of their attention. Whether the present attempt is a happy one, the author is not presumptuous enough to say. The highest wish of his heart would be to have its reception and success commensurate with his esteem and love for those for whose welfare he feels the strongest interest, and for whose benefit he has written.

Scarcely any hour can be more anxious to the parent than that in which he takes leave of his child, after having carried him away from home to some public Institution for the purpose of study. He knows the temptations which will beset his child, without knowing any way by which to shield him. I have tried to make this book such a friend as he will wish to leave with his son, to aid him in forming his character.

The youth who goes from home, and takes his place among his fellows at a strange place, for the purpose of study, feels that it is all new to him: he is inexperienced, and knows not how to form the character which he intends to possess. He has no friend who has been over the ground, and knows it all, to whom he can go for advice, for encouragement, and aid. For such I have endeavored to write this book.

In the different professions, there are multitudes who feel that they are not students, have not the habits, the character of students; and yet they know not where the difficulty is, or what to do. If such do not find hints in this volume which will aid and encourage them, I shall have deep regrets, and no small mortification.

A very few paragraphs in this work will be found in an ephemeral Address which the Author delivered before one of our colleges a short time since.

Some may wonder at the taste which has now and then interspersed a quotation in Latin. Those who are familiar with the taste of students, know how much they admire a beautiful thought in beautiful language, and how much more highly a nut is relished, if they have to crack it.

Why is not the work more decidedly religious? Because the design of it is to aid in forming the *whole* character of the student. The two last chapters, it is hoped, will not be found deficient in this respect.

May He, without whose blessing every attempt at being useful is lost, own it, and make it the instrument of much good to those who are the hope of their friends and the hope of their country.

CONTENTS

CHAPTER I

OBJECT OF STUDY. INTRODUCTORY.

CHAPTER II

HABITS.

CHAPTER III.

STUDY.

CHAPTER IV.

READING.

CHAPTER V.

TIME.

CHAPTER VI.

CONVERSATION.

CHAPTER VII.

POLITENESS AND SUBORDINATION.

CHAPTER VIII.

EXERCISE. DIET. ECONOMY.

CHAPTER IX.

DISCIPLINE OF THE HEART.

CHAPTER X.

THE OBJECT OF LIFE.

THE

STUDENT'S MANUAL.

CHAPTER I.

OBJECT OF STUDY. INTRODUCTORY.

The human mind is the brightest display of the power and skill of the Infinite Mind with which we are acquainted. It is created and placed in this world to be educated for a higher state of existence. Here its faculties begin to unfold, and those mighty energies, which are to bear it forward to unending ages, begin to discover themselves. The *object* of training such a mind should be, to enable the soul to fulfil her duties well here, and to stand on high vantage-ground, when she leaves this cradle of her being, for an eternal existence beyond the grave.

There is now and then a youth, who, like Ferguson,[1] can tend sheep in the field, and there accurately mark the position of the stars, with a thread and beads, and with his knife construct a watch from wood; but such instances are rare. Most need encouragement to sustain, instruction to aid, and directions to guide them.

[1] Note A.

Few, probably, ever accomplish any thing like as much as they expected or ought; and I have thought that one reason is, that students waste a vast amount of time in acquiring that experience which they need. As I look back upon the days when I was a "student," I can see that here I went wrong, and there I mistook; here I missed a golden opportunity, and there I acquired a wrong habit, or received a wrong bias; and as I sometimes walk past a college, as it is lighted up for evening-study, I pause, and sigh, that I cannot go back and begin life again, carrying with me my present experience. I think, too, I can see, that if there had been such a book as I am now attempting to write fo students, put into my hands at an early period, it would have been of incalculable advantage to me. I have strong hopes of saying what will be useful, inasmuch as I shall principally draw from my own experience and from the remembrance of my own wants.

The reader will please to bear in mind, that the only object I have in view, is to be useful to him—to throw out such hints and cautions, and to give such specific directions, as will aid him to become all that the fond hopes of his friends anticipate, and all that his own heart ought to desire.

I would here say to the student, that the character which he now forms and sustains, will cling to him through life. Young men always receive impressions concerning each other which nothing can ever efface.

The very nicknames which are given at this period, and which are generally indicative of some peculiar trait of character, will never be forgotten. His moral and intellectual character, while young, is that by which his class-mates, especially, will invariably measure him through life. Is he unamiable now, or indolent now, or vicious now? Depend upon it, his character is stamped, and no subsequent years of good-nature, or of application, or of moral worth, can ever do away the impressions which he is now making. Ask any educated man about the character of his fellow, and you will notice, that he at once goes back to his College-life, and dates and judges from that period. Thus, every anecdote, every ludicrous circumstance, whether it was a mistake in reciting, or in judgment, or in moral conduct, will be repeated over the land, and his frailties will be known as widely as his class is scattered.

No mistake can be more decided than that of supposing that you are now retired from the world, have no character to maintain, and no responsibility resting upon you. It is far otherwise. And it is peculiarly trying, that, during the very period when the character is forming, it is viewed by all around you as if it were already and unalterably formed, and judged of accordingly. He, who now sits by your side in the recitation-room, has every trait of your character exposed to his view; and he will remember every trait, and he will mark you through life, at the place where you now stand. Never, in fact, does so great a responsibility rest upon you, as while a student; because you are now forming your character and habits, and setting your standard; and because, also, your contemporaries will seldom, if ever, alter their judgment concerning you. If you are stupid and inaccurate during this period, though you should hereafter write dictionaries, and edit classics, and dream in foreign languages, I very much doubt whether your friend, now at your elbow, would ever give you credit for any thing higher than dullness.

Doubtless multitudes are now in the process of education, who *will* never reach any tolerable standard of excellence. Probably some never could; but in most cases they might. The exceptions are few; and probably most, who read these pages, do feel a desire, more or less strong, of fitting themselves for respectability and usefulness. They are, however, ignorant of the way; they are surrounded by temptations and dangers; they soon forget the encouragements, and thus oscillate between hope and fear, resolution and discouragement. It is for such that I write. And such I earnestly entreat not to lay aside this little book till they have read it, weighed it, and, f they please, called the writer whatever hard names occur to them. My pen will probably sometimes seem dull; but if I should, I hope I may apologize for it as the knight did for his slow-pacing horse :—" Hee is a rite gude creetur, and travels all the ground over most faithfully."

" When I turned in at night, the sea was smooth and bright as a mirror ; the vast firmament seemed to descend below us ; the ship appeared to be suspended in the centre of an immense sphere, and, if I may say so, one felt, in awe and silence, the majesty of space. The sails hung idly by the mast, and the officers' tread along the deck was the only sound heard. So I left them.

"About midnight, I was awakened by a heavy swing of my cot, succeeded by a sudden dash to the other side: the water was pouring into our room, and I could hear its rush across the upper decks, where all was noise and rapid motion. I hurried on my clothes, and ran up: the gun-deck was clear; hammocks had already been lashed up and stowed; it was lighted up, and showed it flooded in its whole extent. I ascended to the next: the rain came down in torrents, but I did not feel it, so deeply absorbing was the scene. I wish I could describe it. The sky was in a constant blaze; the sea was not high, but broken, confused and foaming, and taking from the lightning an unnatural hue. Above me were the yards covered with human beings, thrown by each flash into strong outline, struggling hard to secure the canvass and to maintain their precarious footing. The ship rolled tremendously. And now add the wild uproar of the elements, 'the noise of many waters,' the deep and constant roar of the winds, the cries of the men aloft, the heavy and rapid tread of those below, the reiterated commands of officers, and, rising above all this, the firm and composed orders of the trumpet, and then add to this the heavy-rolling thunder, at times drowning all these sounds. The first lieutenant had the deck: he had sprung to it at the first alarm, and, seizing the trumpet, had called Black, his favorite helmsman. The ship was soon under snug sail, and now dashed onward at a furious rate, giving to the gale a yet wilder character.

"All at once a rocky island seemed to start up from the water; but the next broad flash showed a good offing, and we were safe; when suddenly came a loud shout from the forecastle—'A sail close on the larboard bow, sir.' I trembled then—not for ourselves, for we should have gone over them, and have scarcely felt the shock—but for the poor wretches whom it would have been impossible to save. The helm was put hard down: we shot by, and I again breathed freely, when some one bade me look up to our spars. I did so, and found every upper yard-arm and mast tipped with lightning. Each blaze was twice as large as that of a candle; and thus we flew on, with the elements of destruction playing above our heads."

Can any one read this beautiful description of one

of our own proud ships in a storm, and fail to reflect, that *discipline* is the life and salvation of such a ship in such a storm? But I have copied it for a different purpose; and that is, to call the attention of the reader a single moment to the "helmsman Black." Can there be a doubt but the sailor who could take the helm in these circumstances, and hold the ship firmly on her course amid the storm, shunning rocks, and just shooting by smaller vessels, must have courage, presence of mind, and great promptness of character? Or can there be a doubt, but, if he had been properly *educated* when young, he might have stood in the lieutenant's place, and held the trumpet, or even commanded the ship? It is my earnest wish to aid such as have capacity, in seizing the present moment, and, while they have the opportunity, in so laying their plans, and in so forming their habits, as to make the most of all their endowments. There are, doubtless, some who will read these pages without benefit. May I suggest a possible reason? "A mole, having consulted many oculists for the benefit of his sight, was at last provided with a good pair of spectacles; but, upon his endeavoring to make use of them, his mother told him, that, though they might help the eye of a *man*, they could be of no use to a *mole*."

You may converse with any man, however distinguished for attainments or habits of application, or power of using what he knows, and he will sigh over the remembrances of the past, and tell you, that there have been many fragments of time which he has wasted, and many opportunities which he has lost forever. If he had only seized upon the fleeting advantages, and gathered up the fragments of time, he might have pushed his researches out into new fields, and, like the immortal Bacon, have amassed vast stores of knowledge. The mighty minds which have gone before us, have left treasures for our inheritance, and the choicest gold is to be had for the digging. How great the dissimilarity between a naked Indian, dancing with joy over a new feather for his head-dress, and such a mind as that of Newton or of Boyle! And what makes the difference? There is mind enough in the savage; he can almost outdo the instincts of the prey which he hunts; but his soul is like the marble pillar. There is a beautiful statue in it, but the hand of the sculptor has never laid the chisel upon it. That mind of the savage has never been disciplined by study; and it, therefore, in the comparison, appears like the rough bison of the forest, distinguished only for strength and ferocity

I am not now to discuss the question whether the souls of men are naturally equal. If they are, it is certain that, though the fact were proved, it would be of little practical use, since the organization of bodies is so different, that no training can make them alike. But this, I think, may safely be affirmed, that every one has naturally the power of excelling in some one thing. You may not excel in mathematics, or as a writer, or a speaker; but I honestly believe that every one of my readers is capable of excelling in some department, and will surely do so, if faithful to himself.

There was once a boy[1] put under the care of the Jesuits, who was noted for nothing but his stupidity. These teachers tried him abundantly, and could make nothing of him. How little did they think that the honor of being his instructers was to raise their order in view of the world! At length, one of the fathers tried him in geometry, which so suited his genius, that he became one of the first mathematicians of his age. Marcus, the son of Cicero, was sent to Athens, and had all the first masters that could be procured; and he made a perfect —— blockhead. And yet I feel confident, that, had the right place been found for him, he would have been more than respectable in it. *Non omnes omnia possumus.*

I once saw a little boy, on a public occasion, while thousands were gazing at him with unaffected astonishment, climb the lightning-rod on the lofty spire of a meeting-house. The wind blew high, and the rod shook and trembled; but up he went, till he had reached the vane, 195 feet high. All, every moment, expected to see him fall. But what was our amaze-

[1] Note B.

ment to see him mount the vane, and place his little feet upon it, throwing his arms aloft in the air, and turning round, as the wind turned his shaking foot-hold! He stood there till weary, and came down at his leisure. Here was a mind capable, I doubt not, of high enterprise. And yet he has never been heard of since. And why not? Either his mind has not been cultivated, or else his genius has been bent out of its proper channel. I will just add, that the poor boy was fined for setting so dangerous an example before the boys who saw him; but I could not help wishing that, while they sought to restrain him from such physical daring, they had been as careful to direct his fearless genius in a proper channel.

I perceive I have used a dangerous word, though of great antiquity. The word is *genius*. Many train themselves into habits of eccentricity and oddity, and suppose these inseparable from genius. There are some men who think nothing so characteristic of genius, as to do common things in an uncommon way—like Hudibras, to *tell the clock by algebra*, or like the lady in Dr. Young's Satires, "to drink tea by stratagem." Dean Swift, in his celebrated Travels, found whole nations of these geniuses, and tells us that he observed a tailor, with a customer before him, whose measure for a coat he was taking with a quadrant! Never set up any pretensions for a genius nor lay claim to the character. But few such are born into the world; and of those few, though envied greatly, and imitated as greatly, but very few, indeed, leave the world wiser or better than they found it. The object of hard study is not to draw out geniuses, but to take minds such as are formed in a common mould, and fit them for active and decisive usefulness. Nothing is so much coveted by a young man as the reputation of being a genius; and many seem to feel that the want of patience for laborious application and deep research, is such a mark of genius as cannot be mistaken: while a real genius, like Sir Isaac Newton, with great modesty says, that the great and only difference between his mind and the minds of others, consisted solely in his having more patience. You may have a good mind, a sound judgment, or a vivid imagination, or a wide reach of thought and of views; but, believe me, you probably are not a genius, and can never become distinguished without severe application. Hence all that you ever have, must be the result of labor—hard, untiring labor. You have friends to cheer you on; you have books and teachers to aid you, and multitudes of helps. But, after all, disciplining and educating your mind must be *your own* work. No one can do this but yourself. And nothing in this world is of any worth, which has not labor and toil as its price. The zephyrs of summer can but seldom breathe around you. "I foresee, distinctly, that you will have to double Cape Horn in the winter-season, and to grapple with the gigantic spirit of the storm which guards the cape; and I foresee, as distinctly, that it will depend entirely on your own skill and energy, whether you survive the fearful encounter, and live to make a port in the mild latitudes of the Pacific." *

Johnson asserts, that, if any one would be master of the English language, he must give his days and nights to the reading of Addison. It is still more emphatically true, that, if any one would be distinguished, he *must* labor for it. There is no real excellence without patient study. Those who have now and then risen upon the world, without education, and without study, have shed but a doubtful light, and that but for a moment. Many a youth has kindled at the story of TOMASO ANELLO, who was one day hawking fish through the streets of Naples, and the next was master of armies and fleets, and made his will the rule for an empire. The army obeyed him; the banditti quailed before him; and never was a man more absolute in his will. But his short reign of nine days was marked with great folly, cruelty, and despotism; and such examples must ever stand before the world as among the possible things; but also among the improbable, and still more undesirable.

Set it down as a fact, to which there are no exceptions, that we must labor for all that we have, and

* Wirt.

that nothing is worth possessing or offering to others, which cost us nothing. Gilbert Wakefield tells us, that he wrote his own Memoirs (a large octavo) in six or eight days. It cost him nothing; and, what is very natural, it is worth nothing. You might yawn scores of such books into existence; but who would be the wiser or the better? We all like gold, but dread the digging. The cat loves the fish, but will not wade to catch them;—*amat pisces, sed non vult tingere plantas.*

Those islands which so beautifully adorn the Pacific, and which, but for sin, would seem so many Edens, were reared up from the bed of the ocean by the little coral-insect, which deposits one grain of sand at a time, till the whole of those piles are reared up. Just so with human exertions. The greatest results of the mind are produced by small, but continued efforts. I have frequently thought of the motto of one of the most distinguished scholars in this country, as peculiarly appropriate. As near as I remember, it is the picture of a mountain, with a man at its base, with his hat and coat lying beside him, and a pickaxe in his hand; and as he digs, stroke by stroke, his patient look corresponds with his words,—*Peu et peu*—"Little by little."

The first, and great object of education is, to discipline the mind. It is naturally, like the colt, wild and ungoverned. Let any man, who has not subdued his mind, more or less, by close thought, sit down and take hold of a subject, and try to "think it out." The result will be, that he cannot hold his thoughts upon the point. They fly off—they wander away. He brings them back, and determines now to hold his attention there; when, at once, ere he knows how, he again finds himself away. The process is repeated, till he gives it up in discouragement, or else goes to sleep. I once heard a young man complaining that he could not keep his mind fixed on a point. "It rolled off like a barrel from a pin;" and he gave some hints that possibly it might be that his mind was so *great!* His gravity altogether exceeded that of his associates, to whom he was giving the explanation. How many great minds would there be, if such indications were to be relied on!

In the period which belongs to you as a *student*, then, it is not important that you should try to lay up a vast amount of information. Under the chapter on reading, I shall hope to throw out such hints as will enable you to save what you do read. The object now is, to fit the mind for future acquisitions and future usefulness. The magazine will be filled soon enough; and we need not be too anxious to fill it whil we are getting it ready for use. I am desirous that you have it strongly impressed on the memory that the great object now is, to set the mind out on a course which she can successfully pursue herself, and that, too, through life.

You must calculate to improve through life; and, therefore, now try to form habits of study, and learn how to study to advantage. "Newton was in his eighty-fifth year improving his Chronology; and Waller, at eighty-two, is thought to have lost none of his poetical fire."[1]

Make it the first object to be able to fix and hold your attention upon your studies. He who can do this, has mastered many and great difficulties; and he who cannot do it, will in vain look for success in any department of study. "To effect any purpose in study, the mind must be concentrated. If any other object plays on the fancy than that which ought to be exclusively before it, the mind is divided, and both are neutralized, so as to lose their effect—just as when I learned two systems of short-hand: I was familiar with Gurney's method, and wrote it with ease; but when I took it into my head to learn Byrom's, they destroyed each other, and I could write neither."[2] What is commonly called *abstraction in study*, is nothing more than having the attention so completely occupied with the subject in hand, that the mind takes notice of nothing without itself. One of the greatest minds which this, or any other country, ever produced, has been known to be so engrossed in thinking on

1 Note C. 2 Cecil's Remains

a particular subject, that his horse has waded through the corner of a pond, yet, though the water covered the saddle, he was wholly insensible to the cause of his being wet. I mention this, not to recommend such an abstraction, but to show, that he who has his attention fixed, and the power of fixing it when he pleases, will be successful in study. Need I say here, that you can never command the attention, if you are in the habit of yielding to your appetites and passions? "No man," says one who knew, "whose appetites are his masters, can perform the duties of his nature with strictness and regularity. He that would be superior to external influence, must first become superior to his own passions." Why does the boy, who has a large sum upon his slate, scowl, and rub out, and begin again, and grow discouraged? Because he has not yet learned to command his attention. He was going on well, when some new thought flashed into his mind, or some new object caught his eye, and he lost the train of calculation. Why has that Latin or Greek word so puzzled you to remember, that you have had to look it out in your dictionary some ten or dozen times? And why do you now look at it as at a stranger, whose name you *ought* to know, but which you cannot recall? Because you have not yet acquired fully the power of fixing your attention. That word would have been remembered long since, if it had not passed as a shadow before your mind when you looked at it. A celebrated authoress, who states that she reserves all her i's to be dotted, and her t's to be crossed, on some sick day, might have given a more philosophical reason ; and that is, that she could not bear to have her attention interrupted a single moment, when writing with the most success.

The difficulty of confining the attention is probably the secret of the plan of Demosthenes, who shut himself up in his celebrated dark cave for study ; and this will account for the fact, that a person who is unexpectedly deprived of the use of his eyes, will not unfrequently make advances in thought, and show a strength of mind, unknown before. I have frequently seen boys take their books on a summer's day, and flee from their room to the grove, and from the grove back again, full of uneasiness, and in vain hoping that changing the place would give them some new power over the roving attention, and that indescribable restlessness, so inseparable from the early efforts to subdue the mind. It is all in vain. You cannot fly from yourself; and the best way is to sit directly down in your room, and there command your attention to fix itself upon the hard, dry lesson, and master it ; and, when you have thus brought this rover to obey you once, he will be more ready to obey the next time. Attention will more readily come at your call to-morrow than to-day.

Patience is a virtue kindred to attention ; and with

out it, the mind cannot be said to be disciplined. Patient labor and investigation are not only essential to success in study, but are an unfailing guarantee to success. The young man is in danger of feeling "that he will strike out something new. His spirits are buoyant and his hopes sanguine." He knows not the mortified feeling of being repeatedly defeated by himself. He will burst upon the world at once, and strike the blows of a giant, while his arm is that of a child. He is not to toil up the hill, and wait for years of self-discipline, close, patient study, and hard labor—not he; but before you know it, he will be on the heights of the highest Alps, with a lofty feeling, looking down upon the creepers below. Hence, multitudes waste life, and absolutely fritter away their existence, in doing nothing, except waiting for a golden opportunity to do something great and magnificent. Did not Patrick Henry[1] burst upon the world at once, and at once exhibit the strength of a giant? If he did, he is no specimen of ordinary minds, and no man has a right to presume upon any thing more than an intellect of ordinary dimensions as his own. What multitudes of men lie still, and never lift the pen, because the time is not come! When they come out, it must be in a "great book," a splendid address, or some great effort. The tree must not be allowed to grow by inches; no, at once the sapling must be loaded with the fruit of the tree of threescore years.

[1] Note D.

Alas! trees planted and watered by such expectations will never be more than dwarfs. Franklin rose high, and his name is engraven deep and fair on the roll of immortality; but he began his greatness by making an almanac: he continued to make it for years, and rose, step by step, till he was acknowledged at the head of modern philosophers. Every young man ought to remember that he who would carry the ox, must every day shoulder the calf. *Ferret taurum qui tulit vitulam.* That great man, who returned to his study, and, finding that his little dog had turned over the table, and burned up the papers on which he had been engaged for years, yet calmly said, "You have done me a great mischief, Diamond," showed a soul truly great; and its greatness, in this instance, consisted in his patience. Without a murmur, he sat down, and began to do over the same great labor. He lived to complete it; and it was the admiration of the learned world. Yet how few have the patience thus to sit down and labor day by day for years! It is neither a small nor an easy part of education to cultivate this trait of character.

The student should learn to *think and act for himself*. True originality consists in doing things well, and doing them in your own way. A mind half educated is generally imitating others. "No man was ever great by imitation."[1] One great reason is, that it is so much easier to copy the defects and the

[1] Johnson.

objectionable parts of a great man's character, than to imitate his excellences, that we gain only the former. Alexander the Great had a foolish tutor, who used to call him Achilles. He was taught to admire that character. But when he came to imitate Achilles, what did he do? He imitated one of the most cruel and detestable actions in that hero's life. He dragged the governor of a town through the streets after his chariot. This was because the foolish teacher Lysimachus taught him to imitate as well as admire. It has been more than strongly conjectured, that France murdered her king, the inoffensive and amiable Louis XVI., because England once beheaded a king! Strange, that even nations cannot become imitators without copying that which is atrocious! Not a few waste their lives, and lose all discipline and improvement, by an insensible and unconscious habit of imitating others. Of the multitudes who imitated Johnson, was there one who had any thing more than his pompous, inflated language? They seemed to feel that they were wielding the club of Hercules; but the club, in every instance, was hollow, and the blow resulted in nothing but sound. Of the many who tried to follow in the wake of Byron, is there one who will live in song? Not one. They could copy nothing but his measure and his wickedness, borrowing his vileness without his genius. The lion himself is fast turning to corruption, but no honey will be found n the carcass; and as for his followers, the world was relieved from their curse by their decaying before they could taint the moral atmosphere. It is vastly more easy to imitate and borrow, both matter and manner, than to have them of your own. But set it down, that no imitator ever reached any thing like eminence. You must have a character of your own, and rules by which that character is regulated. It has been said of Franklin, that he was a philosopher, because, in his childhood, he formed those rules which regulated him even in old age. "My father," says Andrew Fuller, "was a farmer; and, in my younger days, it was a great boast among the ploughmen that they could plough a straight line *across* the furrows or ridges of the field. I thought I could do this as well as any of them. One day, I saw such a line, which had just been drawn, and I thought, 'Now I have it.' Accordingly I laid hold of the plough, and, putting one of the horses into the furrow which had just been made, I resolved to keep him walking in it, and thus secure a parallel line. By and by, however, I observed that there were what might be termed *wriggles* in this furrow; and when I came to them, they turned out to be *larger* in *mine* than in the original. On perceiving this, I threw the plough aside, and determined *never to be an imitator*." Let it be remembered that we cannot copy greatness or goodness by any effort. We must acquire it by our own patience and dili gence *Nil sine magno vita labore dedit mortalibus.*

Another object of study is, *to form the judgment*, so that the mind can not only investigate, but weigh and balance opinions and theories. Without this, you will never be able to decide what to read or what to throw aside; what author to distrust, or what opinions to receive. Some of the most laborious men, and diligent readers, pass through life without accomplishing any thing desirable, for the want of what may be called a *well-balanced judgment*. The last theory which they hear is the true one, however deficient as to proof from facts; the last book they read is the most wonderful, though it may be worthless; the last acquaintance is the most valuable, because least is known about him. Hence multitudes of objects are pursued, which have no use in practical life; and there is a laborious trifling—*operose nihil agendo*—which unfits the mind for any thing valuable. It leads to a wide field, which is barren and waste. "I once saw a shepherd," says an Italian author, "who used to divert himself, in his solitudes, with tossing up eggs and catching them again without breaking them; in which he had arrived to so great a degree of perfection, that he would keep up *four* at a time for several minutes together, playing in the air and falling into his hands by turns. I think I never saw greater severity than in this man's face; for, by his wonderful perseverance and application, he had contracted the seriousness and gravity of a privy-counsellor; and I could not but reflect with myself, that the same assiduity and attention, had they been rightly applied, might have made him a greater mathematician than Archimedes."

I have known a boy—and such cases are not rare—spend time enough in learning to read with the book bottom upwards—which he did with great fluency—to have made him acquainted with all the minutiæ of the Latin grammar. This is not merely time wasted, but it is cultivating a taste for out-of-the-way things and useless acquirements. It is no small part of education and of study, to know what you do, and what you do not, wish to know.

If, by any thing I have said, an impression has been made that I do not deem it necessary for a man to be familiar with a wide circle of knowledge, in order to become known, influential, and useful, I trust such an impression will be corrected before the reader closes this book. What I wish to say here, is, that the great object of the student is, to prepare his mind to use materials which may hereafter be gathered; but not now to gather them. One of the most distinguished men of this age and nation, whose voice has been heard in lands distant from ours, is said to be remarkable for this faculty—that, when he wants information on any subject, he seems to know, intuitively, who and what shall be laid under immediate tribute. He does not pore over all that this or that man has written, but gets light from all quarters, and then, like the burning-glass, condenses and brings to a focus all the light and heat which are necessary to consume obstacles and objections. Such a habit is worth all the scraps of learning and information which could be laid up in a mind which knows of no use in knowledge but the pleasure which it affords while in the act of acquiring.

The great instrument of affecting the world is the mind; and no instrument is so decidedly and continually improved by exercise and use, as the mind. Many seem to feel as if it were not safe to put forth all their powers at one effort. You must reserve your strength for great occasions, just as you would use your horse—moderately and carefully on common occasions, but give him the spur on occasions of great emergency. This might be well, were the mind, in any respect, like the bones and muscles of the horse. Some, when they are contriving to see how little mental effort will answer, and how far and wide a few feeble thoughts may be spread, seem more like students than at any other time—as if it were dangerous to task the mind too often, lest her stores be exhausted, or her faculties become weakened. The bow may be but half bent, lest it be overstrained, and lose its power. But you need have no such fears

You may call upon your mind, to-day, for its highest efforts, and stretch it to the utmost in your power, and you have done yourself a kindness. The mind will be all the better for it. To-morrow you may do it again; and each time it will answer more readily to your calls.

But remember that real discipline of mind does not so much consist in now and then making a great effort, as in having the mind so trained that it will make constant efforts. *Gutta cavat lapidem, non vi, sed sæpe cædendo.* If you would have the discipline any thing like perfect, it must be unremitted; the mind must be kept clear and shrewd. It is told of our gifted, but infatuated HAMILTON,[1] that, during the periods in which the powers of his mind were put to the highest and severest exercise, he regularly read Euclid through once a month. The Federalist will tell the rest.

The perfection of a disciplined mind is, not to be able, on some great contingency, to rouse up its faculties, and draw out a giant strength, but to have it always ready to produce a given and an equal quantity of results in a given and equal time. This was the glory of the mind of Isaac Newton; and the late venerated Porter, of Andover, could, in any given hour, or day, or week, produce as finished and as ample results, as if he should wait for "some happy hours of thought." He who trains his mind to go by

[1] Note E.

impulses, and must wait for them, will accomplish but very little during his life.

Two monks live near each other at the same time. They both profess to be students. Only one, however, does any thing towards disciplining his mind. One uses language and lamentations as follows :—" They have invented a new language, which they call Greek; you must be carefully on your guard against it; it is the matter of all heresy. I observe in the hands of many persons a book written in that language, and which they call the New Testament. It is a book full of daggers and poison. As to the Hebrew, my dear brethren, it is certain that whoever learns it becomes immediately a Jew." The other monk seizes the New Testament, and applies his habits of study and of diligence to it; and with that Bible he shakes all Europe; he shakes the world, and, in a day, opens upon Christendom the light of thousands of years. Need I say, I mean Martin Luther? Nothing but his disciplined mind, and his habits of using that instrument, could have led him through the thick darkness which surrounded him, to the clear light in which we see him.

The study of *human nature* is a very important part of education. I know it is thought by some, nay, by many, that no one can understand men but those who are moving, and acting, and crowding among them. I grant that such a one is the only man who knows the forms and modes of doing business. But if the student has not, at the close of his academical course, a deep and thorough insight into the nature of man, it is his own fault, or the fault of his instructers. Men in active life will judge very accurately as to the manner in which you may expect men to act in such and such circumstances; but though, in these respects, their conclusions are accurate, yet they see not the motives of action, and look not so deeply into the soul, as the accurate student. Let a man in active life undertake to probe the conscience of an audience; he may have this and that fact, but can he do it as effectually as he who has read human nature, and pondered over it, in all its recesses and windings, in his study? Few men ever lived who moved among men so little as Jonathan Edwards. But did he not understand human nature? Can any one read his writings, and doubt, for a moment, that he knew most accurately what the nature of man is? When such a mind pours out its strength upon the world, it does not make mistakes as to the principles of action. He might mistake in purchasing a horse, or a coat, for he never attended to such small matters; but a surgeon never dissected the body with more accuracy and skill than he does the soul of man. It is a tradition that Edwards knew not his own cows; but, in the world of active, driving, bargain-making men, you will never find one who understands human nature as well as he did. And not he alone; but this is characteristic of all who are real students. They work upon the deep principles of human nature—those principles which are altered neither by time, nor fashion, nor outward circumstances. This is one reason why an educated mind will often send the arrow thro 'gh the heart, while the uneducated man only twangs his bow. He makes more noise, but produces no execution. I doubt not that many will smile at the idea, that the hard student understands mankind; but you might as well smile at the philosopher, who, while he was managing the electricity in the thunder-cloud, could not tell what outward shapes the cloud might, in the mean time, assume, or whether it moved fast or slow.

Self-knowledge is another important end of study. There are some men who have raised themselves to high stations, and maintained them, without a long course of mental discipline. Roger Sherman[1] thus rose from the bench of a shoemaker, till the eyes of a nation gazed on him in admiration. But most are pedants, and self-conceited, unless they have accurately and repeatedly measured themselves by others. It is of great importance that you know what you cannot do, as well as what you can do. For this reason, with all the temptations and dangers attending a public education, I am satisfied it is much to be preferred to a private one. The wisest period in the whole of a man's existence, is when he has just entered college

[1] Note F

And why? Simply because the youth has not yet had the opportunity of measuring his attainments and capacity with that of his fellows. It is not merely that you sharpen the intellect, and add a keenness to the mind, by contact with other minds, but you strengthen it by the contact, and you learn to be modest in regard to your own powers. You will see many with intellects of a high order, and with attainments far beyond any thing which you have dared call your own. There must be some radical defect in that man's nature, who can be associated in study, for years, with those who are severe students, and, at the end of the period, feel that he is a very wise or a very great man. He has then but just stepped upon the threshold of learning, and but just looked out upon that field of knowledge and improvement, which is as boundless as the creation of God. The mouse, which thought his chest was all the world, was astonished, when he stood upon the till, and looked out, to see what a great world lay beyond him. But what is the reason why a man must know himself exactly? What if he does over-estimate himself? I answer—If he presents a draft greater than his deposits, it will certainly be protested There is so much vanity in the heart of every man, that he will not allow any one to claim more than his merits absolutely compel him to allow; so that, if you place yourself on the list of those who over-estimate their own attainments or worth, you injure your usefulness and destroy your happiness. The modest man may, and will, draw vastly harder upon the sympathy and good-will of mankind than the forward man, with the same attainments, will be allowed to do. Modesty, to rest upon any fixed, stable foundation, must rest upon an accurate knowledge of yourself. This will be the result of study. The philosopher whose fame was filling all Europe, was so modest and retiring, that his good landlady, one day, mourned over him, and lamented that "the poor soul could never make any thing more than a *philosopher* after all!"

We are in too great danger of neglecting the memory. It is too valuable to be neglected, for by it, wonders are sometimes accomplished. He who has a memory that can seize with an iron grasp, and retain what he reads,—the ideas, simply, without the language,—and judgment to compare and balance, will scarcely fail of being distinguished. Many are afraid of strengthening the memory, lest it should destroy their inducement and power to originate ideas—lest the light should be altogether borrowed light. The danger does not seem to me to be very great; especially since I have noticed, that those who are so fearful of employing this faculty are by no means to be envied for their originality. Why has that mass of thought, observation, and experience, which is embodied in books, by the multitudes of minds which have gone before us, been gathered if not, that we may use it, and stand on high ground, and push our way still farther into the boundaries and regions of knowledge? Besides, in a world so dark as ours, it is delightful to see a planet rising before us, even though she sheds no light but borrowed. And, after all, the exact amount of original thought which passes through any one mind, is probably much less than is frequently imagined. Who does not know what a delightful freshness there is in the reading of youth! The world is new to him. He treads on ground new and enchanting. I have frequently heard men, in maturer years, wish that they could now sit down and find the same freshness in a book, which they did when young. Why do they not? Because a *new* book, now, is not *new*. They have seen the same ideas, or the shades of them, many times before; and every book takes away from the originality of that which is to follow it. The man who declared that the only two new books in the world were the Bible and Euclid, was not so far out of the way as would at first seem. If, then, there is not so much of originality in men and in books as you at first suppose, it follows, that memory is the grand instrument of conveying knowledge from one man to another. Its cultivation is of the highest importance. I mention it here, not now to direct how to cultivate it, but to state its immense value.

You will see, from what I have said, that the object of study *is to discipline the mind in all its parts; to show it where to find tools, and how to use them.* The exact amount of knowledge which is at any one time in the mind of the student, is not, and need not be, great. Like a good pump, you could soon exhaust it, were it not that it reaches an inexhaustible well beneath, and has all the apparatus for filling itself as fast as emptied. If the knowledge which he now possesses shall evaporate, it will, like the vapors which rise from the ocean, again return to the diligent student, by some other channels. It is thought by some, however, that no item of knowledge, and not a single idea which is once formed in the mind, can ever be lost. It may be forgotten to-day, but it will come again to the notice of the mind in the course of the unending progress which is yet to be made by the human soul. How important that the knowledge which we acquire, and the thoughts which occupy our minds, be such, that, come when they may, we shall recognize them as pleasant companions and worthy friends! The immortality of light which awaits the good, is to be one of thought, of review, and of self-communion; and the night of ages which shall settle down upon the wicked, will not be other than sleepless.

It is not an uncommon thing for the youth to feel

as he is sent away from home, and confined down to books, that it is really a hard way to obtain an education. He thinks of the brooks, the groves, or the hills and ponds near his home, of his skates, his gun, or his fishing-tackle, or of the social circle around his father's fire-side, and sighs, that he must be exiled from all these, and shut up in his naked room, among strangers, and there must unceasingly pore over his books. It is not to be wondered at, that he feels so; but let him reflect, that this is the time to form habits, and to begin a course of mental discipline, which, in a few years, will raise him high in the esteem, the respect, and the honors, of his fellow-men. Every distinguished man has trodden the same path. There is no other road to knowledge, to improvement, to distinction. If the voice of experience could come to your ear, and if you could see the agony of heart which those feel, who once had your opportunities, but misimproved them, you would be astonished to see the real value of your situation. All who have passed through academic or collegiate life, know how very irksome that life is; and the reason is, it is so hard for the mind to be broken in, and subdued by the discipline of the situation: it is like taking the half-grown lion, and putting him in the iron cage, and then teaching him how to obey his master, and, of course, how to subdue himself. But this very discipline is the only thing which can bring the mind under proper subjection, and fit it to become obedient to yourself I hope, in the chapters which are to follow, to mark out the road so plainly, that you will find it more and more pleasant to travel, and, at its end, feel that it has been a journey full of sweet recollections, and one of bright promise.

CHAPTER II.

HABITS.

THE whole character may be said to be comprehended in the term *habits;* so that it is not so far from being true, that "man is a bundle of habits." Suppose you were compelled to wear an iron collar about your neck through life, or a chain upon your ankle; would it not be a burden every day and hour of your existence? You rise in the morning a prisoner to your chain; you lie down at night, weary with the burden; and you groan the more deeply, as you reflect that there is no shaking it off. But even this would be no more intolerable to bear than many of the habits of men; nor would it be more difficult to be shaken off.

Habits are easily formed—especially such as are bad; and what to-day seems to be a small affair, will soon become fixed, and hold you with the strength of a cable. That same cable, you will recollect, is formed by spinning and twisting one thread at a time; but, when once completed, the proudest ship turns her head towards it, and acknowledges her subjection to its power.

Habits of some kind will be formed by every stu

dent. He will have a particular course in which his time, his employments, his thoughts and feelings, will run. Good or bad, these habits soon become a part of himself, and a kind of second nature. Who does not know, that the old man, who has occupied a particular corner of the old fire-place in the old house for sixty years, may be rendered wretched by a change? Who has not read of the release of the aged prisoner of the Bastile, who entreated that he might again return to his gloomy dungeon, because his habits there formed, were so strong, that his nature threatened to sink under the attempt to break them up? You will probably find no man of forty, who has not habits which he laments, which mar his usefulness, but which are so interwoven with his very being, that he cannot break through them. At least he has not the courage to try. I am expecting you will form habits. Indeed, I wish you to do so. He must be a poor character, indeed, who lives so extempore as not to have habits of his own. But what I wish is, that you form those habits which are *correct*, and such as will every day and hour add to your happiness and usefulness. If a man were to be told that he must use the axe, which he now selects, through life, would he not be careful in selecting one of the right proportions and temper? If told that he must wear the same clothing through life, would he not be anxious as to the quality and kind? But these, in the cases supposed, would be of no more importance than is the selection of habits in which the soul shall act. You might as well place the body in a strait-jacket, and expect it to perform, with ease, and comfort, and promptness, the various duties of the body, as to throw the soul into the habits of some men, and then expect it will accomplish any thing great or good.

Do not fear to undertake to form *any* habit which is desirable; for it *can* be formed, and that with more ease than you may at first suppose. *Let the same thing, or the same duty, return at the same time every day, and it will soon become pleasant.* No matter if it be irksome at first; but how irksome soever it may be, only let it return periodically, every day, and that without any interruption for a time, and it will become a positive pleasure. In this way all our habits are formed. The student who can with ease now sit down, and hold his mind down to his studies nine or ten hours a day, would find the laborer, or the man accustomed to active habits, sinking under it, should he attempt to do the same thing. I have seen a man sit down at the table spread with luxury, and eat his sailor's biscuit with relish, and without a desire for any other food. His health had compelled him thus to live, till it had become a pleasant habit of diet. Previous to this, however, he had been rather noted for being an epicure. "I once attended a prisoner," says an excellent man, "of some distinction, in one of the prisons of the metropolis, ill of a typhus fever whose apartments were gloomy in the extreme, and surrounded with horrors; yet this prisoner assured me afterwards, that, upon his release, he quitted them with a degree of reluctance: *custom* had reconciled him to the twilight admitted through the thick-barred grate, to the filthy spots and patches of his plastered walls, to the hardness of his bed, and even to confinement."

I shall specify habits which, in my view, are very desirable to the student, and, at the same time, endeavor to give specific directions how to form them.

1. *Have a plan laid beforehand for every day.*

These plans ought to be maturely formed the evening previous, and, on rising in the morning, again looked at, and immediately entered upon. It is astonishing how much more we accomplish in a single day, (and what of else is life made up?) by having the plan previously marked out. It is so in every thing. This morning a man was digging a path through a deep snow-bank. It was almost insupportably cold, and he seemed to make but little headway, though he worked as if upon a wager. At length, getting out of breath, he paused, and marked out the width of the path with his shovel, then marked out the width of each shovel-full, and consequently the amount of snow at each throw of the shovel. In fifteen minutes, he had done more, and it was done neater and easier, than in thirty minutes previous, when working without a plan. It is of little consequence by what we illustrate, if we make a thing clear, and impress it upon the mind. I have found, in my own experience, as much difference in the labors of two days, when working with, or without a plan, as, at least, one half, without having the satisfaction, in the latter case, of knowing what I have done.

Experience will tell any man, that he is most successful in his own pursuits, when he is most careful as to method. A man of my acquaintance has a small slate, which hangs at his study-table. On that he generally finds, in the morning, his work for the day written down; and in the evening he reviews it, sees if he has omitted any thing, and, if so, chides himself that all is not done. To make this clear, I copy here what was found on his slate for one day, as I saw it this morning:—

a. Horse, errands, and dig paths.

b. Carry my child to school, and pay postage-bill.

c. Write from 9 till dinner [at 1 o'clock].

d. Write to C., inviting him—also to I. at N. H

e. Examine the use of the word ὀργίζεσθε in Ephesians 4. 26.

f. Visit Mr. M. sick, also the two families in Maple Street.

g. Get some straw for horse wherever it can be purchased.

h. Prepare and preach this evening.

i. Examine the sixth vol. of B. [to see if any thing is there which I want].

j. Last, not least, to fix the pump [so that it will not freeze up].

If, at the close of the day, he finds these items all accomplished, and that in such a way as to satisfy conscience, he feels that the day has not been lost. Sometimes he finds he has misjudged, and has marked out more than he can do; sometimes he is hindered by unexpected interruptions, and therefore cannot do all, or even half, he calculated to do. These must be all weighed every night at the review. Be sure and review every night, and when you have balanced the account with conscience, lay out what you will do for the next day.

Such a system will not make a noisy, blustering character. The river, that rolls a heavy burden of water to the ocean, is the stream which keeps the channel, and is noiseless in its course. There is a prescribed routine of duties marked out by your teachers. These, of course, will come in your every-day plans; but, in addition to these, you ought to do something by way of acquiring or retaining information, or something to add to the happiness of your friends or of your companions. Let me suppose you mark out your plan for to-morrow, thus:—

1. Walk to the pond, 1½ mile, immediately after breakfast

2. Lesson and recitation.

3. Write to my mother, acknowledging her letter and bundle.

4. Review, and see if I can read the 6th Eclogue of Virgil without looking into the Dictionary or Grammar. (Regular course of review.)

5. Lesson and recitation. Walk till tea.

6. See if I can go through the 24th proposition of Euclid, 1st B., at once. (Regular review.)

7. Visit Smith's room, and explain the remark which I made to-day, and at which he seemed hurt.

8. Lesson for the morning, &c.

9. Note the three facts respecting Demosthenes in my common-place book.

10. Talk over the question for dispute in the Society with my chum.

11. Read the new magazine which mother has just sent me.

At first you will feel discouraged in not being able to do as much work as you mark out. But you will do more and more, from day to day, as you proceed; and you will soon be astonished at seeing how much can be accomplished. If you choose, you can have a book instead of a slate, which will be also a kind of journal of your life, full of interesting memoranda

2. *Acquire the habit of untiring industry.*

Should you be so unfortunate as to suppose you are a genius, and that "things will come to you," it would be well to undeceive yourself as soon as possible. Make up your mind that industry must be the price of all you obtain, and at once begin to pay down. "Diligence in employments of less consequence is the most successful introduction to greater enterprises." It is a matter of unaffected amazement to see what industry alone will accomplish. We are astonished at the volumes which the men of former ages used to write. But the term *industry* is the key to the whole secret. "He that shall walk with vigor three hours a day, will pass in seven years a space equal to the circumference of the globe."[1] There is no state so bad for the student as idleness, and no habit so pernicious. And yet none is so easily acquired, or so difficult to be thrown off. The idle man soon grows torpid, and becomes the Indian in his feelings, insensibly adopting their maxim—"It is better to walk than to run, and better to stand still than to walk, and better to sit than to stand, and better to lie than to sit." Probably the man who deserves the most of pity, is he who is most idle; for as "there are said to be pleasures to madness known only to madmen, there are certainly miseries in idleness which only the idle can conceive." I am aware that many are exceedingly *busy*, who are not industrious. For it very frequently happens, that he who is most hurried and bustling, is very far from being industrious. A shrewd man can easily discover the

[1] Johnson.

difference. "He that neglects his known duty, and real employment, naturally endeavors to crowd his mind with something that may bar out the remembrance of his own folly, and does any thing but what he ought to do, with eager diligence, that he may keep himself in his own favor."

It is perfectly clear that he who is industrious has really the most of leisure; for his time is marked out into distinct portions, to each of which something is assigned; and when the thing is done, the man is at leisure; but a dead calm settles over him who lives an idle life. Better that the waters be straitened, and burst over their banks, than that they be too sluggish to move at all. Who would not prefer to put to sea, even in a storm, and in a gale hurry over the waters, rather than lie for weeks becalmed? It is said that when Scanderbeg, prince of Epirus, was dead, the Turks wished to get his bones, that each one might wear a piece near his heart, and thus obtain some part of that courage which he had while living, and which they had too often experienced in battle. What a blessing, if the idle might obtain some such charm, that would rouse them up to habits of industry! Seneca assures his friend, in a letter, that there "was not a day in which he did not either write something, or read and epitomize some good author." So universal has the opinion of men been on the point that, in order to excel, you must be industrious, that idlers have received the just appellation of "fools at large." You would be surprised to know how many hours slip away from the man who is not systematically industrious. "Such was his unwearied assiduity and diligence, that he seemed to pray constantly, to preach constantly, to catechize constantly, and to visit the sick, exhorting from house to house, to teach as much in the schools, and spend as much time with the students and young men, in fitting them for the ministry, as if he had been sequestrate from all the world besides, and yet, withal, to write as much as if he had been constantly shut up in his study."*

It is easy for the student to form good plans of study and of daily habits, and to draw them out on paper, all perfected. But the difficulty is, they are found no where but on paper; and because you cannot at once reach them, you sit down and give up an untiring industry. It was a matter of astonishment to Europe, that Luther, amid all his travels and active labors, could present a very perfect translation of the whole Bible. But a single word explains it all. He had a rigid system of doing something every day. "*Nulla dies*," says he, in answer to the question how he did it—"*nulla dies sine versu*;" and this soon brought him to the close of the whole Bible.

I have never known a man whose habits of every-day industry were so good as those of Jeremiah E[illegible]-

* Life of Rutherford.

arts. During years of close observation in the bosom of his family, I never saw a day pass without his accomplishing more than he expected; and so regular was he in all his habits, that I knew to a moment when I should find him with his pen, and when with his tooth-brush, in his hand; and so methodical and thorough, that though his papers filled many shelves, when closely tied up, there was not a paper among all his letters, correspondence, editorial matter, and the like, which was not labelled and in its place, and upon which he could not lay his hand in a moment. I never knew him search for a paper;—it was always in its place. I have never yet met with the man whose industry was so great, or who would accomplish so much in a given time.

"Pray, of what did your brother die?" said the Marquis Spinola to Sir Horace Vere. "He died, sir," replied he, "of having nothing to do." "Alas, sir," said Spinola, "that is enough to kill any general of us all."

Demosthenes, as is well known, copied Thucydides' History eight times with his own hand, merely to make himself familiar with the style of that great man.

There are two proverbs, one among the Turks and the other among the Spaniards, both of which contain much that is true. "A busy man is troubled with but one devil, but the idle man with a thou sand." "Men are usually tempted by the devil, but the idle man positively tempts the devil." How much corrupting company, how many temptations to do wrong, how many seasons of danger to your character, and danger to the peace of your friends, would you escape, by forming the habit of being decidedly industrious every day!

3. *Cultivate perseverance.*

By perseverance, I mean a steadfastness in pursuing the same study, and carrying out the same plans from week to week. Some will read or hear of a plan which somebody has pursued with great success, and at once conclude, that they will do so. The plan will be adopted without consideration, then talked about as a fine affair, and in a few days thrown aside for something else. Such a great man did this, or did that, and I will do so, is the feeling; but as soon as it becomes irksome, as any new habit will in a short time, it is laid aside. I once knew a man, a student, who somewhere read of a great man who wrote over his door, "*Dum loquimur tempus fugit;*" and immediately he had it in staring capitals over his door. Again, he read that a very learned man used to admire Blackstone: at once he drops all, and purchases Blackstone's Commentaries. These he began to read with great eagerness; but, happening to hear that Oliver Ellsworth[1] was in the habit of getting most of his information from conversation, (a fact which I

[1] Note G.

doubt,) he was for dropping Blackstone, and going from room to room, to gather information by conversation! It is hardly necessary to say, that a college full of such students, all condensed into one, would not make a single real student. "The man who is perpetually hesitating which of two things he will do first, will do neither. The man who resolves, but suffers his resolution to be changed by the first counter suggestion of a friend,—who fluctuates from opinion to opinion, from plan to plan, and veers like a weather-cock to every point of the compass, with every breath of caprice that blows,—can never accomplish any thing great or useful. Instead of being progressive in any thing, he will be at best stationary, and more probably retrograde in all. It is only the man who carries into his pursuits that great quality which Lucan ascribes to Cæsar,—*nesciu virtus stare loco*,—who first consults wisely, then resolves firmly, and then executes his purpose with inflexible perseverance, undismayed by those petty difficulties which daunt a weaker spirit,—that can advance to eminence in any line. Let us take, by way of illustration, the case of a student. He commences the study of the dead languages: presently comes a friend, who tells him he is wasting his time, and that, instead of obsolete words, he had much better employ himself in acquiring new ideas. He changes his plan, and sets to work at the mathematics. Then comes anothe friend, who asks him, with a grave and sapient face, whether he intends to become a professor in a college; because, if he does not, he is misemploying his time; and that, for the business of life, common mathematics is quite enough of the mathematics. He throws up his Euclid, and addresses himself to some other study, which, in its turn, is again relinquished on some equally wise suggestion; and thus life is spent in changing his plans. You cannot but perceive the folly of this course; and the worst effect of it is, the fixing on your mind a habit of indecision, sufficient of itself to blast the fairest prospects. No, take your course wisely, but firmly; and, having taken it, hold upon it with heroic resolution, and the Alps and Pyrenees will sink before you. The whole empire of learning will be at your feet, while those who set out with you, but stopped to change their plans, are yet employed in the very profitable business of changing their plans. Let your motto be, *Perseverando vinces.* Practise upon it, and you will be convinced of its value by the distinguished eminence to which it will conduct you." *

We are in danger of ruining our promising plans, in themselves very good, by the habit of putting off till to-morrow what may be done to-day. That letter may be answered to-morrow; that request of my

* Wirt.

friend may be attended to to-morrow, and he will be no loser. True; but you are the loser; for the yielding to one such temptation, is the signal to the yielding up the whole citadel to the enemy. That note and that valuable fact may be recorded in my common-place book to-morrow. True; but every such indulgence is a heavy loss to you. Every hour should be perseveringly filled up. But this is not all. It is not sufficient to take for your motto, with the immortal Grotius,[1] "*Hora ruit;*" but let it be filled up according to some plan. One day filled up according to a previous plan, is worth more than a week, filled up, but without any plan.

It is astonishing to see with what perseverance and inflexibility of purpose those men have pursued the object, the pursuit and attainment of which constituted their greatness. Charles XII. was frequently on his horse for twenty-four hours at once; and thus he traversed most of his dominions. His officers were all tired out; consequently, for the most part, he performed these journeys entirely alone. On one of these excursions, his poor horse fell dead under him. Without any uneasiness, the monarch stripped the dead horse, and marched off with the saddle, bridle and pistols on his back. At the next inn, he found a horse in the stable to his mind, and immediately harnessed him, and was just making off, when the owner came out, and called him to account for stealing his

[1] Note H.

property. The monarch replied, that he took the horse because he was tired of carrying the saddle himself. This not satisfying the owner, they drew swords, and would have shed blood, royal or plebeian, had not the guard rode up and informed the owner that his sword was raised against his king. This was but a single specimen of the untiring perseverance, with which that ambitious man carried out his plans. The same perseverance would place almost any student on a high eminence in a very few years.

4. *Cultivate the habit of punctuality.*

There is no man living who might not be a punctual man; and yet there are few that are so, to any thing like the degree to which they ought to attain. It is vastly easier to be a little late in getting into the recitation-room, and a little late in doing every thing. It is *not* so easy to be a prompt, punctual character; but it is a trait of inestimable value to yourself and to the world. The punctual man can do twice as much, at least, as another man, with twice the ease and satisfaction to himself, and with equal satisfaction to others. The late lord chancellor of England, Henry Brougham, while a kingdom seemed to be resting on his shoulders; who presided in the house of lords and the court of chancery; who gave audience daily to barristers, found time to write reviews, to be at the head of at least *ten* associations which were publishing works of useful knowledge,—was so punctual, that, when these associations met, he was uniformly there when the hour of meeting had arrived, and was in his place in the chair.

We are all so indolent, by nature and by habit, that we feel it a luxury to find a man of real, undeviating punctuality. We love to lean upon such a man and we are willing to purchase such a staff at almost any price. It shows, at least, that he has conquered himself.

Some seem to be afraid of cherishing this habit, lest it border upon a virtue that is vulgar, and is below the ambition of a great mind, or the attention of one who has greater virtues upon which he may presume. Was the mind of Blackstone of a low order? Did he cultivate punctuality because he had not great traits of character on which to rely? Yet, when he was delivering even his celebrated lectures, he was never known to make his audience wait even a minute; and he could never be made to think well of any one who was notoriously defective in this virtue. The reader will be pleased with the following notice of Mr. Brewer, afterwards a valuable minister of the gospel. While a student, he was always known to be punctual in attending the lectures at the tutor's house. The students boarded in neighboring families, and at stated hours met for recitation. One morning, the clock struck seven, and all rose up for prayer, according to custom. The tutor, looking round, and observing that

Mr. Brewer was absent, paused awhile. Seeing him now enter the room, he thus addressed him :—" Sir, the clock has struck, and we were ready to begin ; but, as *you* were absent, we supposed it was too fast, and therefore waited." The clock was actually too fast by some minutes.

It is no great virtue to be punctual in paying a considerable debt, though, even here, too many fail; but it is the every-day and every-hour occurrences, in which we are most apt to fail. "I am too late now, but it is only *once*. I have not been prompt in fulfilling my plans to-day ; but it is only *once*." Such is the language of procrastination. I have myself ridden scores of miles, and been put to inconvenient expense, and a hard week's work in writing, by the want of punctuality in one who failed only five minutes, and that wholly unnecessarily. Be punctual in every thing. If you determine to rise at such an hour, be on the floor at the moment. If you determine to do so much before breakfast, be sure to do it ; if to meet a society, or a circle of friends, be there at the moment. We are apt to be tardy in attending meetings of societies, &c., especially if we have any thing to do. "There is great dignity in being waited for," said one who was in this habit, and who had not much of which he need be vain, unless it was this want of promptness. An assembly will be glad to see you after having waited for you ; but they would have been more glad to see you at your post. When there are two things for you to do, one of which *must* be done, and the other is what you very much *desire* to do, be sure and begin the former first. For example, you may very much *wish* to complete the sheet which you are now writing, and for many reasons you may wish it; but you must recite this evening. Now, the way for you to do, is, *now* to stop writing, and prepare for recitation, else you will write so long, that not only your preparation in study will be slighted, but you will also be in danger of not being punctual. The want of the observance of this rule, very frequently prevents our being punctual in our duties.

5. *Be an early riser.*

Few ever lived to a great age, and fewer still ever became distinguished, who were not in the habit of early rising. You rise late, and of course get about your business at a late hour, and every thing goes wrong all day. Franklin says, "that he who rises late, may trot all day, and not have overtaken his business at night." Dean Swift avers, "that he never knew any man come to greatness and eminence who lay in bed of a morning."

I believe that, with other degeneracies of our days, history will prove that late rising is a prominent one. In the fourteenth century, the shops in Paris were universally open at four in the morning; now, not till long after seven. Then, the king of France dined out at eight o'clock in the morning, and retired to his chamber at the same hour in the evening. In the time of Henry VIII., seven in the morning was the fashionable breakfast hour—ten the dinner hour. In the time of Elizabeth, the nobility, fashionables, and students, dined at 11 o'clock, and supped between five and six in the afternoon.

[1] Buffon gives us the history of his writing in a few words. "In my youth, I was very fond of sleep: it robbed me of a great deal of my time; but my poor Joseph (his servant) was of great service in enabling me to overcome it. I promised to give Joseph a crown every time that he would make me get up at six. Next morning, he did not fail to wake me and to torment me; but he only received abuse. The next day after, he did the same, with no better success; and I was obliged to confess, at noon, that I had lost my time. I told him that he did not know how to manage his business; he ought to think of my promise, and not mind my threats. The day following, he employed force; I begged for indulgence—I bid him begone—I stormed—but Joseph persisted. I was therefore obliged to comply; and he was rewarded every day for the abuse which he suffered at the moment when I awoke, by thanks, accompanied with a crown, which he received about an hour af er. Yes, *I am indebted to poor Joseph for ten or a dozen of the volumes of my works.*"

[1] Note I

Frederick II. of Prussia, even after age and infirmities had increased upon him, gave strict orders never to be allowed to sleep later than four in the morning. Peter the Great, whether at work in the docks at London as a ship-carpenter, or at the anvil as a blacksmith, or on the throne of Russia, always rose before daylight. "I am," says he, "for making my life as long as I can, and therefore sleep as little as possible." Doddridge makes the following striking and sensible remarks on this subject:—"I will here record the observation, which I have found of great use to myself, and to which, I may say, that the production of this work (Commentary on the New Testament), and most of my other writings, is owing, viz. that the difference between rising at five and at seven o'clock in the morning, for the space of forty years, supposing a man to go to bed at the same hour at night, is nearly equivalent to the addition of ten years to a man's life."

In order to rise early, I would earnestly recommend an early hour for retiring. There are many other reasons for this. Neither your eyes nor your health are so likely to be destroyed. Nature seems to have so fitted things, that we ought to rest in the early part of the night. Dr. Dwight used to tell his students "that one hour of sleep before midnight is worth more than two hours after that time." Let it be a rule with you, and scrupulously adhered to, that your light shall be extinguished by *ten* o'clock in the evening. You may then rise at five, and have seven hours to rest, which is about what nature requires.

But how shall you form the habit of getting up so early? Suppose you go to bed, to-night, at ten: you have been accustomed to sit up later: for an hour you cannot sleep; and when the clock strikes five, you will be in a fine sleep. I reply, that, if you ever hope to do any thing in this world, the habit *must* be formed, and the sooner it is done the better. If any money could purchase the habit, no price would be too great. When the writer commenced the practice in earnest, he procured an old clock, at the expense of about two dollars. (This may be placed wherever you please.) He then formed a little machine which went by a weight and string, through the axle of which were four arms of wire, at the ends of which were as many brass buttons. As the weight went down, these revolving buttons struck against a small house-bell. This set up such a tremendous ringing, that there was no more sleep. All this was connected with the wooden clock, in the distant room, by means of wires. He has had the honor to instruct others of his profession into the mystery, and has had the pleasure of hearing the dingling of other bells, which other wooden clocks set a ringing. Some use a small alarm-clock to call them up, and to which they soon acquire a strong attachment, which would be stronger still, could it be made to strike up a light and build a fire. By this, or some such process, you must be regularly waked at an early hour. The students in Yale and Amherst Colleges, have generally the alarm-clock. After you are once awaked, be sure to use the first consciousness in getting upon the floor. If you allow yourself to parley a single moment, sleep, like an armed man, will probably seize upon you, and your resolution is gone, your hopes are dashed, and your habits destroyed. Need you be reminded here, that the young man who is in the habit of early rising, will and must be in the habit of retiring early, and, of course, will put himself out of the way of many temptations and dangers which come under the veil of midnight. Not a few feel that the rules of academies, or colleges, which call them up early, are rather a hardship. They transgress them when they dare. Finding the stolen waters sweet, they do all in their power during vacations, and at other times, to prevent themselves from forming the habit of early rising. They ought not to feel or do so. The business of college, and the business of life, alike require early rising; and you are your own enemy if you cherish the feeling that this is a burden. It ought to be a matter of gratitude that such regulations prevail in our seminaries. One of the most celebrated writers of England was lately asked how it was that he wrote so much, and yet from ten in the forenoon was at leisure through the day. "Because I begin to write at three o'clock in the morning," was the reply. Most confidently do I believe, that he who from his youth is in the habit of rising early, will be much more likely to live to old age, more likely to be a distinguished and useful man, and more likely to pass a life that is peaceful and pleasant. I dwell upon this point, because a love for the bed is too frequently a besetting sin of students, and a sin which soon acquires the strength of a cable.

6. *Be in the habit of learning something from every man with whom you meet.*

The observance or neglect of this rule will make a wonderful difference in your character long before the time that you are forty years old. All act upon it, more or less, but few do it as a matter of habit and calculation. Most act upon it as a matter of interest, or of curiosity at the moment. The great difficulty is, we begin too late in life to make every thing contribute to increase our stock of practical information. Sir Walter Scott gives us to understand, that he never met with any man, let his calling be what it might, even the most stupid fellow that ever rubbed down a horse, from whom he could not, by a few moments' conversation, learn something which he did not before know, and which was valuable to him. This will account for the fact that he seemed to have an intuitive knowledge of every thing. Who but he would stop in the street and note down a word which dropped among the oaths of two angry men,—a word for which he had been looking for months? It is quite as important to go through the world with the ears open, as with the eyes open. "When I was young," says Cecil, "my mother had a servant, whose conduct I thought truly wise. A man was hired to brew, and this servant was to watch his method, in order to learn his art. In the course of the process, something was done which she did not understand. She asked him, and he abused her with the vilest epithets for her ignorance and stupidity. My mother asked her how she bore such abuse. 'I would be called,' said she: 'worse names, a thousand times, for the sake of the information I got out of him.'" It is a false notion, that we ought to know nothing out of our particular line of study or profession. You will be none the less distinguished in your calling, for having obtained an item of practical knowledge from every man with whom you meet. And every man, in his particular calling, knows things which you do not, and which are decidedly worth knowing.

Multitudes of gifted and learned men sat under the ministry of the eloquent and youthful Spencer.[1] They were his superiors in every thing excepting his own profession, and perhaps in that, excepting the point on which he had just been studying, and on which he was speaking. Yet they all felt

[1] See his Life by Dr. Raffles

that they were deriving information, profit, and pleasure, from his ministry. "Old-fashioned economists will tell you never to pass an old nail, or an old horse-shoe, or buckle, or even a pin, without taking it up; because, although you may not want it now, you will find a use for it some time or other. I say the same thing to you with regard to knowledge. However useless it may appear to you at the moment, seize upon all that is fairly within your reach. For there is not a fact, within the whole circle of human observation, nor even a fugitive anecdote that you read in a newspaper, or hear in conversation, that will not come into play some time or other; and occasions will arise when they involuntarily present their dim shadows in the train of your thinking and reasoning, as belonging to that train, and you will regret that you cannot recall them more distinctly."

I do not recommend you to try to learn every thing. Far from it. But while you have one great object in view, you can attend to other things which have a bearing on your object. If you were now sent on an express to Mexico, while the great object before you would be, to do your errand well, and expeditiously, ought you not, as you pass along, to use your eyes, and gaze upon the landscapes, the rivers, the deep glens, the waterfalls, the wild solitudes of nature, which lie in your path? Ought you not to have your ears open, to pick up what information, story, anecdote, fact, every thing of the kind, which you can, and thus return wiser? Would all this hinder you in the least? And would you not be fitting yourself, by every such acquisition, to be a more agreeable, intelligent and useful man? "*Sic, sic se habere rem necesse prorsus est.*"

7. *Form fixed principles on which you think and act.*

A good scholar tries so to fix every word in his memory, that, when he meets with it again, he need not turn to his dictionary. His companion may dispute its derivation, or its gender, and he may not be able to tell just how the word appeared when he looked it out; but he has made up his mind about it, and has a fixed opinion. He may not now be able to tell you by what process he came to that opinion. It should be so with every thing. Do not examine a subject, in order to get some general notion of it, but, if now in haste, wait till you can do it thoroughly. No matter what it be,—of great importance or small,—if it be worth examining at all, do it thoroughly, and do it once for all; so that, whenever the subject shall again come up, your mind will be settled and at rest. It is the possession of established and unwavering principles that makes a man a firm character. These principles relate to right and wrong, and, indeed, to every thing about which the judgment has to balance probabilities. Do not be hasty in coming to conclusions. Young men generally err more by being precipitate, than for want of judgment. If they will only give themselves time to weigh the matter, their conclusions will usually be correct.

"I have long adopted an expedient, which I have found of singular service. I have a shelf in my study for tried authors, and one in my *mind* for tried principles and characters.

"When an *author* has stood a thorough examination, and will bear to be taken as a guide, I put him on the shelf!

"When I have more fully made up my mind on a *principle*, I put it on the shelf! A hundred subtle objections may be brought against this principle; I may meet with some of them, perhaps; but my principle is on the shelf. Generally I may be able to recall the reasons which weighed with me to put it there; but, if not, I am not to be sent out to sea again. Time was when I saw through and detected all the subtleties that could be brought against it. I have past evidence of having been fully convinced; and there on the shelf it shall be!

"When I have turned a character over and over on all sides, and seen it through and through in all situations, I put it on the shelf. There may be conduct in the person, which may stumble others; there may be great inconsistencies; there may be strange and unaccountable turns; but I have put that character on the shelf; difficulties will all be cleared; every thing will come round again. I should be much chagrined, indeed, to be obliged to take a character down which I had once put up, but that has never been the case with me yet; and the best guard against it is, not to be too hasty in putting them there."[1] Those who understand the above keen remarks by experience, well know what a luxury it is, on particular occasions, when the mind is fatigued, or the memory is weak, and doubts are started concerning some point of great importance, to have this "shelf" of established principles to which you can go. I have never been able to read the history of the martyrdom of the venerable Latimer, without being touched, almost to tears, to see him clinging to his long-established principles. They urged him to dispute and prove *his* religion true, and the *popish*, false. He knew that he was old, and had lost somewhat of the strength of his mind. He would not dispute. He left that for young and vigorous minds, while he died simply repeating his belief! He knew very well that he had once examined the subject with all the vigor of his intellect, and he was not to go and take these principles down from the "shelf," and again prove them to be correct. Conduct which stands on such a basis, and character which strikes its roots thus deep, will be such as will bear scrutiny, and such as no storm can shake.

[1] Cecil.

"The man resolved, and steady to his trust,
Inflexible to ill, and obstinately just,
May the rude rabble's insolence despise,
Their senseless clamors and tumultuous cries;
The tyrant's fierceness he beguiles,
And the stern brow and the harsh voice defies,
And with superior greatness smiles."[1]

8. *Be simple and neat in your personal habits.*

It is frequently said, that "some pride is necessary among men, else they would not be decent in their appearance." If the remark means any thing, I suppose it means, that pride adds much and frequently to our personal appearance. But an angel, or any sinless spirit, I doubt not, would be a gentleman in appearance and dress, and that not from pride, but from a desire to be more useful and more happy. Nothing will so uniformly and certainly make you unpopular, as to have any habits that are slovenly.

If you have ever learned to chew or smoke that Indian weed, called tobacco, I beg that you will at once drop all, cleanse your mouth, and never again defile yourself with it. Nicholas Monardus, a German, has written a large folio on the virtues of tobacco; but it would take many such folios to prove it worthy of a place among civilized men. Let a man be thrown from a ship-wreck upon a desert island, and in a state of starvation, and he would rather die than to eat this weed, though the island might be covered

[1] Addison, from Horace, Ode III., Book III.

with it; and no youth can use it, either in chewing or smoking, without decided and permanent injury to his appearance, health, and progress in study. Let a company spend the evening in smoking the cigar, and what is the effect? They all awake, in the morning, restless, feverish, low-spirited, and dissatisfied. The bell grates upon the nerves worse than ever. The mouth is clammy and bitter, the stomach uneasy, and each one feels like pouring out the vital principle in yawning. The custom certainly seems most at home in a filthy ale-house or bar-room. When the fashion was so strong in England, that James I. could get no one to preach against it, his own royal hand took the pen and wrote a treatise which he denominates "*A Counterblast to Tobacco.*" The strength of his princely antidote may be gathered from the following closing paragraph of this royal Counterblast. "It is a custom loathsome to the *eye*, hateful to the *nose*, harmful to the *brain*, dangerous to the *lungs*, and in the black . . . . . . fume thereof, nearest resembling the horrible Stygeian smoke of the pit that is bottomless."

All experienced people will tell you that the habit of using tobacco, in any shape, will soon render you emaciated and consumptive, your nerves shattered, your spirits low and moody, your throat dry, and demanding stimulating drinks, your person filthy, and your habits those of a swine.

Let your dress be neat and simple. Do not feel

that the body, which is merely a case for the soul, is of too great importance. At the same time, he who is a "good and true man," will be likely to keep the outside of his house in good order. In a certain village there is a house, which seems designed to be foppish. Its front is white, its left green, its back yellow, and its right red. Nothing could be more ridiculous, and yet it is not more ridiculous, in reality, than the dress of many a house that the soul must inhabit. I would recommend that your clothes be of good quality,—so good, that you constantly feel that they are worth preserving,—and that you feel anxious to show your economy, by the length of time they last. For exercise, you should have a different dress. No one can enjoy himself who undertakes to study and exercise in the same dress. In your study, use an old coat or gown. You will feel more easy and comfortable, and your dress-coat will last all the better for it. Some wear a baize jacket in study; and this is very well. I know of one who always studies, summer and winter, in his shirt sleeves; and though I have an opinion of him quite as high as he deserves, yet I cannot recommend the practice.

Your dress should be warm. If you wear flannels next the skin, be sure to take them all off when you sleep. Be sure, also, to keep your feet dry and warm. In order to this, you must use them every day in walking. The question in relation to dress should be, not

"How often can I have a new hat or coat?" but "How long can I wear it, and keep it handsome?" He who undertakes to be very nice and finical in his dress, will make but a poor student. He descends towards the animal world. Dryden, in his fable of the Cock and the Fox, seems to have had a dandy before him—

> "Then, turning, said to Partlet, 'See, my dear,
> How lavish Nature hath adorned the year;
> How the pale primrose and the violets spring,
> And birds assay their throats, disused, to sing:
> All these are ours; and I, with pleasure, see
> Man strutting on two legs, and aping me!'"

No slave is so abject, as he who tries to keep near the head in the race of fashions. Alexander is said to have had a neck that was wry; and this created a fashion, so that his courtiers all held their heads on one side. He was most fashionable, who lopped his head the most. Was this more ridiculous than what the votaries of fashion must do continually? But cannot a student be particularly nice about his dress without having his heart all in it? I reply, "that whenever you see the tail of a fox out of the hole, you may be pretty sure that the fox is in the hole." Keep your clothes neat and clean; your coat, your hat, your boots or shoes, and be neat as to your linen; but do not feel that this is by any means the great business of life.

Pay particular attention to your teeth. By this I

mean, simply, cleanse them with a soft brush and with water, in which a little common salt is dissolved, the last thing before you retire at night. This simple direction, faithfully followed, will ordinarily keep the teeth good till old age. I would urge this, because, if neglected, the following are the results:—Your breath will inevitably become offensive from defective teeth; your comfort will be destroyed by frequent tooth-ache; your health will suffer for the want of good teeth to masticate the food; and last, though not least, you will early lose your teeth, and thus your public speaking will be irretrievably injured. These may seem small affairs now, but the habit of neglect will assuredly bring bitter repentance when it is too late to remedy the neglect.

Do not affect singularity in any of your habits. We never feel at home with a man of odd habits; and any such will assuredly increase upon him. He makes a heavy draft upon the kindness of mankind, who is every day demanding that they bear with his eccentricities. You may now recollect a most excellent man, who is often seen in company, with his feet poised upon the top of a chair, and nearly as high as his head, and not unfrequently upon a table. The habit was acquired when a student; and though a whole company has often ached over the habit, yet it remains unaltered. You may be boorish in manners, and be like *Johnson* in *that* respect; but he had talents and industry, which could make him distinguished in spite of his ill manners.

Be particularly attentive to your behavior at table, for, from his situation, the student is peculiarly tempted to err there. There is an abruptness and bluntness in the manners of some professional men—a complete treading under foot of all politeness. It may be attributed to the fact that they probably associated but little with refined society while students; and when they came out into the world, not knowing how to behave, they put on the blunt, hair-cloth mode, as if conscious of abilities which would suffer them to despise form and politeness. But a man is never more mistaken than when he supposes that any strength of mind or attainments will render his company agreeable, while his manners are rude. If you are accustomed to society, behave as you know how; if not accustomed to it, behave modestly, and you will behave well; so that, in all your intercourse with your fellow-students, always maintain the appearance and character of a gentleman, never that of a buffoon, or a sloven. And as your character now is, in these respects, so it is to be through life. I have known students whose wash-stand, and establishment, showed that they were slovens; and they were never known to improve in these respects. Keep your room and person, at all times, just as you would have it if you expected your mother or sister to make you a visit. Neatness is the word by which to designate all that is meant in regard to your personal appearance.

Cleanliness is the first mark of politeness; it is agreeable to others, and is a very pleasant sensation to ourselves. The humor of Swift was not misapplied when he describes himself as recovering from sickness by changing his linen. A clean, neat appearance is always a good letter of introduction. May I request my readers to gather the application and moral of the following beautiful story:—"A dervise, of great sanctity, one morning, had the misfortune, as he took up a crystal cup, which was consecrated to the prophet, to let it fall upon the ground, and dash it to pieces. His son coming in some time after, he stretched out his hand to bless him, as his manner was every morning; but the youth, going out, stumbled over the threshold and broke his arm. As the old man wondered at these events, a caravan passed by in its way to Mecca: the dervise approached it to beg a blessing; but as he stroked one of the holy camels, he received a kick from the beast, which sorely bruised him! His sorrow and amazement increased upon him, until he recollected that, through hurry and inadvertency, *he had that morning come abroad without washing his hands.*"[1]

9. *Acquire the habit of doing every thing well.*

It is well known that Johnson used to write and

[1] Rambler.

send copy to the press, without even looking it over by way of revising. This was the effect of habit. He began by composing slowly, but with great accuracy. We are naturally impatient of restraint, and have so little patience at our command, that it is a rare thing to find a young man doing any thing as well as he can. He wishes to do it quickly. And in the conversation of students, you seldom hear one tell *how well* he did this or that, but *how quickly* This is a pernicious habit. Any thing that is worth doing at all, is worth doing well; and a mind well disciplined in other respects, is defective, if it have not this habit. A young man, who unexpectedly lost the affections of a young lady, of whom he was sufficiently fond, informed his friend, with a good degree of shrewdness, that he doubted not that he lost the prize from a very small circumstance. She handed him a letter which she had been writing to a friend, and asked him to direct it. He did so, but in a manner so hurried and slovenly, (for it was his great ambition to be quick in doing any thing,) that she blushed when she received it. From that little circumstance her affections seemed to cool, until they were dead to him. His friend comforted him by saying that "she was more than half right."

This incident is mentioned, not on account of its dignity, but to illustrate the point in hand. Every thing should be done *well*, and practice wil soon enable you to do it quickly. How many are miserable readers, and miserable writers, as to manner and matter, because they do not possess this habit! Euripides used to compose but three lines, while a contemporary poet composed three hundred; but one wrote for immortality, and the other for the day. Your reading had better be but little, your conversations but few, your compositions short and well done. The man who is in a "great hurry," is commonly the one who hurries over the small stages of the journey, without making the great business of life to consist in accomplishing as much as possible. The great secret of Buonaparte's skill as a warrior, consisted in this; that he did his business thoroughly: if he met an army in two or three divisions, he did not divide his army in the same proportion. No: he brought all his strength to bear upon one point, until that was annihilated. So with McDonough, during our last war. He directed all his force, every gun, against the "big ship" of the enemy. No matter how pressing or annoying others might be; every ball was to be sent towards the "big ship," till her guns were silent. This is a good principle to carry out in regard to every thing.

"How is it that you do so much?" said one in astonishment at the efforts and success of a great man. "Why, I do but one thing at a time, and try to *finish* it once for all." would therefore have you keep this in mind:—Do not send a letter home blotted or hurried, and ask them to excuse it, because you are in a hurry. You have no right to be in such a hurry. It is doing injustice to yourself. Do not make a memorandum so carelessly, that in five years you can make nothing of it. Do not hurry any thing so that you know not what you do, or do not know certainly about it, and have to trust to vague impressions. What we call a superficial character, is formed in this way; and none who are not careful to form and cherish the habit of *doing every thing well*, may expect to be any thing else than superficial.

10. *Make constant efforts to be master of your temper.*

The often-quoted remark of Solomon, in regard to authorship and study, is true to life; and that study which is such a "weariness to the flesh," will almost certainly reach the nerves, and render you more or less liable to be irritated. Who would have thought that the elegant Goldsmith would, in his retirement, have been peevish and fretful? So, we are told, was the fact. And perhaps he who could write the Citizen of the World, and the Deserted Village, and the Vicar of Wakefield, exhausted his nerves, in trying to be kind-hearted and pleasant in his writings; so that, when he fell back into real life, he had no materials left with which to be agreeable. Be this as it may, it is not unfrequently the case, that he who can appear kind and pleasant with his pen, and when abroad, is nevertheless growing sour and crabbed in his study. Hence it has sometimes been said of a student, "He is at times the most agreeable, and at times the most disagreeable of men." It will require no small exertion, on your part, to become master of yourself. He that is master of his own spirit, is a hero indeed. Nothing grows faster by indulgence, than the habit of speaking to a companion hastily: it soon becomes so fixed that it lasts through life. In order to avoid it, cultivate manliness of character. Be frank and open-hearted. Not merely appear so, but really *be* so. There is an openness, a nobleness of soul, about some men, which is quickly discovered, and as highly valued. We know that there is originally a difference in men. Some seem to be born small, close, misanthropic, and their whole contour is on a contracted scale. But there is no reason why they should yield to this constitutional trait, and become more and more so. You may have been neglected in your childhood in this respect; but this is no reason why you should neglect yourself. You will often see students, whose means are small, much respected for their nobleness and manliness of character. I mention this, that you may not forget that it is not the circumstance of being rich or poor, which creates this trait in your character.

Be contented in your situation. Nothing will

sooner render any one disagreeable, or sooner destroy his own peace, than a discontented spirit. Who can expect to master himself, to master languages, to master mathematics, and to master a thousand difficulties, while obtaining a thorough and complete education, without meeting with discouragements? Who ever undertook to explore a great region, without meeting with hot suns, and cold rains, with clouds of dust, and swarms of flies?—Your room is not pleasant. It is to be regretted; but, as the traveller said about his straw-bed on the garret floor, "he could get a great deal of good sleep out of it," you can study hard and thoroughly in it. You will hereafter often be called to task your mind under circumstances vastly worse.—Your room-mate is not good-tempered or agreeable. Very like; but he will become much better by associating with you, if you are faithful to yourself. He may have had poor advantages; he may naturally possess a disposition peculiarly cross-grained; but he is susceptible of great improvement; and if you are faithful, he will alter more than you can now imagine. How many young men have been saved from ruin by the example and kind warnings of their room-mates!—Your boarding-place is not to your mind. Very like; but as the great object is the mind, rather than the body, you will soon cease to regard it, if you do not stop to brood over it.—You see others with more pocket-money, and better dressed, than yourself. True; but remember that the recitation-room is the place where scholars are measured, and that neither broadcloth nor pocket-money will avail there. You will not unfrequently notice a great difference in the appearance of the same scholars when on the promenade and in the recitation-room. You will find many who can do much better in demonstrating the fashions of the day, than in demonstrating the problems in spherical trigonometry, or in construing Thucydides. Will you envy such, and repine at your circumstances?

Another way to avoid discontent and peevishness, is carefully to avoid reverie. Castle-building cannot be laughed out of existence, else had it long since been no more. The mischiefs of it are immense. We are not satisfied with what we now are; we have no patience to dig, and wait, and grow to eminence; and so we go off on the wings of imagination, and range through all desirable conditions, and select one, and at once sit down on empire or greatness. Nature and fortune never combined to create such an Elysium for fallen man as you can at once create for yourself. Fancy soon obtains the victory over the soul; for it is vastly more easy for us to sit in our chair, and dream ourselves into statesmen and orators, rulers, and movers of the world, than to put forth the exertions required to become tolerable in actual life in any profession. The sage, in Rasselas, who spent his time and thoughts, and wore himself down for ten years, in guiding and regulating the planets and seasons, was wise, in comparison with many who live in reverie; for his feelings became mellowed and kind, whereas, in most cases, the whole influence of these day-dreams is bad. *They decidedly sour the feelings.* Notice your own feelings. As you descend upon the world after a season of communing with fancy, it seems like a forsaken castle, cold and cheerless. In these reveries, you will meet with enemies enough; but it is only that fancy may lift you above them, and show you how superior you are to every thing like difficulties or opposition. I am confident that I do not speak at random when I say, I have known young men whose feelings became morose, and their countenances became σκυθρωποι, like those of the Pharisees, wholly in consequence of frequently encountering legions of enemies and troubles in their reveries. Let the imagination become your master, and hold the reins, and you will soon become a discontented spirit. At this point, I am persuaded, insanity frequently begins. Indeed, he who lives in an imaginary world is, *quoad hoc*, insane. Who can be pleasant and good-natured, after having sat an hour, persuading himself that he was electrifying the senate, or melting a jury, or overwhelming a city congregation, with a nation gazing at his greatness, and then suddenly awaking, and finding that he dreads to have the hour of reciting arrive?

11. *Cultivate soundness of judgment.*

Some can decide, almost intuitively, upon the character of the last person they have met. So of a book. They can turn it over, read part of a page here, and a sentence or two in another place, and decide, unhesitatingly, upon its merits. When a prejudice has once entered your mind against a man or an author, it is hard to eradicate it. It warps the judgment and makes you partial. If this habit be indulged, the mind soon becomes habituated to act from prejudice, rather than judgment. "A perfectly just and sound mind is a rare and invaluable gift. But it is still much more unusual to see such a mind unbiased in all its actings. God has given this soundness of mind but to few; and a very small number of those few escape the bias of some predilection, perhaps habitually operating; and none, at all times, are perfectly free. I once saw this subject forcibly illustrated. A watch-maker told me that a gentleman had put an exquisite watch into his hands, that went irregularly. It was as perfect a piece of work as was ever made. He took it to pieces, and put it together again, twenty times. No manner of defect was to be discovered; and yet the watch went intolerably. At last it struck him, that possibly the balance-wheel might have been near a magnet: on applying a needle to it, he found his suspicions true: here was all the mischief. The steel works in the other parts of the watch had a perpetual influence on its motions; and the watch went as well as possible with a new wheel. If the soundest mind be *magnetized* by any predilection, it must act irregularly."

As to judging of your own character, do not forget, that every man is almost sure to over-rate his own importance. Our friends flatter us, and our own hearts still more. Our faults are not seen, or, if seen, passed over, or softened down, by both of these parties. The judgment of our enemies, though more severe upon us, is more likely to be correct. They at least open our eyes to defects, which we were in danger of never seeing. Another thing is to be noticed. The world praises you for this or that thing which you do. If, on examination, you find the motives of that action wrong and sinful, are you, then, judging correctly, if you estimate your character by their judgment? Many of our virtues are of a doubtful nature, and we are in danger of placing all such on the credit side of the ledger.

An officer in our army, of high character and promise, told me that he once sat down to weigh the principle of entire abstinence from ardent spirit, and to decide whether it was his duty, in his circumstances, to adopt it. He took a large sheet of paper, and began by setting down, in regular order, all the reasons why the principle of entire abstinence ought *not* to prevail. The list was somewhat long and imposing. He felt pretty sure that he might safely take that side of the question. But to make it perfectly sure, he began to set down, on another page, the arguments on the other side. They soon began to grow and grow, till he was astonished at their number and weight. They quickly out-numbered their opponents; and it did not at first strike his attention, that he had several put down against entire abstinence which belonged to the other side. These were shifted and altered, till, at last, with one dash of the pen, he blotted out the few that remained; and, though he has now forgotten the steps of the process, yet, from that hour to this, he has never had a doubt on the question. This is what I mean by cultivating soundness of judgment. The process may be slower than to jump to conclusions, but it is much more satisfactory, and will give you the habit of weighing and judging correctly.

12. *Treatment of parents, friends, and companions.* I hope it will appear that I am not out of place in trying to lead you to make the proper treatment of friends a habit. Whether you intend it or not, it will become so. Remember that, when you are away from home, you are more likely to forget and neglect your parents, than they are to forget you. You are in new scenes, forming new acquaintances. They stay at home; they see your room, your clothes-

walk over the rooms where your voice has been so often and so long heard. They follow you away, they miss you at the table, and speak of you; they let no day pass without speaking of you, and at night they send their thoughts away after you, and have a thousand anxieties about you, which nothing but your attentions can remove or alleviate. The poet beautifully compares this anxiety for absent friends to that of the bird which leaves her young. She constantly fears the serpent will find them during her absence, though she knows her presence could do them no good.

> "Comes minore sum futurus in metu,
> Qui major absentes habet;
> Ut assidens implumibus pullis avis
> Serpentium allapsus timet
> Magis relictis: non ut adsit, auxili
> Latura plus præsentibus."[1]

You cannot act the part of a dutiful child, without daily sending your thoughts home. Write to friends often, and *at stated times*. Any correspondence between friends is, in all respects, more valuable, interesting, useful and pleasant to all parties, for being regular and at stated times. You then know when to write, and when to expect a letter, and there is no wondering why a letter does not come, and no chiding for negligence. Enter into no correspondence, unless it be on occasional business, which will not be so val-

[1] Hor. Carm. V.

uable that you wish to continue it; and then have periodical times of writing. To your parents, it should be at least once every month. In these letters, talk out your feelings in that easy, cheerful manner, that you would were you at home, and entertaining the family circle in the vacation. I shall not ask pardon for introducing here a letter from one, whose attentions to the person addressed have never been regretted. The letter needs no expositor, and, as it seems to me, no apology for being inserted here.

"—— *College, Tuesday Evening*

"My dear Mother,

THOUGH I am now sitting with my back towards you, yet I love you none the less; and, what is quite as strange, I can see you just as plainly as if I stood peeping in upon you. I can see you all, just as you sit round the family table. Tell me, if I do not see you. There is mother, on the right of the table, with her knitting, and a book open before her; and anon she glances her eyes from the work on paper to that on her needles; now counts the stitches, and then puts her eye on the book, and starts off for another round. There is Mary, looking wise, and sewing with all her might, now and then stopping to give Sarah and Louisa a lift in getting their lessons, and trying to initiate them into the mysteries of geography. She is on the left of the table. There, in the back ground, is silent Joseph, with his slate, now making a mark, and then biting his lip, or scratching his head, to see if the algebraic expression may have hidden in either of those places. George is in the kitchen, tinkering his skates, or contriving a trap for that old offender of a rat, whose cunning has so long brought mortification upon all his boastings. I can now hear his hammer, and his whistle—that peculiar, sucking-sort of whistle, which always indicates a puzzled state of the brain. Little William and Henry are snug in bed, and, if you will just open their bed-room door, you will barely hear them breathe. And now, mother has stopped, and is absent and thoughtful, and my heart tells me that she is thinking of her only absent child. Who can he be? Will you doubt any more that I have studied magic, and can see with my back turned to you, and many a hill and valley between us?

You have been even kinder than I expected, or you promised. I did not expect to hear from you till to-morrow, at the earliest. But as I was walking, to-day, one of my class-mates cries, "A bundle for you at the stage-office!" and away I went as fast as the dignity of a sophomore would allow me. The bundle I seized, and muffled it under my cloak, though it made my arm ache, and, with as much speed as my "conditions" would permit me, I reached my room. Out came my knife, and, forgetting all your good advice about "strings and fragments," the said bundle quickly owned me victor, and opened its very heart to me; and it had a warm heart too, for there were the stockings, (they are now on my feet, i.e. one pair,) and there were the flannels, and the bosoms, and the gloves, and the pincushion from Louisa, and the needle-book from Sarah, and the paper from Mary, and the letters and love from all of you. I spread open my treasures, and both my heart and feet danced for joy, while my hands actually rubbed each other out of sympathy. Thanks to you all, for bundle, and letters, and love. One corner of my eye is now moistened, while I say, "Thank ye all, gude folks." I must not forget to mention the apples—"the six apples, one from each"—and the beautiful little loaf of cake. I should not dare call it little, if it had not brought the name from you. The apples I have smelled of, and the cake I have just nibbled a little, and pronounce it to be "in the finest taste."

Now, a word about your letters. I cannot say much, for I have only read mother's three times, and Mary's twice. Those parts which relate to my own acts and doings, greatly edify me. Right glad to find that the spectacles fitted mother's eyes so well. You wondered how I hit it. Why, have I not been told from my very babyhood, "You have your mother's eyes?" And what is plainer, than that, if I have her eyes, I can pick out glasses that will fit them? I am glad, too, that the new book is a favorite. I shall have to depend on you to read for me, for here I read nothing but my lexicon, and, peradventure, dip into mathematics. Joseph's knife shall be forthcoming, and the orders of William and Henry shall be honored, if the apothecary has the pigments. "George is delighted with his new sled"—a cheering item; for my thumb has retired into his cot, and growled and ached ever since, and even now, ever and anon, gives me a twinge, by way of recalling the feat of building the sled. And you really think the pigs have profited by my labors, and that, though they have forgotten *me*, yet they like the sty! If they do well, I shall be paid next fall, whether they are grateful or not. Old Charley should be kept warm. He has carried us too many miles to be neglected now. I am sorry I did not have his condition more in mind when at home. Poor fellow, I enjoyed his aid, and helped to make him grow old. And old Rover, let him have his new kennel warm; and if he thinks so much of me as to "go to my room" after me, let him have my old wrapper. One member more,—tell Sukey that, though I mention her after horses and dogs, it is not out of any want of respect. I will wear the mittens which she knit and sent, and, in return, though I cannot approve, will send as much, at least, of "real Scotch," as will fill her box.

I suppose the pond is all frozen over, and the skating good. I know it is foolish; yet, if mother and

Mary had skated as many "moony" nights as I have, they would sigh, not at the *thought*, but at the *fact* that skating days are over. Never was a face more bright and beautiful than the face of that pond in a clear, cold night, under a full moon. Do the boys go down by my willow still? and do they still have the flag on the little island in the centre, where I used to rear the flag-staff once a year? I was going to tell you all about college. But when I think I will begin, pop!—my thoughts are all at home! What a place home is! I would not now exchange ours for wealth enough to make you all kings and queens.

I am warm, well, and comfortable: we all study some; and dull fellows like me have to confess that we study hard. We have no genius to help us. My chum is a good fellow:—he now sits in yonder corner—his feet poised upon the stove in such a way, that the dullness seems to have all run out of his heels into his head, for he is fast asleep.

I have got it framed, and there it hangs—the picture of my father! I never look up without seeing it, and I never see it without thinking that my mother is a widow, and that I am her eldest son. What more I think, I will not be fool enough to say: you will imagine it better than I can say it.

Your gentle hint, dear mother, about leaving my Bible at home, was kind; but it will relieve you to know that I left it designedly, and, in its place, took my dear father's from the upper shelf in our little library room; and what is more, I read it every day.

I need not say, Write! write! for I know that some of you will, at the end of three weeks. But love to you all, and much too. I shall tell you of my methods of economy in my next.

Your affectionate son, &c."

Can any of my readers doubt but a letter like the above, would do much to alleviate the anxiety of the mother, and add greatly to the comfort of the family? Every son can show such attentions, and at the same time keep his own heart warm with tho remembrances of home and kindred. It will add to your ease in letter-writing, and it will cultivate some of the noblest and sweetest virtues of which the heart is susceptible.

I would say a few words on the choice and treatment of friends; and, as this subject is treated of by almost every writer, I shall be brief. You must have some, and will have some, with whom you are more intimate than with the rest of your companions. There are two special difficulties attending friendships; first, it is hard to acquire a real friend; and, secondly, it is still harder to keep him. The acquaintance, which is afterwards ripened into friendship, is, of course, in the first place, casual. And those who are first to extend the hand to embrace you, are seldom those whose friendship continues long. Be cautious in selecting your friends, and look long and well before you allow any one to say, that he is your bosom-companion, and that you share each other's thoughts and secrets. In selecting your friends, you will remember that you will borrow habits, traits of character, modes of thought and expression, from each other; and, therefore, be careful to select those who have not excellences merely, but whose faults are as few as may be. Some rely too much upon friends, and think they will never pass away, and never change. Others, who have known, by experience, that friends may do both, will tell you that friendship is "but a name," and means nothing. Extremes are never in the right. There is much, both of wisdom and beauty, in the following remarks. They are not taken from the writings of Confucius, else had they been set in gold long since.

"Sweet language will multiply friends, and a fair-speaking tongue will multiply kind greetings. Be in peace with many: nevertheless, have but one counsellor in a thousand. If thou wouldst get a friend, prove him first, and be not hasty to credit him; for some man is a friend for his own occasion, and will not abide in the day of thy trouble. Separate thyself from thine enemies, and take heed to thy friends. A faithful friend is a strong defence, and he that hath found such a one, hath found a treasure. A faithful friend is the medicine of life. Forsake not an old friend, for the new is not comparable to him: a new friend is as new wine: when it is old, thou shalt drink it with pleasure. Whoso casteth a stone at the birds frayeth them away, and he that upbraideth his friend breaketh friendships; for upbraiding, or pride, or disclosing of secrets, or a treacherous wound, every friend will depart."

"Verbum dulce multiplicat amicos, et lingua eucharis in bono homine abundat. Multi pacifici sint tibi, et consiliarius sit tibi unus de mille. Si possides amicum, in tentatione posside eum, et ne facile credas ei. Est enim amicus secundum tempus suum, et non permanebit in die tribulationis. Ab inimicis tuis, separare, et ab amicis tuis attende. Amicus fidelis, protectio fortis; qui autem invenit illum, invenit thesaurum. Amicus fidelis, medicamentum vitæ. Ne derelinquas amicum antiquum: novus enim non erit similis illi: vinum novum, amicus novus, veterascet, et cum suavitate bibes illud. Mittens lapidem in volatilia, dejiciet illa: sic et qui convitiatur amico, dissoluit amicitiam: convitiis, et superbia, et mysterii revelatione, et plaga dolosa,—in his omnibus effugiet amicus." *

No one can long be your friend for whom you have not a decided esteem—an esteem that will not permit

* The lover of classical Latin will please to remember, that I no more claim credit for the Latin, than for the beautiful sentiments so inelegantly expressed in it.

you to trifle with his feelings, and which, of course, will prevent his trifling with yours. Great familiarity is inconsistent with any abiding friendship.

> "The man who hails you Tom, or Jack,
> And proves, by thumping on your back,
> His sense of your great merit,
> Is such a friend that one had need
> Be very much his friend indeed,
> To pardon or to bear it."

You will soon be ashamed to love one for whom you have not a high esteem. Love will only follow esteem. In order to have or keep a friend, you must not have a particle of envy towards him, however exalted his character or merits. Says a beautiful writer, "He who can once doubt whether he should rejoice in his friend's being happier than himself, may depend upon it, that he is an utter stranger to this virtue."

You will always observe that those friendships which are the purest, and the most abiding, are chosen for the good qualities of the heart, rather than for those of the head. I should be sorry to give the impression, that the finest qualities of the heart may not accompany the highest intellectual character; and I am satisfied that there is no good reason why they do not. But it has been shrewdly remarked, "I do not remember that Achates, who is represented as the first favorite, either gives his advice, or str kes a blow, through the whole Æneid."

Prudence is a prime quality in a friend; and zeal and noise are not always indicative of the greatest ability or desire to do you good. But in order to have a true friend, you must determine to be to him just what you wish him to be to you. While I would recommend every young man to commit to memory the whole of Cowper's beautiful description of "Friendship," I would particularly request him to keep the following sentiment uppermost:

> "Who seeks a friend, should come disposed
> T' exhibit, in full bloom disclosed,
> The graces and the beauties
> That form the character he seeks;
> For 'tis a union that bespeaks
> Reciprocated duties."

A similarity of inclinations is by no means essential to a perfect and abiding friendship. We admire those traits of character which we do not ourselves possess. They are new to us, and we feel that from them we can supply our own defects.

Although it is considered one great duty of friendship to discover faults, and give reproofs, yet it is a dangerous duty. It must be done very delicately and kindly, and be sure not too frequently. There were once two friends, room-mates, who agreed that, every night, they would tell each other *every thing*, which they had seen during the day, which was in the least degree out of the way. They did so a while. They did it kindly; but it was too much for poor human nature. They soon parted, and took new rooms, but without ever disclosing to each other the true cause even if they were conscious of it at the time. I do not, on the whole, believe it is the appropriate business of a friend to discover faults and reprove you—but it is, *to support you in high and noble pursuits, raising your spirits, and adding to your courage, till you out-do yourself.* Are those families the happiest, where every member is to be tried by a constant or frequent fault-finding? Far from it. If you wish your friend to do well, encourage him, sustain him when in trials or troubles, and thus you become the "medicine of life." Cultivate your old friends: but you must form new ones also; for our changes by removal and death are so frequent, that he who now makes no new friends will soon find himself without any. Need it be said, that a strict and unwavering regard for truth is absolutely essential to having friends? We do not wish to be associated with those whose veracity can, in the least, be suspected. "When speech is employed as the vehicle of falsehood, every man must disunite himself from others, inhabit his own cave, and seek prey only for himself," and in vain ask or seek for a friend.

I have dwelt somewhat on this point,—longer, perhaps, than was to be expected, under the title of this chapter. But it is my wish that all my readers may have friends, select, disinterested friends; and I know that they cannot, unless they make it a part of their daily habits and business to cultivate their own hearts, and render themselves worthy of being beloved. The tree cannot live and thrive without great care; but if it receive that care, it will bear fruit abundantly for many years. How often has the heart of my reader thrilled at the warm greetings of one who said, "Your father and I were friends!" Friendship can lessen no joy by having a sharer. It brightens every one. At the same time, it diminishes sorrow, in every shape, by dividing the burden.

> "Hast thou a friend?—thou hast indeed
> A rich and large supply—
> Treasure to serve your every need,
> Well managed, till you die."

CHAPTER III

STUDY.

When the company had wearied themselves in trying to make an egg stand on its end, they were amazed at the simplicity of the thing, when once they had seen Columbus do it.

"Why, any body can do that!"

"Why, then, did you not?" was the searching reply.

It seems to be an easy affair to study. There is the room, and there the books and there the lesson: what more do you want? You want to know how to go to work—*how to study*. The interruptions to study, even when the student has nothing else to do, —not a care, not a burden of any kind to trouble him, —are numerous and vexatious. Deductions must be made for ill health, and seasons when the spirits droop, and when there is a total disrelish for study, and a want of courage, by which the mind can be brought up to action; for a total ignorance of the best methods of studying; for the interruptions of companions who have yawned over their own books, till they could make little or nothing out of them, and then have come to get sympathy and countenance from others; for the time wasted in reading novels, or other useless books; and, above all, for that natural, inherent indolence, which recoils from the task of rebuking the wandering of the thoughts, and bringing them back to their prescribed tasks. Escaping from home will not relieve the difficulty; neither will removing from one school to another, or changing one college for another. You must make up your mind that no one can go on in a course of study without interruptions from within and from without. Calculate upon this. And it is well that it is so; for, in real life, if you can get two full hours in a week without interruption, you may think it extraordinary. The mind must form the habit of being checked and interrupted, and of bringing itself back to the point from which it was taken off, and at once pursuing the train of mental operations in which it was engaged. Till this power is obtained, you are not prepared for active life; and in proportion as it is acquired, in that proportion will little hinderances appear to you of little consequence. I propose to make some suggestions in the form of hints in relation to study, not so much regarding the order of their introduction, as endeavoring not to omit any that are of real importance.

1. *The number of hours of daily study.*

No fixed time can be marked out for all. This must vary with the constitution of each individual. A mind that moves slowly requires and will bear more time for study. In Germany, the students spend many more hours than we can in this country. I have tried to account for the fact, that, with their preposterous habits of eating and indolence, they can study so many hours in a day, and that to extreme old age. Doubtless national habits do something; individual habits do something; but these will not account for it. Many of them will study sixteen hours a day; few of them less than thirteen. We should all die under it! The difference may be attributed to two causes, for the correctness of which I cannot vouch; viz. their mental operations are slower than ours, and their climate is less variable and better adapted to a student's life. Few, in our own country, ever studied half as much as they have, if hours are to be the criterion. But another remark may here be made. Germany is distinguished for the study of the classics, for the making of lexicons and commentaries, and for studies of such a nature as require diligence and accuracy, but make no very great draft upon the soul. Be this as it may, it is certain that we must do what we do, by way of daily study, in fewer hours; and, in my view, it is vastly better to chain the attention down closely, and study hard, a few hours, than to try to keep it moderately fixed and engaged for a greater length of time Our most successful students seldom study over six hours in a day. In this I include nothing of recita tions, of desultory, half-formed impulses of the mind; but I mean real, hard, devoted study. He who would study six hours a day, with all the attention of which the soul is capable, need not fear but he will yet stand high in his calling. But mark me,—*it must be study as intense as the soul will bear.* The attention must all be absorbed; the thoughts must all be brought in, and turned upon the object of study, as you would turn the collected rays of the sun into the focus of the glass, when you would get fire from those rays. Do not call miscellaneous reading, or any thing which you do by way of relief or amusement, study: it is not study. Be sure to get as much of your study in the morning as possible. The mind is then in good order. *Aurora musis amica, necnon vespera.*

2. *Have regard to the positions of the body while engaged in study.*

Some men, from early life, habituate themselves to study, sitting at a low, flat table. This ought to be avoided; for, as you advance in life, that part of the body which is between the shoulders and hips, becomes more and more feeble, and consequently the stooping habit is acquired. Few literary men walk or sit perfectly erect. Standing is undoubtedly the best method of study, if you will only begin in this way. In writing, in the study of languages, and most kinds of mathematics, you must be confined to one spot. If you can change positions, and stand a part, and sit a part of the time, it will be well; but the former should preponderate. As you advance in life, you will naturally sit more and more, till the habit becomes fixed. Few men are seen standing at their books after forty years of age. The late talented, and lamented Grimke,[1] informs us that he uniformly stood, and did most of his studying while walking in his room. If you are composing, or reading, or committing to memory, this position is a desirable one. Be sure you have your table high enough, and keep clear of the rocking-chair, with a writing leaf on the arm of it. Sitting in such a chair gives the body a twisting position, which is almost sure to lead to poor health, and not unfrequently to the grave. If possible, place your table, the top of which should so slope a little, that the light may fall upon you from behind. This will be a kindness to the eyes. In the evening, it is well to have the lamp shaded, or to have a shade drawn over the eyes. I would hope, however, that you keep your lessons so much in advance, that the necessity of putting your eyes to a severe trial, will be avoided. If your eyes are weak, be careful that a glare of light does not fall upon them; and be sure to wash them in cold water the last thing at night, and the first in the morning. The great desideratum in the choice of positions, is, to keep the body as straight as possible. A bending at the chest is by all means to be avoided. Your

[1] Judge of the Supreme Court of S. Carolina

dress, even to the slipper, should sit as loosely as possible; and the house which is now to stand still, and in which the mind is to labor, should be as easy as it can be, without assuming a position which, by long habit, will court the embrace of sleep.

3. *Let there be no conversation in the hours of study.*

This direction goes on the supposition that you have a room-mate, which is usually the case. A lesson is easily spoiled by being interrupted, every now and then, with some question, raised on that, or on some other subject. You cannot study to advantage if *any* conversation is allowed in the room. But what if you find a word in your lesson, whose meaning or whose parsing you cannot determine? What is to be done? May you not ask your friend? I reply, no. Keep the room silent. If you wish to review and compare together, then begin a half hour earlier, and leave off half an hour before reciting, and in this time, go over the lesson together. Have the words, about which you doubted, just marked with a pencil, and then settle their meaning and their relations. This review should not take place till you have each exhausted your own efforts upon the lesson, and until you have definitely settled every word and every sentence.

Some are in the habit of studying aloud together, or in small clubs;—a very bad practice. The habit is soon formed, so that the mind refuses to make any efforts alone; and then it becomes necessary to have a constant "Bee" to aid it, just as the partially civil ized tribes of the Pacific ocean, refuse even to thatch a cottage, unless they have a great company to work together. This cannot be the mode of study through life; and no habit should now be allowed, which will be troublesome hereafter. The sagacity and perseverance of our own minds are to be the ultimate resources on which we shall all be obliged to rely. But if the tongue refuses to be silent, and conversation cannot be banished from your room, be careful to have it on the lesson, and on no other subject.

4. *Be thorough in every study.*

Passing over a field of study has been graphically compared to conquering a country. If you thoroughly conquer *every thing* you meet, you will pass on from victory to victory; but if you leave here and there a fort or a garrison not subdued, you will soon have an army hanging on your rear, and your ground will soon need re-conquering. Never pass over a single thing, however minute, or apparently of little consequence, without understanding all that can be known about it. "Socrates ille non hominum modo, verum etiam Apollinis oraculo, sapientissimus judicatus, et perennis Philosophiæ Fons, dicere solet: 'Radicem quidem eruditionis peramarum esse, sed fructum habere jucundissimum; initioque magnos adferre labores, sed honestissimum sudantibus præmium reponere.' Ergo, O Tu, quisquis es, cui ignea vis in pectore exarsit, cui flamma in præcordiis micat, procul absint mollia, lenia, facilia, blanda, quæ animi ineptum extinguere solent. Dura petamus."

He who accustoms himself to pass over a word or sentence, or a single point of mathematical inquiry, without thoroughly understanding every thing that can be known about it, will soon be known as an inaccurate scholar; will feel but half confident on any subject; and, what is worse, will have acquired a habit which will forever make his knowledge vague and uncertain, both to himself and to others. There is such a constant mortification and loss of self-respect attending the habit of going upon the surface, that, were it only for personal comfort, you should be thorough. At the first setting out, your progress will be slower —perhaps very slow; but, in the long race before you, you will be the gainer. How often have I seen a man, with a mind originally bright, chagrined and humbled at his want of accuracy! He makes an assertion, and calls it a quotation from some distinguished author. "Does Burke say so, and advocate that sentiment? I never understood him so," says an accurate listener. He now begins to hesitate—apologizes—says it is a great while since he read Burke, but such is his impression. Has he not fallen in the estimation of every one present, and in his own also? And yet, such is the habit fixed upon him, that he will go and again tread over the same ground with hesitating steps

Two farms may lie side by side; the one may be "run over" by the hand of the cultivator. Here, is a poor spot of mowing, and there, a miserable-looking corn-field, and yonder, a wretched fern pasture. It covers a great extent of territory, but no part of it is subdued or cultivated. The other farm has its fences in order, its mowing lots all side by side, and its fields, so far as any thing is done, perfectly subdued. Every acre that claims to have been subdued, will bear a certain, a definite, and a full crop. Is there any doubt which of the two farms is more profitable, or which method of cultivation is the most wise?

How much better is knowledge—something that you *know*—than any amount of conjecture formed somewhere in the region of knowledge! Have you never seen the face of an educated man—i. e. of one who ought to have been educated—gather a blank upon it, at the sound of a Latin or Greek quotation? Like the hero in one of Molière's comedies, he understands it, but wishes it translated. The aptness and humor of the case will justify my quoting it.

"*Le M. de Phil.* Ce sentiment est raisonnable; *nam sine doctrinâ vita est quasi mortis imago.* Vous entendez cela, et vous entendez le Latin sans doute?

"*M. Jour.* Oui, mais faites comme si je ne le savais pas: expliquez-moi ce que cela veut dire!

"*Le M. de Phil.* Cela veut dire, que sans la science, la vie est presque l'image de la mort.

"*M. Jour.* Ce Latin-la a raison."

Every thing should be understood as far as you go; and never should you allow yourself to think of going into the recitation-room, and there trust to "skinning," as it is called in some colleges, or "phrasing," as in others, or "mouthing it," as in others. No man who regards his reputation as a scholar, will ever do this.

One lesson or one book, perfectly and thoroughly understood, would do you more good than ten lessons, or ten books, not half studied. Mr. Evarts, to whom allusion has already been made, read his Greek Testament so thoroughly while fitting for college, that he was in the habit, through life, of readily repeating any passage to which allusion was made. And several of our best scholars committed and recited the whole of Virgil without carrying a book into the recitation-room. One of them, at least, did the same with the whole of Horace.

"When you have a mind to improve a single thought, or to be clear in any particular point, do not leave it till you are master of it. View it in every light. Try how many ways you can express it, and which is shortest and best. Would you enlarge upon it, hunt it down from author to author; some of which will suggest hints concerning it, which, perhaps, never occurred to you before; and give every circumstance its weight. Thus, by being master of every subject as you proceed, though you make but a small progress in [the number of books which you study,] you will make a speedy one in useful knowledge. To leave matters undetermined, and the mind unsatisfied in what we study, is but to multiply half-notions, introduce confusion, and is the way to make a pedant, but not a scholar."

Some plausible and ingenious things have been said in favor of using translations to Latin and Greek authors. My own observation has not been as extended as that of very many; but, so far as it does go, I can unhesitatingly say, that I never knew any other than miserable scholars made by the use of translations. I have seen scholars use a translation of Virgil, another of Horace, and as many as they could get to authors selected in Græca Majora; and though they recited smoothly at the time, and perhaps even better than those who dug it all out, yet I am confident they knew less about Latin and Greek at the end of every year. I am sorry to disturb the feelings of any reader who has a faithful translation carefully put away in his drawer or desk, and at which he now and then so stealthfully peeps; but let him continue to use it, and I will warrant him that soon, though the reason may not be assigned, or even known, he will lose all that respect which belongs solely to a thorough student. I have known those who studied Horace with a translation, and though they went off "*smartly*" at the time, not able, at the end of two years, to read an ode. "Go to the fountain head. Read original authors, rather than collect translated and retailed thoughts. It will give you more satisfaction, more certainty, more judgment, and more confidence, when those authors are the subjects of conversation, than you can have by taking your knowledge of them at second hand. It is trusting to translations, quotations, and epitomes, that makes so many half-scholars so impertinently wise."

Some friend may offer to aid you by translations, or by books interlined with a pen, or by furnishing you with mathematical problems all wrought out. Such kindnesses ought to be shown only to an enemy, whom he would have pursued by his vengeance through life. They are the greatest cruelties which an enemy could possibly invent. If you cannot stand on your own feet, do not borrow crutches which will be taken from you soon, and which will effectually prevent you from ever having strength to walk alone.

5. *Expect to become familiar with hard study.*

Study, which is hard for one man, is easy for another. Not only so, but the study which is easy to you to-day, may be intolerably irksome at another time. This is owing to the difficulty of confining the attention closely. The health being the same, study would at all times be equally agreeable, had we the same command over the attention. But who that has tried it, does not know how much easier it is to study on a cold, stormy day in winter, when every thing without is repulsive, than on the warm, bright day of spring, when all nature seems to invite you out, and when the soul seems to disdain and rebel against the restraints of study? You must make your calculations to study many hours, and at many seasons when it is disagreeable—when the mind feels feeble, and the body is languid, or is even in pain. "Other things may be seized on by might, or purchased with money; but knowledge is to be gained only by *study*."

So great is the advantage of being able to confine the attention, that men who have by some unexpected providence lost their sight, have felt willing to exchange all that is beautiful, lovely, and cheering, which the eye drinks in, for the increased power over the attention which this loss gave them. The truly great President Dwight used to consider the loss of his eyes, a great blessing to him, inasmuch as it strengthened the power of attention, and compelled him to think. You may point to men, and say, that "this and that distinguished man was not celebrated for scholarship, or any thing, unless for stupidity, in his younger days. He had no appointment in college—no rank as a scholar." Not unlikely. But be sure of one thing; and that is, he never became distinguished without, some time or other, passing through a severe course of dry, hard study. He might have omitted this when young; but, if so, the task was harder when he did undertake to perform it. But undertake it he must, and he did.

> "Pater ipse colendi
> Haud facilem esse viam voluit, primusque per artem
> Movit agros, curis acuens mortalia corda."

The remarks of the lamented Wirt should be treasured up by every student. A few of the points upon which he touches are so much to my purpose, that I should do injustice to my reader not to quote them. "*Take it for granted, that there is no excellence without great labor.* No mere aspirations for eminence, however ardent, will do the business. Wishing, and sighing, and imagining, and dreaming of greatness, will never make you great. If you would get to the mountain's top, on which the temple of fame stands, it will not do *to stand still*, looking and admiring, and wishing you were there. You must gird up your loins, and go to work with all the indomitable energy of Hannibal scaling the Alps. Laborious study and diligent observation of the world, are both indispensable to the attainment of eminence. By the former, you must make yourself master of all that is known of science and letters; by the latter, you must know *man* at large, and particularly the character and genius of your own countrymen. We cannot all be Franklins, it is true; but, by imitating his mental habits and unwearied industry, we may reach an eminence we should never otherwise attain. Nor would he have been the *Franklin* he was, if he had permitted himself to be discouraged by the reflection that we cannot all be *Newtons*. It is our business to make the most of our own talents and opportunities; and, instead of discouraging ourselves by comparisons and impossibilities, to believe all things imaginary possible, as, indeed, almost all things are, to a spirit bravely and firmly resolved. Franklin was a fine model of a *practical man*, as contradistinguished from a *visionary theorist*, as men of genius are very apt to be. He was great in the greatest of all good qualities—*sound, strong common sense*. A mere bookworm is a miserable driveller; and a mere genius, a thing of a gossamer, fit only for the winds to sport with. Direct your intellectual efforts principally to the cultivation of the strong, masculine qualities of the mind. Learn (I repeat it) *to think—think deeply, comprehensively, powerfully*; and learn the simple, nervous language which is appropriate to that kind of thinking. Read the legal and political arguments of Chief Justice Marshall, and those of Alexander Hamilton which are coming out. Read them, *study them*; and observe with what an omnipotent sweep of thought they range over the whole field of every subject they take in hand,—and that with a scythe so ample and so keen, that not a straw is left standing behind them. Brace yourself up to these great efforts. Strike for this giant character of mind, and leave prettiness and frivolity to triflers. It is perfectly consistent with these Herculean habits of thinking, to be a laborious student, and to know all that books can teach. You must never be satisfied with the surface of things; probe them to the bottom, and let nothing go till you understand it as thoroughly as your powers will enable you. Seize the moment of excited curiosity on any subject, to solve your doubts; for, if you let it pass, the desire may never return, and you may remain in ignorance. The habits which I have been recommending are not merely for college, but for life. Franklin's habits of constant and deep excogitation clung to him to his latest hour. Form these habits now. Look at Brougham, and see what a man can do if well armed and well resolved. With a load of professional duties that would, of themselves, have been appalling to the most of our countrymen, he stood, nevertheless, at the head of his party in the house of commons, and, at the same time, set in motion and superintended various primary schools, and various periodical works, the most instructive and useful that have ever issued from the British press, for which he furnished, with his own pen, some of the most masterly contributions, and yet found time, not only to keep pace with the progress of the arts and sciences, but to keep at the head of those whose peculiar and exclu sive occupations these arts and sciences were. There is a *model of industry and usefulness worthy* of all your emulation."

Under this head, I would add, that he who expects to discipline his mind by hard study, and to build up the mind by the habit of severe thinking, will not be the man to quarrel with *what* he studies. How often do we hear students complaining that they are put to studies which can be of no possible use to them in after life! One is to be a merchant: why should he be drilled in Latin and Greek for years? Another is to study medicine; and why should he be poring over conic sections for months? Multitudes complain that their instructers understand their business so poorly, that the very things for which they will never have any use, are forced upon them as studies! Little do such complainers understand the object of an education. Keep it in mind, that the great object of study is to fit the mind to be an instrument of usefulness in life. You are now upon a dry, hard, uninteresting study. It contains not a single thing which you can ever use hereafter. Be it so. But if you can compel your mind to take hold and master that dry, hard, uninteresting study, you are fitting it to obey you through life, and at any time to do what you bid it do. Suppose your teachers should put you to studying magic—I do not pretend that it would be the best possible study—but if they *should*, take hold and study it without quarrelling with it. There may be nothing in magic which can be of any practical use in life; but perhaps it may do you good to know that there is nothing useful in it; and, at any rate, the discipline of mind acquired by wading through an uninteresting study, is of immense value. It will be time enough to study such things as you propose to use, when you have your mind fitted to master them, and when they are needed. The chancellor of the state of New York was noticed, last summer, morning after morning, on a beautiful young horse, accompanying the rail-road cars, as far as he could go, before they left him by their superior speed. The horse was afraid and unruly, and somewhat dangerous at first, but grew more and more gentle. Why did he do this? Not for pleasure—not to aid him in the severe duties of his responsible station—not because he delighted to travel on that road—but to *discipline his horse, and fit it for future service.*

You study geometry to-day. Perhaps your life may be so busy, and your time so occupied hereafter, that you may forget every proposition, and nothing but the name of the book may remain to you. But Plato, and every other man who has studied geometry, will tell you that it will strengthen your mind, and enable it to think with precision. Geography and chronology are not now needed, but will soon be, in order to trace philosophy through all her branches, in order to acquire a distinct and accurate idea of history and to judge of the propriety of the allusions and com parisons every where meeting you in the works of genius. Philosophy seems to open the mind, and to give it eyes, like the wings of the cherubim, in Ezekiel's vision, within and without it. It subjects all nature to our command, and carries our conceptions up to the Creator. The mind is liberalized by every such study, and without these, it can never become really great or tasteful.

While I would urge you to hard study and severe application, each being a *sine qua non* to success, you must, at the same time, feel sure that a steady, persevering course of study will certainly place you on an eminence. But press onward in a steady course of daily application. A beautiful writer, with great vivacity and spirit, says, "The most usual way, among young men who have no resolution of their own, is, first to ask one friend's advice, and follow it for some time; then to ask advice of another, and turn to that; so of a third, still unsteady, always changing. However, be assured that every change of this nature is for the worse. People may tell you of your being unfit for some peculiar occupations in life; but heed them not. Whatever employment you follow with perseverance and assiduity, will be found fit for you; it will be your support in youth, and comfort in age. In learning the useful part of every profession, very moderate abilities will suffice; even if the mind be a little balanced with stupidity, it may, in this case, be useful. Great abilities have always been less serviceable to the possessors than moderate ones. Life has been compared to a race; but the allusion still improves, by observing that the most swift are ever the least manageable."

Henderson gives an interesting account of his meeting with an Icelander, a poor man, in the common walks of life, who, to his surprise, could read German with great ease. On inquiring how he came to understand the German language, he replied, that he once met with a German book, and so great was his desire to know what it contained, that he could never rest till he had acquired the language so as to read it with confidence.

We are in great danger of being willing to excuse ourselves from severe study, under the idea that our circumstances are not favorable. We are apt to fall in with the common notion that men are made by circumstances—that they are called forth, and their characters are thus formed; and that almost every man would be great, and decided, and effective, were he only sufficiently hedged in and pressed by circumstances. There can be no doubt but that men are naturally and practically indolent, and that they need powerful stimulants and a heavy pressure, to awaken their powers and call forth exertions. We know that most men accomplish but very little. But would they under any circumstances? Might not the tables be turned, and might we not with as great propriety say, and perhaps with equal truth, that men make circumstances? Was it the circumstances of the times, or the character of Hannibal, that enabled him, at the age of twenty-four, to guide the legions of Carthage over the everlasting, untrodden Alps, and thunder at the gates of Rome? Look at John Milton. What was there in his circumstances to press him into greatness? Shut out from the light of heaven by blindness, most, in his situation, would have thought that they did well, could they have sung a few tunes, and earned their bread by making baskets. But Milton!—he has thrown a glory over his age, and nation, and language, which can be impaired only by blotting the world out of existence.

Look at Andrew Fuller;—without education, without opportunities, without circumstances which can, in any way, be denominated favorable, like the birch rising up in the cleft of the rock, he stood far above the age and the generation in which he lived.

But the cry is, "We have no favorable circumstances—no opportunities—no tools; we can do nothing." Can do nothing! If we have any thing of the deathless Roman fire within—*alta petens,—aliquid immensum, infinitumque*—we have every needed help. Many a beautiful ship has sat like a swan upon the dark-blue waters, which never had a tool upon her sides, save the axe, the auger, and the knife. Hear what a master-spirit says on this point—a man whose example has often reproved me, and thousands like me.

"If a man really loves study, has an eager attachment to the acquisition of knowledge, nothing but peculiar sickness or misfortunes will prevent his being a student, and his possessing, in some good degree, the means of study. The fact is, that when men complain of want of time for study, and want of means, they only show that, after all, they are either attached to some other object of pursuit, or have no part nor lot in the spirit of a student. They will applaud others, it may be, who do study, and look with a kind of wonder upon their acquisitions; but, for themselves, they cannot spare the time nor expense necessary to make such acquisitions; or they put it to the account of their humility, and bless themselves that they are not *ambitious*. In most of all these cases, however, either the love of the world or genuine laziness lies at the bottom. Had they more energy and decision of character, and did they redeem the precious moments, which they now lose in laboriously doing nothing, or nothing to the purpose of the church, they might open all the treasures of the east and the west, and have them at their disposal. I might safely promise a good knowledge of Hebrew and Greek to most men of this sort, if they would diligently improve the time that they now absolutely throw away, in the course of three or four years. While one man is deliberating whether he had better study a language, another man has obtained it. Such is the difference between decisive, energetic action, and a timid, hesitating, indolent manner of pursuing literary acquisitions. And what is worst of all, in this temporizing class of students, is, that, if you reason with them, and convince them that they are pursuing a wrong course, that conviction operates no longer than until the next paroxysm of indolence, or of a worldly spirit, comes on. These siren charmers lull every energetic power of the mind to sleep. The mistaken man, who listens to their voice, finds himself, at the age of forty, just where he was at thirty. At fifty, his decline has already begun. At sixty, he is universally regarded with indifference, which he usually repays with misanthropy. And if he has the misfortune to live until he is seventy, every body is uneasy because he is not transferred to a better world." *

6. *Remember that the great secret of being successful and accurate as a student, next to perseverance is*, THE CONSTANT HABIT OF REVIEWING.

I have already spoken of the memory. I would here say a word as to its use in your definite studies. Have you never tried to banish a thought, or a train of

* Professor Stuart.

thought, from your memory, and could not? Have you never tried to recall some idea, or some train of thought, and the more you tried, the more you seemed to forget it? The reason is, that the memory loves freedom, and disdains to be forced. The correct path, then, in which to tread, is to cultivate the memory as much as possible, without weakening it by restraint. It loves to try its powers spontaneously. Little children will frequently learn a long list of Latin or Greek words, without designing it, merely by hearing others repeat them. And I have known an ignorant Catholic, who could repeat the most of the Lord's Prayer, and a good part of the Missal, all in Latin, without knowing what it meant, simply by hearing it frequently repeated. Those who have been most successful in fixing language in the memory, have uniformly done it by repeated readings of the thing to be retained. In committing grammar, for example, to memory, you should not attempt to confine the mind to it too long at a time, but bend the whole attention to it while you do study, and repeat the process often: repeat the lesson aloud, that it may come to the mind through the ear, as well as through the eyes, and then use the pen, and, laying aside the book, write it all out. In this process, you use the eyes, the ears, and you also give the mind an opportunity to dwell upon every letter, and syllable, and sound. This will be slow, at first, but it will effectually do the thing; it will make you thorough, and soon give the courage of the war-horse. No new encounters will, in the least, appal you. The great difficulty in committing grammar, consists in the similarity of the words and things that are brought together. Similarity confuses the mind. If you were to go into a jeweller's shop, and see a card containing twenty watches, though each had a different name, yet, the next day, you could not tell one from another. But suppose you go for five days in succession, and examine four watches each day. The jeweller carefully points out the difference. This is a common watch: he shows you its mechanism, and all its parts. That is a patent lever: he shows you how it differs from the former. The third is a lepine: its parts are very different still. The next is a chronometer, and differs widely from any you have yet seen. He tells you the properties of each one, and compares them together. The second day, you review and recall all that he told you, and you fix the name, the character, and the properties of each in the memory. You then proceed to the second four. You go through the same process, every day reviewing what you learned on the preceding day. At the end of five days, you can repeat from memory, the name and powers of each watch, though, before the process, all you could remember was, that their number was twenty, and that they stood in five different rows. Now, study the grammar with the same p.e cision, and in the same manner, and the memory will not complain that she is confused, and cannot retain what you ask her to keep.

But what I have said of reviewing, pertains more especially to the lessons which you prepare for the recitation-room, and which are to be reviewed and repeated at your room. The indefatigable Wyttenbach[1]—and few could speak more decidedly from experience—says, that this practice will have "*an incredible effect in assisting your progress;*" but he adds, "it must be a real and thorough review; that is, it must be *again* and *again* repeated. What I choose is this; *that every day the task of the preceding day should be reviewed; at the end of every week, the task of the week; at the end of every month, the studies of the month; in addition to which this whole course should be gone over again and again during the vacation.*" Again; this great scholar tells his pupils, "*You will not fail* to devote one hour, or part of an hour, at least, every day, to these studies, on the same plan which you have followed under me; for *there is no business, no avocation whatever, which will not permit a man who has an* INCLINATION, *to give a little time every day to the studies of his youth.*" I would add, that one quarter of an hour, every day, devoted to reviewing, will not only keep all that a man has ever gone over, fresh in mind, but advance him in classical study. And no man may hope to become a thorough scholar, who does not first fix this habit upon

[1] Note J

himself. It will be irksome at first, but only at first "In reading and studying this work, [the Memorabilia of Xenophon,] I made it a rule never to begin a section without re-perusing the preceding one, nor a chapter, nor book, without going over the preceding chapter and book a second time; and finally, after having finished the work in that manner, I again read the whole in course. This was a labor of almost three months; but such constant repetition proved most beneficial to me. The effect of repetition seemed to be, that when I proceeded from a section or a chapter which I had read twice, to a new one, I acquired an impulse which bore me along through all opposing obstacles; like a vessel,—to use Cicero's comparison in a similar case,—which, having once received an impulse from the oar, continues her course even after the mariners have suspended their operations to propel her."

How very different this from the practice of too many! That part of the path over which they have passed, is covered with a thick fog, and they can look back and see nothing but the fog. They look forward, and the atmosphere is, if possible, still more dim. The road seems long, and they are constantly in doubt where they are. Any one can travel in a fog, but with no comfort or certainty at the time, and with no impression upon the memory to recall at some future time.

It is not for me to say that our colleges and schools

should insist on such reviews in the recitation-room It would probably be impracticable; but the youth ought to be encouraged and urged to do it at his room, again and again. We are told that there is a fine, and a more than human emotion produced by reading Demosthenes. But who feels it? Read over the first and second Olynthiac, and do you feel it? No; nor can you, till you have reviewed every sentence, and paragraph, and section, again and again, and that, probably, to the twelfth time. *Then*, if you are faithful, you will begin decidedly to feel it. You cannot but feel it. The influence of Plato's genius is thought to be distinctly felt through the whole world of letters. Does the student see any thing of this by dipping into Plato? No! nor can he ever do so, unless he train himself to the constant, invariable habit of reviewing every sentence, and every page, and that, too, many times. Try it for six months, and my poor reputation shall be staked on the result. Get, by any labor, your author's meaning and spirit. What Quintilian says of eloquence, is doubly applicable to this point: "Prima est eloquentiæ virtus, perspicuitas; et quoquisque ingenio minus valet, hoc se magis attollere et dilatare conatur: ut statura breves in digitos eriguntur, et plura infirmi minantur."

7. *Be faithful in fulfilling your appointed exercises.*

It has been said of the promising and lamented

Professor Fisher,[1] that, during his collegiate course, he never missed a recitation of his class, and was never known to have his name handed in by the monitors. And all those men, who have ever become influential among us, almost without exception, began to be distinguished for a conscientious discharge of all appointed exercises, while obtaining their education. You may feel unwell to-day; you have over-eaten, or abused the body in some other way; and now you have but little courage to master your lesson. You are tempted not to try to learn it. But I beg of you not to lay it by. You will lose in self-respect; you will have yielded to a temptation that will often assail you; you will have lowered yourself in the estimation of others. No call of friends, no preparation for a society, no writing to friends, should ever turn you aside from getting that lesson which is shortly to be recited. The strong language of the late venerable President Porter ought to be hung up in the room of every student. It is the testimony of one who was so careful and so judicious an observer of men and things, that he seldom made mistakes. "Regular, prescribed exercises have the first claim on your time, and should never be thrust aside by incidental things. It should be a point of conscience with every member of this seminary, for his own good, as well as in conformity with his sacred promise at matriculation, never to neglect these regular exercises, unless disabled by Providence. I

[1] Note K

was detained by company, is sometimes offered as a reason for such neglect, and it *may* be a good reason; *very rarely*; but in my own case as a student, from twelve years of age, through college, it never *once* was regarded by me as a reason for such neglect; *never once has it been so, in the nineteen years of my connection with this seminary.* Take the catalogue of our seminary from the beginning, and mark the men, if you can, on that honored list, who, since they have left us, have been most distinguished for usefulness as ministers and missionaries, and also the men, not a few, who have been elected presidents and professors in colleges and theological seminaries, and then remember, that the same men were distinguished for *punctuality*, and industry, and *conscientious regard to order*, while they were here."

These remarks apply with as much force to every other student as to the student in theology. "Les hommes sont a peu pres tous faits de la même maniere; et ainsi ce qui nous a touche, les touchera aussi."

8. *Learn to rest the mind, by variety in your studies, rather than by entire cessation from study.*

Few can confine the mind down to severe thought, or to one study, long at a time, and therefore most, when they relax, throw the thoughts loose, and do not try to save them. You are studying Homer, or algebra, for example. You apply yourself some two or three hours at a time. Your body becomes weary, and the mind is jaded. You stop, and throw aside your books, and rest, perhaps, quite as long as you have been studying. Now, all this time is lost, or nearly so. You forget that the mind is as much refreshed by *variety* as by *idleness*. When you lay aside your algebra, take up your Livy, or Tacitus, and you will be surprised to find that it is a refreshment, as you review your last lesson. Or make those minutes in your common-place book of what you last read; or turn your thoughts, and ponder over the subject of your next composition. You may save a vast amount of time in this way.

We wonder how our fathers, and how the students of Germany, at the present time, can study sixteen hours a day. They never could do it, were it not that they pursue one study till the mind reluctates; they then turn to another, by which the mind is relieved, and at once becomes buoyant. This is the difference between him who loses no time, and him who loses very much. The men who accomplish so much in life, are those who practise on this plan. This will account for the fact, that the same man will not unfrequently hold several offices which require talents and efforts seemingly incompatible with each other, and yet promptly execute the duties of all. He is thus continually busy and continually resting.

In this way the justly distinguished Dr. Good long

before he was forty years old, amid the incessant and anxious duties of a laborious profession, had gained prizes by writing essays; had mastered at least eleven different languages; had aided in making a Universal Dictionary in twelve volumes; had written his celebrated Study of Medicine; and was constantly writing and translating poetry. His "Book of Nature" will give the reader an admiring conception of the variety and the accuracy of his attainments. Instead of being thrown into confusion by such a variety and pressure of occupations, he carried them all forward simultaneously, and suffered none to be neglected, or but half executed. His practice was like that of the indefatigable, but somewhat eccentric Dr. Clarke,[1] who said, "I have lived to know the great secret of human happiness is this,—never suffer your energies to stagnate. The old adage of 'too many irons in the fire,' conveys an abominable lie. You cannot have too many; poker, tongs, and all—keep them all going." This habit of keeping the mind employed, will soon destroy the common habit of reverie. The soul will be too busy for reverie; and then, if she gains nothing by change of occupations, by way of acquisition, she gains the satisfaction hat she is not wandering off on forbidden ground.

[1] Note L.

CHAPTER IV.

READING.

THE genius of Shakspeare has shed a glory around the name of Brutus, which the iron pen of history cannot do away. The historian and the poet are certainly greatly at variance in regard to him: the latter has made him so amiable and exalted a character, that we feel unwilling to know the truth about him. I am not now to act as umpire between them; but there is one spot where we see him in the same light, both in history and in poetry. It is this. The night before the celebrated battle of Pharsalia, which was to decide the fate of the known world, Brutus was in his tent *reading*, and making notes from his author with the pen!

The elder Pliny seldom sat down to eat a meal, without having some one read to him; and he never travelled without having one or more books with him, and conveniences for making extracts or memoranda.

The amiable Petrarch never felt happy a day, if, during it, he did not read or write, or do both. One of his friends,[1] fearing it would injure his health, begged him to lend him the key of his library. Petrarch, without knowing the design, granted it. His

[1] Cardinal Colonna.

friend locked it up, and forbade him to read any thing for ten days. The poet consented with great reluctance. The first day seemed longer than a year; the second produced a hard headache from morning till night; and on the morning of the third day, he was evidently in a fever. His friend, touched with his situation, restored the key, and with it his health and spirits.

All distinguished men have been given to the habit of constant reading; and it is utterly impossible to arrive at any tolerable degree of distinction without this habit. "Reading," says Bacon, "makes a *full* man; conversation a *ready* man; writing an *exact* man." That which he means by *full* can never be attained, except by an extensive and thorough acquaintance with books. No genius, no power of inventing and creating thoughts, can ever supply a deficiency in this respect. The mightiest mind that was ever created, could, perhaps, here and there, strike out a road; but who would wish it to spend itself in beating about to discover a path, and even to make it, when the united minds of the generations who have gone before us, have done this for him? In order to have a judgment sound and correct, you must travel through the history of other times, and be able to compare the present with the past. To have the mind vigorous, you must refresh it, and strengthen it, by a continued contact with the mighty dead who have gone away, but left their imperishable thoughts behind them. We want to have the mind continually expanding, and creating new thoughts, or at least feeding itself upon manly thoughts. The food is to the blood, which circulates through your veins, what reading is to the mind; and the mind that does not *love* to read, may despair of ever doing much in the world of mind which it would affect. You can no more be the "full man" whom Bacon describes, without reading, than you can be vigorous and healthy without any new nourishment. It would be no more reasonable to suppose it, in the expressive and beautiful language of Porter, "than to suppose that the Mississippi might roll on its flood of waters to the ocean, though all its tributary streams were cut off, and it were replenished only by the occasional drops from the clouds." Some will read works of the imagination, or what is called the light literature of the day, while that which embraces solid thought is irksome. The Bishop of Winchester (Hoadley) said that he could never look into Butler's Analogy without having his head ache—a book which Queen Caroline told Mr. Sale, she read every day at breakfast. Young people are apt—and to this students are continually tempted—to read only for amusement. Pope says, that, from fourteen to twenty, he read for amusement alone; from twenty to twenty-seven, for improvement and instruction; that in the former period, he wanted only to *know*, and in the second, endeavored to *judge*.

The object of reading may be divided into several branches. The student reads for relaxation from more severe studies; he is thus refreshed, and his spirits are revived. He reads for facts in the history and experience of his species, as they lived and acted under different circumstances. From these facts he draws conclusions; his views are enlarged, his judgment corrected, and the experience of former ages, and of all times, becomes his own. He reads, chiefly, probably, for information; to store up knowledge for future use; and he wishes to classify and arrange it, that it may be ready at his call. He reads for the sake of style,—to learn how a strong, nervous, or beautiful writer expresses himself. The spirit of a writer to whom the world has bowed in homage, and the dress in which the spirit stands arrayed, is the object at which he must anxiously look.

It is obvious, then, that, in attaining any of these ends, except, perhaps, that of amusement, *reading should be performed very slowly and deliberately.* You will usually, and, indeed, almost invariably, find that those who read a great multitude of books, have but little knowledge that is of any value. A large library has justly been denominated a learned luxury—not elegance—much less utility. A celebrated French author was laughed at on account of the poverty of his library. "Ah," replied he, "when I want a book, I make it!" Rapid readers generally are very desultory; and a man may read much, and know but very little. "The *helluo librorum* and the true scholar are two very different characters." One who has a deep insight into the nature of man, says that he never felt afraid to meet a man who has a large library. It is the man who has but few books, and who thinks much, whose mind is the best furnished for intellectual operations. It will not be pretended, however, that there are not many exceptions to this remark. But, with a student, in the morning of life, there are no exceptions. If he would improve by his reading, it must be very deliberate. Can a stomach receive any amount or kind of food, hastily thrown into it, and reduce it, and from it extract nourishment for the body? Not for any length of time. Neither can the mind any easier digest that which is rapidly brought before it. Seneca has the same idea in his own simple, beautiful language— "Distrahit animum librorum multitudo:—Fastidientis stomachi multa degustare, quæ ubi varia sunt et diversa, inquinant, non alunt."

It is by no means certain that the ancients had not a great compensation for the fewness of their books, in the thoroughness with which they were compelled to study them. A book must all be copied with the pen, to be owned; and he who transcribed a book for the sake of owning it, would be likely to understand it. Before the art of printing, books were so scarce, that ambassadors were sent from France to Rome, to beg a copy of Cicero de Oratore, and Quintilian's Institutes, &c., because a complete copy of these works was not to be found in all France. Albert, abbot of Gemblours, with incredible labor and expense, collected a library of one hundred and fifty volumes, including every thing; and this was considered a wonder indeed. In 1494, the library of the Bishop of Winchester contained parts of seventeen books on various subjects; and, on his borrowing a Bible from the convent of St. Swithin, he had to give a heavy bond, drawn up with great solemnity, that he would return it uninjured. If any one gave a book to a convent or a monastery, it conferred everlasting salvation upon him, and he offered it upon the altar of God. The convent of Rochester every year pronounced an irrevocable sentence of damnation on him who should dare steal or conceal a Latin translation of Aristotle, or even obliterate a title. When a book was purchased, it was an affair of such consequence, that persons of distinction were called together as witnesses. Previous to the year 1300, the library of Oxford, England, consisted only of a few tracts, which were carefully locked up in a small chest, or else chained,[1] lest they should escape; and at the commencement of the 14th century, the royal library of France con

[1] One may still be seen in the library of Hereford Cathedral

tained only four classics, with a few devotional works. So great was the privilege of owning a book, that one of their books on natural history contained a picture, representing the Deity as resting on the Sabbath, with a book in his hand, in the act of reading! It was probably no better in earlier times. Knowledge was scattered to the four winds, and truth was hidden in a well. Lycurgus and Pythagoras were obliged to travel into Egypt, Persia, and India, in order to understand the doctrine of the metempsychosis. Solon and Plato had to go to Egypt for what they knew. Herodotus and Strabo were obliged to travel to collect their history, and to construct their geography as they travelled. Few men pretended to own a library, and he was accounted truly favored who owned half a dozen volumes. And yet, with all this scarcity of books, there were in those days scholars who greatly surpassed us. We cannot write poetry like Homer, nor history like Thucydides. We have not the pen which Aristotle and Plato held, nor the eloquence with which Demosthenes thrilled. They surpassed us in painting and in sculpture. Their books were but few. But those were read, as Juvenal says, *ten* times—"decies repetita placebunt." Their own resources were tasked to the utmost, and he who could not draw from his own fountain, in vain sought for neighbors, from whose wells he could borrow.

How very different with us! We read without

measure, and almost without profit. "Aliud enim est scire, aliud sapere. Sapiens est, qui didicit non omnia, sed ea quæ ad veram felicitatem pertinent, et iis quæ didicit afficitur ac transfiguratus est."

If, at the close of any given year, you will examine the register of the librarian of any of the literary societies in college, you will find, almost without exception, that those who have taken out most books, have accomplished least in preparing the mind for future usefulness. It is a good maxim, in regard to your reading—*Non multa, sed multum.*

Beware of bad books. Some men have been permitted to live and employ their powers in writing what will continue to pollute and destroy for generations after they are gone. The world is flooded with such books. They are permitted to lie in our pathway as a part of our moral discipline. Under the moral government of God, while in this state of probation, we are to be surrounded with temptations of every kind. And never does the spirit of darkness rejoice more, than when a gifted mind can prostitute itself, not merely to revel in sin itself, but to adorn and conceal a path which is full of holes, through which you may drop into the chambers of death. Books could be named, were it not that there is a possibility that even the information conveyed in naming them might be perverted and used to obtain them, which, seemingly, could not be excelled by all the talents in hell, if the object were to pollute and to ruin. These are to be found every where. I do entreat my young readers never to look at one—never to open one. They will leave a stain upon the soul which can never be removed. I have known these books secreted in the rooms of students, and lent from one to another. They are to be found too frequently. And if you have an enemy, whose soul you would visit with a heavy vengeance, and into whose heart you would place vipers which will live, and crawl, and torment him through life, and whose damnation you would seal up for the eternal world, you have only to place one of these destroyers in his hand. You have certainly paved the way to the abodes of death; and if he does not travel it with hasty strides, you have, at least, laid up food for many days of remorse.

What shall be said of those who print and sell such works to the young?—of those who go out on purpose to peddle them? They are the most awful scourges with which a righteous God ever visited our world. The angel of death can sheath his sword, and stay his hand in the work of death. But these wretches! they dig graves so deep that they reach into hell. They blight the hopes of parents, and pour more than seven vials of wo upon the family whose affections are bound up in the son who is thus destroyed.

In connection with these books, allow me to lift up a loud voice against those rovings of the imagination, by which the mind is at once enfeebled, and the heart and feelings debased and polluted. It is almost inseparable from the habit of reverie: but, in this life, a heavier curse can hardly hang upon a young man than that of possessing a polluted imagination. The leprosy fills the whole soul. Time only increases it, and even the power of the gospel can seldom do more than restrain, without subduing, when the disease is once fixed.

While I thus briefly allude to these wanderings of the imagination, by which the mind is debilitated, the sou polluted by a stain which tears cannot wash out, nor the deepest repentance fully do away, I cannot satisfy my conscience without going a step further, and saying what others have, to my certain knowledge, wished to say, and ought to say, but which no one has yet had the courage to say, in tones loud and distinct. May I entreat the young man who reads these pages not to pass the following paragraph without reading and pondering it. I have chosen to risk the charge of pedantry rather than not say what I could not say in English.

*Lux nulla, illâ Diæ ultimæ exceptâ, ut frequenter et assidue, consuetudinem * * * effundendi manu* [ONANIS SCELUS,] *revelare possit. Adolescentulos quamplurimos novi, in singulatos dies, in hac re, seipsos turpantes, et hoc, per annos multos. Incitamentum ad hoc crimen, cum pene omnibus, permagnum est. Casum multorum quos, de causâ execrabile solâ, vidi occumbere prema-*

turæ morti, gemui,—aliquos in aulis academicis, et nonnullos citissime post digressum e collegio et ex aliquovis gradu exornatos. Plurimi hanc consuetudinem defendere conati sunt, quasi instinctu quodam et imperio impulsi, et sic voluerunt Deum ipsum esse hujus stupri auctorem. "Hoc prætexit nomine culpam." Turpissima simulatio! Ethnici ipsi, luce naturæ ducti, cum verbis multis hanc culpam reprobaverunt. V. C. "*Veneri servit—manus! Hoc nihil esse putas? scelus est, mihi crede; sed ingens, quantum vix animo concipis ipse tuo;—parce solicitare manu. Lævibus in pueris plus quam hæc—peccat.*"

Deus, quoad hoc crimen, mentem ejus lucidissime indicavit. Indignatio et ira Dei illis adsequentur. "Scimus vero judicium Dei esse secundum veritatem adversus eos qui talia agunt. Putas autem hoc, O qui facis ea, fore ut tu effugias judicium Dei?"*

Memento fructus hujus consuetudinis esse—

(1.) *Memoriam esse maxime debilitatam;*

(2.) *Mentem esse valdè dejectam atque stulte imbecilem;* †

* Gen. 38:9, 10. 1 Cor. 6:9. 2 Cor. 12:21. Gal. 5:19 Eph. 5:3, 5.

† See a thrilling and harrowing chapter in Rush on Diseases of the Mind. Physicians testify, that probably this is a greater source of derangement than all other causes. The very intelligent and respectable Superintendents of the Insane Hospitals at Worcester and at Hartford will say, not only that this is the cause of bringing many of their patients there, but an almost insuperable obstacle in the way of their recovery.

(3.) *Semina letiferi morbi, et mortis ipsæ in corpore sparsa;**

(4.) *Omnia quæ ad animam pertinent ruere in pejus;*

(5.) *Tribulationem a Deo, qui te aspicit in occulto, certissime venturam fuisse. Oculus ejus, semper vigilans, te spectat. "Nam omne opus Deus Ipse adducet in judicium cum omni re occulta." "Nam quæ, fiunt ab istis, turpe est vel dicere." Fuge, fuge, pro vita, pro anima. "Obsta principiis." Hoc scelus vincere non poteris, nisi effugiendo. Quicunque in timore Dei versatur, te docebit, "hic viæ ad sepulchrum," hic viæ descendentes ad penetralia mortis.*

What shall be said of such works as those of Byron? May not a young man read those? Can he not learn things from him which cannot be learned elsewhere? I reply, Yes, just as you would learn, while treading in burning lava, what could not be learned elsewhere.

* It is awfully certain, too, that it is very frequently the cause of sudden death. The apoplexy waits hard by, as God's executioner, upon this sin. May not the pale-faced youth, in feeble health, frequently imputing his disease to the dyspepsia, or something like it, tremble as he looks off the abyss on which he has placed himself? I do hope what I have said will lead many to fear and to beware. These remarks may be condemned by some; but I shall have two sources of consolation,—first, that I have discharged a sacred duty; and, secondly, that those who are offended are those for whose special benefit these remarks are made.

But would the knowledge thus obtained be worth the agony of the fire, and the scars which would remain through life? It is breathing the air which comes up from a heated furnace; and though you may see a brightness and a glow in that furnace, as you gaze into it, which is no where else to be found, yet you will feel the effects of what you breathe a long time. There are many bright spots in such writings; but while one ray of pure light is thrown upon the soul, it must find its way through volumes of Egyptian darkness. There are beautiful pearls in the slimy bottom of the ocean, but they are found only here and there; and would you feel it worth your while to dive after them, if there were many probabilities that you would stick and die in the mud in which they are imbedded, or, if not, that you certainly shorten and embitter life, in the process of diving and obtaining them?

Would you thank a man for fitting up your study, and adorning it with much that is beautiful, if, at the same time, he filled it with images and ghosts of the most disgusting and awful description, which were to abide there, and be continually dancing around you all your life? Is he a benefactor to his species, who, here and there, throws out a beautiful thought, or a poetic image, but, as you stoop to pick it up, chains upon you a putrid carcass which you can never throw off? I believe a single page may be selected from Byron, which has done more hurt to the mind and the heart of the young than all his writings have ever done good. But he will quickly pass from notice, and is doomed to be exiled from the libraries of all virtuous men. It is a blessing to the world, that what is putrid must soon pass away. The carcass hung in chains will be gazed at for a short time in horror; but men will soon turn their eyes away, and remove even the gallows on which they swung. "But," say you, "has my author ever read Byron and Moore, Hume and Paine, Scott, Bulwer and Cooper?" Yes, he has read them all, and with too much care. He knows every rock and every quicksand; and he solemnly declares to you, that the only good which he is conscious of ever having received from them is, a deep impression that men who possess talents of such compass and power, and so perverted in their application, must meet the day of judgment under a responsibility which would be cheaply removed by the price of a world. Those who wrote to undermine or to crush the belief of the Christian—those who wrote to show how they could revel in passion, and pour out their living scorn upon their species—and those who wasted life and gigantic powers merely to amuse men—have come far short of answering the great end of existence on earth. Talents and influence were given for purposes widely different. But is it not necessary to read works of this kind, especially those whose design is only to amuse and awaken the interest of the reader? There a no more necessity than there is to be acquainted with all the variety of dishes with which the palate may be pleased, and the body stimulated, and the stomach weakened. Were these the only books in the world, the case would be different. But who does not know that they who are given to reading works of fiction, leave a mass of most valuable and solid reading untouched and unknown? When you have read and digested all that is really valuable, and which is comprised in what describes the history of man in all lights in which he has actually been placed, then betake yourself to works of imagination. But can you not, in works of fiction, have the powers of the imagination enlarged, and the mind taught to soar? Perhaps so. But the lectures of Chalmers on Astronomy will do this to a degree far beyond all that the pen of fiction can do. Will they not give you a command of words and of language which shall be full, and chaste, and strong? Perhaps so. But if that is what you wish, read the works of Edmund Burke. There you will find language, gorgeous at times, but, for copiousness and wealth, hardly to be equalled by any uninspired pen. He is a master on this subject; and I hope no one, who intends to strike for a character for language or thoughts, strength or beauty, will ever be trying to clothe himself with the puissance of a novel, when he can boast the language of Burke as being his mother tongue.

The question in regard to works of fiction usually has a definite relation to the writings of Walter Scott. There is such a magic thrown around him, that it cannot be but we are safe there. Is t so? Because the magician can raise mightier spirits than other magicians, and throw more of supernatural light about him than others, is he therefore the less to be feared? No; the very strength of the spell should warn you that there is danger in putting yourself in his power. While I have confessed that I have read him—read him entire—in order to show that I speak from experience, I cannot but say, that it would give me the keenest pain to believe that my example would be quoted, small as is its influence, after I am in the grave, without this solemn protest accompanying it.

How shall you know what to read?—a very important question; for some books will positively injure, if they do not destroy you. Others will have no positive good effect; and from all, a tincture, like that left upon the mind by the company you keep, will be left. Do not expect to read all, or even a small part of what comes out, and is recommended, too, in this age of books. You take up a book, and read a chapter. How shall you know whether it is worth your reading, without reading it through? In the same way that you would know whether a cask of wine was good. If you draw one glass, or two, and find them stale and unpleasant, do you need to drink off the whole cask, to decide that you do not want it? "I have somewhat else to do, in the short day allotted me, than to read whatever any one may think it his duty to write. When I read, I wish to read to good purpose; and there are some books, which contradict, on the very face of them, what appear to me to be first principles. You surely will not say, 'I am bound to read such books.' If a man tells me he has a very elaborate argument to prove that two and two make five, I have something else to do than to attend to his argument. If I find the first mouthful of meat which I take from a fine-looking joint on my table is tainted, I need not eat through it to be convinced I ought to send it away." But there is a shorter route, and one every way still more safe; and that is, to treat books as you do medicines; have nothing to do with them till others have tried them, and can testify to their worth. There are always what are denominated *standard* works at hand, and about which there can be neither doubt nor mistake. You cannot read every thing; and if you could, you would be none the wiser. The lumber would bury up and destroy all the valuable materials which you were laying up. Never feel any obligation to read a trifling author, or one whose thoughts are spread out like gold-leaf over a wide surface, *quite* through, in hopes of finding something better as you proceed. You will be disappointed. An author may reserve some of his happiest thoughts for the close of his book; but he has great poverty of intellect if he makes you travel over a long, sandy road, without any spots that are refreshing. Leave such books—you will find better; and you are not bound to spend time and strength on a mere possibility. Will you stand till wearied, to hear a dull, impertinent coxcomb talk, when, by turning away, you can find instructive company?

How shall you begin to read a book? Always look into your dish and taste it, before you begin to eat. As you sit down, examine the title-page; see who wrote the book—where he lives; do you know any thing of the author? where, and by whom published? Do you know any thing of the general character of the books published by this publisher? Recollect what you have heard about this book. Then read the preface, to see what kind of a bow the author makes, and what *he* thinks of himself and his work; why he has the boldness to challenge the public to hear him. Then turn to the contents, see what are the great divisions of his subject, and thus get a glance of his general plan. Then take a single chapter or section, and see how he has divided and filled that up. If, now, you wish to *taste* of the dish before further examination of the contents, then turn to the place where some important point is discussed, and where some valuable thought professes to be expanded or illustrated, and see how it is executed. If, after some few such trials, you should find your author obscure, dull, pedantic, or shallow, you need not longer fish in these waters. It will be hard to catch fish here, and, when caught, they will be too small for use. But if you find the author valuable, and worth your attention, then go back to the contents. Examine them chapter by chapter; then close the book, and see if you have the plan of the whole work distinctly and fully in your mind. Do not proceed till this *is* done. After you have this map all distinctly drawn in the mind, then get the first chapter vividly before you, so far as the contents will enable you to do it. Now proceed to read. At the close of each sentence, ask yourself, "Do I understand that? Is it true, important, or to the point? Any thing valuable there which I ought to retain?" At the close of each paragraph, ask the same questions. Leave no paragraph till you have the substance of it in your mind. Proceed in this manner through the chapter; and, at the close of the chapter, look back, and see what the author *tried* to accomplish by it, and what he really *has* accomplished. As you proceed, if the book be your own, or if the owner will allow you to do it, mark with your pencil, in the margin, what, according to *your* view, is the character of each paragraph, or of this or that sentence. To illustrate what I mean, I will mention a few marks which I have found very useful to myself: these, or any thing similar, will answer the end to be attained. Perhaps the remark had better be made here, that you can never read to advantage unless you feel well, and the mind and spirits are buoyant. Otherwise, any author will be stupid. "No one will read with much advantage, who is not able, at pleasure, to evacuate his mind, and who brings not to his author an intellect defecated and pure; neither turbid with care, nor agitated with pleasure."

|| Signifies, that this paragraph contains the main, or one of the main propositions to be proved or illustrated in this chapter; the staple, or one of the staples, on which the chain hangs.

<| This sentiment is true, and will bear expanding, and will open a field indefinite in extent.

>| This, if carried out, would not stand the test of experience, and is therefore incorrect.

?| Doubtful as to sentiment.

?!| Doubtful in point of fact.

S| Good, and facts will only strengthen the position.

∞ | Bad; facts will not uphold it.

ϑ | Irrelevant to the subject; had better have been omitted.

φ | Repetition; the author is moving in a circle.

♯ | Not inserted in the right place.

O | In good taste.

Θ | In bad taste.

Such marks may be increased at pleasure. I have found the above sufficient. These need not be adopted, as each one can invent them for himself; but care should be taken always to make the same mark mean the same thing. But will not this method of reading be *slow?* Yes, *very slow, and very valuable.* A single book read in this way, will be worth a score run over. It will compel you to *think* as well as read, to judge, to discriminate, to sift out the wheat from the chaff. It will make thought your own, and will so fix it in the mind, that it will probably be at your command, at any future time. The first thing to be done, in order to make what you read your own, is to think as you read; think while you read; and think when you have closed the book

It is also very important to talk over the subject upon which you are reading, with a friend. Be candid enough to tell him that you have just been reading, so that he may know that you do not claim what you have, as your own. If the circle embrace several who really wish to fix what they read in the mind by conversation, so much the better.

> "Thought, too, delivered, is the more possessed:
> Teaching, we learn, and giving, we receive."

"Quicquid didiceris id confestim doceas; sic et tua firmare, et prodesse aliis potes. Ea doce quæ noveris, eaque diversis horis, aliis atque aliis conveniet inculcare. Satis sit, si quispiam te audiat, interea exercitatione miram rerum copiam tibi comparaveris."

If your friend is reading the same book, or if one is reading to the other, the advantages of conversation will still be greatly increased.

No small part of the time should be spent in *reviewing* what you have read. The most eminent scholars think that one fourth of the time spent in reading should be thus spent. I believe the estimate is none too great. But is it not evident, that, if you read with the marginal marks made by the pencil in your hand, as described above, you can review the author, and your own judgment too, in a very short time? One glance of the eye will show you what is the character of each paragraph. You will see just *where* the fish is, and *what* he is, and at once you can put your hook in and take him out.

There is another very important thing to be attended to in reading. I mean *classification.* We need a power, which, in the present state of our existence, we do not possess,—a power of keeping *all* that ever passes through our mind which is worth keeping. Erasmus *(de Rat. Stud.)* dwells upon this point with great beauty and force. "Inter legendum auctorem non oscitanter observabis, si quod incidat insigne verbum, si quod argumentum, aut inventum acute, aut tortum apte, si qua sententia digna quæ memoriæ commendetur: isque locus erit apta notulâ quapiam insigniendus." "Quanto pluris feceris exiguum proventum, tanto ad altiora doctrinæ vestigia es evasurus. Qui vilissimos quosque nummos admirantur, intuentur crebro, et servant accurate, ad summas sæpenumero divitias perveniunt; pari modo, si quis aptavit sudorum metam bene scribere, discat mirari bene scripta, discat gaudere, si vel nomina duo conjunxerit venuste."

We cannot write out, or copy, what we read. We can remember but a very small part of it. What shall we do? For one, I have been in the habit of making an *Index Rerum* of my reading. The book is so classified, that, in a single moment, I can refer to any thing which I have ever read, and tell where it is found,—the book and the page. It saves the labor of a common-place book, and yet preserves all that can be preserved. About a year since, I published the plan of my own Index Rerum. And as I have not, from the first, had any pecuniary interest in it, I may say that the plan is highly approved. One large edition has been sold, and a second widely scattered. I find, also, since its publication, that the late venerable President Porter made himself such an index, on principles somewhat similar, which he used all his life. This plan, pursued for a very few years, will give you an index of inestimable value. A single year will convince you that you cannot afford to lose its benefits.*

What shall be said of the newspapers and magazines with which we are flooded? Few things weaken the mind of the student more than light, miscellaneous reading. You find it the fashion to have read a world of reviews, magazines and papers. They are not written with the expectation of being remembered. And after you have spent hours over them, it is very doubtful whether you have done any thing more than crowd the mind with vague images and impressions, which decidedly weaken the memory. Every time you crowd into the memory what you do not ex-

* I may respectfully refer to my Index Rerum for the plan and explanation of the work. While the kindest things have been said in regard to it, nothing to the contrary has ever been said by *those who have used it*. It, or something like it, should be the constant companion of every student

pect it to retain, you weaken its powers, and you lose your authority to command its services. The fewer of such things the student reads, the better. Perhaps you may, now and then, crowd sweet-meats into the stomach, which it neither can nor will digest; but the fewer, the better.

There is another very important point to be kept in mind; and that is, that, in reading, you should always have your pen by you, not merely to make a minute in your index, but to save the thoughts which are started in your own mind. Did you never notice, that, while reading, your own mind is so put into operation, that it strikes out new and bold trains of thinking,—trains that are worth preserving, and such as will be scattered to the winds, if not penned down at the moment of their creation? A wise man will be as careful to save that property which he himself makes, as that which he inherits. The student should be; for it will be of vastly more value to him.

I cannot close this chapter without saying what seem to me to be distinctly the three great objects of reading.

1. *Reading forms your style.*

It is impossible to bring your mind, for any length of time, under the influence of another mind, without having your language and modes of thinking influenced by that mind. Suppose you wish to write in an elevated, measured, dignified style,—could you easily avoid doing it, were you first to sit down a fortnight and read Johnson's works? If you wish to write in a style pure, simple, *Saxon*, read John Bunyan's Pilgrim's Progress through some half a dozen times, and you will write thus. Could you walk arm in arm with a man for days together, without catching his step and gait? It is a law of nature that our minds insensibly imbibe a coloring from those with whom we associate, whether they are brought in contact by the living voice or on the written page. The insect that lives on the bark of the tree is no more certain to be of the color of that bark. Hence the importance of reading good authors,—those who, in all respects, make a good impression upon you. Books probably do more than all other things to form the intellectual and moral habits of the student. A single bad book will frequently give a tone and a bias to the mind, both as to thought and language, which will last during life. Hear the testimony of the late distinguished President Porter. "If I may be allowed here to speak of my own experience, as a theological student, I would say that to Edwards on the Will, which I read at three several times, before I entered the ministry, besides frequent reviews of it since, I am more indebted than to all other human productions. The aid which it gave was to me invaluable."

A lady, who now and then writes in rhyme, informed me that she first discovered that she possessed any of the rhyming powers, after having made a business, for some time, of copying the poetry of others. Owing to this insensible, undesigned and certain imitation, such writers as Addison are always recommended to the young. I may mention the author from whom I just quoted, as an example of pure, clear and beautiful style. Be as careful, then, not to read what would vitiate your style, as you would not to keep company with those who would corrupt your manners.

2. *Reading stocks the mind with knowledge.*

This is the grand object of reading. We come into the world ignorant of every thing. The history, the experience of other men and other generations, can be ours only by reading. Human nature, in all ages, is the same. The laws of mind and of matter do not alter; and thus we can, in a short life, know as much, and judge as accurately, by the use of books, as we could by living centuries, having no light to guide us, except that of our own individual experience. He who would be compelled to go across the Atlantic to obtain a narration of facts which can be read in two hours, would need the years of the antediluvians, and then die a very ignorant man. "Without books," says the quaint but enthusiastic Bartholin, "God is silent, justice dormant, physic [natural science] at a stand, philosophy lame, letters dumb, and all things involved in Cimmerian darkness."

You must not only read, and make books the fountain from which you draw* your knowledge, but you must expect to draw from this fountain through life. What you read to-day, will soon be gone—expended, or forgotten; and the mind must be continually filled up with new streams of knowledge. Even the ocean would be dried up, were the streams to be cut off, which are constantly flowing into it. "How few read enough to stock their minds! And the mind is no widow's cruise, which fills with knowledge as fast as we empty it. It is the 'hand of the diligent which maketh rich.'"

3. *Reading stimulates and puts your own mental energies into operation.*

If you were driven into a corner, and compelled to produce something as your own thoughts and opinions on an important point, at once, you would wish to stimulate your mind, and key it up to the highest point. How would you do it? You might reach it through the body, and, by stimulating that with wines or opium, might excite the mind. But then, the results thus produced would be uncertain. They might be correct, and they might be like the ravings of the mind excited by disease. But, at any rate, the body and mind would both suffer by this unnatural excitement. The reaction is awfully great; and, therefore, you may not do it. What can you do? I reply, that you can stimulate your mind at any time, when the body is healthful, by reading. No one can read the speeches of Burke, of Chatham, and of our own Patrick Henry, without being moved. No matter what you are writing upon, or upon what you are to speak, you cannot read a good book without being stimulated. The dream of Clarence, and the speeches of Hamlet, in Shakspeare; the speeches of men in the senate; the addresses of men from the pulpit; and, above all, the overwhelming torrent of clear thought, in burning language, which the masters of ancient times poured out,—will swell the bosom, rouse the soul, and call all your own powers into action. This effect of books will last through life; and he who knows how to read to advantage, will ever have something as applicable to his mental powers, as electricity is to move the animal system. The man who has sat over the workings of a powerful mind, as exhibited on the written page, without being excited, moved, and made to feel that *he* can do something, and *will* do something, has yet to learn one of the highest pleasures of the student's life, and is yet ignorant of what rivers of delight are flowing around him through all the journey of life.

I close by repeating, Do not read too many books: read thoroughly what you undertake. Buy but few books; and never buy till you can pay for what you buy. You cannot more than half enjoy any thing for which you owe. Make *all* that you do read your own; and you will soon be rich in intellectual wealth, and ever be making valuable additions to your stores.

CHAPTER V.

TIME.

THERE is no point, upon which I wish to touch, so difficult as this; and yet not one upon which so much good might be done, if the right things could be said, and said in a right way. It is easy enough to write prettily about the shortness and the fleetness of time, but not so easy to give specific rules how to improve it as it flies; but it is far easier to do this, than to confer the disposition, and create the determination, to use it to the best possible advantage. A miser will frequently become wealthy,—not because he has a great income, but because he saves with the utmost care, and spends with the greatest caution. This is a precept taught us in the very morning of life, but generally not learned till late in the evening. "It is a prodigious thing to consider that, although, amongst all the talents which are committed to our stewardship, time, upon several accounts, is the most precious; yet there is not any one of which the generality of men are more profuse and regardless. Nay, it is obvious to observe, that even those persons who are frugal and thrifty in every thing else, are yet extremely prodigal of their best revenue, time; 'of which,' as Seneca nobly says, 'it is a virtue to be covetous.' It is amazing to think how much time may be gained by proper economy."

This is a hard lesson, but it must be learned. "Ad summa perveniet nemo, nisi tempore, quo nihil esse fugacius constat, prudenter utatur."

The celebrated earl of Chatham performed an amount of business, even minute, which filled common improvers of time with utter astonishment. He knew, not merely the great outlines of public business, the policy and intrigues of foreign courts, but his eye was on every part of the British dominions; and scarcely a man could move, without his knowledge of the man, and of his object. A friend one day called on him when premier of England, and found him down on his hands and knees playing marbles with his little boy, and complaining bitterly that the rogue would not play fair, gaily adding, "that he must have been corrupted by the example of the French." The friend wished to mention a suspicious looking stranger, who, for some time, had taken up lodgings in London. Was he a spy, or merely a private gentleman? Pitt went to his drawer, and took out some scores of small portraits, and, holding up one which he had selected, asked, "Is that the man?" "Yes, the very person." "O! I have had my eye on him from the moment he stepped on shore."

All this was accomplished by a rigid observance of

time, never suffering a moment to pass without pressing it into service.

No one will try to improve his time, unless he first be impressed with the necessity. Remember that, at the very best calculation, we can have but a short time in which to learn all, and do all, that we accomplish in life. There is something melancholy in the following picture, drawn by the great hand of Johnson:—"When we have deducted all that is absorbed in sleep; all that is inevitably appropriated to the demands of nature, or irresistibly engrossed by the tyranny of custom; all that passes in regulating the superficial decorations of life, or is given up in the reciprocations of civility to the disposal of others; all that is torn from us by the violence of disease, or stolen imperceptibly away by lassitude and languor,—we shall find that part of our duration very small, of which we can truly call ourselves masters, or which we can spend wholly at our own choice." At the beginning of each day, see what, and how much, you want to accomplish before you sleep, and then at once begin to execute your plans, suffering no time to run waste between planning and acting. At the close of the day, be impartial and thorough in reviewing the day, and noting wherein you have failed. There is much to be learned from the somewhat humorous account of the Indian Gymnosophists, in their plans for educating their disciples. The account is from Apuleius, a Platonic philosopher of the second century. "When their dinner is ready, before it is served up, the masters inquire of every particular scholar how he has employed his *time* since sun-rising: some of them answer, that, having been chosen as arbiters between two persons, they have composed their differences, and made them friends; some, that they have been executing the orders of their parents; and others, that they have either found out something new, by their own application, or learned from the instructions of their fellows. But if there happens to be any one among them who cannot make it appear that he has employed the morning to advantage, he is immediately excluded from the company, and obliged to work, while the rest are at dinner." I shall be excused, if I here introduce the dream of the amiable Bolton. If my young readers have met with it before, they will see that it will bear a review.

"Dipping into *Apuleius* for my afternoon's amusement, the foregoing passage was the last I read, before I fell into a slumber, which exhibited to me a vast concourse of the fashionable people at the court-end of the town, under the examination of a Gymnosophist, how they had passed their morning. He began with the men.

"Many of them had only risen to dress—to visit—to

amuse themselves at the drawing-room, or coffee-house.

"Some had, by riding or walking, been consulting that health at the beginning of the day, which the close of it would wholly pass in impairing.

"Some, from the time they had got on their own clothes, had been engaged in seeing others put on theirs—in attending levees—in endeavoring to procure, by their importunity, what they had disqualified themselves for, by their idleness.

"Some had been early out of their beds, but it was because they could not, from their ill luck, the preceding evening, rest in them; and when risen, as they had no spirits, they could not reconcile themselves to any sort of application.

"Some had not had it in their power to do what was of much consequence: in the former part of the morning, they wanted to speak with their tradesmen; and in the latter, they could not be denied to their friends.

"Others, truly, had been reading, but reading what could make them neither wiser nor better—what was not worth their remembering, or what they should wish to forget.

"It grieved me to hear so many of eminent rank, both in the sea and land service, giving an account of themselves that levelled them with the meanest under their command.

"Several appeared with an air expressing the fullest confidence that what they had to say for themselves would be to the philosopher's entire satisfaction. They had been employed as virtuosi should be,—had been exercising their skill in the liberal arts, and encouraging the artists. Medals, pictures, statues, had undergone their examination, and been their purchase. They had been inquiring what the literati of France, Germany, and Italy, had, of late, published; and they had bought what suited their respective tastes.

"When it appeared that the completing a *Roman* series had been their concern who had never read over, in their own language, a *Latin* historian; that they who grudged no expense for originals, knew them only by hearsay, from their worst copies; that the very persons who had paid so much for the labor of Rysbrack, [an Italian landscape-painter,] upon Sir Andrew's judgment, would, if they had followed their *own*, have paid the same sum for that of Bird's; that the book-buyers had not laid out their money on what they ever proposed to read, but on what they had heard commended, and what they wanted to fit a shelf, and fill a library that only served them for a breakfast-room;—this class of men the sage pronounced the idlest of all idle people, and doubly blamable, as wasting alike their time and their fortune.

"The folly of one sex had so tired the philosopher, that he would suffer no account to be given of the other. It was easy for him to guess how the females must have been employed, where such were the ex amples in those they were to *honor and obey*."

There are certain thieves who hang around a student, and who daily destroy much which might be of great value to him. I will mention some of these, that you may know when you even hear their footsteps; for hear them you certainly will, and, if you have any thing of the desires of a student, will often cry out, "O fures,—latrones—O tyrannos crudelissimos quorum consilio mihi unquam periit Hora!"

1. *Sleep.*

Nothing is easier than to cultivate the habit of sleep so that the system demands, and will be deranged if the demand be denied, eight or ten hours out of the twenty-four. Physicians usually say that six hours are sufficient for all the purposes of health; and, were the eyes to close the moment you reach the pillow, perhaps six hours would be sufficient for the bed. But suppose you allow seven, and rigidly adhere to that number as a rule. Would you not have much more time than you now have? Were you faithfully to apply that time to your studies, which is now occupied by your bed, over and above the seven hours, would you not make great advances in almost any department of study? But the waste of time is not all. The whole system is prostrated by indulging the luxury of sleep; and you are as really and as certainly disqualified for severe study, after ten hours of sleep, as if you had over-loaded the stomach with food. The body and mind are both weakened by it. Take, then, two hours from the sleep of most who call themselves students, and add to it the value of two hours more, saved by increased vigor of mind, by the diminution of sleep, and you have a decided gain. What shall be said of the practice of sleeping after dinner? A few words will suffice. If you wish for a dull, feverish feeling, low spirits, prostration of strength, full, aching head, and a stomach that refuses to work for such a master, then be sure to eat hearty dinners, and sleep immediately after them. The call will be as regular as the dinner. But your fate, as a student, is sealed, if the practice be continued

2. *Indolence.*

Indolence differs from sloth and idleness in the same way that the parent differs from the child. It consists in the indulgence of a heavy, inactive disposition, entreating you to delay, till some future time, what ought to be done now. This will beset you by day and by night, unless you act from principle, and a high sense of moral responsibility. It can be resisted and overcome only by making your studies a duty, rather than a pleasure. They may, at times, be a pleasure, but should always be a duty. Dr. Fothergill, an eminent Quaker physician, says, "I endeavor to follow my business, because it is my *duty*, rather than my interest: the latter is inseparable from a just discharge of duty; but I have ever looked at the profits in the last place."

3. *Sloth.*

This has frequently and justly been denominated the rust of the soul. The habit is easily acquired; or, rather, it is a part of our very nature to be indolent. It grows fast by indulgence, and soon seizes upon the soul with the violence and strength of an armed man.

The exhibitions of human nature, in the time of Seneca, were the same as at our day. "Quædam tempora eripiuntur nobis; quædam subducuntur: quædam effluunt; turpissima tamen est jactura quæ per negligentiam venit."

The great mistake with us seems to be, that we feel that we cannot do any great thing, unless we have all our time to devote to that particular thing. "If I only had the time to go and sit down, day after day, for a number of days, or weeks, to examine that subject, and to write on that point, I could then do something." But, as it is, what can you do with such fragments as you gather, here and there, by sitting up late, or robbing your pillow at the dawn of day? Can you do any thing with them? No; you must wait for leisure, and for some great change in your outward circumstances, before you can hope to accomplish much! This is a great mistake. Madame de Genlis tells us, that, when a companion of the queen of France, it was her duty to be at the table and waiting for her mistress just fifteen minutes before dinner. These fifteen minutes were saved at every dinner, and a volume or two was the result. No change, great and marked, in your general course, is necessary to make new and rich acquisitions; only save every moment of time which you now throw away, and you will be able to do any thing. If I may speak from my own experience, I can testify that very nearly all that I have ever attained, or done, out of the regular routine of my professional duties, has been by taking those odd moments which are so easily thrown away. There are little vacancies, in the most crowded periods of every man's duties, which are thrown away in resting from the great object of pursuit. But there is no way of resting the mind more effectual, than to have something on hand to occupy it. The mind is not like a hand-organ, which wears as fast after you have shifted the key, and taken a new tune, as before. I have a friend, who is most laborious in his profession, and so active in his duties, that one would think he could never enter his study; and yet, should he live and labor for the coming ten years as he has for the last five, he will die with a celebrity, as an author, that will not be doubtful. He accomplishes it all by improving the fragments of time. The well-known Erasmus spent the greater part of his life in wandering from country to country, chasing promises of patronage, which were held out only to deceive. Yet, by an undeviating and vigilant improvement of those hours which will always remain amid the greatest activity, this poor scholar, compelled by poverty to solicit from the great, continued to write more valuable books than most men, in like circumstances, would have felt able to read. Johnson declares that he will forever stand in the first rank of literary heroes, having transmitted the most complete and perfect delineations of the manners of his age.

4. *Visiting.*

There can be no doubt but some of our time should be given to the cultivation of the social affections. But if the visiting be formal and ceremonious, it cannot well be too seldom, or too short. It is frequently said that the student should visit, and, in the society of the ladies, to relax his mind. I could never feel that this is any thing different from an insult to the sex. If you do visit with them, it should, in part, be, to be instructive and useful to them, and not to consider them in the mere light of "parlor ornaments," with the admiration of which it is very pleasant for you to relax your mind after severe study.

And how many dinner or evening parties can the student attend weekly, and yet be a student? Not any. He who would obtain knowledge, must have his body in the proper condition, his mind in his room his attention all his own. You will find many students who visit much; but they are not what we mean by good scholars. But how shall you ever become acquainted with society, and become familiar with good manners? I answer, By your vacations. Nearly a quarter of your time is given up to vacations for this and similar purposes; and is not this sufficient?

5. *Reading useless books.*

After what has been said on reading, perhaps you will feel impatient that it should be introduced again. But you are probably not aware how much time is consumed in many colleges and academies in reading such books. Clubs exist for the very purpose of purchasing and reading novels; and circulating libraries are exhausted of their trash. A club of such worthies have been known to be all in their places in the chapel on the Sabbath, each with a novel under his cloak, which he most assiduously read during the services. I once heard it asserted in "great company," where the voices were too many and too loud to be resisted by my feeble remonstrance, that "nine tenths of all the students in our colleges spend most of their time in reading novels." The assertion is not true; but there is too much truth in it. A noble mind and a manly spirit can soon become so much interested in what will be of use in future life, as not to need or even to relish the morbid excitement of fiction.

6. *Improper method of study.*

May I not hope that what I have said under the chapter on Study, will enable you to understand what is meant by study, and also to form habits which will soon make it pleasant? Many students will begin studies which have no present use, and no immediate relation to their prescribed course. They are useless or puerile. You may conquer them; but *cui bono?* A gentleman was riding through one of our large towns, when a dog came out and began to bark at the chaise. He began to strike at him with his whip. This only increased the clamor of the dog, which brought some ten or a dozen more to his aid. It now became a serious business. All the doors were on jar, and the old women and children laughing at the contest. What was to be done? Was a gentleman to be put down so? No. He descends, ties his horse, applies his whip, and actually whips and drives away the yelping tribe. But as the conqueror ascended his chaise, his laurels began to wither, as an old lady cried after him, "Why, after all, you have only chased away a dog!" Are there not many such battles fought by students who pursue studies that are out of the way, and which, if chased, are as honorable as the conquest just mentioned? These remarks do not apply to any thing in the course prescribed for the class.

Music, painting, drawing, and the like, are appropriate, and very desirable, in their places; but how many have wasted their time in their pursuit, and thus not merely thrown away their opportunities for making solid attainments, but acquired wrong habits, which clung to them through life! Leave your flute at home, and let it be one of the many things to cheer you during vacations, and one of the pleasures which you forego in term-time, to avoid temptations.

7. *We lose time by pursuing a study when the mind is wearied.*

There is danger in mentioning this, lest you mistake that restlessness, and that uneasiness of mind, so uniformly attending early discipline, for real weariness. But the mind, as well as the body, may be jaded; and even a horse, in that condition, ought not to be spurred. *Nil invita Minerva.*[1] Relief and refreshment will be quickly found by turning to some other study. "Post lectione seu stylo defessus, nihil nitor repugnante natura; sed exercitii genus aliud quæro, quo tædium varietas minuat."

8. *Having our studies press us in consequence of procrastination.*

It is impossible to have the mind free and unembarrassed, if you suffer your studies to be driving you. If you defer your lesson to the very last moment in which you can possibly get it, you are n your own

[1] Hor. Ars Poet.

master. A man may do a full day's work in the afternoon; but if he puts it off till that time, he will be unhappy all the morning, over-laboring in the afternoon, and sick in the evening. He who does any thing in haste, no matter what his powers of mind may be, cannot do it well. If I have fifty miles to ride today, I *can* do it all after dinner; but to undertake it would be unwise, and cruel to myself and my horse. There should be no loitering in the morning, because you can retrieve the loss in the evening. Punctuality in getting your lessons is of the very first importance. "It is like packing things in a box: a good packer will get in half as much more as a bad one. The calmness of mind which it produces is another advantage of punctuality. A disorderly man is always in a hurry: he has no time to speak with you, because he is going elsewhere; and when he gets there, he is too late for his business, or he must hurry away to another before he can finish it. It was a wise maxim of the Duke of Newcastle—'I do one thing at a time.' Punctuality gives weight to character. 'Such a man has made an appointment; then I know he will keep it.' And this generates punctuality in you; for, like other virtues, it propagates itself. Appointments, indeed, become debts: I owe you punctuality, if I have made an appointment with you, and have no right to throw away your time, if I do my own."

9. *We lose time by beginning plans and studies which we never complete.*

If the habit of entering upon what is not carried out and completed, be allowed in early life, the evil increases as long as we live. A friend put into my hands a bundle of papers which belonged to one who was reputed a genius. "Were they worth publishing?" was the question. Honesty required the answer to be—"No." There was hardly a single thing completed. Here was a poem begun; there a sonnet *nearly* completed; there a calculation of an eclipse, about two thirds finished, with great accuracy and beauty; there a composition commenced, or a letter about half finished—evidence sufficient that he possessed mind, and even genius; but had he lived, with those habits, he could never have arrived at eminence Never begin any thing, without carrying it through, unless in so doing you must sacrifice some moral feeling or principle. He who desists, *re infecta*, not only loses all his labor, but allows himself in a vicious habit. The man who begins to build, but, for some reason or other, cannot finish, has been the object of ridicule for centuries. It is not essential that you devote all your time to the point on which you wish to receive or bestow light; but do something every day, and in time the thing will be completed, however formidable it appears at the commencement

Order is essential to a proper division and improvement of our time. Any one who has never made the trial, is an utter stranger to the calmness and pleasure with which the soul meets her daily duties, however various, or however arduous, if they return periodically at the same hour. There will be a sufficiency of variety to afford relief, and also stimulus. But the order should be as complete as possible. A wheel that turns constantly may move a vast power, if every cog of the wheel be right; but if there be one broken here, and another there, the whole machinery will suffer, and eventually break in pieces. So, if you try to have order in all your arrangements of study, you will suffer whenever it be broken in upon. The result will be, that you will abandon it, and let the ship go as she pleases, and how she pleases, or you will seize the helm with an arm more resolute and nerved, and keep her true to her course.

If you would make time valuable, beware of low and trifling pursuits. Do nothing of which you will ever be ashamed, either here or hereafter. Is it right that one who has your advantages and your responsibilities should be descending to tricks, or even to trifles? What is the verdict of a world against Nero, who, when emperor of Rome, went up and down Greece, challenging the fiddlers to beat him? Æropus, king of Macedonia, spent his time in making lanterns,—a very useful article, but no business for a king

Harcatius, king of Parthia, employed his time in catching moles, and was one of the best mole-catchers in the kingdom; but does it tell to his credit? Was Biantes, of Lydia, a useful man, or worthy ruler, though he was excellent at filing needles? In the tenth century, there was a patriarch in the church, by the name of Theophylact, who had his time employed in rearing horses. He had in his stable above two thousand hunting horses, fed upon the richest dates, grapes, and figs, steeped in wines. To say nothing about the waste of money, does not the voice of mankind execrate such an abuse of time, and talents, and station? And yet, what is the difference between such a waste of life, and that which too many young men make, excepting that, in the former case, the responsibility may be greater? What "diseases of labor" truly!

By many, much time is wasted in dressing the person. You will not unfrequently find those who will spend from one hour to two and a half every morning in shaving and dressing. What do they accomplish in life? They usually have smooth chins and look neat. As for accomplishing any thing good or great, they will never do either. Dress and neatness are highly commendable; but we cannot have our wagons of mahogany, and highly varnished, if we expect to carry heavy loads over mountains with them.

I shall speak of the necessity of exercise in another

place; but, instead of that exercise which is to refresh and invigorate, how many spend much of their time in sports, and call them recreations! We may have sauces to our dinner; but he who should try to live solely upon them, would find himself shortly becoming lean. Taylor calls such diversions "garments made all of fringes," neither comfortable nor becoming. You are in danger from any recreation which you love much; for men always give their time freely to what they love.

He who can make two spires of grass grow where but one grew before, is said to be a benefactor to his species; and I doubt not that he who would show you a method by which you could double or treble the length of your existence on earth, would be a benefactor also. It seems to me that this may be done.

Locke observes "that we get the idea of time or duration, by reflecting on that train of ideas which succeed one another in our minds; that, for this reason, when we sleep soundly without dreaming, we have no perception of time, or the length of it, while we sleep; and that the moment wherein we leave off to think, till the moment we begin to think again, seems to have no distance. And so, no doubt, it would be to a waking man, if it were possible for him to keep only one idea in his mind without variation, and the succession of others; and we see, that one who fixes his thoughts very intently on one thing, so as to take but little notice of the succession of ideas that pass in his mind, while he is taken up with the earnest contemplation, lets slip out of his account a good part of that duration, and thinks the time shorter than it is." Hence, on this principle, you will notice that life always seems short, in looking back, to those who have been troubled with but few thoughts. Idiots, and sick people, frequently have weeks pass away, while to them they seem scarcely so many days. Of course, it follows, that he who has the most thoughts pass through his mind, and the most rapid succession of distinct ideas, will take most notice of time, and, in the same space of time, will live the longest; so that the curious remark of the philosopher Malebranche is far from being improbable. The thought is beautiful, as well as curious. "It is possible that some creatures may think half an hour as long as we do a thousand years, or look upon that space of duration which we call a minute, as an hour, a week, a month, or a whole age." If Locke's theory be correct, it follows that time will seem long or short, just in proportion as our thoughts are quick or slow. Hence he who dies in the very morning of life, not unfrequently lives longer than another who falls at threescore and ten. Hence, too, the prediction of the prophet may be literally true—"The child shall die an hundred years old." The Eastern nations have long, to all appearance, had this thought. I will give the exquisite illustration drawn by the masterly pen of Addison.

"In the Koran, it is said, that the angel Gabriel took Mahomet out of his bed one morning, to give him a sight of all things in the seven heavens, in paradise, and in hell, which the prophet took a distinct view of, and, after having held ninety thousand conferences with God, was brought back again to his bed. All this, says the Koran, was transacted in so small a space of time, that Mahomet, on his return, found his bed still warm, and took up an earthen pitcher which was thrown down at the very instant that the angel Gabriel carried him away, before the water was all spilt!

"There is a very pretty story in the Turkish Tales, which relates to this passage of that famous impostor, and bears some affinity to the subject we are now upon. A sultan of Egypt, who was an infidel, used to laugh at this circumstance in Mahomet's life, as what was altogether impossible and absurd; but, conversing one day with a great doctor in the law, who had the gift of working miracles, the doctor told him he would quickly convince him of the truth of this passage in the history of Mahomet, if he would consent to do what he would desire of him. Upon this, the sultan was directed to place himself by a huge tub of water, which he did accordingly; and as he stood by the tub amidst a circle of his great men, the holy man bid him plunge his head into the water and draw it up again. The king accordingly thrust his head into the water, and at the same time found himself at the foot of a mountain on the sea shore. The king immediately began to rage against his doctor for this piece of treachery and witchcraft; but, at lengtn, knowing it was in vain to be angry, he set himself to think on proper methods for getting a livelihood in this strange country. Accordingly, he applied himself to some people whom he saw at work in a neighboring wood. Those people conducted him to a town that stood at a little distance from the wood, where, after some adventures, he married a woman of great beauty and fortune. He lived with this woman so long, that he had by her seven sons and seven daughters. He was afterwards reduced to great want, and forced to think of plying in the streets as a porter for his ivelihood. One day, as he was walking alone by the sea side, being seized with many melancholy reflections upon his former and his present state of life, which had raised a fit of devotion in him, he threw off his clothes, with a design to wash himself, according to the custom of the Mahometans, before he said his prayers.

"After his first plunge into the sea, he no sooner raised his head above the water, but he found himself standing by the side of the tub, with the great men of his court about him, and the noly man at his side. He immediately upbraided his teacher for having sen him on such a course of adventures, and betrayed him into so long a state of misery and servitude, but was wonderfully surprised when he heard that the state he talked of was only a dream and a delusion; that he had not stirred from the place where he then stood; that he had only dipped his head into the water, and immediately taken it out again.

"The Mahometan doctor took this occasion of instructing the sultan, that nothing was impossible with God; that he, with whom a thousand years are but as one day, can, if he pleases, make a single day, nay, a single moment, appear to any of his creatures as a thousand years."

If life may thus be prolonged, why will it not hang heavy upon us, as it does with many now? The reason is this, that he who has a constant stream of useful and valuable thoughts passing through his mind, will enjoy each one of them, while he who has few thoughts, will have more passions in exercise; and the soul soon palls upon being forced to attend only to the passions. "The latter is like the owner of a barren country, that fills his eye with the prospect of naked hills and plains, which produce nothing either profitable or ornamental; the other beholds a beautiful and spacious landscape, divided into delightful gardens, green meadows, fruitful fields, and can scarce cast his eye on a single spot in his possessions, that is not covered with some beautiful plant or flower."

Some men, while young, rush into open, high-handed sin, and plunge headlong into guilt, which quickly leads them to the slaughter-house, or which, if they survive, lays up food for future repentance and deep remorse. But this is not the history of the great majority of our educated men. But the sin which, of all others, most constantly lies at their door, is the waste of time while young, and, indeed, all the journey of life. An evening is spent in chatting and smoking; it seems a small space of time; but when life closes, and we leave time to go into eternity, how many of these fragments lie scattered and murdered by the way-side! How deep will be our repentance when too late to remedy the defect, if not too late to seek forgiveness! There is no one thing of which students are so prodigal, as of their time. There are some exceptions—*rari nantes*; but multitudes would be amazed at their conduct, had they been as prodigal of any thing else. You cannot read that page in Tacitus readily; you never read any of the Latin poets except the drudgery spent on Virgil and Horace; but have you not wasted moments and hours sufficient to have made you at home in Latin? You cannot run that Greek verb through all the synopsis, and are blank at a page in Homer; but might you not have made yourself an adept in Greek, and conquered the dialects, and the idioms, had you wasted no time? You neglect duties, public and private, and satisfy conscience, that you have not time to fulfil them all. But the wasted hours cry out against you. They should have been seized and stamped with what would have met the approbation of conscience and of God, as they winged their way to his throne.

In this place I may add, that your time will pass neither smoothly nor profitably, unless you seek and receive the blessing of your Maker upon you daily. I am not now speaking as a theologian, but as an observer of men; and I can unhesitatingly assure you, that there is no one, and no ten things that will so much aid you to improve your time as the daily practice of prayer. "Bene precasse est bene studuisse," according to a great master in study. In the morning, ask the blessing of God upon your studies, that he who created the mind, and has his finger upon it every moment, would keep it sound and clear, and instruct it; that he give you a disposition to spend all your time in his fear, and to improve it for him. In the evening, recall the day, and the hours, and see wherein you have come short of duty, and what you have this day done, or omitted doing, which the conscience, quickened by prayer, tells you should have been done. Alas, how many have squandered this precious gift, and then, when they came to lie on the bed of death, have reproached themselves with a keenness of rebuke, which language was too poor to convey! The lofty Queen Elizabeth, on her dying bed, cried out, "Millions of money for one inch of time!" How many such inches had she thrown away! The piercing cry came too late. "O," said one, as he lay dying, "call back time again: if you can call back time again, then there may be hope for me; but time is gone!"

"Where is that thrift, that avarice of time,
(Blest avarice,) which the thought of death inspires?
O time! than gold more sacred; more a load
Than lead to fools; and fools reputed wise.
What moment granted man without account?
What years are squandered, wisdom's debt unpaid!
Haste, haste! he lies in wait, he's at the door,
Insidious Death! should his strong hand arrest,
No composition sets the prisoner free.
Eternity's inexorable chain
Fast binds, and vengeance claims the full arrear.
On all important time, through every age,
Though much and warm the wise have urged, the man
Is yet unborn who duly weighs an hour.
Who murders time, he crushes in the birth
A power ethereal, only not adored."

CHAPTER VI.

CONVERSATION.

"What a delightful evening we have spent!" said a student to his companion, as they were returning home from a visit during vacation.

"Yes, I do not know as I ever spent one more agreeably; and yet I cannot tell exactly what it was that rendered it so agreeable. The circle all seemed to be happy, and parted so; but, for myself, I was so taken up with the conversation of that stranger, that I took little notice of what the rest were doing."

"That was precisely my own case. Without seeming to know it, he possesses uncommon powers of conversation."

And this was the whole secret of the pleasures of the evening—that there was one in the circle, who, by nature and education, was fitted to instruct and please by his conversation.

There are few things more neglected than the cultivation of what we denominate conversational powers; and yet few which can be more subservient to bestowing pleasure and advantage. The man who knows precisely how to converse, has an instrument in his possession with which he can do great good, and which will make him welcome in all circles.

Take notice as you are introduced to a stranger In a short time, you find he is interesting. You are in the stage; you hear him, and forget the time, and are surprised at the rapidity with which you approach the place at which you must part. What makes him so interesting? It is his powers of conversation.

The advantages of this mode of communicating ideas need not be dwelt upon here. It is the method devised by the infinite Creator for the happiness of man, in all circumstances. It is the most perfect way of giving and receiving instruction. It is simple, as are all his works. We may produce strong, dazzling lights, by chemical combinations; but the pure light of heaven is the most perfect. We may tickle the appetite by artificial drinks, but the pure water which God has provided for man, in all circumstances, is the most perfect drink. Speech, between man and man, is the universal medium of transmitting thought, and it is, by far, the best that can be devised. We now wish to know how we may best cultivate and use this faculty. Every one feels the importance of this knowledge. If you have a friend whom you wish to warn, or upon whose mind you wish to make a deep impression, you know the most perfect way of doing it, is with the tongue. You first think over his situation, his prospects and dangers; you think over all his temptations, what apologies can reasonably be offered, and what he will probably offer for himself; you then think of the motives with which to impress him. You then go to him; you try, by tones and voice, to convince him that you are his friend; you tell him your fears in language chosen and tender, and then you pour out your heart upon him, just as you had planned beforehand. You are perfectly aware that you have used the best and most appropriate means in your power, when you have exhausted your powers of persuasion in conversation. If you cannot reach his heart and conscience in this way, you despair of doing it.

If you wish for information on a particular subject, and there is a book which has it all drawn out on paper, and there is a friend who perfectly understands it, why do you go to that friend and hear him converse, rather than to the book? Because you know that the latter method is not the most interesting and easy way of obtaining information. You can ask light on particular points; you can state your objections; you can compare with what you already know; you can soon know all that your informer knows. Varilles has said that, "Of ten things which he knew, he had learned nine from conversation."

Make it a matter of study, then, to understand this subject, and not merely try to free yourself from faults, but t make it an accomplishment,—a part of your education. There is scarcely any way by which you can gain a stronger hold upon the circles in which you may move, or in which you may do more good. In conversation all are free-booters, and may carry away and appropriate to themselves as much as they can; and there is a vast quantity of thought and information afloat upon the great mass of intelligent mind, which never has been, and never will be, committed to paper. He who is permitted to draw from this great fountain, can hardly fail of having thought poured upon him sufficient to render him intelligent, even though he should never open a book. You will see this every day in our cities. There the mass of men are too busy and hurried to read. They do not read; and yet, when you meet a man from the city, you expect to find him an interesting and an intelligent man. If he has long resided there, you will hardly be disappointed. The reason is obvious: he is thrown where all this thought is floating from mind to mind; where mind is constantly coming in contact with mind; and he feels the influence. A light that is hardly seen when standing alone, will, when placed among others, not only give but receive light.

This constant, direct contact of mind with mind, invariably tends to soften and refine the feelings; so that, when you hear it said of a man, that he keeps the best of company, you have no doubt but he is a man of refinement and politeness. The language which he has been accustomed to use has, at least, the appearance of conveying refined thought and feeling, and we insensibly conform our feelings to the dress in which we clothe them. An actor who personifies a king or a hero, and uses his language, frequently feels that he is what he represents; and were he never to put off the habits and language which he represents for a few hours, he would soon use the language of kings as his own, and have his feelings correspond. There are two dangers to which people in cities, and to which those who are similarly situated, may be exposed: the one is, that of using the language of kindness and refinement till it becomes a habit, when they do not feel it, and thus make dupes of others, and soon make dupes of themselves. Any hypocrisy may be practised till it no longer seems a borrowed character. At any rate, there is danger that, when the forms are greatly studied, the heart, under those forms, is seldom exercised. The other danger is, that the information gathered from conversation alone, be incorrect, and yet be esteemed of good authority. No information thus acquired can be relied upon. Books are the only correct reporters of facts; and even they will sometimes invent facts, and imagine history. A man who relies solely upon conversation and society for stocking his mind, will be a very ready man, a very inaccurate man, and, consequently, incapable of being an accurate judge

He can amuse you—he can interest you—he can give you new views of things; but you cannot rely upon the soundness of his judgment.

The student has an immense advantage over all other classes of the community; for he can unite the two most perfect and desirable methods of gaining information—the accuracy and profound thoughts which can be found only in books, and the general information concerning men and things, which conversation and society will bestow. Consequently, under certain restrictions, it becomes as really his duty to improve by conversation as by books. But as conversation is a kind of commerce, towards which every person ought to pay his share, you act against all honorable rules of commerce, if you are not so prepared as to furnish your quota. If you would draw out facts and information, and elicit mental effort from others, which may be useful to you, it is certainly your duty to cultivate your talents and powers, so that they may, in turn, derive the same benefit from your society. You act an ungenerous part, if this be not the case.

Allow me to continue to be specific in my hints, as it is always true, that, when judicious advice is given, the more specific it is, the more valuable.

1. *Do not waste your time, and that of the company, in talking upon trifles.*

The amount of attention bestowed upon trifles and

follies, frequently renders conversation so nauseous to an intelligent mind, that it is disgusted. The consequence is, that such a man withdraws from company, and loses all the advantages of society. He cannot bear to spend hours of precious time in hearing the narrow-minded dwell upon the merest trifles in the world. He has no taste for entering into them, and he sits silent till he takes a final leave. While I would not applaud a taste that is delicate and fastidious to a fault, and which could endure nothing short of the exquisite, I would, at the same time, earnestly request every trifler, in society, to inquire if he is aware that, by his flat and trivial conversation, he is driving every sensible man from the circle in which he moves. But the man of sense ought not to withdraw. He must have courage to turn the tide. You need not sit silent because the rest are talking trifles. In every circle, you will find, at least, one who is able and willing to communicate instruction. Seek him out; ply him with interrogations, and be in earnest to obtain information which you need. In this way, every one will be able to learn, if he chooses. If there are not two, at least, in the circle, who are engaged in profitable conversation, it is your fault, and you ought not to complain that the company was dull or trifling. It is to be lamented, that even gifted minds and exalted talents are frequently of no other use, in company, than to give countenance to trifling, when they migh and ought to be used to give a right direction to the conversation, and rightly influence the excited, interested minds present. There should be a bearing towards usefulness which is systematic. The want of this is a great deficiency. Even Robert Hall failed here. "Often, indeed, has Mr. Hall lamented this defect: often, as we have been returning from a party, which he kept alive by the brilliancy and variety of his observations, has he said, 'Ah, sir, I have again contributed to the loss of an evening, as to every thing truly valuable: go home with me, that we may spend, at least, one hour in a manner which becomes us.'"[1]

A man given to severe study and thought, is in peculiar danger here; for, when he goes into society, he drops all study, forgets the train of thought in which he had been engaged, and at once has his spirits, not elastic, merely, but even, at times, highly excited. Then the temptation is, to forget that he ought to use his knowledge and talents to instruct and enlighten that circle of friends; and that, if he does not improve the opportunity, he throws all the weight of his character into the vote to drive all valuable thoughts and conversation from the room. I do not mean that you are to strive to monopolize the conversation, to shine and show yourself, and your attainments. Far otherwise. But I mean that you should not waste your time, and the time of those who are kind enough to hear what you have to say, in saying things

[1] Sir James Mackintosh.

which might be said and repeated to the end of time, and no human being would be either the wiser or the better. Do nothing which has the appearance of superiority; but he who relies upon his "small talk" to render him long useful or agreeable in society, has much mistaken human nature. It may be pleasant and pretty; but who would thank you to invite him to dine frequently upon custards and ice-creams? If you leave a company without being able to reflect that you are wiser, or have made somebody else wiser, than when you entered it, there is something wrong in the case.

2. *Beware of severe speaking in company.*

No matter whether the company be large or small, you may be sure that all you say against an absent person will reach him. You have done wrong, and an avenger will be found. I admire the warning which St. Austin is said to have had inscribed in the centre of his table at which he entertained his friends—

> "Quisquis amat dictis absentem rodere amicum,
> Hanc mensam indignam noverit esse sibi."

There is an almost universal propensity in mankind to slander each other, or, at least, to throw out hints which detract from the good opinion which they suppose may be entertained of their fellows. The detractor cheats himself most egregiously, but never others. He tacitly believes that he is pushing this one, and thrusting that one, with the charitable purpose of keeping the unworthy out of the seat of those who merit the esteem of all. "I remember to have read in Diodorus Siculus an account of a very active little animal, which, I think, he calls the ichneumon, that makes it the whole business of his life to break the eggs of the crocodile, which he is always in search after. This instinct is the more remarkable, because the ichneumon never feeds upon the eggs he has broken, nor any other way finds his account in them. Were it not for the incessant labors of this industrious animal, Egypt, says the historian, would be overrun with crocodiles; for the Egyptians are so far from destroying these pernicious creatures, that they worship them as gods."

Do not those who may be denominated detractors of mankind, congratulate themselves that they are disinterested, like this little animal, and are really acting the part of benefactors of mankind? They probably deceive themselves so frequently; but the deception is only upon themselves. But how do others view them? The rest of the world know that, if you detract, it is for the same reason that the Tartars are eager to kill every man of extraordinary endowments and accomplishments, firmly believing that his talents, how great or high soever, and what station soever they qualified him to occupy, will, upon his death, become, as a matter of course, the property of the destroyer. Were this theory correct, it would be an apology for those who indulge in severe remarks upon the absent; for, in most cases, it would be their only hope of possessing great excellencies of character. What you say in detraction will not merely reach the ear of the individual against whom it is said, but it will prejudice the circle against him. We love to be prejudiced against people; and while you may say ten clever things of him which are forgotten, the two or three which you say against him, will be remembered. Nor is this all. Such remarks leave a sting in your own conscience. You cannot thus speak disparagingly of the absent, without giving conscience the right to call you to an account, and tell you, in language which cannot be misconstrued, you have done wrong, and not as you would be done by.

Aristophanes was the enemy of Socrates: he slandered him and abused him, and even wrote a comedy to ridicule him, and especially his notions of the doctrine of the immortality of the soul. As Socrates was present to see the comedy acted upon the stage, and was not at all moved, it was thought that he did not feel this dastardly treatment. But it has been remarked, by an acute observer, that he did feel it most deeply, though too wise to show it; for, as he was taking the bowl of poison, and about to drink it off, as he was entertaining his friends and strengthening his own mind by a conversation on the immortality of the soul, he remarked, that he did not believe the most *comic* genius could blame him for talking on such a subject at such an hour. He probably had his detractor, Aristophanes, in his mind, on making this remark.

'He that indulges himself in ridiculing the little imperfections and weaknesses of his friend, will, in time, find mankind united against him. The man who sees another ridiculed before him, though he may, for the present, concur in the general laugh, yet, in a cool hour, will consider the same trick might be played against himself; but, when there is no sense of this danger, the natural pride of human nature rises against him, who, by general censure, lays claim to general superiority." Unless you have had your attention particularly called to this subject, you are probably not aware how many of these light arrows are shot at those who are absent.

An honest fellow was introduced into the most fashionable circle of a country village; and though he was neither learned nor brilliant, yet he passed off very well. But he had one incorrigible fault: he always staid so as to be the last person who left the room. At length, he was asked, categorically, why he always staid so long. He replied, with great good-nature and simplicity, that "as soon as a man was gone, they all began to talk against him; and, consequently, he thought it always judicious to stay till none were left to slander him."

The habit of flattering your friends and acquaint

ances is pernicious to your own character. It will injure yourself more than others. It is well understood among men, that he who is in the habit of flattering, expects to be repaid in the same coin, and that, too, with compound interest. This is a very different thing from bestowing that encouragement upon your friend in private which he needs for the purpose of calling forth praiseworthy efforts. Flattery is usually bestowed in public—probably for the purpose of having witnesses, before whom your friend now stands committed, to return what you are now advancing to him. But judicious encouragement will always be given in private. If you flatter others, they will feel bound to do so to you; and they certainly will do it. They well know that there is no other way in which they can cancel the obligations which you have imposed upon them; because no compensation but this will be satisfactory. Thus you hire others to aid you to become your own dupe, and over-estimate your excellencies, whatever they may be. For a very obvious reason, then, you will deny yourself the luxury of being flattered. And especially do not fish for such pearls. You cannot do it, in a single instance, without having the motive seen through. You may have been astonished at seeing young men greedily swallow praise, when they could not but know that he who was daubing was insincere. It used to be a matter of surprise to me, how it is that we love praise, even when we know that we do not deserve it. Johnson, at a single plunge, has found the philosophy of the fact. "To be flattered," says he, "is grateful even when we know that our praises are not believed by those who pronounce them; for they prove at least our power, and show that our favor is valued, since it is purchased by the meanness of falsehood." The desire of the approbation of others, for their good opinion alone, is said to be the mark of a generous mind. I have no doubt it is so. Against this desire I am breathing no reproach. It is the character ascribed to Garrick by Goldsmith, against which I am warning you.

"Of praise a mere glutton, he swallowed what came,
And the puff of a dunce, he mistook it for fame;
Till, his relish grown callous almost to disease,
Who peppered the highest was surest to please.
But let us be candid, and speak out our mind:
If dunces applauded, he paid them in kind."

3. *Never indulge in levity upon what is sacred.* It is nearly impossible to treat any sacred subject with levity, in a mixed company, without greatly wounding the sensibilities of some one. It is no mark of strength of intellect, or of freedom from prejudice, or of any good quality, to do it. It shows nothing but a heart that sins without excitement and without temptation. He who can speak lightly of God, his Maker, and his best Friend, or of any thing that pertains to him, will always be known to carry a

heart that will easily yield to a temptation to treat an earthly friend in the same way. You may set it down as a rule to which there are no exceptions, that he who treats religion, or any of the ordinances of his God, with lightness and irreverence, carries a selfish heart, and is not fit to be your bosom friend. Levity of manner, or matter, in regard to sacred things, will ruin your character, or that of any other man. Hear the testimony of one who was "unquestionably one of the first preachers—perhaps the very first preacher—of his time." "I set out with levity in the pulpit. It was above two years before I could get the victory over it, though I strove under sharp piercings of conscience. My plan was wrong. I had bad counsellors. I thought preaching was only entering the pulpit, and letting off a sermon. I talked with a wise and pious man on the subject. 'There is nothing,' said he, 'like appealing to facts.' We sat down and named names. We found men in my habit disreputable. This first set my mind right. I saw such a man might sometimes succeed; but I saw, at the same time, that whoever would succeed in his general interpretations of Scripture, and would have his ministry that 'of a workman that needeth not to be ashamed,' must be a laborious man. What can be produced by men who refuse this labor?—a few raw notions, harmless, perhaps, in themselves, but false as stated by them."

I need hardly allude to the practice of profane

language; for I have no expectation that any one, who has so far forgotten what self-respect demands,—to say nothing about higher claims,—as to use such language, will read a book like this. Such are seldom seen in company as reputable as a book designed to do them good. But still, some may be exposed to the temptation, who never yet yielded to it. Lord Chesterfield, who is universally quoted as a master in the school of politeness, declares that such language is never that of a gentleman. When you hear any one use profane language, you will not wrong him if you conclude, that this is only one of a nest of vipers which he carries in his heart; and although this is the only one which now hisses, yet each, in his turn, is master of the poor wretch who is giving his life-blood to feed them.

In France, men frequently hold both civil and ecclesiastical offices. An elector, who was also an arch bishop, was one day very profane before a peasant. Seeing the man stare, he asked him at what he was so much amazed.

"To hear an arch-bishop swear," was the reply.

"I swear," said the elector, "not as an arch-bishop, but as a prince."

"But, my lord," said the peasant, "when the devil gets the prince, what will become of the arch-bishop?'

"A Persian, humble servant of the sun,
Who, though devout, yet bigotry had none,
Hearing a lawyer, grave in his address,
With adjurations every word impress,
Supposed the man a bishop, or, at least,—
God's name so much upon his lips,—a priest,
Bowed, at the close, with all his graceful airs,
And begged an interest in his frequent prayers."[1]

Every approach to any thing like profaneness ought, at once and forever, to be banished. If you wish to fit yourself for the dark world, it will be time enough to learn its language after you have prepared for it by more decent sins. I am happy to say, that an oath is now seldom heard among people who lay any claim to respectability, and that I have not heard one for years, except where I had evidence that it was stimulated, and was borne on breath tainted and poisoned by ardent spirit. Politeness needs not embellishments which belong to spirits accursed; and truth and sincerity always despise and disdain such auxiliaries.

4. *Be careful in introducing topics of conversation.* There are some people, who move in a sphere so contracted, and the range of their thoughts is in so narrow a circle, that you can anticipate what are to be the topics of conversation, what stories you must hear repeated, and where the circle will return into itself. If you allow yourself to have favorite topics, you will

[1] Cowper.

insensibly and surely run into this habit. Nothing can be more tiresome and unwelcome than such a talker. The same round is to be passed over, the same compliments repeated, the same jests broached. To avoid the possibility of this, some writers will advise you to make use of your last reading in conversation; and thus you will have topics and a store of information to communicate. The objections to making this a rule, in my mind, are great. It does not seem to me to be honest. Your hearer is led to suppose that you are now using information which you have some time or other acquired—that it is a part of your capital, and not that which you have just borrowed. Is it fair for a scholar, who has just laid down the writings of Aristophanes, to come into company and talk about "the Crown;" how keen it was; how Socrates winced under it; and how much ground there was for the satire? Perhaps I have never heard of "the Crown" before, nor have any of the company. Perhaps he had not, two days since. He may inform us of his discovery, and amuse and instruct us with the information; but if he talks about it as if it were one among the thousand things which he knows, and thus palms it off upon us as if it were a part of his capital, he deceives us, and it is dishonorable to do so.

Some will go out of their way to harp upon topics which they suppose particularly agreeable to you, and thus flatter you by talking upon what they suppose you are particularly pleased with; just as if they were to invite you to dine, and then load your plate with some odd food, of which they supposed you were peculiarly fond, though they and the rest of the company loathed it. It is worse than insulting you, because you have all the mortification of the insult, without the power of resenting it. If, for example, a man knows me to be a Calvinist in my religious opinions, and spends his breath, every time he meets me, in lauding John Calvin—in praising the Puritans—when I know that, in his heart, he despises both—I do not thank him for taking all this pains to tickle me. If he sincerely desires information on these, or any other subjects with which he supposes me to be acquainted, he does me a kindness by giving me the opportunity to communicate what I know; but if the subject be dragged in, and that frequently, few things can be more nauseous. The reproof which was given to one who indulged in this practice was severe, but just. A man supposed his acquaintance particularly fond of conversing about the characters drawn in Scripture, and took every opportunity to bring these upon the tapis. "I affirm," said he, on one of these occasions, "that this Samson was the strongest man that ever lived, or ever will live."

"It is not so," said he for whose special gratification the subject was introduced—"it is not so: you yourself are a stronger man than Samson."

"How can that be?"

"Why, you have just lugged him in, by head and shoulders!"

Conversation is an intellectual feast; and it cannot be enjoyed if each one must have a particular dish by himself; and to suppose that you cannot eat the same dish that the rest do, is treating you unhandsomely. You do not wish to have a little table spread in the corner for yourself alone, but to enjoy the feast in common. Remember, then, that the treatment which would be disagreeable to you, will be equally unpleasant to others; and be careful to avoid a practice very common, but which always gives pain.

As a topic of conversation, you cannot do better than to introduce *yourself* as little as possible. We are all in danger of this; but, probably, the danger decreases from youth to old age. "It is a hard and nice subject for a man to speak of himself," says Cowley; "it grates upon his own heart to say any thing of disparagement, and the reader's ears, to hear any thing of praise from him." It is especially dangerous to speak of yourself, if your circumstances are such that you are, in any way, tempted to ask for aid. A beggar will be relieved, if his wants are real, and known. But if he takes pains to expose his sores, those who would otherwise befriend him, turn away in disgust. Say as little about yourself, your friends, your deeds, as possible; for if you say any thing, it is supposed to be done for the purpose of challenging admiration or pity. A good writer recommends his readers not to talk about themselves, unless they are of some considerable consequence in the world. But this rule is unsafe. For who is there that is not, in his own opinion, of consequence enough to be the subject of conversation?

If not exceedingly careful, you will be in danger of repeating old jests as if new, and, perhaps, of appropriating to yourself, as your own, what was said generations before you were born. You have heard, or have read, the *bon mot:* the circumstance of reading or hearing it has escaped your mind, while the jest remains. You repeat it, and will be mortified, at some future time, to find in print what, for years, you had supposed your own property, honestly acquired. It is better to pass for a man of plain, common sense, in ordinary conversation, than to attempt to be brilliant or facetious at an expense which you cannot well bear for any length of time. Few can deal in this commodity without feeling their need of borrowing; and he who is in the habit of borrowing, will soon cease to remember that what he freely uses, is not his own.

While upon this subject, I may say that, if you are tempted to indulge in humor and wit, you are beset in a weak and dangerous spot. Wit, and the faculty of producing smart sayings, may be cultivated. They are so; and I have known a company thrown into shouts of laughter by sallies and strokes which were taken to be impromptu, but which would have been welcomed with coolness, had it been known that they were studied and arranged in private. This must always, more or less, be the case with smart sayings; and the great talent displayed, is in passing them off as if they were the creations of the moment. There are two special dangers in the indulgence of wit: the one is, that it is impossible to flourish a tool so sharp without wounding others. Strive against it as much as you please, your best jokes, and keenest arrows, will be spent upon men and upon living characters. This will cause enmities and heart-burnings. Enemies, and bitter enemies, he must have, who tries to be a wit. And when you hear of a man who "had rather lose a friend than a joke," you may be sure that he will soon cease to be troubled by the officiousness of friendship. Every man knows that he has peculiarities and weaknesses of his own; but they are a part of his nature; and he cannot, and will not, love a man who wounds him through these. These weaknesses are ours; and, though we may feel ashamed of them, as we are of our "poor relations," yet we do not like to have them ridiculed. We repel the man who feels so conscious of superiority, that he may sport with the characters of others. He may excite the laugh, and he may be flattered for a while, but it must be among those whom he has tacitly promised to spare.—The second danger of trying to be a wit, is, that you injure your own mind. No one can be a wit without assiduously cultivating peculiar and odd associations of ideas. The thoughts must run in channels unknown to common ......ds. A strange light must invest every thing at which you look; and the mind soon becomes habituated to eccentric associations. The result will be, that the mind ceases to be a well-balanced instrument of acquiring or communicating information. And the man who sets out to be a wit, will probably succeed so far as to be second-rate, and useless for every thing besides. The character of a witling, as drawn by the pen of Gil Blas, is true to the life. "He is, moreover, the most self-conceited man in Spain, though he spent the first sixty years of his life in the grossest ignorance; but, in order to become learned, he employed a preceptor, who has taught him to spell in Latin and Greek. Besides, he has got an infinite number of good stories by heart, which he has repeated and vouched so often, that, at length, he actually believes them to be true. These he brings into conversation; and one may say, *that his wit shines at the expense of his memory.*" It is important, also, to remember, that he who says a great many brilliant things, says a vast many that are weak and foolish; for pearl-divers always find that the waters which yield the most sparkling pearls, yield also the most shells. The best that can be hoped for, is, that the few witty things that are said, may be retained and repeated, while the worthless may be forgotten.

"Silva," said one of the archest among them, "we shall make something of thee, my friend. I perceive thou hast a fund of genius, but dost not know how to use it to advantage. The fear of speaking nonsense hinders thee from talking at a venture; and yet, by this alone, a thousand people now-a-days acquire the reputation of wits. If thou hast a mind to shine, give rein to thy vivacity, and indifferently risk every thing that comes uppermost: thy blunders will pass for a noble boldness; and if, after having uttered a thousand impertinences, one witticism escapes thee, the silly things will be forgot, the lucky thought will be remembered, and the world will conceive a high opinion of thy merit. This is what every man must do who aspires to the reputation of a distinguished wit."

You will be careful, also, in conversation, not to make any display of knowledge or superior learning. No company likes to confess that they are ignorant; and when one makes a parade of his learning, it is a silent invitation for them to acknowledge his superiority, and to confess that all the rest are ignorant. No invitation could scarcely be more unpleasant. I once knew a student do his utmost to be popular in the social circle, but without success. It was difficult to discover the reason; but a single evening explained

10

the whole. He quoted Latin and talked in Greek, and took great delight in tracing things up to their sources: thus, for example, he took great pains to show the company that the term *comedy* had somewhat lost its original meaning, for it was composed of κωμη, *street*, and ωδη, *song*, meaning a street-song, which they used to act in a cart in the streets of the city. This was all true, but the pedantry was insufferable. It is no evidence of learning, since a single hour spent over Webster's large Dictionary would produce learning enough to torment a circle the whole evening. He who is really a scholar, will make but little noise about it. The half-educated physician, who is constantly afraid that you will suspect him of ignorance, is the man who uses the hard technicalities of the profession, and turns even the precise terms of the pharmacopœia into bombast. It is probably for this reason, also, that pedantry is so odious. If you meet a man who spouts Latin, and bores you with Greek, you may generally suppose that his learning is about as deep as is the courage of the impudent house-dog, who barks loudly whenever you pass his master's house. If you are among students alone, the case is altered; but, in mixed companies, the cases are rare in which even a pun or a jest is welcomed, if it must come in an unknown tongue.

In all your conversation, be careful to maintain purity of thought. All approaches towards what is in delicate, will be at once discountenanced by all good society. Indeed, you can find none who are pleased with it. The vilest person is displeased with *double entendres*, and the like, in company. The reason is obvious. None love to have so much disrespect shown them as must be, when you take it for granted that they will be pleased with such conversation. It is a downright insult to a man of pure mind and pure morals. And never have I known any thing but disapprobation expressed, and felt, on occasions when things thus improper have been introduced, even by those whose hearts were known to be impure. Never allow any thing to drop from your lips which you would not be willing to have your sister or your mother hear you say. Your recitals of facts, anecdotes, and all that you say for the purpose of enlightening or amusing others, should be pure in language and pure in thought.

How are anecdotes and stories to be used? They are of great importance and value, when properly used, and worse than useless when employed improperly. You have known men, of all professions, who are forever relating anecdotes and telling stories. Their fund seems inexhaustible when you first become acquainted with them; but, on further acquaintance, you will find the stock really limited, and that the same things are repeated and laughed at many times every year. One is noted as "an old story teller another is remarkable for keeping the company in good humor, or in shouts of laughter, by the hour together. And yet these individuals are not, and cannot be, as a general thing, very highly respected. No one would esteem it an enviable point to gain, if he might gain the same distinction. And yet every one is in danger of becoming one of these "hoary buffoons," if he indulges in stories and anecdotes. At the same time, stories and anecdotes are facts which illustrate important principles, and cannot well be dispensed with. How shall you avoid Scylla, and not fall upon Charybdis? I answer, You may and ought to use stories and anecdotes. They are very important; and you cannot interest, and instruct, and impress without them. You may make abundant use of them; I had almost said, you cannot make too much. But there are two important cautions to be given here.

1. That you use the fact just as it occurred. Do not add, nor take from it in the least, for the sake of embellishing or making it more striking and to the point. You belie history, if you add or diminish aught. Some men cannot repeat a fact in the shape of anecdote without having it so distorted and discolored, that you would hardly know it to be the same thing. The habit is bad; for you will soon be unable, if it be allowed, to state an interesting fact as it was.

2. The second caution is, do not tell stories, or repeat anecdotes, for *their* sake, and to amuse by them

Their use is, to illustrate what you are talking or writing about. When they are used otherwise than to illustrate, they are out of their place. Never commence a conversation, or pen a paragraph, for the sake of the anecdote which will be brought out by way of illustration. A guide-board is a very convenient thing as you travel a tedious and difficult road; but, though every road ought to have them at its branches and corners, yet what would you say of the man who should lay out and build a road for the sake of its guide-boards? He who is in the habit of investigating subjects by analogy, will be very likely to illustrate them in the way in which they are presented to his own mind. Let your comparisons, figures, and illustrations, all be natural. Were I to see a man building a house, and, all at once, as he wanted a stick of timber, easily and naturally take his axe and go out into the woods and cut it, and bring it, and put it in its place, my opinion of the man would be raised; but if he evidently built the house for the purpose of showing that he could do such things, he would fall, and that greatly, in the estimation of all.

In these remarks I hope I shall not be understood to advise that you be in the habit of tedious minuteness in all your relations of facts and anecdotes. This is intolerable. It is like trying to eat some of our small fish—slow in process; and when you have done, you remember the *bones* while you forget the meat.

A man in haste would not thus dine, if he could well avoid it.

Keep your conversation clear of envy;—and to do it, the heart must be kept clear. I shall not stop to write a tirade against this crying sin. But I will point you to a noble example. Virgil and Horace were contemporaries—both poets—both panting after distinction—both patronized by the same hand—both caressed by the same nation—and both living and laboring for an immortality on earth; and yet they ate at the same table, and, in all their race, were friends. Envy and jealousy never soured their dispositions, never marred their peace. Envy is one of the besetting sins of the student. He is sensitive, nervous, and longs for the approbation of men. He sees others, by some apparently fortuitous circumstances, prospered, caressed and honored, while he is forgotten and passed by. What is more natural than that he should feel envy, and should show it in words, in severe, perhaps unjust remarks? Guard against this temptation. Envy is a demon which invariably dances attendance on men of small minds; and, so far as it is shown, all understand it to be so.

Be cheerful in all your conversation. It can be made a habit, and will always render you agreeable. We have so many weaknesses, so many crosses, and so much that is down-hill in life, that we love to meet a friend that is cheerful. The veriest cripple, and the sour est of men, love to pause and forget themselves, while they listen to the prattle and the cheerful shouts of the group of children. The cultivation of cheerful tones, and a cheerful manner of conversation, will add to your own comfort, and also to that of all with whom you associate. The hares of the sensitive Cowper were his evening companions; and he informs us that their cheerfulness and frolicsomeness beguiled his hours of sadness.

The following are the rules, much abridged, which the judicious Mason gives to the student, in regard to conversation.

1. Choose your company for profit, just as you do your books. The best company and the best books are those which are the most improving and entertaining. If you can receive neither improvement nor entertainment from your company, furnish one or both for them. If you can neither receive nor bestow benefit, leave that company at once.

2. Study the character of your company. If they are your superiors, ask them questions, and be an attentive hearer; if your inferiors, do them good.

3. When the conversation droops, revive it by introducing some topic so general that all can say something upon it. Perhaps it will not be amiss to stock your mind, beforehand, with suitable topics.

4. When any thing is said new, valuable, or instructive, enter it in your memorandum-book. Keep

all that you can lay your hand on that is worth keeping; but reject all trash.

5. Never be a cipher in company. Try to please, and you will find something to say that will be acceptable. It is ill manners to be silent. What is trite, if said in an obliging manner, will be better received than entire silence; and a common remark may often lead to something valuable. Break a dead silence, at any rate, and all will feel relieved and grateful to you.

6. Join in no hurry and clamor. If a point is handled briskly, wait till you have seen its different sides, and have become master of it. Then you may speak to advantage. Never repeat a good thing in the same company twice.

7. Remember that others see their foibles and mistakes in a light different from what you do; therefore, be careful not to oppose or animadvert too freely upon them in company.

8. If the company slander or are profane, reprove it in words, if that will do; if not, by silence; and if that fails, withdraw.

9. Do not affect to shine in conversation, as if that were your peculiar excellency, and you were conscious of superior ability.

10. Bear with much that seems impertinent. It may not appear so to all, and you may learn something from it.

11. Be free and easy, and try to make all the rest

feel so. In this way, much valuable thought may be drawn out.

To these I would add, never get out of temper in company. If you are ill treated, or affronted, that is not the place to notice it. If you are so unfortunate as to get into dispute with a loud, heated antagonist, keep cool—perfectly so. "It is cold steel that cuts," and you will soon have the best end of the argument. The sympathy and respect of the circle will always move towards him who is cool under provocation. "If a man has a quarrelsome temper, let him alone. The world will soon find him employment. He will soon meet with some one stronger than himself, who will repay him better than you can. A man may fight duels all his life, if he is disposed to quarrel." What is usually understood by dispute, i. e. something in which the feelings are strongly enlisted, and in which there is strife for victory, ought never to be admitted into company. The game is too rough. And discussion, when it approaches that point, should be dropped at once.

I cannot close this Chapter without reminding my reader, that the power of communicating our thoughts and feelings by conversation, is one of the greatest blessings bestowed on man. It is a perpetual source of comfort, and may be an instrument of great usefulness. The tongue is an instrument, also, of vast mischief. It is our chief engine for doing good or mis chief. The gift brings a vast responsibility upon us The emotions of the soul, when expressed in language, will always affect others, more or less. If they are rightly affected, good is done; if improperly, evil is the result. You will never pass a day without having a heavy responsibility rest upon you for the use of this gift. Every word is heard by him who planted the ear; and, for every word, you are bound over to give an answer at the great day of accounts. The student, with a cultivated mind, with a fund of ready knowledge, with manners and habits that make him welcome wherever he goes, with an influence which cultivation always gives,—the student can do much for the good of man, the honor of his God, and for his own future peace, by the manner in which he uses his powers of conversation. His words, his tones, will pour delight into the soul of friendship; they will form the character of the little prattler who listens to him; they will pave his way to high and glorious scenes of usefulness;—or they will fall heavy on the ear of affection, and will roll a deep night of sorrow back upon his own soul. Remember that every word you utter wings its way to the throne of God, and is to affect the condition of your soul forever. Once uttered, it can never be recalled; and the impression which it makes, extends to the years beyond the existence of earth.

CHAPTER VI.

POLITENESS AND SUBORDINATION.

THE students of a certain literary institution were assembled in commons at tea, at the commencement of a new academical year. A new class were thus, for the first time, brought to eat together. Their advancement in life and in education was such, that each one ought to have been a gentleman. As they sat down, one says to his friend at his right, "We shall soon see who is who." Presently a large, brawny hand came reaching along up the table, pushing past two or three, and, seizing the brown loaf, in a moment had peeled it of all its crust, and had again retired with its booty to the owner. "Hold, there!" cries one, "to say nothing about politeness, where is the justice of such a seizure?" "Oh! I love the crust the best." "Very like; and *perhaps* others may also have the same taste." Here the conversation ended. But that unfortunate *coup-de-main* fixed an impression concerning the student which was never removed. He was at once marked as a man destitute of politeness, and justly, too. All believed that his heart was more to blame than his hand.

If my readers have ever watched at the door of the

stage-office, as the load of wearied passengers came out, one by one, they are aware that we almost instinctively and almost invariably judge of men by their first appearance—their address. They will notice, too, as they enter a stage for a journey, the inquiring glance goes eagerly round the circle, and at once, unhesitatingly, and almost intuitively, each one has made up his mind who are, and who are not, polite men in the company. In any company, a polite man will be selected as the one in whom all feel that they have a kind of friend and protector—one who will neither disregard their rights nor suffer others to do so. When among strangers, at the public table, the politest man is selected to carve and distribute to the company, because all have confidence in the uprightness and goodness of his heart. And such a man always carries, in his very manners, what is better than a letter of commendation. The letter may deceive, or it may be seen but by few, while his manners will be seen by all. As politeness will not only add to your personal comfort, and the comfort of all among whom you move, but will also greatly add to your usefulness, I feel that no apology is necessary for introducing the subject here. Indeed, I should feel that the book was very deficient without it

Nations and communities differ as widely in respect to politeness as, perhaps, any one thing. The French are polite to a proverb; but we, as a people, seem to be characterized as being a very impolite nation. I need not stop to vindicate our national character, even if it can be vindicated. But this is certain, that we can lay no claims to be considered in danger of being too polite. I have seen a gentleman in a large circle, in attempting to sit down, supposing a chair stood behind him, fall flat on his back. The company all laughed or tittered at his awkward situation, excepting a French gentleman present, who ran to him, helped him up, hoped it had not hurt him, gave up his own chair, and at once entered into a lively conversation, to make him forget the accident. The company all felt rebuked by the politeness of the Frenchman; but I doubt whether, had the same accident recurred the next evening, they would not have repeated the same conduct. Politeness was a *habit* with him; but with the rest of us, it was not a habit. In the same walk in a city, I have inquired at an American store for a place which I wished to find, and received an answer that was hardly civil, and no direction that was of any use. On inquiring at a French store, a few rods distant, the polite owner came out, showed me the street, and even went with me till the house was in sight. Which of these was the polite man?—and at which shop would I be likely to stop and make purchases in future? Yet it was not this motive that induced the man to be polite. It was his habit.

Perhaps no class of men are in greater danger of neglecting to cultivate politeness, at the present day, than students. I will suggest some of the causes of this danger.

The habits of children are formed very differently, now, from what they used to be. Formerly, there was a distance—I will not say it might not have been too great—between the parent and the child. The child was taught to reverence his parents, and to feel that he must look up to them, through all the years of childhood and youth. A child was not then brought forward and exhibited as a prodigy in geometry, in languages, or in oratory. But now, we have mathematicians at four and five, deep proficients in languages at seven, orators that can vie with Pitt at ten, and finished statesmen before the teens. The result is, that these learned children are brought forward, and, like the hot-bed plants, force themselves into notice even before the spring opens. The tokens of respect which used to be paid to age, and worth, and parental care, are all prostrated. The child is not to be blamed; but if, when he becomes a student, his manners are even tolerable, he is greatly to be commended. It is not now thought proper to enforce family-government in the old-fashioned way marked out by Solomon; and thus you will find children in early life wiser than their parents in every thing wherein the will of the parties comes in contact. And he who, from his childhood, has been permitted to show a want of respect and deference to his parents, will not, in manhood, be polite to the rest of mankind. If the principles of a polite, deferential behavior be not planted in early life, they will rarely become a part of a man's character.

Many students, and the very best too, were originally from humble life, and unaccustomed to society. When they began to study, they were secluded from society, and confined to their books; and, not knowing the forms of politeness, nor its uses, they soon learned not merely to neglect, but to despise both. They thus commenced habits which will effectually prevent their ever becoming polite men. Mistaken in the notion, that no one can cultivate politeness unless he moves in a brilliant circle, they neglect their daily habits, till they are clowns for life.

Religious young men are even still more exposed to danger. They are looked upon as the promise and the hope of the church, and are treated with the utmost kindness. They are the sons of the church of God, and all feel something of the partiality of parents towards them. They are in great danger, consequently, of being much more ready to receive attentions than to bestow them—to receive, or even exact deference, than to bestow it upon those whose years and character should at once make them forget themselves. There is an impertinence, a sort of smirking manner, about some young men, which is endured only because the kind hope is indulged, that experience will correct the evil, and some other hand will deal the rough blows necessary to bring them to their proper places; just as the tender mother spares her child, in hopes that he will do better as he grows older; by which she means, that she hopes others will bestow those corrections which he so richly deserves, but which she cannot inflict. I most sincerely wish that young men of this class, who are thus exacting the attentions which old soldiers only deserve, could hear even but a part of the severe remarks which are made upon them the moment they have left the company. The evil of which I am speaking, and speaking, too, with the kindest of feelings, would be quickly remedied.

It is frequently supposed, that the vacations of students will enable them to throw off the stiffness of their habits, and to become polite. This ought to be their effect. But if you will watch the progress of a student's life, you will find that there is danger of having a contrary habit formed by vacations. We will suppose you have studied closely and faithfully through the term, have passed the customary examination at its close, and are now prepared to go home. You are weary, worn down, and almost sick. You reach home with a countenance pale, and eyes sunken. Your parents find that, for the last week or two, you have been drooping. Your brothers and sisters dance around you in pure joy. You are now to be a visitor for a short time, are to be nursed and revived, and sent back in good health, and in fine spirits. Every one in the family is to do all for you in his power, to make your visit pleasant and cheering. The walks, the rides, the visits, every thing, even to the diet, is regulated with a regard to your happiness. What is the result? You are happy, you are gratified; and vacation is delightful; but I ask you, are you not in danger, by these delightful attentions, of receiving all this as your due, and of expecting it all, without feeling a corresponding obligation to return kindnesses, and to make others as happy? Are you not in danger of feeling that these kind attentions are something which are the right of the student, and, consequently, of expecting them from all men, and of feeling disappointed if you do not receive them? Beware of cherishing the feeling, that you are not bound to bestow attentions and kindnesses, as well as to receive them.

Some depend upon becoming polite men and gentlemen from the fact, that, during vacations, they visit much, and, especially, that they then associate much with the ladies. With all due respect to their influence, I must be allowed to say, that every association of the student, connected with their society, is too ideal to do much towards forming habits of politeness It is thought, that any thing which intoxicates for a season, is pernicious to regular habits of life. If the remark is ever true, it probably is in this case.

The radical notions of the present day, so prevalent in regard to almost every subject and department of life, with how much good soever they may be associated, have certainly a deadly influence upon habits of politeness. He who believes mind and matter to be of equal worth, and that the great thing necessary, to recover a planet which has wandered from its orb, is to put it in a whirl, is not very likely to be the man who will acknowledge real worth, and pay deference to genuine merit,—much less to be an angel in kindness towards equals and inferiors. But few men are radical in theory ; but lest they should be thought too far removed from it, too many sacrifice their politeness as a peace-offering to this divinity.

Perhaps students in New England are in special need of caution in regard to their manners. The very air we breathe is republican ; and nothing is current among us but pure republicanism. I am proud to have it so ; and may there never be a breeze, which shall pass over the blue hills and the sweet valleys of New England, which shall not give breath to men of these principles. But, at the same time, while we cultivate iron sinews, high enterprise, and freedom of thought and feeling, there is no need of downright roughness of manners, or savage tones ot peech

We justly admire the easy, graceful politeness of our southern brethren. They are always welcomed among us, and make all happy among whom they move. We may and ought to have more of their pleasing manners, without sacrificing any thing of the New England character, which is truly valuable. From their infancy, they exceed us, altogether, in reverence for their parents, deference to superiors, and urbanity towards their associates.

Professional men are too frequently destitute of real politeness, and in very many cases wofully so. I shall try to account for this shortly. But, lest the position should be doubted, look at a few facts. The good people of New York city are in the habit of opening their houses every spring, to receive clergymen who may wish to attend the anniversaries of the religious societies. A few years since, long and imposing cautions were published in their papers, guarding the clergymen who might attend, against spitting on carpets, and other acts of impoliteness of a similar nature. Without asking whether such a public reproof was altogether delicate or not, it shows the light in which the profession is viewed by a city population. The offices of lawyers and of physicians can seldom boast of any thing that looks towards refinement, unless it be the occupant. And even at the capitol, at Washington, it is said that, when Congress adjourns, they leave the halls in a situation which indicates that almost any thing has been there, rather than the most refined gentlemen of whom our land can boast. The manners of professional men, too, are frequently blunt, slovenly, and boorish. The remark is not to be confined to any one profession. And why is it so? Why are not professional men among the most refined and polite in their manners? I will tell you. Their profession is their character. Upon this they rely, and upon this wholly. It is not that they despise dress and politeness, but because they do not give them their real value. An advocate can manage a cause, and make a plea, so that the whole court will bow to his learning and powers. He relies upon this character, and neglects manners, which, it may be, are all that another man has for his support. That physician, whom you see walking the streets, would not be tolerated in refined society, with his present manners, were it not that he stands so high in his profession. And that clergyman, so eccentric, and so uncouth, even at table, would be intolerable, were it not that, in the pulpit, he can show a powerful, cultivated intellect, and a warm heart. Is not this just as well as if professional men were more particular, and as if every one was a model of politeness? I reply, no. Look a moment at the philosophy of the thing. Every one loves to gaze upon a beautiful picture, or a beautiful statue. You can gaze for the hundredth time, and, at each look, receive an emotion of pleasure. This is true of every man, whoever he may be. We all love to look at what is refined and beautiful; and, when the thoughts recur to it, we dwell longer and more intently upon what is graceful and beautiful The consequence is, that a man, with the same talents and attainments, who is a refined and a polite man, is looked at and remembered with vastly more pleasure than his equal, who is awkward, uncouth, and impolite in his manners. The French lady who declared that she could not read her prayers with any comfort, except from a beautifully-printed and elegantly-bound Prayer-Book, based her remark, not upon fancy, but upon true philosophy. If, then, the physician would be remembered with interest, and have his image recalled with pleasure by his feverish, suffering patient, let him be a polite, finished gentleman in all his appearance and demeanor. If the lawyer would have his skill and his eloquence remembered, let them be associated with manners refined and inviting, and they will be the more often recalled, as they will be associated so intimately with his person If the clergyman would have his instructions take deep hold on the affections of his people, and his visits at their houses hailed with warm greetings, let him cultivate manners that bring no associations connected with his person which are not decidedly pleasurable.

Some trample on all the forms of politeness, for the purpose of challenging and receiving attentions, especially in public places But they greatly mistake human nature. Who does not know that he receives, and welcomes, and waits upon a polite man, at his own house, with much more cheerfulness and alacrity than he does one who has an opposite character? If you would be waited upon and receive the attentions of others, by all means be a man of politeness yourself.

Some feel that politeness is inconsistent with independent feeling. The reverse is true. He who cannot but half respect himself, and can place but half a confidence in himself, is the man to be jealous of others, and to demand of them by impudence what he fears they will not yield him without. "An envious and unsocial mind, too proud to give pleasure, and too sullen to receive it, always endeavors to hide its malignity from the world and from itself, under the plainness of simple honesty, or the dignity of haughty independence." You may regard the convenience of others, and do all that politeness requires, and your own independence will be actually strengthened by it.

Others feel that it is the mark of genius, or of a great mind, to be slovenly in appearance and uncouth in manners. If this be a sure index, the world is certainly in no danger of suffering for the want of genius and talents. A man may be great and influential in spite of his manners; and so can the elephant do wonders with his trunk. The most refined lady cannot thread her needle quicker than he can; but would she be improved by exchanging her hands for his trunk? If genius requires such manners, the Graces should have been hawkers of fish in the streets, and Genius himself a canal-digger.

No station, rank, or talents, can ever excuse a man for neglecting the civilities due from man to man. When Clement XIV ascended the papal chair, the ambassadors of the several states represented at his court, waited on his holiness with their congratulations. As they were introduced, and severally bowed, he also bowed, to return the compliment. On this the master of ceremonies told his holiness that he should not have returned their salute. "O, I beg your pardon," said he; "I have not been pope long enough to forget good manners."

The following hints are suggested as worthy of your consideration:—

1. *That good humor is essential to politeness.*

Perhaps you will think I should have used the term *good nature.* But that seems to be usually confined to a negative character. By good humor I mean "the habit of being easily pleased." The poet has beautifully said, that the art of love ought, on Saturday, to sup at the house of the art of pleasing; that is, if I rightly understand him, the art of pleasing comes next to that of loving.

"Au nom du Pinde et de Cythère
Gentil Bernard est averti,
Que l'art d'ainner doit samedi
Venir souper chez l'art de plaire."

Addison has beautifully illustrated this trait of character in his somewhat whimsical description of his walk with his friend Will Honeycomb It seems that Will had picked up a pebble, which, on account of its shape, he determined to present a friend of his who was gathering such valuable articles. In the mean time, he discovered, by the looks of his friend, that he wished to know the time of day. Pulling out his watch, he "told me we had seven minutes, good. We took a turn or two more, when, to my great surprise, I saw him squir away his watch a considerable way into the Thames, and, with great sedateness in his looks, put up the pebble, he had before found, in his fob. As I have naturally an aversion to much speaking, and do not love to be the messenger of ill news, especially when it comes too late to be useful, I left him to be convinced of his mistake in due time, and continued my walk."

I trust I have said sufficient, under the head of conversation, to prevent my being misunderstood, and to prevent your mistaking good humor for any thing like buffoonery. It must arise from kind feelings within; and a smile must be ready to aid those feelings in expressing themselves. It may be an encouragement to know that every exercise of these kind feelings will surely increase them; so that what is begun as a duty, will soon become a pleasure. We all know that outward expressions of kindness have no value any further than as they are an index of the feelings within ; but it is a kind provision of Providence, that even the outward expression of kindness has a tendency to cultivate the feelings of good will.

2. *That the cultivation of the conscience will increase your politeness.*

The very spirit of the gospel is, that you love your neighbor as yourself; and all know that this is true politeness; so that, when you see an impolite man make great pretensions to religion, you give him credit for having probably deceived himself. You may now be able to think of a man who is notorious for being wicked. Look at him, and see if he be not far from being a man of politeness. Look again, and see if his wickedness did not first commence at the point of being impolite towards men ; for impudence towards men will almost invariably lead to disrespect of God, so that he who begins by throwing aside kind and proper feelings towards his fellows, will most assuredly end in despising the commands of his Maker. The best way, then, to become a man of politeness, is to begin with the heart, to act on the principle of making every one as happy as in your power, because you would have all others do so to you. No one can act on this principle, for any length of time, without possessing all the essentials of politeness. You should, therefore, never try to see how much of kindness you can express, but how much you can feel. Every feeling of deference towards your Maker ; every feeling of contrition before him; every season of self-abasement for your sins,—will bring you nearer and nearer that state in which you will hardly fail of being a man of politeness. If we were made for ourselves alone, and had no other aim but to demand new indulgences from others, we might say nothing about the heart. But if you are to love your neighbor as yourself, and if there be a score, a hundred, or a thousand, who are so situated that they are your neighbors,—then, as you divide off the happiness which you distribute, you will seek but your share; of course, your great object will be to distribute to others.

3. *That cheerfulness is essential to a polite man.*

A gloomy, melancholy man can never think of much except himself. He cannot forget so important a personage to attend to you. He may have cause for all his bad feelings, sufficient to excuse them; but you cannot count any of them as being very kindly towards others. A sick man, as he lies on his bed, will hear the voice of one man as he enters the house, and dread to see him. Why? Because he knows that he has so long brooded over himself, that he has not a single kind, cheerful expression for any one else. Another man enters, and the very sound of his voice cheers him, and the smile and the visit are a reviving cordial. He is a man of cheerful feelings and habits; and, having these, he tries to communicate them to others. When you cultivate cheerfulness, then, you cultivate, at the same time, the habit of politeness. There is a keenness, a razor-like irony, about some men, which assumes the airs of cheerfulness, but which, in reality, is only a genteel way of snarling. Much that is impolite, and really bitter, escapes in this way.

For the purpose of appearing cheerful, you must really feel so; and to feel cheerful, you must be in good health. No one can feel cheerful with a severe toothache upon him, or when turning and tossing under a burning fever. Your health must be good, and kept good by a frugal diet, and a regular course of bodily exercise. It is impossible for the mind to be cheerful and the spirits buoyant without this. No man ought to undertake to pass himself off in company, or expect to render himself even tolerably agreeable, for a single day, unless he has prepared himself by some suitable exercise. The cheerfulness and buoyancy of a hunting party is proverbial: it is owing to the fact that they are all taking an agreeable exercise, without having an object before them of importance enough to do any thing more than barely excite them. "There is no real life but cheerful life; therefore valetudinarians should be sworn, before they enter into company, not to say a word of themselves until the meeting breaks up." Never suffer your body to droop, for the want of exercise, so as to sink below the power of wishing to please and to be pleased.

The cultivation of friendship will add to your politeness; for, so far from rendering the heart selfish by giving warm affections to a few choice friends, it will become more generous towards others. "He that has no one to love, or to confide in, has little to hope. He wants the radical principle of happiness;" and he who wants this, will in vain strive to be a happy man, or to confer happiness upon others.

I shall do great injustice to my readers unless I speak on the subject of SUBORDINATION with great plainness. What need be said will not occupy a long space, especially as I shall pretend to offer no new theory on the subject.

The mind loves to be free; and so strongly does it disdain confinement, and a relinquishment of its own wishes, that it is not unfrequently unwilling to see the necessity for its doing so.

"Order is Heaven's first law." From the earliest dawn of reason to the hour of death, when we reluctantly take the last bitter medicine, we have to submit our wills, more or less, to the will of others. We cannot, in childhood, see that the motive which induces our parents to lay us under restraints, is a regard to our future happiness. It seems to us to be caprice, or, at least, arbitrary dictation. But we learn to submit our wills to theirs; and here is the foundation of government, and here commences a system of bonds and obligations which abide on us through life.

As we advance in life, we see that the reason of family-government is not a love of authority, or of an infliction of punishment; but it arises from compassion to our ignorance, and a desire to form our characters for the world in which we are to live and act.

As we leave the paternal roof, the laws of the state reach us, and throw their obligations around us. If we violate them, the laws to which all have agreed to abide, take hold of us. The judge is only the mouth of the law, and the magistrate who punishes is only the hand. But it is the law, the naked law, which no one or two can alter, which reaches the highest and the lowest in the community with entire impartiality, that compels us to bow our wills to its mandates. Without this, no community could be safe or prospered. Life, character, and property, would alike be a prey to the wicked, without this power and majesty of law.

If you step aside from the laws of the land, and seek for a circle of most valued friends where the heart may revel in its freedom, you will find that even here there are the nicest of laws, which you must obey, or you are expelled from that circle, and your friends renounce you. These laws are not the enactments of legislatures or senates, but they are as well defined and settled as if they were, and their infraction will as surely and as speedily be visited with punishment as if the magistrate stood with his sword to revenge their violation. The most delicate and nice laws must be obeyed, if you would have friends. The cords are silk, and the first thread that is broken will bring retribution upon you.

Even the loose acquaintance of the street in which you daily walk, throws its laws over you, and you must obey them; be civil in your appearance and manners; return kind salutations and kind looks; or you lose character and friends also. It would be easy for you to ruin your influence, and almost your character, by a violation of these unwritten rules. I once saw a student standing under a tree at the corner of the street, sketching a building with his pencil. Another student came sauntering along with his companion, arm in arm. As they passed the corner, one says to the other, "Well, well, something is now to be done!" in a tone which can be conceived, but not expressed on paper. The poor limner blushed, crammed his paper into his pocket, and walked away; but the sting of that rudeness will never entirely leave his heart. The form, the gait, the tones, of that rude young man, will ever remain vividly before him. Was there any need of such rudeness? Were not the laws of good breeding violated?

You cannot expect, then, to go to an academy, a college, or to any other institution, at which scores and hundreds of youth are educated, without finding laws,—laws that are definite, tangible, and which are made to be obeyed, and which must be obeyed, or the character of the institution is gone.

One of the most useful books that could be written, would be a particular and accurate "*History of College Rebellions;*" and I cannot but hope that some one—and the individual could easily be selected—who is well qualified, will undertake it. The only danger would be, that the work would be too voluminous. As you open the work, the chapters would read something like the following:—'A brief history of the *Great Stomach Rebellion;* wherein is set forth how a whole class refused to eat—how they assembled and defied the faculty—their eloquent speeches reported —how half the class, including every rebel, were expelled from college, and went home in disgrace—how many of them became dissipated, and all of them disappointed the hopes of their parents, and their own, and never accomplished any thing which endears their memory to their survivors,' &c. 'A concise history of the *Green-pea Rebellion,* which arose because that when the steward obtained all the peas which he could, he did not obtain more; and which resulted in the final expulsion of only sixteen from the College.' 'An authentic history of the *Window-breaking Rebellion,* wherein is set forth the severity of the faculty, inasmuch as they would not commute the punishment of one who broke seven windows in one night, though the class petitioned it; but, on the contrary, on receiving the vote of one third of the class, that they would not recite till said class-mate was restored, proceeded to discipline the third.' 'The melancholy history of the *Gunpowder Rebellion;* showing the arbitrary proceedings of the faculty in punishing ten of the most promising young men that ever lived, for the trifling, inconsiderate amusement of blowing up five of the out-buildings with ten pounds of powder; with an appendix, containing the votes and speeches of the students, together with their thrilling and soul-harrowing appeal to the public.'

These are but the mere specimens of the titles of the chapters. The book should be faithfully written, and if it could be embellished with a portrait or two of the greatest sufferers, in each chapter, it would be a most valuable vade mecum for the student.

Now, before you ever engage in a rebellion, there are four points of consideration at which I beg you carefully to look:—

1. That, at such times, the faculty are always acting on right principles, and the students always on wrong.

In every contest of the kind, you will remember that you are to act against, and measure strength with men, who have the coolness of age and the wisdom of experience. In your vacations, or at any other time, you would be highly offended at the suggestion that your instructors are not men of candor, of judgment and of kind feelings. But you come back, and, at some unexpected turn of affairs, all on a sudden, these men are so changed that they are neither wise nor prudent, neither just nor humane. How came they to be altered so greatly, and so suddenly? Is it so that they *have* altered? or do you now look at them through the medium of excited passion? You will remember that their age will not be likely to permit your teachers to be thrown into acts of indiscretion by passion: their character, their reputation, their interests, their standing before the community, all unite to urge them to treat you fairly, and honorably, and kindly. Even if they were all bad men, and had scarcely a particle of moral feeling in exercise, every selfish motive of the human heart forbids their abusing any power which they may have over you. In a country like ours, where the very breath of our nostrils is the good opinion of the public, and where schools and colleges are so numerous, that each has to be very circumspect in order to get its share of students, the danger is very small, indeed, that the hand of oppression will be heavy upon the students. I am not anxious to press this view of the subject, because it is unnecessary. Men cannot be found, intrusted with our high literary institutions, who are capable of being on the wrong side of the question, when a contest arises between them and the students.

2. The second suggestion is, that, in every rebellion, public sentiment will always set against the students.

Multitudes have been disappointed in this respect, and that, too, most grievously. A great number get excited on some subject,—a subject about which, individually, they would be ashamed to murmur, if they had to do it alone: they have meetings, they talk, they make most thrilling speeches, and work the thing up, till, in the medium through which they are looking, their sufferings are intolerable, and the conduct of the faculty is atrocious. Never were young men of such character and promise so treated before. They pass resolutions heated in the furnace of passion; they transmit these to their instructors, and then breast themselves in their positions, and, in tones of defiance, ask, in all the spirit of a command, that the faculty meet their wishes. The faculty have seen such storms before: secure in their own upright designs—secure in the confidence of the whole community—they coolly tell their threatening pupils, that *they* are the party to yield, to submit to law, to acknowledge wrong, and promise to do better. But they will not yield,—not they. They will strike a blow which will shake the institution to its very foundations. They will leave, and appeal to the public. To the public they appeal, in tones loud and high-wrought. The good public hears them; and, here and there, a very radical newspaper utters a faint echo of sympathy; but, for the most part, at least in ninety-nine cases out of a hundred, the good public laughs at the appeal, despises the threatenings, mocks at the idea that these misguided youth are not lost to any useful purpose, turns and applauds the firmness of the institution, and gathers round it with new confidence. Others now rush to fill their places, rejoicing to put themselves under men who have laws and regulations, and who will, at any rate, see that these laws are respected and obeyed.

3. The third suggestion is, that, in these cases, the students always miss their aim.

The aim of every rebellion is, to free the students from the exercise of severe, arbitrary power. But, so far from doing this, the very first moment you rebel, you place yourself entirely within the grasp of that power. While you obey the laws, they are your protection, and no injustice can be done to you; but, the very moment that you violate them, you lie at the mercy of those who execute those laws. You hold your place in your class, and in the institution, entirely by courtesy; and, of all the situations for a noble mind to be placed in, this is the most humiliating. "A great mind disdains to hold any thing by courtesy, and therefore, never usurps what a lawful claimant may take away." Such is the testimony of one whom every student in the world reverences. Do the young men think of this, when they rush into a rebellion? Like the poor fly attempting to free himself from a web, into which he voluntarily thrusts himself, every plunge, and every agony of passion, only takes from his strength, and places him more and more at the mercy of his destroyer. Was a class, or any part of a class, ever known to better themselves, in any respect, by a rebellion? It is a very expensive way of gaining redress; and, what is worse, the redress is never gained. A man, who has been considered almost an oracle to the nation, once contrived a new kind of saw-mill. It was to go by wind. But, for the purpose of having the wind, he built it on the highest hill in the region. There the wind was strong and unfailing. The mill was built, and worked to admiration. But there was one capital defect, after all. *The hill was so high and so steep, that he could never get a log to his mill.* It would repay for the great efforts necessary to get up a rebellion in college, were there any possible way of making it of any use, when once excited. But this will always be an unanswerable objection to the whole system.

4. The fourth suggestion is, that a rebellion generally results in the ruin of several members of the institution.

When an excitement first begins, it is usually among some two or three, who feel that they possess popularity among their fellows, and who are conscious that they are none too popular with their instructors. They raise the cry of oppression, and, in order to lead others forward, at once make two or three plunges, which, they are aware, put their own characters beyond recovery. Their all is now staked, and the more they can draw away with them, the better they will feel; just as highwaymen are said to feel that their vocation is honorable in proportion to the number of outlaws they can muster. Having once committed themselves, their song is,

> "Rebellion is my theme all day;
> I only wish 'twould come
> (As who knows but perhaps it may?)
> A little nearer home."

The excitement becoming more general, the great body who fall in and plunge with the rest, do not stop to ask whether they have a cause that will justify them in so doing; nor do they ask who are the leaders in it, nor what will be the results; but they are afraid of losing popularity by any appearance of reluctance. They cannot stand before the finger of contempt, which, at once, points at them, nor endure those names and keen reproaches which are so intolerable to a man of generous spirit, if in any measure deserved. Four fifths, at least, who are drawn into a rebellion, do it from fear of losing their popularity among their fellows. I have known those who could bluster at a public meeting, and talk of trampling the "sheep-skin," or diploma, under foot with contempt, go away to their rooms and weep at the thought that they were preparing a cup of sorrow for a father, whose heart was bound up in his son, or were about to dash the hopes of the fond, widowed mother, who had denied herself all the luxuries, and many of the comforts of life, for years, that she might educate her son. And then, there is an affectation of manly feeling, the show of a spirit that can rise above the loss of hopes and prospects, and dare to make its own destiny. Few things are more insupportable to the young man than to have his courage challenged. He will throw himself headlong into a rebellion to show that he is a lad of spirit and courage. Brave youth! he need not pay such a price for what is already acknowledged to be his. Nobody will, or does, doubt the courage of our young men at our seminaries. Educated as they are, they have a courage which death could not destroy. Why should they commit suicide to prove what needs no proof?

I beseech my young friends to consider the results of a rebellion. It may not injure him who is now reading these lines. But a rebellion must and will result in prodigious evils. Seldom does an institution pass through such a scene without having a third, a half, and not unfrequently the whole, of a class expelled, or sent away with such marks of disgrace and disapprobation, that no respectable college will hereafter receive them. The result will be, that the rebellion is purchased by the ruin of nearly all those who are sacrificed in the contest. You may take the names of all those who have thus violently broken away from college, and you will be surprised to see how few of them ever reach eminence, or even respectability, in any profession. It has always been so, and must continue to be so. There are two reasons why it must be so. First, a young man cannot go through a rebellion, and be sent from college, without receiving such a shock in the process, that it will be next to impossible to recover from it. No sudden changes can be otherwise than injurious to the mind. Scarcely any change can be greater than takes place when a student is, in a moment, thrust from the bosom of his college into the world, with a character unformed, and without the power of retrieving his loss. He may laugh at his prospects, talk with contempt about being "incapacitated from admission into every institution of our country, and writhing beneath the indignation of a father, and the weeping reproaches of a mother;" but when the die is once cast, and he is thrown out upon the world, and separated from the cheering voices of those who are in like condemnation with himself, he will find his heart is desolate indeed. Home, the most delightful spot upon earth, can bring no joy to him. He goes there, and meets the face of the father whose goodness he has abused, and whose hopes he has blasted; of the mother whose sorrows and anxieties he has repaid by dashing the fond pride of one whose heart's blood would freely flow for him; of the sisters who used to come around him as their guide, and cheer him on by every means in their power. All is disappointment at home. Does he leave home and turn to his acquaintances? They despise one who could thus throw away the highest advantages, and prefer his will, at the expense of the happiness of his family, and of his own prospects. His soul has been frenzied almost to madness, and the passions have been called up till the reason sunk under them; and now, when the boiling waters subside, and Reason once more looks abroad, she sees what was before a rich and beautiful vale, now desolated and seared by fire. Of all who know him, he can receive sympathy from none, whose sympathy is not a disgrace. He is now in great danger of flying to stimulants to relieve and drown his troubles, or of sinking down in misanthropy and inactivity. The shock which his whole character and plans have received is inconceivably great. The bankruptcy of the merchant who falls from profuse wealth even to eating the bread of charity, will not, in any measure, compare with it. Few can ever hope to recover from such a fall.

The second reason why such young men as are thus sent from college can hardly ever reach respectability, is, that they forever deprive themselves of the very discipline of mind which is absolutely essential to form a distinguished character. I am not wishing to pass a universal censure, nor to say that there may not be, here and there, a rare instance in which the loss has been made up, and the young man has been saved. These, if the cases do ever occur, are exceptions. But break off a young man from his studies when he has but just commenced the discipline of his mind, shut him out from every institution in the land, and let him feel that he has committed an error which can never be retrieved, and where is he to obtain that mental discipline, and that thorough education, which are essential to his future success? His plans are all broken up; his associates in study are all dissevered from him; his instructors are all taken from him; and his prospect of ever becoming what he once justly hoped, is small indeed. You will never find a man over the age of forty, who ever was engaged in a college rebellion, or who ever saw one, who will not speak of it in terms of the most decided disapprobation.

Besides, are you acting a generous, manly part? You have voluntarily placed yourself under the laws of your college, and under the men who administer those laws; you have promised solemnly to obey them. And now, what shall be said about the honor of a young man who engages in a rebellion, and talks about his "honor," while he is violating that honor which he pledged when he became a member of that institution? If you feel that you are not dealt with justly and fairly—that you are degraded and abused—ask and receive at honorable dismission, and go to some other college, where you will be properly treated. But do not plunge yourself, your class-mates, your parents, and the whole circle of friends, into deep trouble and lasting sorrow, with the vain hope of making it clear that you are a young man of honor, nice feelings, or of true courage. No one doubts that you possess all these. But you run too great a hazard, when you stake your character, and that of others younger than yourself, who will follow you, upon the desperate attempt of dictating conditions to a literary institution. It is thoughtlessness of the consequences, rather than deep depravity, which draws so many into these troubles. If you are such a genius that it must work out of your fingers' ends, and your hands cannot keep out of mischief, go home, and employ those hands in some mechanical business. But do not stay where you are acting a part dishonorable to your own feelings, which will, sooner or later, end in lasting disgrace. Have the hardihood, if it be required, to overlook petty inconveniences and vexations in your present situation, and, while you are a student, stand up in all the strength of an honorable, high-minded man.

> "Os homini sublime dedit
> ———— Cœlumque tueri."

That you will meet with many things, in themselves disagreeable, and trying to your habits and your patience, you must expect. The whole season of study is one of unpleasant restraint and of severe discipline. It will cost many sacrifices of feeling to obtain a good education; but, when once obtained, you will be your own master, and will be fit to govern yourself, and will feel amply repaid for all that you endure. But if you would respect yourself through life, be free from perpetual mortification, ***never engage in a college rebellion.***

CHAPTER VIII.

EXERCISE. DIET. ECONOMY.

So much has of late been written on the subject of exercise, that it is in danger of becoming a stale subject, even before it is understood, and long before it is reduced to systematic practice. It must be plain to my reader, in the very outset, that the whole hopes, prospects, every thing dear to the student, must depend upon his health. If the powers of the body be palsied or prostrated, or in any way abused, his mind must so far sympathize as to be unfitted for making progress in study. You may let the system run down and lose its tone by neglect, and, for a time, the mind retains its activity, as the fires created by some kinds of fuel burn brighter and brighter, till they sink away at once. Sometimes, while the poor house in which the soul resides is rapidly preparing to fall, the mind is even more active as decay approaches, and the fires of the soul burn with a more beautiful and intense glow. So it is said, that the ear will frequently become so exquisite, just before dissolution, that it can gather music from the room of death; the harp is about to be crushed in pieces, but, ere it breaks, it sends forth notes that are sweet beyond expression, till it breathes itself away into ruins.

In other employments, if health fails, it may be recovered, in very many cases, by care and exercise. The business goes on, and the loss of time and property usually do not suffer at once. Not so with him whose all depends upon the constant employment of the mind. Three months' loss of time, while in college, will blast many fair hopes and bright prospects: it will depress you and perplex you as a scholar, and, probably, have a material influence upon you through the whole of life. You may be poor—you may have had but small advantages heretofore; but above these, by industry and application, you may rise. But if your health be gone, you are, at once, cut off from doing any thing by way of study. The mind cannot, and will not, accomplish any thing, unless you have good health. Resolve, then, that, at any rate, so far as it depends upon yourself, you will have the *mens sana in sano corpore.*

It is frequently the case that the student, as the fields of knowledge open before him in all their boundless extent, feeling strong in the buoyancy and elasticity of youth, and knowing that his character must all depend upon himself, sits down closely to his books, resolved to stop for nothing, till his scholarship is fair and high. The first, the second, and the third admonitions, in regard to his health, are unheeded, till, at last, he can study no longer, and then, too late, he discovers that the seeds of death are planted in him. The more promising the student, the higher are his aims, and the stronger are the aspirations of his genius, the greater is the danger. Multitudes of the most promising young men have, within the last few years, found an early grave;—not because they studied too intensely, but because they paid no attention to the body. The beautiful lament which was sung over the gifted White might be repeated every year, and be equally applicable to many who were of equal promise, though their names are "unknown to song.

"Oh! what a noble heart was here undone,
When Science' self destroyed her favorite son!
Yes, she too much indulged thy fond pursuit;
She sowed the seeds, but Death has reaped the fruit.
'Twas thine own genius gave the final blow,
And helped to plant the wound that laid thee low:
So the struck eagle, stretched upon the plain,
No more through rolling clouds to soar again,
Viewed his own feather on the fatal dart,
And winged the shaft that quivered in his heart.
Keen were his pangs; but keener far to feel,
He nursed the pinion which impelled the steel;
While the same plumage that had warmed his nest
Drank the last life-drop of his bleeding breast."

It may, no doubt, be true, that the man who sits down to study, and gives his whole soul to it, without much if any regard to health, may, for a time, impro fast, and mature with great rapidity. He may pass over the ground fast, and appear a prodigy of genius. But it is almost certain that such a one is soon to reach the limits of his attainments, and, if he does not speedily find his grave, will soon be too feeble to do any thing but drag out a discouraging existence. For one, I do not feel that it is so *very* desirable to mature the mind as early as some strive to do; and, perhaps, we labor under a great mistake, on this point, in this country. Our country is a youth, and nothing but what is elastic and youthful, is in fashion. Our legislators, our professional men, must all be young to be popular. The stars are to be looked at only while they are rising. A man of fifty is considered almost superannuated, with us. Such is the fashion. It is not so in other countries. Even La Fayette would not have been considered fit to stand at the head of a great national army, in times of revolution, in this country, after he was eighty. In England, the throne is usually surrounded by a galaxy of talent which is the admiration of the world. Are they men who matured in boyhood, and whose education was completed at twenty-five? Far from it. They are usually old men, whose minds have been slow in becoming mature, whose judgment has been made sound by reading, by thought, by observation, and by years. I make these remarks, because I would have our young men feel that the business of study is for life; and that, instead of trying to do all that can be done in a very short time, they should lay their plans and make their calculations to live long, and for many years be improving and ripening for usefulness.

It is impossible for any man to be a student without endangering the health. Man was made to be active. The hunter, who roams through the forest, or climbs the rocks of the Alps, is the man who is hardy, and in the most perfect health. The sailor, who has been rocked by a thousand storms, and who labors day and night, is a hardy man, unless dissipation has broken his constitution. Any man of active habits is likely to enjoy good health, if he does not too frequently over-exert himself. But the student's habits are all unnatural; and by them nature is continually cramped and restrained. "Men err in nothing more than in the estimate which they make of human labor. The hero of the world is the man that makes a bustle,—the man that makes the road smoke under his chaise-and-four,—the man that raises a dust about him,—the man that ravages or devastates empires! But what is the real labor of this man, compared with that of a silent sufferer? He lives on his projects; he encounters, perhaps, rough roads, incommodious inns, bad food, storms and perils, weary days and sleepless nights;—but what are these? His project, his point, the thing that has laid hold on his heart, glory, a name, consequence, pleasure, wealth—

these render the man callous to the pains and efforts of the body. I have been in both states, and therefore understand them; and I know that men form this false estimate. Besides, there is something in bustle, and stir, and activity, that supports itself. At one period, I preached and read five times on a Sunday, and rode sixteen miles. But what did it cost me? Nothing! Yet most men would have looked on, while I was rattling from village to village, with all the dogs barking at my heels, and would have called me a hero; whereas, if they were to look at me now, they would call me an idle, lounging fellow. 'He gets into his study—he walks from end to end—he scribbles on a scrap of paper—he throws it away, and scribbles on another,—he sits down—scribbles again—walks about!' The man cannot see that here is an exhaustion of the spirit which, at night, will leave me worn to the extremity of endurance. He cannot see the numberless efforts of mind, which are crossed and stifled, and recoil on the spirits like the fruitless efforts of a traveller to get firm footing among the ashes on the steep sides of Mount Etna."

There can be no room for doubt, in the mind of an attentive observer, that one cause why so many of our promising young men sink into a premature grave, is, that they try to do so much in so short a time. By this I mean, that they feel that the great work of disciplining and stocking the mind must be done before the age of twenty-five. Whoever embraces this notion must, at once, abandon the idea of ever excelling, or else he must sit down to his books with an intensity of application that cannot but endanger life.

There are several difficulties in the way of your taking regular, vigorous exercise.

1. *You do not now feel the necessity of it.*

We take no medicine till necessity compels us; and exercise to the student is a constant medicine. You are now young; you feel buoyant, have a good appetite, have strength, fine health, and fine spirits. Time flies on downy wings. Why should you teach yourself to be a slave to exercise, and bring yourself into habits which would compel you, every day, to take exercise? It seems like fitting yourself with a pair of heavy crutches, when you have as good legs to walk with as ever carried an emperor. Let those who are in danger of the gout, or of falling victims to disordered stomachs, begin the regimen; but for yourself, you do not feel your need. No, nor will you feel it, till you are probably so far gone, that exercise cannot recover you. On this point, you *must* take the testimony of the multitudes who have gone over the ground on which you now stand, and who understand it all. They will tell you, that it is not at your option whether you will take exercise or not; you must take exercise, or you are lost to all your hopes and all your prospects.

2. *You feel pressed for time, and therefore cannot take exercise.*

Your hours of reciting are all marked out. The bell will ring at the moment, and, prepared or not, you must be at recitation. You have such a pressure of studies—perhaps labor under some peculiar disadvantages—and so many extra efforts to make out of the regular study hours, that you really cannot find time to exercise. Let me tell you that you miscalculate on one important point. If you will try the plan of taking regular, vigorous exercise every day for a single term, you will find that you can perform the same duties, and the same amount of study, much easier than without the exercise. The difference will be astonishing to yourself. The time spent in thus invigorating the system will be made up, many times over, in the ease and comfort with which your mind takes hold of study.

3. *You do not feel interested in your exercise, and therefore do not take it.*

Many schemes have been devised, by which the student will take regular exercise, and, at the same time, be interested in it. The manual labor system has been greatly extolled. The gymnastic system was no less so. In the latter, I have never had any confidence; and, though I would not speak decidedly against the former, inasmuch as it may, in certain cases, do good, yet I must say that I do not believe it will prevail in our systems of education, to any great extent. The system must stand, if at all, by appealing to the selfishness or wants of the student, and telling him that in this way, he can earn money. But this will not be true in all cases, and probably not in a majority of instances. But there seems to me one great objection to it; and that is, it is too monotonous. When you lay aside your books, you want something to do which will not merely relax the mind from the fatigue of study, but which will also tend to enliven it, and render it cheerful. The monotony of the work-shop will hardly do this. Judging from experience, I decidedly prefer *walking* to all other exercise for the student. Buchan urges it as the best possible exercise, as it calls more muscles into motion than any other which is not positively painful. The advantages of this mode of exercise are, that it is simple. The apparatus is all at hand complete. You need not wait for any importation of machinery. It is in the open air, so that the lungs can, at once, receive the pure air of heaven, and the eye gaze upon hill and dale, upon trees and flowers, upon objects animate and inanimate. The very objects of sight and sound cheer and enliven the mind, and raise the spirits. The noise of the hammer or saw, the walls of the shop, and whole interior of the work-shop, have a very different effect upon the feelings and spirits. If any one is skeptical on this point, a few months' trial in the two places will remove all doubt. Another advantage of walking is, that you can have a friend to walk with, and unbend the mind, and cheer the spirits, by pleasant conversation. This is a point of great consequence; and it can be attained only in walking. You hear the same sounds, you see the same objects, you relieve the way, and the fatigues of exercise, by conversation. For this reason, you should calculate, in most cases, to have company in your walks. Once try the method of walking with a friend regularly for a few weeks, and you will be surprised at the results. On those afternoons in which study is not required, be sure and take long walks, and lay up health for days to come. I once knew two students who invigorated their constitutions astonishingly by this simple process. During one summer, they walked over two hundred miles in company, counting no walk which was under five miles. In a short time, you will feel so much at home in the exercise, that you will not inquire what weather it is, but, Has the hour for walking arrived?

4. *The habits of the student make any bodily exertions fatiguing; and therefore you neglect exercise.*

There is no need of going into the physician's department, and assigning the reasons why, by disuse, the body soon comes to a state in which we feel it a burden to make exertions. The fact is unquestionable. You may go to your books, and shut yourself up in your room for weeks almost constantly, and the idea of walking two or three miles will almost fatigue you of itself. The muscles, the joints, the whole house, reluctates at the thought of moving. The limbs will ache in a few moments, and the will has not the power to enforce obedience. Every day you put off the *habit* of exercise, the difficulty becomes greater; so that he who has not regular times for taking exercise, will soon cease to take any. Nothing can make it pleasant, or even tolerable, but the constant practice of it. You cannot snatch it here and there, and find it an amusement, as you can take up a newspaper; for it will be a burden. Many have, now and then, taken what they call "a dish of exercise;" and when over, they felt worse than when they took none; indeed, it came near making them sick; and so they sagely conclude that exercise does not agree with them. Like the Indian, with a single feather under his head on the rock, and which made him wonder how any one could sleep on a whole bed of feathers, they wonder what they do who exercise daily. Exercise is pleasant or otherwise, not in proportion to its being light or heavy, but to its regularity. The habits of the mind, and more especially those of the body, will forever forbid your enjoying the luxuries and the benefits of it, unless it be regular. Keep this in mind, and it will probably account for much of the unwillingness which you may now feel to taking exercise.

Exercise, then, to be a blessing to you, must be qualified by the following rules:—

(*a.*) It must be regular, and daily.

Nature has planted hunger within us, so that we shall daily bring supplies, to meet the wastes of the body. But, without exercise, the system has not the power to appropriate these supplies, and reduce them, so that they become nutriment. Be as regular in taking exercise, as you are in taking your food. There can be no good excuse, so long as you have feet, which, in a few moments, will give you the best of exercise.

(*b.*) It should be pleasant and agreeable.

The tread-mill would afford regular and powerful exercise; but it would be intolerably irksome. It might give you iron sinews, but the soul would be gloomy and cheerless. It is of the first importance, that you take pleasure in the exercise. Walking is good, but not—if you must walk in a bark-mill. Riding is good, but not—if you had to ride a wooden horse, or a trip-hammer. Be sure and have your hour of exercising cultivate cheerfulness. "Writers, of every age, have endeavored to show that pleasure is in us, and not in the objects offered for our amusement. If the soul be happily disposed, every thing becomes a subject of entertainment, and distress will almost want a name. Every occurrence passes in review like the figures of a procession: some may be awkward, others ill-dressed; but none but a fool is for this enraged with the master of the ceremonies."

(*c.*) It should relax the mind.

Philosophy can teach us to be stubborn or sullen when misfortunes come; and religion can enable us to bear them with resignation; but to a man whose health and spirits are good, they never come with their full power. We should aim to keep both the mind and body in such a condition, that our present circumstances are pleasant, and the future are undreaded. But this cannot be done if the mind be always keyed up like the strings of the musical instrument. The mind that attains the habit of throwing off study and anxiety, and relaxing itself at once, has obtained a treasure. It was this that gave the famous Cardinal De Retz his power over his circumstances, and which could enable him to smile at his destiny. When fallen into the hands of his deadliest enemy, and confined a close prisoner, he laughed at himself and at his persecutor. "In this mansion of distress, though secluded from his friends, though denied all amusements, and even the conveniences of life, teased every hour by the impertinences of the wretches who were employed to guard him, he still retained his good humor, laughed at all their little spite, and carried the jest so far as to be revenged, by writing the life of his jailer."

(*d.*) It should be increased at convenient seasons.

My reader will understand by this that I mean, he should improve his vacations to recover from the fatigue of the past, and gather strength and health for the future. At a very trifling expense, two young men can set off on foot, and, while they are at entire leisure, can perform a long journey, see a great variety of new objects and curiosities, become acquainted with a variety of character, have their spirits raised, the tone of the whole system regulated, and all this during each vacation. I would urge this, because it is naturally impossible for a student to live long, without some such course. All professional men must have the relaxation of travelling. Lawyers have more or less of it in attending courts. Physicians are constantly moving; and clergymen must take a journey almost every season, or they sink into the grave. I have heard, now and then, a severe and captious remark on this point. Must professional men, and especially clergymen, every year or two, take this expensive journey? Farmers and mechanics do not. True; but they would be compelled to do it, if they used their minds, and that to the necessary neglect of the body. But did not Paul preach continually, labor vastly more than we do, and yet live to old age, without relaxation? I answer, no. Far from it. In the first place, he travelled almost the whole of the time while preaching; sometimes by land, and then again a passenger on the water; but most of the time on some journey. His circuit lay round Jerusalem, the diameter being about a thousand miles. In the second place, Providence so ordered it, that he was, every now and then, taken off from his labors, and shut up in prisons. Here he had no desponding feelings, for his religion supported him; here his friends visited him; and here, necessarily, he relaxed and rested, long enough to recover from the wearing of preaching, and yet not long enough to sicken for the want of exercise.

I should be sorry to have my remarks construed as tending to discountenance any manual labor by which the student or the professional man may benefit himself. Many illustrious men have alternately followed the plough, harangued in the forum, commanded armies, and bent over their books. The patriarchs and the distinguished son of Jesse were shepherds, as were Moses and some of the prophets. Paul, though no mean scholar, was a tent-maker. Cleanthes was a gardener's laborer, and used to draw water and spread it on his garden in the night, that he might have time to study during the day. He was the successor of Zeno. Æsop and Terence, whose names will live while language lives, were slaves. Cæsar, as every student knows, studied in the camp, swam rivers holding his writings out of the water in one hand; while his clothing was spun and woven by his sisters. Mahomet "made his own fires, swept his own house, milked his ewes, and mended his shoes and pantaloons, with his own sacred hand." Charlemagne, great in war, and greater in peace, filled his palace with learned men, founded schools and academies through his dominions, and yet was so industrious that he could frame laws even to the selling of eggs. Of Gustavus Vasa it is said, "a better laborer never struck steel." It is by no means certain that these men would ever have been as distinguished for mental excellence, had they not endured all these fatigues of the body. If you can feel as cheerful and happy in the garden, the field, or the work-shop, as you can while walking with a companion, it is altogether to be preferred to walking. But that regular daily exercise which is most pleasant to you, is that which, of all others, will be the most beneficial.

Permit me to say, in a word, that no student is doing justice to himself, to his friends, or to the world, without being in the habit of a uniform system of exercise; and that for the following reasons:—

1. Your life will probably be prolonged by it.

It is little less than suicide to neglect to do that, without the doing of which you are almost sure to shorten your days. The Creator has not so formed the body, that it can endure to be confined, without exercise, while the mind burns and wears upon its energies and powers every moment.

2. You will enjoy more with than without exercise.

This remark is to be applied only to those who exercise daily; and to such it does apply with great force. Every one who is in this habit will bear ample and most decided testimony to this point.

3. You add to the enjoyment of others.

A cheerful companion is a treasure; and all wil gather around you as such, if you are faithful to yourself; for exercise will make you cheerful, and cheerfulness will make friends.

4. Your mind will be strengthened by exercise.

Were you wishing to cultivate a morbid, sickly taste, which will, now and then, breathe out some beautiful poetical image, or thought, like the spirit of some most refined essence, too delicate to be handled or used in this matter-of-fact world, and too ethereal to be enjoyed, except by those of like palate, you should shut yourself up in your room for a few years, till your nerves only continue to act, and the world floats before you as a dream. But if you wish for a mind that can fearlessly dive into what is deep, soar to what is high, grasp and hold what is strong, and move and act among minds conscious of its strength, firm, resolved, manly in its aims and purposes, be sure to be regular in taking daily exercise.

"We consist of two parts, of two very different parts; the one inert, passive, utterly incapable of directing itself, barely ministerial to the other, moved, animated by it. When our body has its full health and strength, the mind is so far assisted thereby, that it can bear a closer and longer application; our apprehension is readier; our imagination is livelier; we can better enlarge our compass of thought; we can examine our perceptions more strictly, and compare them more exactly; by which means we are enabled to form a truer judgment of things; to remove, more effectually, the mistakes into which we have been led by a wrong education, by passion, inattention, custom, example; to have a clearer view of what is best for us, of what is most for our interest, and thence determine ourselves more readily to its pursuit, and persist therein with greater resolution and steadiness."

In regard to DIET, no class of men are more apt to go from one extreme to another than students. You will see one, to-day, swallowing hot bread and cold, meats and vegetables, and whatever else may fairly come in his way. He takes more food into the stomach than it can manage, feels sick, and takes to a rigid system of dieting, which lasts—till he gets well. He hears of such a distinguished man who uses no meat, and he must, from his success in study, be considered right. Another uses milk only, and has become a great man; and therefore the milk diet must be the best. He flies from one thing to another, is capricious and variable, usually for two good reasons—First, he exercises so little, or so irregularly, that no kind of food can sit kindly upon his stomach; and, secondly, his appetite demands more in quantity than a sedentary man should eat. Hence the student has no confidence in his own judgment or experience, and thus frequently presents a ludicrous picture of inconstancy. He is really a dyspeptic, and has a weight upon him, which, with his habits, must be heavier and heavier, till he cannot support it. "Propter stomachum, homo est, quod est," is a maxim which carries too much of truth in its very face at this day. The calls of appetite are listened to till the appetite becomes morbid, the stomach oppressed for weeks; and then the spirits sink, resolution droops, and nothing can now give a start to the clogged machinery but the prescriptions of the physician. When you have come regularly under the influence of medicine, and must rely upon that to do for you what diet and exercise should have done long ago, you are far down the hill.

"The first physicians by debauch were made;
Excess began, and sloth sustains the trade.
By chase our long-lived fathers earned their food:
Toil strung the nerves and purified the blood:
But we, their sons, a pampered race of men,
Are dwindled down to threescore years and ten:
Better to hunt in fields for health unbought,
Than fee the doctor for a nauseous draught;
The wise, for cure, on exercise depend:
God never made his work for man to mend."

In this case, as in most others, the cure of the student must consist in prevention. He can, by care and prudence, in most cases, live long, enjoy good health, be a severe student, and do a great amount of good; he may also, by carelessness, in a short time, seal his own fate, and ruin himself. There are a few hints which I am wishing to suggest on the subject of diet, which may be expressed briefly.

1. *Your diet must correspond with your exercise in the open air.*

Many shut themselves up entirely, in unpleasant weather, during the long winter, or whenever they find a pressure of business within, or unpleasant weather without; and yet they eat just as voraciously as if they took exercise every day. To say that no attention is to be paid to diet, is madness. You *must* pay attention to it sooner or later. If you are faithful to take regular, vigorous exercise every day in the open air, then you may eat, and pay less attention to quantity and quality. But if you take but little exercise, you may be sure that you are to be a severe sufferer if you do not take food in the same proportion. I do not ask you to *diet*, i. e. to be as difficult, and as changeable, and as whimsical, as possible, as if the great point were to see how much you can torment yourself and others; but I do ask you to beware as to the quantity of food which you hurry into the stomach three times each day, without giving it any rest. It is the *quantity*, rather than the kinds of food, which destroys students: it is certainly true, that the more simple the food, the better. If you are unusually hurried this week; if it storms to-day, so that, in these periods, you cannot go out, and take exercise, —let your diet be very sparing, though the temptation to do otherwise will be very strong. When, by any means, you have been injured by your food, have overstepped the proper limits as to eating, I have found, in such cases, that the most perfect way to recover is to abstain *entirely* from food for three or six meals. By this time, the stomach will be free, and the system be restored. I took the hint from seeing an idiot who sometimes had turns of being unwell: at such times, he abstained entirely from food for about three days, in which time nature recovered herself, and he was well. This will frequently, and perhaps generally, answer instead of medicine, and is every way more pleasant. The most distinguished physicians have ever recommended this course. It is a part of the Mahometan and pagan systems of religion, that the body should be recruited by frequent fastings. "Let a bull-dog be fed in his infancy upon pap, Naples' biscuit, and boiled chicken; let him be wrapped in flannel at night, sleep on a good feather-bed, and ride out in a coach for an airing, and if his posterity do not become short-limbed, puny, and valetudinarian, it will be a wonder." If there is any one thing in the history of the celebrated Mathers which tends to account for their long lives, notwithstanding their astonishing labors as students, it is their frequent and stated days of fasting. A man of property, who had for years been abusing his stomach, at last found his health on a rapid decline. Nature could endure it no longer. He went to consult the celebrated Dr. Spring, of Watertown, Mass. He stated the symptoms of his case so clearly, that the learned physician could not mistake the nature of the disease. "I can cure you, sir," said he, "if you will follow my advice." The patient promised most implicitly to do so. "Now," says the doctor, "you must steal a horse." "What! steal a horse?" "Yes,—you must steal a horse. You will then be arrested, convicted, and placed in a situation where your diet and regimen will be such, that in a short time your health will be perfectly restored."

2. *Be regular in your diet.*

Nature loves regularity. She will permit you to dine at any hour you please, and will conform to your wishes in almost every thing, if you will only allow her to depend upon regularity. Some will tamper with themselves, and cultivate a morbid appetite, by eating something, if it be nothing of more worth than a handful of hot peppermints, between almost every meal. And then, at night, among the last things they do, they eat something before retiring to rest. That weariness and faintness which are the calls of nature for rest and sleep, are met by a new supply of food. One of the best remarks that Jefferson ever made, was, "that nobody ever repented having eaten too little." This is true to the letter, in regard to eating between meals. I do not wish to go into particulars; but the habit of closing the day or evening by loading the stomach with fruit or food, will, sooner or later, visit you with fearful retribution.

3. *Be simple in your diet.*

In no profession of life are men likely to accomplish any great and good enterprise, who are in any measure slaves to their palates. Buonaparte was temperate and simple to notoriety during his wonderful career as a general; and Washington, during all his campaigns, was remarkable for the simplicity of his diet. Many times he was known to sit on his horse all day, making his dinner of bread and a slice of pork. The habits of the epicure are the last which the student should cherish. No one thing should be considered as essential to your comfort. A distinguished lawyer used to congratulate himself that the only luxury in which he indulged, was good coffee in the morning: to make it to his taste, it amounted to just half as much ground coffee as he drank liquid. He shone brightly while he lived, but, without any disease or sickness upon him, he sunk into the grave before the age of forty. He died worn out, and seemed an old man. Without wishing to descend to particular articles of food, it should be a general rule to be as simple as possible at the table.

I cannot persuade myself that I need say a word on the subject of stimulating drinks; for I cannot believe that any one, who has self-respect enough to read a book designed for his improvement, will need a single caution on this point. Many classes of men are more frequently in the way of temptation from this quarter, than the student; but no class has half the temptation from within. There is a depression, and a sinking of the animal spirits, at times, which makes the desire for artificial stimulants almost irrepressible. And when the experiment has been once made, and the appetite once indulged, you are, probably, too completely in the hands of your enemy to be saved. Let it alone: never suffer a bottle, a decanter, a wine-glass, to come into your room, or to touch your lips. You could be pointed to men who, in their several professions, were brilliant while they lived, and whose tongues and pens were made eloquent by artificial stimulants. Their suns, almost without exception, set in clouds, and what they wrote will lie unread, at least till the memory of the authors has passed away. But if you could take the catalogue of our colleges, and hear the history of those who, by the star, are marked as having gone to the grave, you would be astonished at the number who were destroyed by this fatal in dulgence. The student who, even occasionally, uses strong drinks, may be marked as one who will soon cease to be in your way as a rival, and whose career will probably be marked, hereafter, only with shame and degradation. While I feel that I almost insult my reader by cautioning him on this subject, I must be permitted to say that the danger, to the student, is very great, and that, owing to the peculiar excitability of his nerves, and the relaxed state of his system, he probably receives treble the injury, by stimulants, that any other man does.

I shall close this chapter with some remarks upon ECONOMY.

The great mass of our students are any thing but wealthy. There are many who, to render their standing in life respectable, go through college, when they have no expectation of relying upon themselves for support. Few of these lay any claim to the character of students. They rely upon their wealth for character and influence in life. Among these there are some who make fine scholars; but, though their number is greater than we should expect, it is small. Those who are to inherit wealth, as a class, will never feel a pressure sufficient to make them severe students. And those who are seeking wealth, will never seek it in the way of study. If it be your object to become rich, you can find a thousand paths which will lead you to wealth, before that of study.

No class of men in the world, considering the amount of capital expended in obtaining an education, and the amount of labor in their professions, are so poorly paid as professional men. It has been said, with emphasis and truth, "that merely to obtain wealth, a man would be more likely to succeed, to begin with a wood-saw and axe, than with an education, which cost him ten years of hard study, and all the money he could borrow." A professional man, in this country, by untiring industry and economy, may have a competency, in most cases; but it will require the union of these two qualities to give it. You will see the necessity, then, of looking at the subject now, and of beginning life with those habits and views which will be safe. It is certainly true, that without economy no student will ever be rich; and, perhaps, it is equally true, that with it very few will ever be poor through life.

Set it down as an axiom, that poverty will do you no injury as a student. While multitudes have been ruined by wealth, few have ever been, by being poor; for there is no pressure so direct, so constant, and so powerful, as that of poverty. Pythagoras long ago remarked, "that ability and necessity dwell near each other:" they usually inhabit the same building. The strong, gigantic character of Johnson was probably owing, in a very great measure, to his poverty. He used to say, that Richard Savagé and himself often walked till four in the morning,—in the course of their conversation, reforming the world, dethroning princes giving laws, &c.,—till, fatigued with their legislative office, they began to want refreshment, but could not muster more than four-pence-half-penny between them. If, in a country where so much is thought to depend on hereditary rank and affluence, poverty only presses a man into greatness, it is no less true, certainly, that, in this country, it cannot injure you. Savage composed his most admired productions while walking over the corn-fields; and then, stepping into the shops and begging a pen, he wrote on scraps of paper picked up in the street, what he had composed during his rambles. And that burning, indescribable passion for knowledge and high attainments which the student ought to have, can no more be quenched by his poverty, than the deep river will cease to roll on with its burden of waters, because you cut off a mountain rill. Indeed, the circumstance of his being poor, is decidedly favorable to the hope that he will stand high as a student; for who does not love to rise above obstacles which, being no reproach to us by lying in our path, and which, being seen by all, only show the strength of character and of purpose which can carry us over them? The discipline which poverty adds to the character is often more severe than language can describe; but the spirit that can bow to its yoke, and, under it, carry forward all the burdens connected with study, is the spirit to be hereafter felt and revered by others. The temptations to dissipation, to dress, and extravagance, to take the mind away from his books, are greatly lessened by his being poor. Look at the men on the stage of life, whose voice, whose pen, whose influence are felt the widest, and who are the ornaments of our country. Were many of them cradled in affluence? Did they acquire their strength on beds of roses? Or are they those who have made themselves by their own efforts, little aided by circumstances that may be denominated fortuitous? The most indigent student in the land need not fear the results of such an investigation.

Never be ashamed to have it known that you are poor, provided that your poverty is owing to no mismanagement of yours. The remark, that "it is the eyes of other people which cost us so much," is so true, that, to attract those eyes, some will be extravagant, and others will be odd, in their appearance. "A celebrated old general used to dress in a fantastic manner, by way of making himself better known. It is true, people would say, 'Who is that old fool?' but it is also true, that the answer was, 'That is the famous General ———, who took such a place.' No one ever stands high in the estimation of others, who goes beyond his means to adorn his person; and while the student should, in all respects, study to be a gentleman in his deportment, it is no more desirable for him to rely upon dress for character, than it is for a lady to adorn her face with chalk, which the rain will wash off, or with paints, which the sun will melt away.

As far as possible, *keep out of debt.* Nothing, short of loss of character, ever weighs down the spirits of a student, like a load of accumulating debts. To say nothing about independent feeling, which he can no more enjoy, than an "empty bag can stand upright," there is an agony about it of which the stirring, active, bargain-making man cannot conceive. It haunts the soul day and night; and the man who can prosper in his studies while sinking in debt, must have feelings peculiar to himself, and be made of "sterner stuff" than most men. All the efforts of denying yourself the luxuries, and even the comforts of life, are light, in comparison with the burden of owing.

But perhaps you will say, that your circumstances are such, that you must relinquish your studies, at once and forever, or be in debt. What shall you do in such a case? I reply that, if you must meet an evil, and carry a burden on your back for years, make every effort to have it as light as possible. You must be in debt, we will suppose. Try, then, and see how little you can be in debt, and possibly get along. In this case, in order to have the mind as free as you can, borrow your money at one place, and in sums sc large, that you need have no small debts upon which you think, and over which you ache, every time you walk out. Keep a small book, in which you register all the items of your expense, and frequently look it over, and see if there be an item registered which you might have saved, by the most rigid economy.

If the taste of a young man improves as it should during the progress of study, he will be in danger, when he makes purchases, of consulting his taste and fancy, rather than his judgment or his means. It is natural, if the taste be cultivated, to be unsatisfied with purchases which do not bear marks of having been prepared for a refined taste; and such preparations are always to be paid for dearly. You must resist this appetite, and consult your judgment, rather than your taste, or be very sparing in your purchases. I have known a poor student pay thirty or thirty-five dollars for a flute, when one seventh of the sum would have procured one of a tone every way as good; and the instrument, inasmuch as he never made any thing more than an ordinary proficient upon it, every way as valuable to him. Pay as little to gratify your taste as you please, at present. You can at any future time do that.

Buy nothing because it is offered cheap. The question should be, not, Is this article worth, and more than worth its price? but, Can I not possibly get along without it? For this purpose, keep away from places where cheap things are to be sold, such as auction-rooms, and the like. "He who buys what he does not need, will often need what he cannot buy." Nor can you expect to purchase any thing like *all* that you want—all that would add to your comfort. We must not only deny ourselves many things which would be pleasant, but also many which, at first view, seem essential. Beware of buying books. The temptation is great here. But there are obvious reasons why you should resist it. One is, that few books will be sufficiently valuable to you to be worth the interest of your money. Another is, that every year brings books more and more within your reach, as every edition of a valuable work is likely to be cheaper than the preceding. You may think you get this and that volume cheap; but, ten years hence, you will not think so. I could mention a gentleman who entered his profession under an embarrassment of four hundred dollars, for books. But before he could possibly pay the debt, the interest which he paid on the money would have purchased what would have been more valuable to him. Excepting your text-books, purchase but few books—perhaps some three or four volumes a year;—the Institution at which you study, will furnish you with books during term-time, and your own purchases will fill up the vacations. It is amusing, in reading the correspondence of the amiable Cowper, to see him borrowing most of the books which he read, because his finances would not allow him to purchase,—and debts he could not endure.

The habits of economy which you now form are for life; and upon these habits are to depend the questions, whether your journey through life be one of independence and comfort, or of mortification and inquietude. If you will read over the curious document embracing the minute expenses of Washington, during the whole of the revolutionary war, and which he kept with his own hand, you will be struck with his economical habits, and feel that such traits properly go into a great character. That is a mistaken notion which supposes that a want of economy is a mark of genius, and that profusion, extravagance, and debts, are inseparable from a man who is to be distinguished for mental attainments. Nothing is beneath you, which will keep you from anxiety, and permit the mind to pursue the paths of knowledge unclogged and unfettered. While it should be impressed on the student, that "wealth cannot confer greatness, because nothing can make that great which the decrees of nature have ordained to be little; that the bramble may be placed in a hot-bed, but can never become an oak;" it should, at the same time, be equally impressed upon him, that he must feel prodigal of his mental powers who can strike for a high character, knowing that much of the strength of these powers is to be expended in the embarrassments of debts. As to being useful, there ever has been, and ever will be, so much of disgrace connected with being in debt, that you cannot be as useful while you owe. If you must be in debt, strive to make the bondage as light as possible, and seek for freedom the first hour that you can.

Finally, one of the very best safeguards against the least waste of property, is to consider yourself accountable to God for all that you have,—that you must answer to him for its use or abuse; and especially if you have not of your own, but live by borrowing of others, will he hold you most strictly accountable for all that you expend. While you have no items on your book at which you cannot look with pleasure, be careful, also, to have your conscience, on this subject, enlightened by a regard to the eye of your God.

CHAPTER IX.

DISCIPLINE OF THE HEART.

My reader will have noticed, that I have said little or nothing thus far on the high subject of the moral feelings. The omission was designed; not that I deem this subject of small importance to the student, but because I wished to present each topic by itself, hoping thereby that the light which fell upon each would be stronger, and that thus each would make a deep and a distinct impression. The two chapters which now remain of this little book are, in my view, by far the most important of any; and I cannot but hope that they will receive the attention of the reader in proportion as they are important.

One of the first steps to be taken, if you would have a character that will stand by you in prosperity and in adversity, in life and in death, is *to fortify your mind with fixed principles.*

There is no period in life in which the heart is so much inclined to skepticism and infidelity as in youth. Not that young men are infidels, but the mind is tossed from doubt to doubt like a light boat leaping from wave to wave. There is no positive settling down into deism or infidelity, but the heart is so full of doubt ing, that the mind has no position, in morals or religion, fortified. If the restraints of education are so far thrown off as to allow you to indulge in sin which is in any way disgraceful if known, you will then easily become an infidel. "The nurse of infidelity is sensuality. Youth are sensual. The Bible stands in their way. It prohibits the indulgence of 'the lust of the flesh, the lust of the eye, and the pride of life.' But the young mind loves these things, and therefore it hates the Bible, which prohibits them. It is prepared to say, 'If any man will bring me arguments against the Bible, I will thank him; if not, I will invent them.' I never gathered from infidel writers, when an avowed infidel myself, any solid difficulties, which were not brought to my mind by a very young child of my own. 'Why was sin permitted?—What an insignificant world is this to be redeemed by the incarnation and death of the Son of God!—Who can believe that so few will be saved?' Objections of this kind, in the mind of reasoning young persons, prove to me that they are the growth of fallen nature. As to infidel arguments, there is no weight in them. They are jejune and refuted. Infidels are not themselves convinced by them. What sort of men are infidels? They are loose, fierce, overbearing men. There is nothing in them like sober and serious inquiry. They are the wildest fanatics on earth. Nor have they agreed among themselves on any scheme of truth and felicity. Look at the need and necessities of man. 'Every pang of grief tells a man that he needs a helper; but infidelity provides none. And what can its schemes do for you in death?' Examine your conscience. Why is it that you listen to infidelity? Is not infidelity a low, carnal, wicked game? Is it not the very picture of the prodigal,—'Father, give me the portion of goods which falleth to me?' *Why*, WHY will a man be an infidel? Draw out the map of the road of infidelity. It will lead you to such stages, at length, as you could never suspect."

This is the testimony of one who had faithfully travelled the road of infidelity; a man whose testimony would have rung through the world, had he continued a low, grovelling, sensual infidel; but whose testimony has never been noticed by infidels, since he became a better man, and an eminent Christian. I will here put it to my reader to say, whether he can recollect, in all he has known of men from history or observation, a great, discriminating and efficient mind, —a mind that has blessed the world in any degree,— which was thoroughly imbued with infidel principles? Take the writings of such a mind, and you will be astonished at the vulgarity, sophistry, puerility, and weakness, which are continually marking its progress. Suppose him a politician. In the unpublished language of a young friend of mine, "it may be said that his religion has nothing to do with his political opinions. But this is not clear: it is justly remarked by some writer, I know not whom, 'that the mind which has been warped and biased upon one great subject, is not safely trusted upon another.' And can we say of a man, 'It is true that the evidences of the Christian religion, which carry along with them the soundest judgments, and the most profound minds, did not meet a reception in his? It is true that his intellect did not lead him to such conclusions on *this* subject as we consider to be the necessary conclusions of a balanced mind,—but yet, in politics, he was great, deep, searching, divine!" Learning, poetry, and literature, walk hand in hand under the light of the gospel. They are destined to do so; and no where else on earth can they now be found. It is absolutely impossible for any mind, amid all this light, to veil itself in infidelity, and expect to be known, revered, or influential among men. Were there no warpings of the mind, and no outrages committed upon it, when it was led to embrace infidelity, still it asks too much of its fellows, when it demands admittance to their communion, and asks permission to reach other minds, when it pretends to pour nothing but the cold light of a December evening upon them. There is so little of sympathy between the mind of an infidel and the enlightened, Christian part of the community, that, if he hopes to have any influence upon men, it must be upon those who have already made shipwreck of character and hopes, and who will hear him speak or write, because he holds out the last, faint glimmering of hope to them, ere they are thrust off upon the dark waters, upon which nothing else sheds a ray of light.

Should you be among those who have no fixed principles in morals and religion, for your own peace and usefulness, I beg you to settle this subject at once and forever. Has God ever spoken to man? If so, when and how? These are the most important questions ever asked. And they should be answered and settled, so that the mind may have something to rest upon so firm that nothing shall move it. "We are mere mites creeping on the earth, and oftentimes conceited mites too." We can easily unsettle things, but can erect nothing. We can pull down a church, but, without aid, cannot erect a hovel. The earlier in life you settle your principles, the firmer, more mature, more influential, will your character be. Search the Bible, and try it as you would gold in the furnace. If you doubt its inspiration, sit down to its examination with candor, and with an honest desire to know what is truth: let the examination be as thorough as you please; but, when once made, let it be settled forever. You will then have something to stand upon. You will have an unerring standard by which to regulate your conduct, your conscience, and your heart. The ship that outrides the storm with the greatest ease, is the one which has her anchors out, her cables stretched, and her sails furled, before the strength of the storm has reached her; and the navigator, who must stand at the helm through the long, dark night, does not wait till that night comes, ere he sees that his compass is boxed and properly hung. He who has his religious principles early fixed, has nothing to do but at once, and continually, to act upon them—to carry them out in practice. He has not the delays and the vexations of distrust and doubt every little while, when he stops to examine and settle a principle. Every reader will be convinced of this, who will read over the seventy resolutions of President Edwards, all of which were formed before he was twenty years old, and the most important of them before he was nineteen. No mind could form, and act upon, such principles from early life, without becoming great and efficient. I cannot refrain from selecting a few of these as a specimen.

"1. Resolved, that I will do whatsoever I think to be most to the glory of God, and my own good, profit, and pleasure, in the whole of my duration, without any consideration of the time, whether now, or never so many myriads of ages hence. Resolved, to do whatever I think to be my *duty*, and most for the good and advantage of mankind in general. Resolved, so to do, whatever *difficulties* I meet with, how many soever, and how great soever."

"4. Resolved, never to do any manner of thing,

whether in soul or body, less or more, but what tends to the glory of God, nor *be*, nor *suffer* it, if I can possibly avoid it.

"5. Resolved, never to lose one moment of time, but to improve it in the most profitable way I possibly can.

"6. Resolved, to live with all my might while I do live.

"7. Resolved, never to do any thing, which I should be afraid to do, if it were the last hour of my life."

"20. Resolved, to maintain the strictest temperance in eating and drinking.

"21. Resolved, never to do any thing, which, if I should see in another, I should count a just occasion to despise him for, or to think any way the more meanly of him."

"34. Resolved, in narrations never to speak any thing but the pure and simple verity."

"46. Resolved, never to allow the least measure of any fretting or uneasiness at my father or mother. Resolved, to suffer no effects of it, so much as in the least alteration of speech, or motion of my eye, and to be especially careful of it with respect to any of our family."

The whole of these seventy resolutions are every way worthy the attention and the imitation of every young man. And while this example is before you allow me to present a few brief resolutions which were formed by a young man before he entered college, and which formed a character known and revered widely, and whose death was sincerely lamented.

"For the future direction of my life, I resolve,

"1. That I will make religion my chief concernment.

"2. That I will never be afraid or ashamed to speak in defence of religion.

"3. That I will make it my daily practice to read some part of the Holy Scriptures, that I may become acquainted with the will of God, and be quickened and comforted, and qualified to serve Christ and promote the interests of his kingdom in the world.

"4. That I will every day reflect upon death and eternity.

"5. That I will daily pray to God in secret.

"6. That, upon all proper occasions, I will reprove vice, and discountenance it, and, to my utmost, encourage virtue and religion.

"7. That I will dispute only for light, or to communicate it.

"8. That I will receive light wherever and however offered.

"9. That I will give up no principle before I am convinced of its absurdity or bad consequences.

"10. That I will never be ashamed to confess a fault to an equal or to an inferior.

"11. That I will make it a rule to do no action, at

any time or place, of which action I should not be willing to be a witness against myself hereafter."

It is frequently the case that young men have an idea that there is something in the cultivation of the heart, and in the restraints of religion, which degrades or cramps the soul; that a mind which is naturally noble and lofty, will become grovelling and contracted by submitting to moral restraints. This is a mere prejudice; and it does little good to deny a prejudice. But go into that library, and examine the shelves, and see who are those who have penned what will be immortal, and influence other minds as long as earth shall endure. In almost every instance, the work which will hold its place the longest, was dictated by a Christian heart. The loftiest minds, the most cultivated intellects, and the most solid judgments, have bowed at the altar of God, and have been quickened and ennobled by the waters which flow from his mount; and if we go up from man to those higher orders of beings who compose "the presence" of the Eternal, we shall find them, after having shouted for joy over the creation of this world, when the morning stars sang together; after having watched the providences of God, and seen empires rise and fall; after having hung around the good in all their wanderings on earth, still studying the Gospel, to have their views enlarged, their conceptions of the infinite wisdom expanded, and still d siring to look into these things. May not the sublime idea of the modesty of these "angelic students" rebuke the ignorance, the darkness, and consummate pride, of those who feel that their greatness would be diminished by bowing to the gospel of God? The angels diligently look into the mystery of the gospel; and they are the companions and fellow-students of all who thus study it.

By disciplining the heart, I mean, bringing it into subjection to the will of God, so that you can best honor him, and do most for the well-being of men. I shall suggest some means by which the heart may be disciplined and the feelings cultivated.

1. *Let it be your immediate and constant aim to make every event subservient to cultivating the heart.*

We are in danger of acknowledging the importance of this subject, but at the same time of putting it off to a convenient season. You suppose your present circumstances are not favorable. There are difficulties now, but you are looking forward to the time when things will be different. Your studies will not hurry you so much; they will become much easier; and you will have conveniences which you have not at the present time. But when you shall go to another place, or commence a new study, or enter upon a more pleasant season of the year, or have a new companion in your room, then you can begin to take care of your heart, and have intercourse with God. But you greatly misjudge. Every thing, every circumstance in our condition, is designed by Infinite Wisdom as a part of our moral discipline; and He who watches the sparrow when she alights, and directs her how and where to find the grain of food, he directs all things relating to your situation; and he designs to have every thing contribute to your moral improvement. There is not a temptation which meets you, nor a vexation which harasses you, nor a trouble which depresses you, but it was all designed for your good. Do not put off, and plead that the path in which your Heavenly Father is leading you is different from what you would have chosen, and therefore you are excusable for not doing his will. No principle of action is of any worth, unless it leads you continually to take care of the heart. I have spoken already of the difficulty in subduing the mind, so as to make study easy. You will find the heart no more readily subdued. Every indulgence of vice, every neglect of duty, strengthens the habits and propensities to do wrong and to go astray.

Should the hand of Providence strike down your best earthly friend, you would feel that you were called upon to make the event contribute to moral culture. But do you feel that it is best to wait for such providences?—to tempt God thus to visit you with afflictions? Every event under his government is designed to do you good; and he who does not make it his daily business to cultivate his heart, will be in great danger of never doing it. You cannot do it at any time, and in a short period. A virtuous and holy character is not built up in a day: it is the work of a long life. Begin the work at once, and make it as really a part of your duties daily to cultivate the heart, as it is to take care of the body, or to cultivate the intellect.

2. *Make it a part of your daily habits to cultivate your conscience.*

A man never became intemperate or profane at once. He never became a proficient in any sin by a single leap. The youth first hears the oath, blushes as he falters out his first profane expression, and goes on, step by step, till he rolls "sin as a sweet morsel under his tongue." It is so with any sin. In this way, the conscience is blunted and the heart hardened. In this way, too, the conscience is recovered, and made susceptible to divine impressions. Were you seeking only for a powerful motive to impel you onward in your studies, and were you regardless of your moral culture, still I would urge you, on this ground alone, to cultivate conscience most assiduously. I will tell you why.

There are but few men who can be brought to task their powers so as to achieve much by motives drawn from this world only. With the mass of educated men this is true. Wealth cannot bribe to steady, unwearied efforts; ambition may lay an iron hand on the soul, but it cannot, excepting here and there, do it with a grasp sufficient to keep it in action: the soft whispers of pleasure can do nothing towards shaking off the indolence and sluggishness of man; and fame, with a silver trumpet, calls in vain. These motives can reach only a few. But conscience is a motive which can be brought to bear upon all, and can be cultivated till she calls every energy, every susceptibility, every faculty of the soul into constant, vigorous, powerful action. Every other motive, when analyzed, is small, mean, contemptible, and such as you despise when you see it operating upon others. The soul of man is ashamed to confess itself a slave to any other power. But this is not all: any other motive soon loses its power. Trials, and misfortunes, and disappointments, damp, kill any other governing motive. But this is not so of the man who acts from conscience. You can crush him only by destroying his life. Shut him up in the prison, and he writes the Epistle to the Hebrews—a work which is yet to do wonders, I doubt not, when the "scattered, peeled" sons of Israel are called in. Shut him up in prison, and his conscience arouses him, and carries him onward to exertions unthought of before. The cold walls of his dungeon grow warm while he describes the Pilgrim's Progress up to eternal day, and scatters the food of angels over the earth;—while he describes the Saint's Everlasting Rest,[1] and actually

[1] Note M.

does more for the good of man, under the pressure of conscience, in adversity, than during all the days of his prosperity.

Only fix the impression on the mind so that it will be abiding, that we are accountable to God for all that we accomplish, and the amount of effort and success will be almost unmeasured. Connect the immeasurable demands of eternity with every effort to conquer sin, to subdue your appetites and passions, and thus make the soul and body more disciplined instruments of doing good, together with every noble resolution, and every exertion, whether it be for life or for a moment,—and you will not do small things; you will not walk through life unfelt, unknown, and you will not go down to the grave unwept. Every unholy desire that you conquer; every thought that you treasure up for future use; every moment that you seize as it flies and stamp with something good, which it may carry to the judgment-seat; every influence which you exert upon the world for the honor of God or the good of man,—all, all is not only connected with the approbation of God and the rewards of eternal ages, but all aids you to strike for higher and nobler efforts still, till you are enabled to achieve what will astonish even yourself. Think over the long list of those men who have lived and acted under the direct and continued influence of a conscience which chained every exer tion and every thought directly to the throne of God. Go, stand at the grave of one of these men; and you will go away musing and heart-smitten, to think that he finished his work, and did it so soon, and went home to his rest in the morning of life, while you have never even contemplated doing but little good. The stone over the dust of such a one will soon crumble away; but the light which surrounds that grave will grow brighter and brighter, till seen the earth over, because his faculties were under the continued direction and control of conscience.

Had I no other aim, then, than merely to excite you to high and noble enterprise, to make great efforts while you live, that motive which I would select as incomparably superior to all others, to lead you to effort, is a cultivated, sanctified conscience. But I have an aim higher than even this, in urging you to cultivate your conscience.

The path of life is beset with temptations. This is a part of our moral discipline. We must meet them every day; we cannot go round them, nor go past them, without being solicited by them; and nothing but a conscience increasingly tender will enable us to meet and overcome them. For example, you will, every week, if not every day, find seasons when you are tempted to be idle, to waste your time. There is no motive at hand which will arouse you. These fragments of time are scattered all along your path

Nothing but a cultivated conscience will enable you to save them. But this will. It cannot be created and brought to bear upon you when indolence has seized you. No, it must be done before.

You will often be tempted to smite with the tongue. The company indulge freely in their remarks upon absent characters. Opportunities occur in which you can throw in a word or two handsomely, and therefore keenly. You can gain credit by the shrewdness with which you judge of character, and for your insight into human nature. No motive of kindness, of politeness, no sense of justice, will now avail to meet this temptation: nothing but a tender conscience will do it.

You are a student. Your health may not be good, —your nerves are easily excited,—you are easily thrown off your guard, speak quickly, and evidently with a great loss of self-respect, which aids in increasing your ill-humor and your tartness. You cannot reason yourself or shame yourself into a good temper: a cultivated conscience is the only thing which will sweeten the temper.

In the course of your life, you will be making bargains, and be more or less in habits of dealing with men. You may intend to be an honorable and an honest man; but you will be strongly tempted, at times, to cheapen what you buy, and over-praise what you sell, or to do as you would not that others should do unto you, unless you are under the direction of a clear, discriminating conscience.

You know how much we esteem our character in the sight of men. Many will fight for it, and quarrel for it, and prefer death a thousand times to the loss of character, in the eyes of their fellow-men. This love of character is as it should be. But what is it to be judged of men, in comparison to being judged of God? Of what consequence is it what men say of us, or think of us, in comparison to what God thinks of us? Who, that believes in the justice of God, and in the immortality of the soul, would not prefer to have his approbation to that of the universe besides? But you can never gain his approbation; you can never stand fair in his sight; you can never have him for your friend, unless you have a heart that is continually under the discipline of a well-regulated, cultivated conscience.

3. *Avoid temptations.*

It is wisdom in beings as frail as we are, not only to use every possible means to overcome sins which beset us, but, as far as possible, to avoid meeting them. If you are on a journey, with a high object in view to be attained, and you may be beset with enemies, you will feel anxious, not merely to be so well guarded that they cannot overcome you, but, as far as possible, to avoid meeting them. There is something in the simple piety of Baxter which pleases us, when he gravely tells us what a blessing he received in narrowly escaping getting a place at court in the early part of his life. We all believe in a superintending Providence; and we know that many of the best men who have ever lived, have been not merely shut out from wealth, and station, and honors, but made objects of suffering, and even of derision to the rest of mankind. The hand that covers them seems rough, and frequently oppressive. But multitudes, who have been ornaments to society, and blessings to their species, and who, after having done their work here, have gone to the rewards of the perfect, have owed their character chiefly to the fact, that their circumstances shielded them from temptations. Were you to mark any number of young men in the same class, who you would fear will accomplish little or nothing for the good of man, you would be likely to select those who, by their situations, are peculiarly exposed to temptations.

There are said to be certain peculiar sins which easily beset every man; and there are certainly temptations which are peculiar to every one. Into some you fall oftener and more easily than into others. Some will meet you in one place, and some in another; some in one shape, and some in another. It is important, for any improvement in moral character, to know where you are peculiarly exposed; and at those points set a strong and wakeful guard.

There are certain individuals with whom you cannot associate, with whom you cannot spend an hour, without hearing things said, and receiving impressions, which tend to lower your standard of honorable feeling, and of purity of heart. Their society may, in many respects, be enchanting, their conversation bewitching, while, at the same time, there may be a subtle poison which will gradually destroy your moral sense. You love to walk with some of these; you love to visit them in their rooms; and you hope you may have some good influence upon them. Perhaps you will have; but the danger is all on your side. The impressions which the soul receives, and the modes of feeling into which the heart is gradually led, will not be likely to startle you at first, even though their end is moral death. How can you hope to strengthen your moral habits, and grow in character, if you frequently yield to the temptation of conversation which deadens the moral sensibilities? Here is one plain temptation; and the way to grow in purity of heart is, not to frequent such company, and there try to throw some feeble influence in favor of virtue, and then go away, and lament and pray over the instances in which you yielded to temptation; but keep clear of the danger; break off from all associates whose influence is against the great object of disciplining the heart.

Some sins meet you at particular seasons. For example, you notice that, after study, or after tea, or at some particular hour of the day, you have less patience than usual. You are inclined to be irritable, or you are low in spirits. You are in danger of cultivating a bad habit of feeling and speaking, and of trying the temper of others. Here you are beset at a particular time of the day ; set a watch over yourself, and avoid the danger. You can easily see the rock, for it is above the waves.

At some particular time of the day, or in some particular situations, you find yourself exposed to debasing and corrupting thoughts. They fill the mind and crowd out every thing that is good. These associations arise only when you are alone, or when you are conversing on some particular topics, or when something is recalled by the memory. Can you hope to conquer these legions, and drive away all these unclean birds, by any other means than by fleeing from them? As there are some demons which, it is said, cannot be cast out except by prayer and fasting, so these can be overcome only by avoiding and resisting them, when they approach the heart, and by the most sincere prayer when they have once entered it.

Suppose you were attempting to grow in moral character and worth, and yet should, now and then, indulge yourself in reading a bad book. The book seems to have fallen into your hand by accident. You do not often read it, but sometimes look into it ; or, if you do not own it, some one may, who offers to loan it to you. Here is a temptation thrown before you. You may never know what that book contains, if you do not now learn it; and should you not know what such books contain, in order to warn others against their influence? I reply, Beware; and yield not to this temptation. One yielding, when thus tempted, may be your ruin; or, if it be not, it will take you a long time to recover from the mischiefs which you are bringing upon yourself. Temptations should be met at a distance: if you see the bird once gaze upon the serpent, she begins to fly round and round, and at every revolution coming nearer and nearer, till she falls into the mouth of the devourer.

You have what are usually called "failings," or "little failings." By a proper attention and study of yourself, you can know what these are; but if you find any difficulty in discovering, you have only to ask your near neighbor, and he will name many which you never had claimed as yours. Now, what are these failings, except places at which you are constantly yielding to temptations? And how can you hope to cure yourself of them, except by avoiding them? Suppose you are naturally of a turn of mind which is bold, impetuous, and forward. It leads you to make remarks that are rash, and to do things which you ought not. Should you not avoid every temptation to it? If Peter be naturally impetuous, and in danger of striking at the first head which he meets, ought he not to leave his sword behind him? You may be of such a temperament, that all company excites your animal spirits, and you are so easily elated, that you lose your balance at the time, and have an equal degree of depression following it. In this case, are you wise to allow yourself to run into temptation? Suppose a man have an innate propensity to be dishonest, so that he can hardly touch the property of others without appropriating something of it to himself; can he hope to clear his hands and his heart so long as he continues in the place of temptation? Should Judas carry the bag, when he has fully proved to himself that he cannot do it without stealing from it? Should a passionate man, whose temper is easily excited, throw himself in situations in which he will certainly be tempted to anger? Whatever be your weakness, or the spot at which you fall, beware of it, and shun it. I once knew a gifted young man, who, in very early life, had indulged a love for ardent spirit, which was almost fatal. Under the influence of conscience and religion, he finally conquered himself, and for years did not taste a drop. In a conversation with him on the subject, he told me that so strong was his appetite, that, even then, the sight of a decanter was painful; and that, whenever he heard liquor running from the cask in a store, he immediately ran out as fast as possible, whether his errand was or was not done. His safety was only in flying

So it is in regard to any temptation. The best way to overcome sin, is to flee from its approach. He who tampers with a temptation is already under its power. The lion will frequently let his victim move, and will play with it before he crushes it.

4. *Watch over your temper.*

There is much said about the natural disposition and temper of men; and the fact, that any one has a temper which is unhappy and unpleasant, is both accounted and apologized for, by saying that his temper is "naturally" unpleasant. It is a comfortable feeling to lay as much blame upon nature as we can; but the difficulty is, that the action, to use a law term, will not lie. No one has a temper naturally so good that it does not need attention and cultivation; and no one has a temper so bad, but that, by proper culture, it may become pleasant. One of the best-disciplined tempers ever seen was that of a gentleman who was, naturally, quick, irritable, rash, and violent; but, by having the care of the sick, and especially of deranged people, he so completely mastered himself, that he was never known to be thrown off his guard. The difference in the happiness which is received or bestowed by the man who guards his temper, and that by the man who does not, is immense. There is no misery so constant, so distressing, and so intolerable to others, as that of having a disposition which is your master, and which is continually fretting itself. There are corners enough, at every turn in life, against which we may run, and at which we may break out in impatience, if we choose.

No one can have an idea of the benefits to be derived from a constant supervision and cultivation of the temper, till he try them ; not that you will certainly cultivate the moral feelings, if the temper be subdued ; but you certainly will *not*, if it be not subdued. Few men ever had, naturally, a more unmanageable disposition than he who, at forty, frequently appears among the most amiable of men. Look at Roger Sherman. He made himself master of his temper, and cultivated it as a great business in life. There are one or two instances which show this part of his character in a light that is beautiful. He was, one day, after having received his highest honors, sitting and reading in his parlor. A roguish student, in a room close by, held a looking-glass in such a position as to pour the reflected rays of the sun directly in Mr. Sherman's face. He moved his chair, and the thing was repeated. A third time the chair was moved, but the looking-glass still poured the sun in his eyes. He laid aside his book, went to the window, and many witnesses of the impudence expected to hear the ungentlemanly student severely reprimanded. He raised the window gently, and then—shut the window-blind! I cannot forbear adducing another instance of the power which he had acquired over himself.

"He was naturally possessed of strong passions; but over these he at length obtained an extraordinary control. He became habitually calm, sedate, and self-possessed. Mr. Sherman was one of those men who are not ashamed to maintain the forms of religion in his family. One morning, he called them together, as usual, to lead them in prayer to God; the 'old family Bible' was brought out and laid on the table. Mr. Sherman took his seat, and beside him placed one of his children, a small child—a child of his old age; the rest of the family were seated round the room; several of these were now grown up. Besides these, some of the tutors of the college were boarders in the family, and were present at the time alluded to. His aged and now superannuated mother occupied a corner of the room, opposite the place where the distinguished judge of Connecticut sat. At length, he opened the Bible and began to read. The child, which was seated beside him, made some little disturbance, upon which Mr. Sherman paused, and told it to be still. Again he proceeded; but again he paused, to reprimand the little offender, whose playful disposition would scarcely permit it to be still. At this time, he gently tapped its ear. The blow, if it might be called a blow, caught the attention of his aged mother, who now, with some effort, rose from her seat, and tottered across the room. At length, she reached the chair of Mr. Sherman, and, in a moment most unexpected to him, she gave him a blow on the ear, with all the power she could summon. '*There*,' said she, '*you strike your child, and I will strike mine!*'

"For a moment, the blood was seen rushing to the face of Mr. Sherman; but it was *only* for a moment, when all was calm and mild as usual. He paused—he raised his spectacles—he cast his eye upon his mother—again it fell upon the book, from which he had been reading. Not a word escaped him; but again he calmly pursued the service, and soon after sought, in prayer, an ability to set an example before his household, which should be worthy of their imitation. Such a victory was worth more than the proudest victory ever achieved in the field of battle."

Suppose, at the close of the day, as you look back upon what you have done and said, you see that, in one instance, you answered a companion short and tartly; in another, you broke out in severe invective upon one who was absent; in another, you were irritated and vexed at some trifle, though you kept it to yourself, and felt the corrosions of an ill temper without betraying your feelings, otherwise than by your countenance. Can you now look back upon the day with any degree of comfort? Can you feel that you have made any advancement in subduing yourself, so that you can look at yourself with cheerfulness and respect, during this day? And if they be so, from day to day, and from week to week, can you expect that your heart will be more and more subdued? You may be sure, that no one, who so gives way to his temper, during every day, that, at night, he has to reproach himself for it, can be growing in moral excellence.

You need not be discouraged in your attempts to correct a quick, an irritable and a bad temper, even though, at first, unsuccessful. Success, on this point, will certainly follow exertion. It is one mark of a great, as well as a good man, to have a command over the temper. Sir Walter Raleigh was challenged by a hot-headed young man; and, because he coolly refused to fight, the young man proceeded to spit in his face, in public. Sir Walter took his handkerchief, and, calmly wiping his face, merely made this reply:—"Young man, if I could as easily wipe your blood from my conscience as I can this injury from my face, I would this moment take away your life." The great Dr. Boerhaave[1] was always unmoved by any provocation, though the practice of medicine is by no means well calculated to soothe the nerves. Upon being asked how he obtained such a mastery over himself, he stated, that "he was naturally quick of resentment, but that he had, by daily prayer and meditation, at length attained to this mastery over himself."

You will have strong temptations to irritability of temper; for it is impossible to be a student, and not

1 Note N.

have the system in such a state that little vexations will jar upon your nerves. But the indulgence of such a temper will not merely mar your present peace, injure you in the eyes of all who know you, hurt your usefulness, hasten on a premature old age, but it is fatal to that peace of mind which consists in "a pure conscience." The heart sickens in despondency, when, at the close of the day, you go to the closet and have to reflect, that your temper is still unsubdued; and that, while you ought to be above being moved by the little troubles which meet you, they constantly oppress you. If you now have no more of character than to give way to your disposition, while in the retirement of the study, what will you do when the multiplied vexations of active life come upon you?

5. *Be careful to improve your thoughts when alone.*

There will be seasons recurring frequently, when you must be alone. You will walk alone, or you will sit in the evening shade alone, or you will lie on a sleepless pillow alone. Every student ought not only to expect this, but to desire it; and never, if faithful to himself, need he be less alone than when alone. The appetites and passions are so apt to ramble, that we esteem him to be good at self-government who subdues them; but the thoughts are but little behind in giv'ng the conscientious man trouble. The two diffi ulties which will meet you most consta ly are, to keep the thoughts from wandering, and from wandering in forbidden paths. What is vain and visionary will easily steal in upon you when alone, and you will soon become a most wretched companion to yourself, and your own tempter. You can easily get into the habit of looking back, and recalling what you have read or studied, and examining what way-marks you have put up, or of reviving the memory of information and knowledge which you have received by conversation; but if you do not cultivate this habit, there will be one at your elbow ever ready to enter the heart and become the strong man of the house. The memory and the judgment may both be cultivated by employing your thoughts upon whatever you have been studying or reading for the last twenty-four hours. Your process will be, first, to recall any thing valuable which you have met with, and then classify it, and weigh it, and judge as to the occasions in which you may wish to use it.

I have spoken of the practice of building castles in the air,—a practice which will be very apt to steal in upon you till it becomes a regular habit, unless you are very careful. You can hardly be too solicitous to keep clear of this habit. I have also spoken of worse results of permitting the thoughts to wander when alone,—evils which want a name, to convey any conception of their enormity.

There are many great advantages in taking frequent opportunities of employing your thoughts alone.

The mind and feelings are soothed by the process; and this is an object every way desirable. Who can rush into the responsibilities, the anxieties, and the labors of the student without strong excitement? Who can see the field of knowledge continually and boundlessly opening before him, with multitudes who, like himself, have staked their character, hopes and happiness upon success, ready to compete with him, without having the excitement continually increasing and growing upon him? There will be little disappointments frequently, little trials, mistakes, which harass and vex you beyond measure. You need seasons of meditation, by which the feelings become soothed and softened, and the judgment rendered clear and decided.

The future lies before you. It will come—it will bring changes to you; some of them will be severe and heavy to bear. There will be sorrows and disappointments in your progress. You need to anticipate the future, so far as you can do it by sitting down and looking calmly at the possible events which may be before you. He who never looks out and anticipates a storm, will be but poorly prepared to meet it when it comes. I do not mean that you should go into the future, and there take a possible calamity, and then grapple with it as with your destiny, and thus mentally endure evils which probably will never come; for no one is likely to hit upon the real evils which will overtake him; but I mean that the thoughtless man, who never communes with himself, is the man who meets troubles with the least resignation.

You have plans, too, for the future, which need to be laid in your own bosom first—matured there—reviewed there till they are perfected, under all the light which frequent contemplations can throw upon them. Your thoughts, while alone, are the best instruments with which to ripen the fruit of future exertions.

Some are afraid of themselves, and dread few things more than to find themselves alone. Every thought of the past or of the future only discourages; and they can be comfortable only by forgetting themselves. But this is not wise. Were it possible for a friend to whisper all your failings, deficiencies and faults into your ear, without wounding your feelings, and causing you to revolt under the discipline, it would be an invaluable blessing to you. What such a friend might do, you can do for yourself, by your thoughts, when alone, and that without any mortification. A man can thus be his own teacher, and, after repeated trials, can weigh his actions, conduct and character very accurately.

He who does not know himself, will never be read-so to make allowances for others, as to be greatly beloved. He will be in danger of being harsh and censorious. While he who is in the habit of measuring himself, in the cool moments of retirement, will seldom fail of knowing so much of himself that he will regard with tenderness the failings of others. In studying your own character, you have a wide field opening before you. You will fail of doing yourself any good, if, in looking at yourself, you do not make it your determination faithfully to reprove yourself for your failings and faults. Mark the places where you trip, and be sure to shun them the next time. Note every instance in which you trespassed upon the kindness, the feelings, or the rights of others; and in all cases in which you have failed to observe the golden rule, reprove yourself with due severity, and see that you amend. You will find that, at some particular places, you have shown a heart that was selfish or wanton—a temper that was revengeful and unkind—a spirit that was jealous, or envious, or malicious—a self-conceit that was unpleasant—or a positiveness that required others to acknowledge your infallibility. No one can be alone, and look over his character, and the manifestations of that character, long, without seeing numerous deficiencies, and marking many places, at which he will set a guard in future.

One of the best criterions by which to judge of your character, is, to examine the characters of those of whose society you are especially fond. You will be more intimate with some than with others. They will be more likely to flatter you; and no better index can ever be found to a man's real character, than those who are his flatterers. If you can discover—and who cannot, if he tries?—who are most frequently flattering you, it will be easy for you to see where you stand. In no moral excellence will you be likely to be above those who pay for your company by their flatteries. You can, in this way, most accurately know the state of your heart; and in your hours of meditation you will be unwise to neglect to submit your life to this ordeal.

By attention to your thoughts when alone, you can obtain what can in no other situation be obtained—definite and correct views of the character of God. No reading, or preaching, or conversation, can ever give you clear conceptions on this great subject, without meditation. From our infancy we hear the character of God described; we read the descriptions of his character in his word; but, after all, we are not likely to attach correct and precise ideas to this language, unless we reflect much alone. On other subjects it is not so. If, from your infancy, you should hear the characteristics of a steam-engine described, as you grew up, your ideas would become definite and settled by experience. You would see the engine frequently, or converse with those who had seen it. But our conceptions of the character of our Maker do not become definite by experience. The same terms may convey wrong impressions, all the way through life, if we never make this the subject of meditation. Let my young reader try it, and he will find that a single hour of close thought alone will give him views of the character of God which are more definite, clear, and satisfactory, than any thing of which he has ever made trial.

6. *Be in the daily practice of reading the word of God.*

The whole journey of life is a continued series of checks, disappointments, and sorrows. In other words, all the dealings of Providence towards us are designed for the purposes of moral discipline. On no other supposition can we reconcile his dealings with his infinite benevolence, or feel resigned in the circumstances in which we are frequently placed. But those views of God, and of ourselves, which are essential to our peace, and discipline of heart, are to be found only in the word of God. I have often been struck with a passage in the Travels of the celebrated Mungo Park, describing his situation and feelings when alone in the very heart of Africa. "Whichever way I turned, nothing appeared but danger and difficulty. I saw myself in the midst of a vast wil derness, in the depth of the rainy season, naked and alone, surrounded by savage animals, and men still more savage. I was five hundred miles from the nearest European settlement. All these circumstances crowded at once on my recollection, and I confess that my spirits began to fail me. I considered my fate as certain, and that I had no alternative but to lie down and perish. The influence of religion, however aided and supported me. I recollected that no human prudence or foresight could have arrested my present sufferings. I indeed was a stranger in a strange land; yet I was still under the protecting eye of that Providence who has condescended to call himself the stranger's friend. At this moment, painful as my reflections were, the extraordinary beauty of a small moss in fructification irresistibly caught my eye. I mention this to show from what trifling circumstances the mind will sometimes derive consolation; for, though the whole plant was not larger than the top of one of my fingers, I could not contemplate the delicate conformation of its roots, leaves, and capsula, without admiration. Can that Being, thought I, who planted, watered, and brought to perfection, in this obscure part of the world, a thing which appears of so small importance, look with unconcern upon the situation and sufferings of creatures formed after his own image? Surely not. Reflections like these would not allow me to despair. I started up, and, disregarding both hunger and fatigue, travelled forwards, assured that relief was at hand; and I was not disappointed."

This is a touching incident in the life of a brave man, and is beautifully expressed. But let us notice the fact that God has made two distinct revelations of himself to this world, each of which is perfect in its kind. The one is by his works,—so clearly revealing his eternal power and Godhead in these, that the very heathen are inexcusable for not worshipping him. The heavens, the earth, all his works, even to the little "moss" which lifts its humble head in the sands of the desert, unite in teaching his wisdom, his power, and his goodness. And it was very natural for Park thus to gain confidence and instruction from this microscopic forest, planted and watered by an unseen hand; but I am confident, that, had he, at the same time, looked at the other revelation which God has made, and drawn from the Bible, he would have had a confidence still stronger, and even joy in again committing himself to One who suffers not the sparrow to fall without his special direction. In the nineteenth Psalm is a beautiful parallel drawn between these two revelations of heaven, and the superiority of the written most decidedly extolled. The monarch of Israel seems to have been walking on the top of his palace, on one of those clear, delightful evenings which hang over Palestine, and contemplating the works of his Maker. He breaks out in praise, declar ing that the heavens and the starry firmament beam out the glory of God; and looking down upon the earth, he says that every day speaks to the one that is to follow it, and every night to its successor—declaring the character of God; and though no speech is heard, and no language is uttered by the works of God, yet they reveal him through all the earth, wherever the sun shines. He then seems to forget all the brightness of the heavens and the glories of earth as he turns away to the word of God,—that better revelation of himself. His harp rises in its strains as he celebrates that; for here is a revelation which is perfect, complete, reaching the soul, commending itself to the conscience, gladdening the heart, enlightening the understanding, enduring in its effects upon the soul, gratifying the taste, and, beyond all, restraining from sin and purifying the heart. This spontaneous burst of the sweet singer of Israel is probably the most perfect eulogy upon the word of God which the world has ever seen.

Perhaps the best uninspired eulogy upon the Bible is from the pen of that masterly scholar, Sir William Jones.[1] It was written on a blank page in his Bible, and also inserted in his eighth Discourse before the Society for Asiatic Researches. "The Scriptures contain, independently of a divine origin, more true sublimity, more exquisite beauty, purer morality, more important history, and finer strains both of poetry and

[1] Note O.

eloquence, than could be collected, within the same compass, from all other books that were ever composed in any age, or in any idiom. The two parts of which the Scriptures consist, are connected by a chain of compositions, which bears no resemblance, in form or style, to any that can be produced from the stores of Grecian, Indian, Persian, or even Arabian learning The antiquity of those compositions no man doubts; and the unstrained application of them to events long subsequent to their publication, is a solid ground of belief that they were genuine predictions, and consequently inspired."

Deists and skeptics, in swarms, have studied the revelation of nature, and professed to see and know God; but from this source they draw no truths in which they can agree, no precepts which in any measure break the power of sin within the heart, no consolations which bow the will to that of God in the hour of suffering and trial, and no hope that can sustain and cheer the soul when she is called to feel her house shake and fall in pieces.

"The Bible resembles an extensive and highly cultivated garden, where there is a vast variety and profusion of fruits and flowers; some of which are more essential or more splendid than others; but there is not a blade suffered to grow in it, which has not its use and beauty in the system. Salvation for sinners is the grand truth presented every where, and in all points of light; but *the pure in heart* sees a thousand traits of the divine character, of himself, and of the world,—some striking and bold, others cast, as it were, into the shade, and designed to be searched for and examined,—some direct, others by way of intimation or inference."

You cannot enjoy the Scriptures unless you have a taste for them; and, to this end, it is absolutely essential that you read them *daily*. Many have tried to read the Bible, and were entirely unsuccessful. They have obtained new editions, in different forms, and yet there was no enjoyment in reading. One reason was, that they never were in the habit of reading the Bible every day; and unless you have this habit, it is in vain ever to hope to see or feel any of those excellences which others praise. You could enjoy no study, if taken up only now and then. Every student knows that he feels interested in any study in proportion as he continues to attend to it day after day for some time. This is true of the mathematics, where the taste has but little to do. Take up Euclid once in a year, and look over a few propositions, and you feel but little interest in it. Open Shakspeare once in many months, and you read with no interest; and the longer the intervals are between reading him, the less is the disposition to recur to him. So of any other book.

Perhaps few characters have ever had their time more fully engrossed with business than Queen Elizabeth; yet she is said to have found time to read the

Scriptures daily, and to have acquired a decided taste for them. "I walk," says she, "many times in the pleasant fields of the Holy Scriptures, where I pluck up the goodlisome herbs of sentences by pruning, eat them by reading, digest them by musing, and lay them up at length in the high seat of memory by gathering them together; so that, having tasted their sweetness, I may perceive the bitterness of life."

A little before his death, the great Locke, being asked how a young man could, "in the shortest and surest way, attain a knowledge of the Christian religion, in the full and just extent of it," made this memorable reply: "Let him study the Holy Scriptures, especially the New Testament. Therein are contained the words of eternal life. It has God for its author, salvation for its end, and truth, without any mixture of error, for its matter."

I would not only most earnestly recommend you to read the Scriptures daily, but would add a few hints as to the best method of doing it.

(1.) *Read the Bible alone in your retirement.*

The reason of this is obvious. Your mind will be less distracted, the attention less likely to be called off, your thoughts less likely to wander. You can read deliberately, slowly, understandingly, and with personal application. It will soon become a delightful habit; and you will shortly greet the time when you are to be alone with your Bible, with as much interest as if you were to be with your dearest earthly friend. No taste is so much improved by habit and cultivation as the taste for the word of God. There is a condensation in language, a power in the poetry and eloquence of the Bible, aside from its moral influence, which brings the taste of the reader to its own standard, with astonishing rapidity.

(2.) *For all practical purposes in your daily reading, use the common translation of the Bible.*

For accurate and critical study, the student will of course go to the original, and to commentators. But to obtain a general knowledge of the revelation in our hands, and to cultivate the moral feelings of the heart, the common translation is incomparably superior to any thing else. It is of great importance to obtain such a knowledge of the Bible as you will obtain by reading it in order. I suppose the word of God was given in parcels, from time to time, as was best adapted to the state of the world, and best adapted to give us correct conceptions of the character and government of God. I would have one part of your time employed in reading the books in order, going regularly through the Bible in this way as fast as your circumstances will admit. At another sitting, and in another part of the day, I would read some part that is strictly devotional, such as the Psalms, the Gospels, or the Prophets. No young man can be too familiar with the book of Proverbs. There is an amazing amount of practical wisdom treasured up there; and the young man who should have that at his command, will be likely to do wisely. All the proverbs and wise sayings of the earth can bear no comparison to those of Solomon for value; and there is scarcely one of any value, the essence of which is not already in his. I would not recommend commentaries of any kind for your daily reading. They are like putting crutches under the arms of a man nearly well. They will aid him now for a short time, but will eventually do injury. He who uses a commentator constantly will soon feel that it is essential; that the Scriptures contain but little, while the commentary is rich; and that he must rely upon it for all his opinions. What opinions you have, will also leave you at once; for what comes easily, will be sure to go as easily.

(3.) *Read the Scriptures with an humble, teachable disposition.*

The strongest of all evidence in favor of the inspiration of the Bible is the internal—that which the good man feels. This, indeed, is such as no arguments of the infidel can shake. On other evidence you can throw doubts for a moment, bring objections which cannot at once be answered, suggest difficulties which perplex;—but you may heap difficulties up like mountain piled upon mountain, and the good man *feels* that his Bible is from God. This is just as you would suppose it would be with a book from heaven

But, aside from this, there is evidence enough to crush every doubt forever. It is well to measure the base and examine the foundations of the building, if your circumstances will allow of it; but if you cannot do it just now, reserve it for some future time. But you cannot derive good from the Bible, unless you have an humble mind. A child might say that the sun and stars all moved round the earth; that his reason taught him so; and that it was befitting that God should thus form the universe. But the reason of the child cannot decide such points. You must not say that you can decide what and how much God ought to reveal. We cannot explain or understand the mysteries which hang around every grain of sand and every drop of water; much less can we expect at once to have a revelation about a Being whom no eye ever saw, and a country from "whose bourne no traveller" ever returns, without meeting with difficulties and mysteries. Humility will teach us to sit at the feet of Revelation, and receive her instructions without cavilling. Reverence towards the author, the contents of the Scriptures, and our own everlasting welfare, demand that we read with humility. We must be docile. We are ignorant, and need instruction; we are dark, and need illumination; we are debased by our passions and sins, and need elevating. The torch of reason cannot enlighten what hangs beyond the grave; the conjectures of the imagination only bewilder; and without receiving the Bible with the spirit of a child, you will conjecture, and theorize, and wilder, till you find yourself on an ocean of uncertainty, without a chart to guide you, a compass by which to steer, or a haven which you can hope to make.

(4.) *Read the Scriptures under a constant sense of high responsibility.*

If the book in your hand be the only revelation which has been made to man, and if God has spoken his mind and will in that, then you have a standard to which you can at all times bring your conscience, by which you can cultivate your heart and grow in purity. You have a book which is able to fit you for the highest usefulness,—to point out the noblest ends of your existence,—the best method of attaining those ends;—which can soothe you when the heart is corroding by vexatious cares, which can humble you when in danger of being lifted up by prosperity; which can sustain you when your own strength is gone, and which, after having led you as the star led the wise men of the East, through life, will at last lead you to a world where the soul shall live and act in her strength, the mind be enlarged to the utmost of its capacity, and where your wishes will only be commensurate with your enjoyments. Can you neglect this book without doing yourself injustice? You are but of yesterday, and have had time to learn but little of what is around you; and without divine aid, you never would learn what is the destiny of your nature, nor the path which lies before the soul in the eternal world; but God has given you his own word to teach, to direct, and to sanctify you. If you have any thing of wisdom, you will read the Scriptures daily: if you do not do it, you may be sure the reason is, that you are so in love with sin, that you are unwilling to have a light poured upon you which would rebuke you.

7. *Be in the habit of faithfully reviewing your conduct at stated seasons.*

When these stated seasons shall be, and how often they shall recur, is not for me to say. But they should recur often, and periodically. A heathen philosopher strongly urged his pupils to examine, every night before they slept, what they had been doing that day, and so discover what actions are worthy of pursuit to-morrow, and what vices are to be prevented from slipping into habits. There are particular times when, by the providences of God, we are especially called to examine our conduct, which are not periodical. For example, if the hand of sickness has been laid upon you, and you have been made to feel your weakness and helplessness, the time of your sickness and of your recovery should both be seasons in which to pause and hold close counsel with your heart. If you change places, go from home, or go to a new institution for study, such a change affords you the best possible opportunity to examine and see what habits, what moral delinquencies you ought to change for the better,—what have been the rocks of temptation on which you have split, —what the companions who have led you astray,—what the sins you have fallen into which would grieve your parents, which have pierced your own soul with sorrow, and which, if persisted in, will eventually destroy you for any service, in the holy kingdom of God. These changes in your circumstances ought always to be made pausing places, at which you faithfully review all your life, and, with penitence for the past, and new resolutions, set out for a better life in future.

But these are not the periodical times which I am especially urging. At the close of every Sabbath, you should make a conscience of performing the duty, and retire and review the week which is now past. It is a good time. You have had the soothing rest of the Sabbath, and you are now one week nearer the hour of dying, and the hour of being judged. You have had the advantages of another week; now is the time to see how you have improved them: you have had another week in which to influence others; now is the time to see what that influence has been: you have had the responsibilities of forming a character, under the highest possible advantages, for the service of God during the past week; now is the time to inquire how you have acted under such responsibilities. Make this review thorough, and be sure not to omit it once. If you allow the season to pass you without this close self-examination, you will be likely to do it again and again; for there is no duty in all that pertains to the discipline of the heart so irksome as that of self-examination. Some will say that they had rather their friends would point out their defects. But why should you be like the child who asks for a looking-glass in which to examine his hands, to see if they need washing? No doubt it is more agreeable to have a friend to do this, than to do it yourself; and for the obvious reason that you will see a thousand sins, and a thousand wrong motives, which his eye cannot reach. If I may be allowed to suggest, I know of no one thing, aside from the Bible, so useful to aid in examining the heart, on these occasions, as Buck's Closet Companion. It is clear, brief, and to the point. Every question is searching; and he who will use that little treatise in his attempts at examining his heart on the evening of the Sabbath, will not long fail of having definite views of himself, and very moderate views of his excellencies. Such a season, too, is exceedingly well fitted to close the Sabbath, and to fasten upon the soul those sacred impressions for which that day is especially designed.

It has been said by some, that we can judge of the bent of our characters by examining every morning to see about what our thoughts have been employed during the night, as it is supposed we shall, of course, when off our guard during sleep, go about the business which we should like best, if our inclinations might be followed. There may be some truth in this, but not enough, probably, to enable you to make it any criterion by which to judge of your character; for every student knows that a noise like the falling of a pair of tongs, may hurry him away to the field of battle; a single coverlet too much, may cause him to groan with a mountain upon him; and a single movement of his bed-fellow, may cause him to commit murder—in his sleep. This much is generally true; that, if you have a troubled night, you have either abused the body by eating or drinking too much, or tasked the brain by too great a draft upon its functions at a late hour at night. Dreams will at least indicate how much you are abusing your corporeal and mental powers.

But at night—at the close of the day, when you have passed through the day; have added it to the days of your existence on earth; when its hours have fled to the judgment-seat and reported all your doings, all your words and thoughts—the day which must inevitably have more or less effect in shaping your destiny forever;—this is the season when you ought to review, most faithfully and most strictly, all your conduct. You may not at once see the advantages of doing so; but they are really greater than language can describe

You will find duties omitted during the day;—will not the examination lead you to repent of what was wrong, and to avoid it to-morrow? You will find time wasted, an hour here, and half an hour there;—will not the examination do you good? You will find that you have spoken unadvisedly with your lips,—that you have said what will wound the sensibilities, either natural or moral;—and ought you not to know of these instances? You will find that you have sinned with the thoughts, and that you have spread out feelings which the Divine Mind, of course, must retain forever, and which were vile;—will it not do you good to recall these instances? Perhaps you have made one effort to resist temptation, and to do your duty;—and it will cheer you to recall it. To-morrow you will be still more likely to be successful. Every man, at night, can tell whether he has made, or squandered, or lost, property during the day; and so every one, by proper care, can tell whether he has gone backward or forward in disciplining his heart, at the close of every day. He who passes on for weeks and months without this frequent, faithful review, will wonder, at the end of these long periods, why he has not grown in moral character, and why he has no more confidence in his hopes for the future. The fact is, we may live, and be heathen, under the full light of the gospe , and perhaps, too, while we are cherishing some of ts forms. But life w'll pass f om you while you are making good resolutions, and hoping to do better, unless you bring yourself to account daily; and when death shall come to call you away, you will find the touching and affecting language of the dying heathen philosopher most suitable to your case:—*Fœde hunc mundum intravi, anxius vivi, perturbatus egredior,—causa causarum miserere mei*:—"I was born polluted, I have spent my life anxiously, I die with trembling solicitude,—O thou Cause of causes, have pity on me." The pain which our deficiencies and sins give us on the review, will be salutary, desirable, and necessary; and it is at a fearful hazard that any one under as great responsibilities as those under which we are placed, ever retires to rest without such a review of the day as I am recommending.

8. *Be in the habit of daily prayer.*

Though much of the novelty of the style and manner of Johnson has passed away, yet his works will ever bear the impress of a great mind; and as long as the English language exists, he will stand high in the estimation of the student. Yet Johnson, as far as he was from enthusiasm, is found making use of an humble and beautiful form of prayer when taking his pen to write a work which will be immortal. The most distinguished authors—such, I mean, as have been the most widely useful—have always sought the blessing of God upon their studies. Doddridge used to observe frequently, "that he never advanced well in human learning without prayer, and that he always made the most proficiency in his studies when he prayed with the greatest fervency." When exposed to dangers which threaten the body, such as the perils of a journey, the malignant plague, the storm at sea, or the rockings of the earthquake, no one esteems it enthusiasm or weakness to ask aid and protection from God. But how many feel, that, when they sit down to study, when they are tempted to go astray in a thousand paths of error, when liable to have their opinions, views, plans, habits, all the traits of their character, wrong, they have no need of prayer! The very heathen felt so much need of aid in their mental researches, that they seldom, if ever, began a study or a book, without invoking the aid of the gods. Surely the student who knows his dependence upon the true God, and who knows how easily the mind of man is thrown off from its balance,—how important it is that the mind be clear, and all its powers in full vigor,—will not feel that, *as a student*, to say nothing about a higher character or destiny, he can do his duty to himself with forming and cultivating the habit of daily prayer.

I know that thousands, when pressed on this point, will say that they have no time,—their studies are so pressing, so urgent, that they have neither the time nor the spirit necessary for prayer. I reply, that it will not hinder your studies. On the contrary, the mind will be calmed, rested, and refreshed, by being daily turned off from your studies for prayer. Ask any distinguished man, who has ever tried both methods of study, and he will tell you that he has been prospered in his studies in proportion to his faithfulness in performing this duty. What shall be said of such a man as Andrews,[1] who was such a proficient in study, that he could read fifteen different languages, and yet never spent less than five hours daily in private devotion?

You will find, as I trust, the following hints of advantage to you in the performance of this duty.

(1.) *Have regular hours of prayer.*

Habit, in regard to every duty, is of the first importance; but for none is it more important than in regard to prayer. You cannot walk and lift your heart to God, or sit in your room and do it, as well as to be retired. The direction of Christ, to enter the closet, was founded on the philosophy of human nature. Have particular seasons, and when the hour arrives, you will hail it as that which is the most pleasant in the whole day. The return of the hour brings to mind the duty, which might otherwise be crowded out of mind. System should be rigidly adhered to, in this duty, for the sake of insuring its

[1] Note P

prompt performance, and especially for the sake of enjoyment. No man ever enjoyed his religion who had not regular seasons devoted to prayer.

(2.) *These hours should be in the morning and in the evening.*

In the morning the mind is calmed; the temptations of the day have not beset you; the duties of the day have not filled the mind and begun to vex you. Before you go to the duties of the day, to its cares, and anxieties, and temptations, begin the day with prayer. Temptations you certainly will meet; trials of virtue and patience will overtake you; and many times before night, you will need the aid of your Father to shield you. Go to him, and ask his counsel to guide you, his power to uphold you, his presence to cheer you, his Spirit to sanctify you. Then will you have done what is equivalent to half the duties of the day, when you have thus engaged his care and assistance. And when the evening comes, when you have done with the duties of the day, the body is wearied, and the mind is jaded, when the world is shut out by the shades of night, when you come to look back and review the day, when you see how many deficiencies have marked the day, how many imperfections still cluster around you, how many sins stare you in the face, how little you have done for yourself or for others, or for God, the day past, *then*—is the hour of prayer. It will be sweet to feel that you have one to whom you can go, and who will hear you; one who will forgive you, if you are penitent, and ask in the name of Jesus Christ; one who will accept your evening sacrifice, and give you strength for the morrow, and gird you with his own righteousness. This hour, if rightly improved, will be like the cheering countenance of a most beloved friend. Take care that nothing comes between you and these hours devoted to God. "Think of Daniel, prime minister of Persia, with the affairs of one hundred and twenty provinces resting on his mind, yet finding time to go 'into his chamber, three times a day, that he might pray and give thanks to God.' Think of Alfred, with the cares of monarchy; of Luther, buffeted by the storms of Papal wrath; of Thornon, encompassed with a thousand mercantile engagements, yet never allowing the hurry of business to intrude on their regular hours of devotion."

(3.) *Keep your conscience void of offence in other respects, if you would enjoy prayer.*

If you are aware of any sin, be it what it may, in which you allow yourself, you may be sure that will ruin your devotional hours. Either that, or communion with God must be relinquished, and certainly will be. If you do not keep the Sabbath; if you are light and foolish in conversation, jealous and censo

-ious upon others, or given to the indulgence of vile thoughts and practices in secret, you cannot welcome the hour of prayer.

It may seem strange to some of my readers, that I urge this duty upon them, when they do not profess to be Christians, or religious people. But am I to blame, if they do not even profess to wish to obey and honor their God? Are they in any way above the reach of want, so that they need not prayer? What if you have no relish for prayer; will neglecting the duty cultivate, or even create, such a relish? If you have lived so long under the government of God, under all the advantages which you have enjoyed, under all the responsibilities which have been resting upon you, and still are living without prayer, are you in the path of duty to plead this neglect of prayer, as a reason why it should not be urged upon you? Shall I be a faithful friend to admit this excuse, and to allow, that, because you have so long tried to escape the eye of God, and have neither thanked him for his mercies nor asked him for his goodness, neither sought his friendship nor deprecated his displeasure, you ought still to be left, and no warning voice reach you? No. And if you urge that you have not been in the habit of prayer, I assure you that you are inexcusable; that you are losing great peace of mind, and daily satisfaction in laying all your wants and trials before Him who can relieve them: you are losing those great principles which make character good, great, and stable, and you are losing opportunities which are passing away rapidly, and whose misimprovement will hereafter bring down great anguish upon you.

(4.) *Offer your prayers in the name of Jesus Christ.*

He is the only Mediator between God and man. He it is who sits with the golden censer in his right hand, and who ever lives to intercede for us. He is a great and a merciful High Priest, who can be touched with a feeling of our infirmities. We have no righteousness of our own; we can have no confidence in offering prayer in our own names. But he who has most of the spirit of Christ; who comes near to him in his contemplations and devotions; who has the most exalted views of the Redeemer, and the most abased views of himself,—will enjoy most at the throne of grace. Your prayers will be cold unless they go from a heart warmed by his love. Your petitions will not be fervent unless you feel your need of an almighty Saviour.[1] The songs which are the loudest and sweetest in heaven, we are told, are kindled by the exhibitions which he has made, of what he has done for us.

(5.) *Ask the assistance of the Holy Spirit.*

When God directs us to pray, it is not that he may sit at a distance, and, in the coldness of a sovereign

[1] See Bickersteth on Prayer, and H. More's Private Devotions.

monarch, hear our prayers, and receive our homage; but it is, that we may draw ourselves near to him, as one in a boat, with a boat-hook, would not draw the shore to the boat, but the boat to the shore. His promise of the Holy Spirit to those who ask him, was sincere; and no gift can be compared to this. All that is done for man in the way of calling his attention to eternal things, sanctifying the heart, and preparing the soul for the service of God here and here after, is done by the Holy Spirit as the agent. Solemn warnings are given in the Bible lest we should abuse this last, best gift of Heaven. He is the Sanctifier to purify your heart, the Comforter to sustain and cheer in life and in death. Ask his assistance, and you will be shielded from temptation, trained for usefulness here, enlightened in your views, expansive in your feelings, pure in your aims, contented in your circumstances, peaceful in your death, and glorious in immortality beyond the grave.

CHAPTER X.

THE OBJECT OF LOVE

How many beautiful visions pass before the mind in a single day, when the reins are thrown loose, and fancy feels no restraints! How curious, interesting and instructive would be the history of the workings of a single mind for a day! How many imaginary joys, how many airy castles, pass before it, which a single jostle of this rough world at once destroys! Who is there of my readers who has not imagined a summer fairer than ever bloomed,—scenery in nature more perfect than was ever combined by the pencil,—abodes more beautiful than were ever reared,—honors more distinguished than were ever bestowed,—homes more peaceful than were ever enjoyed,—companions more angelic than ever walked this earth,—and bliss more complete, and joys more thrilling than were ever allotted to man? You may call these the dreams of the imagination, but they are common to the student. To the man who lives for this world alone, these visions of bliss, poor as they are, are all that ever come. But good men have their anticipations—not the paintings of fancy, but the realities which faith discovers. Good men have the most vivid conceptions. Witness those of old. As they look down the vale of time, they see a star arise,—the everlasting hills do bow, the valleys are raised, and the moon puts on the brightness of the sun. The deserts and the dry places gush with waters. Nature pauses. The serpent forgets his fangs; the lion and the lamb sleep side by side, and the hand of the child is on the mane of the tiger. Nations gaze till they forget the murderous work of war, and the garments rolled in blood. The whole earth is enlightened, and the star shines on till it brings in everlasting day. Here are glowing conceptions, but they are not the work of a depraved imagination. They will all be realized. Sin and death will long walk hand in hand on this earth, and their footsteps will not be entirely blotted out till the fires of the last day have melted the globe. But the head of the one is already bruised, and the sting is already taken from the other. They may long roar, but they walk in chains, and the eye of faith sees the hand that holds the chains.

But we have visions still brighter. We look for new heavens and a new earth wherein dwelleth righteousness. No sin will be there to mar the beauty, no sorrow to diminish a joy, no anxiety to corrode the heart, or cloud the brow. Our characters may be tested, in part, by our anticipations. If our thoughts and feelings are running in the channel of time, and dancing from one earthly bubble to another, though our hopes may come in angel-robes, it is a sad proof that our hearts are here also.

Is there any thing of weakness in these hopes of good men? Are we not continually seeking rest for the soul?—A few years ago, a youth went up to the mast-head of a large whale-ship, and there sat down to think. He was the only child of his mother, and she a widow. He had left her against her wishes and remonstrances, her prayers and tears. He had for many years been roaming over the seas, and was now returning home. He was thinking of the scenes of his childhood,—all the anxious hours which he had cost that mother,—all the disobedience on his part, and that love on hers which no waters could quench. Would she be sleeping in the grave when he once more came to her door? Does his home still look as it used to? —the tree, the brook, the pond, the fields, the grove, —are they all as he left them? And his mother,—would she receive him to her heart, or would she be sleeping in death? Would she recognize her long-absent boy, and forgive all his past ingratitude, and still love him with the unquenchable love of a mother? And may he again have a home, and no more wander among strangers? The pressure of these thoughts was too much. He wept at the remembrance of his undutifulness. Troubles and hardships did not break his spirit, did not subdue his proud heart; but the thoughts of home, of rest, of going out no more, suffering no more, engrossing the love of a kind parent, melted him. Is not this human nature? And is it weakness in a good man to rejoice at the thought of that day, when death shall be swallowed up in victory? when the Lord God shall wipe away all tears, and take away the rebuke of his people, that they may be glad and rejoice in his salvation? "I am going," said the great Hooker, "to leave a world disordered and a church disorganized, for a world and a church where every angel and every rank of angels stand before the throne in the very post God has assigned them."

The world, the great mass of mankind, have utterly misunderstood the real object of life on earth, or else he misunderstands it who follows the light of the Bible. You look at men as individuals, and their object seems to be to gratify a contemptible vanity, to pervert and follow their low appetites and passions, and the dictates of selfishness, wherever they may lead. You look at men in the aggregate, and this pride and these passions terminate in wide plans of ambition, in wars and bloodshed, in strifes and the destruction of all that is virtuous or lovely. The history of mankind has its pages all stained with blood; and it is the history of a race whose object seemed to be, to debase their powers, and sink what was intended for immortal glory, to the deepest degradation which sin can cause. At one time, you will see an army of five millions of men following a leader, who, to add to his poor renown, is now to jeopardize all these lives, and the peace of his whole kingdom. This multitude of minds fall in, and they live, and march, and fight, and perish, to aid in exalting a poor worm of the dust. What capacities were here assembled! What minds were here put in motion! What a scene of struggles was here! And who, of all this multitude, were pursuing the real object of life? From Xerxes, at their head, to the lowest and most debased in the rear of the army, was there one, who, when weighed in the balances of eternal truth, was fulfilling the object for which he was created, and for which life is continued? Look again. All Europe rises up in a phrensy, and pours forth a living tide towards the Holy Land. They muster in the name of the Lord of Hosts. The cross waves on their banners, and the holy sepulchre is the watchword by day and night. They move eastward, and whiten the burning sands of the deserts with their bleaching bones. But of all these, from the fanatic whose voice awoke Europe to arms, down to the lowest horse-boy, how few were actuated by any spirit which Heaven, or justice, to say nothing about love, could sanction! Suppose the same number of men, the millions which composed the continent which rose up to exterminate another, and who followed the man who was first a soldier and then a priest and hermit, and who has left the world in doubt whether he was a prophet, a madman, a fool, or a demagogue, had spent the same treasures of life, and of money, in trying to spread the spirit of that Saviour for whose tomb they could waste so much; and suppose this army had been enlightened and sanctified men, and had devoted their powers to do good to mankind, and to honor their God, how different would the world have been found to-day! How many, think you, of all the then Christian world, acted under a spirit, and with an object before them such as the world will approve, and especially such as the pure beings above us will approve?

Look a moment at a few of the efforts which avarice has made. For about four centuries, the avarice of man, and of Christian men too, has been preying upon the vitals of Africa. It has taken the sons and daughters of Ham, and doomed soul and body to debasement, to ignorance, to slavery. And what are the results? Twenty-eight millions—more than twice the population of this country—have been kidnapped and carried away from the land of their birth. The estimate is, that the increase in the house of bondage since those times, is five-fold, or nearly one hundred and seventy millions of human, immortal beings, cut off from the rights of man, and, by legislation and planning, reduced far towards the scale of the brutes. This is only a single form in which avarice has been exerting its power. Suppose the same time and money, the same effort, had been spent in spreading the arts of civilization, learning, and religion, over the continent of Africa, what a vast amount of good would have been accomplished! And at the day when the recording angel reads the history of the earth, how very different would be the picture, and the eternal condition of untold numbers! If the marks of humanity are not all blotted out from that race of miserable men, it is not because oppression has not been sufficiently legalized, and avarice been allowed to pursue its victims, till the grave became a sweet asylum.

I am trying to lead you to look at the great amount of abuse and of perversion of mind, of which mankind are constantly guilty. When Christianity began her glorious career, the world had exhausted its strength in trying to debase itself, and to sink low enough to embrace paganism; and yet not so low, as not to try to exist in the shape of nations. The experiment had been repeated, times we know not how many. Egypt, Babylonia, Persia, polished Greece, iron-footed Rome, mystical Hindooism, had all tried it. They spent, each, mind enough to regenerate a nation, in trying to build up a system of corrupt paganism; and when that system was built up—let the shape and form be what it might—the nation had exhausted its energies, and it sunk and fell under the effects of misapplied and perverted mind. No nation existed on the face of the earth, which was not crumbling under the use of its perverted energies, when the gospel reached it. Our ancestors were crushed under the weight of a Druidical priesthood, and the rites of that bloody system of religion.

Another striking instance of the perversion of mind, and the abuse of the human intellect and heart, is the system of the Romish church. No one created mind, apparently, could ever have invented a scheme of delusion, of degradation of the soul, the intellect, the whole man, so perfect and complete as is this. What minds must have been employed in shutting out the light of heaven, and in burying the manna, which fell in showers so extended! What a system! To gather all the books in the world, and put them all within the stone walls of the monastery and the cloister,—to crush schools, except in these same monasteries, in which they trained up men to become more and more skilful in doing the work of ruin,—to delude the world with ceremonies and fooleries, while the Bible was taken away, and Religion muttered her rites in an unknown tongue,—and all this the result of a settled plan to debase the intellect and mock poor human nature! And, when the Reformation held up all these abominations to light, what a masterpiece was the last plan laid to stifle the reason forever!—the inquisition. It was reared through the Christian world: the decree, by a single blow, proscribed between sixty and seventy printing presses, and excommunicated all who should ever read any thing which they might produce. A philosopher, who, like Galileo, could pour light upon science, and astonish the world by his discoveries, must repeatedly fall into the cruel mercies of the inquisition. The ingenuity of hell seemed tasked to invent methods by which the human mind might be shut up in Egyptian darkness; and never has a Catholic community been known to be other than degraded, ignorant, superstitious and sunken. Let light in, and all who receive it rush to infidelity. But what a mass of mind has been, and still is, employed in upholding this system! And what a loss to the world has it produced, in quenching, in everlasting darkness, the uncounted millions of glorious minds which have been destroyed by it! If I could find it in my heart to anathematize any order of men,—and I hope I cannot,—it would be those who are thus taking away the key of knowledge, and preventing all within the compass of their influence from fulfilling the great object for which they were created.

Was man created for *war*? Did his Maker create the eye, that he might take better aim on the field of battle? give him skill, that he might invent methods of slaying by thousands? and plant a thirst in the soul, that it might be quenched with the blood of men? What science or art can boast of more precision, of more to teach it, to hail it with enthusiasm, and to celebrate it in song? Genius has ever sat at the feet of Mars, and exhausted his efforts in preparing exquisite offerings. Human thought has never made such gigantic efforts as when employed in scenes of butchery. Has Skill ever been more active and successful—has Poetry ever so kindled, as when the flames of Troy lighted her page? What school-boy is ignorant of the battle-ground, and the field of blood, where ancient and modern armies met and tried to crush each other? Has Music ever thrilled like that which led men to battle, and the plume of the desert-bird ever danced so gracefully as when on the head of the warrior? Are any honors so freely bestowed, or cheaply purchased, as those which are gained by a few hours of fighting? See that man, who, so late, was the wonder of the world, calling out, marshalling, employing and wasting almost all the treasures of Europe, for twelve or fifteen years. What multitudes of minds did he call to the murderous work of war!—minds that might have blessed the world with literature, with science, with schools, and with the gospel of peace, had they not been perverted from the great and best object of living! Says a philosophical writer, speaking on this subject, "I might suppose, for the sake of illustration, that all the schemes of ambition, and cruelty, and intrigue, were blotted from the page of history,—that against the names of the splendid and guilty actors whom the world, for ages, has wondered at, there were written achievements of Christian benevolence, equally grand and characteristic,—and then ask what a change would there be in the scenes which the world has beheld transacted, and what a difference in the results! Alexander should have won victories in Persia more splendid than those of Granicus and Arbela; he should have wandered over India, like Buchanan, and wept for another world to bring under the dominion of the Saviour; and, returning to Babylon, should have died, like Martyn, the victim of Christian zeal.* Cæsar should have made Gaul and Britain obedient to the faith, and, crossing the Rubicon with his apostolic legions, and making the Romans freemen of the Lord, should have been the forerunner of Paul, and done half his work. Charlemagne should have been a Luther. Charles of Sweden should have been a Howard; and, flying from the Baltic to the Euxine, like an angel of mercy, should have fallen, when on some errand of love, and, numbering his days by the good deeds he had done, should have died like Mills in an old age of charity. Voltaire should have written Christian tracts. Rousseau should have been a Fenelon. Hume should have unravelled the intricacies of theology, and defended, like Edwards, the faith once delivered to the saints."

We call ours the most enlightened nation on earth

inferior to none in owning the spirit of Christianity; and we claim this as an age behind none ever enjoyed, for high moral principle and benevolent, disinterested action. But what is this principle in the great mass of mankind! When clouds gather in the political horizon, and war threatens a nation, how are the omens received? How many are tnere who turn aside and weep, and deprecate the guilt, the wo, and the indescribable evils and miseries of war? The great majority of the nation feel that the path of glory is now opening before them, and that the honor which *may* possibly be attained by a few bloody battles, is ample compensation for the expense, the morals, the lives, and the happiness, which *must* be sacrificed for the possibility. Let that nation rush to war for some supposed point of honor. Watch the population as they collect, group after group, under the burning sun, all anxious, all eager, and all standing as if in deep expectation for the signal which was to call them to judgment. They are waiting for the first tidings of the battle, where the honor of the nation is staked. No tidings that ever came from Heaven can send a thrill of joy so deep as the tidings that one ship has conquered or sunk another.

Was it any thing remarkable, that, in the very heart of a Christian nation, a single horse-race brought over fifty thousand people together? Were they acting so much out of the character of the mass of mankind as to cause it to make any deep impression upon the moral sensibilities of the nation?

Suppose it were known that a mind was now in process of training, which might, if its powers were properly directed, be equal to Milton or Locke; but that, instead of this, it will waste its powers in creating such song as Byron wrote, or in weaving such webs as the schoolmen wove. Would the knowledge of such a waste of mind, such perversion of powers, cause a deep sensation of regret among men? or have such perversions been so common in the world, that one such magnificent mind might be lost to mankind, and no one would mourn? The answer is plain. The world has become so accustomed to seeing mind prostituted to ignoble purposes, and influence which might reach round the globe like a zone of mercy thrown away forever, that we hardly think of it as greatly out of the way.

A generation of men come on the stage of action; they find the world in darkness, in ignorance, and in sin. They live, gain the few honors which are easily plucked, gather the little wealth which toil and anxiety will bestow, and then pass away. As a whole, the generation do not expect or try to throw an influence upon the world which shall be redeeming. They do not expect to leave the world materially better than they found it. Why do we not mourn that such myriads of immortal minds are destined to pass away, and never to break out in acts of mercy and kindness to the world? Because we have so long been so prodigal of mind, that we hardly notice its loss.

For thousands of years the world has slept in ignorance, or groped in utter darkness. Nations have come up, and bowed and worshipped the sun, or wood, or brass, stone, or reptile, and then have passed away. The heart of man has been broken by vain superstitions, by cruelties, by vileness, under the name of religion; and, aside from the Bible, we see no hope that it will be otherwise, for as long a period to come. But does this immense waste, this immeasurable loss, for time and eternity, trouble mankind? Is the world at work for its redemption, and disenthralment? By no means! A small portion of the Christian world alone have even looked at it with any interest. This small part are making some efforts. They are taking the gospel of God, and with it carrying the arts of civilization, the light of schools, the sacredness of the Sabbath, and the influences and hopes of immortality, to the ends of the earth. But how are these labors esteemed by the mass of society? Where is the sympathy for the solitary missionary of the cross, as he takes his life in his hand, and goes to the dark places of the earth, full of the habitations of cruelty? The world laughs at the idea that the earth can be recovered; and, though lions and tigers are constantly tamed, and the deadly serpent is charmed, yet there is no faith that the moral character of man is ever to be any better. The schemes of the missionary are fanatical, the Bible is powerless as the cold philosophy of the world, and preaching has no power but that which depends upon the eloquence of the tongue which utters it. But the question is, How do you account for it, that the community at large so coolly make up their minds, that the world can never be any better, and each one goes about his business, as if it were all of no sort of consequence? I account for it, by saying that mankind are supremely selfish; so much so, that the situation of a world lying in wickedness, does not move them—that the great majority of men always have, and do still, mistake the true object of life.

"Nothing in man is great, but so far as it is connected with God. The only wise thing recorded of Xerxes, is his reflection on the sight of his army, that not one of that immense multitude would survive a hundred years. It seems to have been a momentary gleam of true light and feeling. The history of all the great characters of the Bible is summed up in this one sentence;—they acquainted themselves with God, and acquiesced in his will in all things;" and no other characters can be called great, with any propriety.

Look at individuals. You walk down on the wharf of one of our large cities. You notice a man by himself alone. He walks with a quick, feverish step, backwards and forwards, and, every few moments, looks away at that dark speck, far off on the "dark blue sea." He is waiting for that ship to loom up, that he may see his own flag at mast-head. For nearly three years she has been gone, and comes home now, probably, richly freighted. During all this time, he has followed her, in his thoughts, day and night: when it was dark—when the storm rushed—when the winds moaned—he thought of his ship; and not for a single waking hour at a time has that ship's image been out of his mind. His whole soul went with her; and yet, all this time, he never lifted a prayer to Him who holds the winds and the waves in his hand; and even now, when his heart is swelling with hopes that are realized, still he thinks not of raising a breath in thanksgiving to his God; thinks of no acts of mercy which he will perform; feels no accountability for his property. Is such a man, living for property alone, pursuing the real object of life?

Look at another man. He is walking his closet: his brow is contracted; his countenance faded; his eye sunken, and he is full of troubled anxiety. He looks out of his window for his messenger, and then sinks down in deep thought. It would seem as if nothing less than the salvation of his soul could cause such an anxiety. He is a cunning statesman, a crafty politician, and is now waiting to learn the result of a new scheme, which he is now executing, with the hope that it may aid him in climbing the ladder of ambition. He eyes every movement in the community, watches every change, and carries a solicitude which, at times, must be agonizing. There are thousands of such minds, trying to make men their tools, regardless of means or measures, provided they can fulfil their great desire—exalt themselves. Are such men pursuing the real object of life?

Look again.—There is a man of cultivated taste and refined feeling. His soul is full of poetry, and his feelings alive to every charm that is earthly. He can look out on the face of the evening sky, or watch the tints of dawn, and admire such beauties; but his soul never looks up "through nature's works to nature's God." He can enter into deep communion with what is perfect in the natural world, but he holds none with the Father of his spirit. Music, too, is his delight. He can eagerly give himself away to the melody of sweet sounds; but, with all this, he stands without the threshold of the moral temple of God, and has no wish to enter in and eat the food of angels. The thorns which grow on Sinai are unpleasant to his soul; but not more so than are the roses which bloom on Calvary. The blending tints of the summer-bow awaken a thrill of pleasure; but the bow of mercy which hangs over the cross of Jesus, has in it nothing that can charm. He lives, plans, and acts, just as he would were there no God above him, before whom every thought lies naked. Is this man—this refined, cultivated scholar—pursuing the object for which he was created? And if every cultivated man on earth should do precisely as he does, would the world advance in knowledge, virtue, or religion? Man was created for purposes high and noble—such as angels engage in, and in comparison with which, all other objects sink into insignificance, and all other enjoyments are contemptible as ashes.

The distinguished Pascal has a thought which is well worth examination, especially by all those who are conscious of living for other aims than those which ought to be the real end of life. "All our endeavors after greatness proceed from nothing but a desire of being surrounded by a multitude of persons and affairs that may hinder us from looking into ourselves; which is a view we cannot bear." Probably few are conscious that this is the reason why they so busily waste their lives in unworthy pursuits, though none can be insensible of having the effect produced.

Every youth who reads these pages expects to be active, to be influential, and to have some object of pursuit every way worthy of his aims. That object will be one of the four following—pleasure, wealth, human applause, or genuine benevolence.

I shall not stop to dwell upon these. No argument need be urged to show how utterly unworthy of his education, of his friends, and of himself, he acts, who so degrades himself as to make the appetites and passions of his animal nature the object of life, and who looks to them for happiness. Let him know that there is not an appetite to be gratified, which does not pall and turn to be an enemy the moment it has become his master. It makes him a slave, with all his degradation and sorrows, without any of the slave's freedom from thought and anticipation. You cannot give way to any appetite, without feeling instant and constant degradation; and he who sinks in such a way that he despises himself, will soon be a wretch indeed. Conscience can be deadened and murdered in no way so readily as by such indulgence: the mind can be weakened, and every intellectual effort forever killed in no way so readily as in this. If you would at once seal your degradation, for time and eternity, and forever blast every hope of peace, greatness, or usefulness, I can tell you how to do it all. You have only to cultivate your appetites, and give way to the demands of your passions, and drink of those stolen waters which are sweet, and eat of that bread, in secret, which is forbidden, and you may rest assured that you have chosen a path which is straight—but it is straight to ruin.

The pursuits of wealth are less debasing, more refined, and every way more honorable. But they are not worthy of you. You can pursue wealth and cultivate selfishness at every step: you may do it with a heart that idolizes what it gains, and, could it know that what it gathers to-day would continue in the family for centuries, and be constantly increasing, would idolize it still more. But here let me say, that if wealth be your object, you have mistaken your path. A student seeking wealth! There is no situation in the land in which you could not obtain it easier and faster, than by study. No class of men are in so poor a situation to become wealthy as students; and no class of men, in proportion to their time, their labor, and their efforts, are so poorly paid as professional men; and if wealth were my object, I hardly know of any business which I would not rather undertake as a means by which to obtain it, than either of the professions, in this country. A student cannot become wealthy, in ordinary circumstances, without contracting his soul to a degree which destroys all his claims to be a student.

But the strongest temptation which will beset you, is to live and act under the influence of ambition, and to sell your time, and efforts, and yourself indeed, for human applause. There is no stream so sweet as that which flows from this fountain. But you little know the dangers which wait around the man who would drink here—the archers which lie in ambush. There are so many things to diminish the gratifications which ambition bestows, that, were there no higher, no nobler end of existence, it would seem dangerous to pursue this. How many begin life with high hopes, with expectations almost unbounded, who, in a little time, sink down into discouragement and listlessness, because they find the tree higher up the mountain than they expected, and its fruit more difficult to be obtained! But suppose a man be successful, and the measure of his desires begins to be filled. As you come close to him, you discover spots which were not seen at a distance, and blemishes which the first glare of brightness concealed. These weaknesses are noted, trumpeted, magnified, and multiplied, till it seems astonishing how a character can be great under such a load of infirmities. These are vexations; they are like little dogs which hang upon your heels all the day, and which give you no peace at night. But these you can endure. You may live in spite of having every blemish, which your public character exposes, published abroad. But suppose you make a single false step, as you mount the hill—where then are you? How many, who have made the applause of men the breath of their nostrils, have seen all their hopes dashed, in the very morning of their lives, by some step which they took in furtherance of their object, but which, in fact, was a mistaken step! The wheel was broken at once, and with it, their schemes, and perhaps their hearts. But this is not the worst of what is before you, if you live for applause. Admiration for any thing on earth cannot endure long. It will always be short-lived; and there is quite as much difficulty in keeping up a reputation, as in gaining it at the first. It takes us but a short time to say all our pretty sayings, and all our smart things. A reputation which has cost you years of toil to obtain, is no less difficult to keep than to acquire. If that reputation be not still rising and increasing in splendor, it will soon begin to droop and decay. Your best actions must become better still—your highest efforts must become higher still—or you sink; and, after all, do what you will, and as well as you will, still you do not more than barely meet expectation. You exert yourself, and you make a fine speech; or you produce a masterly dissertation; or you write an interesting and a valuable book; and the question is, not whether you have fallen below the subject, or below yourself, but have you not fallen below the standard which others have capriciously set for you? If you have, you are going down the hill, in fame. A man writes a book:—it is his first effort. There was no expectation about it. It is received well, even with applause. He writes another; and now he is not to be measured by what he did before. He must be measured by the standard of public opinion; and a reception which would raise a new author, is ruin to him. All this price you must certainly pay, if you live for the applause of your fellow-men. They will bestow no more of it than they can avoid; they will recall it as soon as an opportunity allows; and they will feel that neglect is your due, in future, as a counterweight to what has been so liberally thrown into the other scale. The pursuits of ambition are successions of jealous disquietudes, of corroding fears, of high hopes, of restless desires, and of bitter disappointment. There is ever a void in the soul—a reaching forth towards the empty air, and a lighting up of new desires in the heart. It seems to me to have been mere affectation in Cæsar, who said—and his *repeating* it so often strengthens the supposition of affectation—that he "had enough of fame"—*se satis vel ad naturam, vel ad gloriam vixisse.* Few can believe that the emperor could have been sincere in this declaration.

There are other vexations, and certain disappointments, attending him who lives for the good opinion of men, which are unknown till they come upon you, but which are distressing in the extreme, when they do come. That desire after fame which moves you, soon becomes feverish, and is constantly growing stronger and stronger. And in proportion to your desire for applause, and the good opinion of men, is your mortification deep and distressing, when applause is withheld. If praise elates and excites you, the withholding that praise will proportionably sink your spirits and destroy your comfort. You are thus a mere foot-ball among men, thrown wherever they please, and in the power of every man; for every man can take away your peace, if he pleases, and every man is more tempted to bestow censures than applause.

One thing more. If you set your heart on the applauses of men, you will find that, if you receive them, the gift will not, and cannot, bestow positive happiness upon you, while the withholding of them will clothe you with certain and positive misery. A disappointed man of ambition is miserable, not because his loss is really so great, but because his imagination has, for years, been making it appear great to him. I could point you to the grave of a most promising man, who lived for honors solely. The first distinct object on which he fixed his eye, was to be a representative in congress. For this he toiled day and night. He was every way worthy; but just as he was on the point of succeeding, when the convention had met to nominate him, one of his best friends felt that such an appointment would interfere with his own schemes of petty ambition, and, therefore, he stepped in and prevented the nomination. The poor man returned home sick, cast down, and broken-hearted. The loss of that election certainly was not of any great consequence, but he had brooded over it till it was of immense consequence, in his view. The blow withered him, and in a few months he went down to his grave, the prey of disappointment. Is such a pursuit worthy of man? Is this the high end of life on earth? A distinguished writer, who thus lived for fame, not only outlived his fame, but the powers of his own mind; and many were the hours, in broken old age, which he spent in weeping, because he could not understand the book:

which he wrote when young. What a picture could the painter produce, with such a subject before him!

"We blush, detected in designs on praise,
Though for best deeds, and from the best of men·
And why?—because immortal. Art divine
Has made the body tutor to the soul:
Heaven kindly gives our blood a moral flow;
Bids it ascend the glowing cheek, and there
Upbraid that little heart's inglorious aim,
Which stoops to court a character from man:
Ambition's boundless appetite outspeaks
The verdict of its shame. When souls take fire
At high presumptions of their own desert,
One age is poor applause: the mighty shout,
The thunder by the living few begun,
Late time must echo, worlds unborn resound.
We wish our names eternally to live.
Wild dream! which ne'er had haunted human thought,
Had not our natures been eternal too.
Fame is the shade of immortality,
And in itself a shadow;—soon as caught,
Contemned, it shrinks to nothing in the grasp.
Man must soar.
An obstinate activity within,
An insuppressive spring, will toss him up
In spite of fortune's loads.
And why?—because immortal as his Lord
And souls immortal must forever heave
At something great—the glitter or the gold—
The praise of mortals, or the praise of Heaven."

This brings me to the point at which I am wishing to come. This "something great," at which we "heave," may be great in reality, or only great because we make it so. But while I have thus briefly tried to show you that in neither of the ways described will you find what ought to be the object of living, you will understand that there is nothing in the spirit or philosophy of the gospel, which throws the soul back upon herself without giving her any object upon which her powers may be exerted. If we would drive the love of pleasure, the love of wealth, and the love of human applause, from the heart, we do not propose to leave that heart cold and desolate, with nothing to cheer or warm it, or to call forth its warmest, holiest, noblest sympathies. Far from it. But what I wish is, that you may so lay your plans, and so pursue the object which you place before the mind, that you may have continued contentment and peace while pursuing it, the consciousness of not living in vain, while your soul is expanding in all noble, heavenly qualities, and preparing for a destiny which is blessed with the pure light of immortality.

> "At tibi juventus, at tibi immortalitas:
> Tibi parta divium est vita. Periment mutuis
> Elementa sese et interibunt ictibus.
> Tu permanebis sola semper integra,
> Tu cuncta rerum quassa, cuncta naufraga,
> Jam portu in ipso tuta, contemplabere."

He who has the advantages and the responsibilities of the student, needs to act under a motive which is all-pervading, which guides at all times, in all circumstances, and which absorbs the whole soul. It should be such as will lead to a high, noble standard of action and feeling, and as will call forth the highest efforts of the whole man, body and soul, in enterprise which will do good to men. There is but one motive which has these qualities; and that is, to secure the approbation of God, and act on a scale which measures eternity, as well as time. Under the light of the Bible, with the wish to do what God would have you do, you will not fail of meeting and fulfilling the great object of life.

You will naturally ask here, is it *practicable* to have the high standard of acting for the glory of God constantly before you? I reply, unquestionably yes.

You know that we have the power of choosing any object on which to fix the heart, to look at the motives which should gather the affections around that object, and then we have the power of bending the whole energy of the soul to the attainment of that object. Demosthenes was an ambitious young man. He is thought to have had very little principle; but he fixed his eye on fame—on that species of popular applause which eloquence alone can command. The mark at which he gazed was high. From it he never turned his eye a single moment. Difficulties, which nature threw in his way, were overcome. He gave his heart, his soul, to seeking enown; he climbed up a hill where most would have slid down, and, with his own hand, he wrote in the book of immortality, at the top of the hill, his own deathless fame. His admirer, Cicero, tells us, that he *always* had a standard of greatness before him which was unmeasured—infinite. He determined to stand by the side of Demosthenes. He labored; he toiled; he achieved the victory, and stands, perhaps, as high up the hill of fame as his master. He made himself. We often speak of self-made men, of high renown and wonderful deeds. What made them great? What made Buonaparte the terror of the earth? He fixed his eye on the dominion of Europe at least, and towards that goal he ran like a strong man; and *to* it he would have attained, had there not been an Omnipotence in heaven which can make the strong man as tow. He made himself his own idol, and determined that the whole world should bow to it.

What made Paul the man that he was? It was his fixing his eye on one vast object, and never looking away. That object was, to bring the whole world to a knowledge of the gospel, to the obedience of the faith, and to lead them up the paths of life. No smaller object filled his vision; and with such a purpose filling his soul, he could trample on earth, and walk upon the thorns which persecution threw in his path, as if they were roses. What made David Brainerd? He forgot himself; he threw himself away;

he fixed his heart on bringing the wanderers of the desert to sing of redeeming mercy. For this he lived, toiled, wore out, and came to his rest in the grave, till the morning of the resurrection.

You know that this man has the power of fixing his heart on ambition, and dreaming over his schemes, till they swallow up every thing else;—that another can fix his heart on wealth; and another on the pleasures of sensual indulgences; and every man on the object which is most congenial to himself. Can you doubt that you have the power of making the glory of God the polar star of life?—of living for it and to it?—of rising high and strong in action?—high and bright in personal holiness, and having the image and superscription of God engraven on your heart?

Is it your *duty* to make the will of God your only standard of life?

Ask your reason. What says she? "Shall I give my heart to seeking wealth, and the treasures of earth?" No: it will take to itself wings and fly away. Death will shortly be here, and seize you with a grasp so firm, that you must let go of wealth. You sigh after gold deeply: you must shut your eyes, shortly, upon all that is called wealth. Remember that he who "maketh haste to be rich shall not be innocent." But your soul spreads in her desires; she thirsts; she rises: and do you suppose that any amount of wealth which you *can* obtain will satisfy her? Will the little time which it is yours, cheer the soul in her everlasting progress? No: the bag in which you drop your gains will have holes in it. Every river which flows over golden sands, like the river of Egypt, will turn to blood.

Ask reason, "Shall I give my heart to honors?—to seeking the notice of men?—to draw their attention by this or that effort?" How poor will be your reward for your pains! If you draw the eyes of man towards you, *he* will envy you. If you do not, *you* will be bitterly disappointed. There is no house on the shores of time, which the waves will not wash away; there is no path here which the foot of disappointment will not tread; there is no sanctuary here which sorrow will not invade. There is a home provided for the soul, but you can reach it only by living for God; to none others than those who thus live will its doors be opened.

Consult your conscience also. What does she say is the great end of life? Listen to her voice in the chambers of your own heart. She tells you that there is only one stream that is pure, and that stream flows from the throne of God; but one aim is noble and worthy of an immortal spirit, and that is to become the friend of God, so that the soul may wing her way over the grave without fear, without dismay, without condemnation. There is only one path passing over the earth which is safe, which is light, and which is honorable. It is that which Jesus Christ has marked out in his word, and which leads to glory. Let conscience speak, when you are tempted to waste a day, or an hour, or to commit any known sin, to neglect any known duty, and she will urge you, by all the high and holy motives of eternity, to live for God, to give your powers to him, to seek his honor in all that you do.

My young reader will now permit me to present what appear to me the motives which ought to bear upon the mind, to lead it thus to act—making the honor of God the great end of life.

We naturally love to have the soul filled. We gaze upon the everlasting brow of the mountain which rises beetling and threatening over our heads, and the feeling of admiration which fills the soul is delightful. We gaze upon the ocean rolling in its mighty waves, and listen to its hoarse voice responding to the spirit of the storm which hangs over it, and we feel an awe, and the emotion of sublimity rises in the soul. So it is with the desires. There is something inexpressibly delightful in having the mind filled with a great and a noble purpose—such a purpose as may lawfully absorb all the feelings of the heart, and kindle every desire of the soul. Who ever reared a dwelling perfect enough to meet the desires of the soul? Who ever had a sufficiency of wealth, or of honors, when these were the grand objects of pursuit? Who ever had the thirst quenched by drinking here? And who ever had an earthly object engrossing the heart, which did not leave room for restlessness, a desire of change, and a fretting and chafing in its pursuit? Not so when the glory of God fills the soul, and the eye is fixed on that as the great end of life. You may live near him, and draw continually nearer; and the soul does not feel the passion of envy, or jealousy, or disappointment, as she comes near the object of her desires. Having, increases the desire for more, and more is added; for sin has no connection with the gift. They who are near the throne are full of this one thought,—how can we do most to promote the glory of Him who is over all, God blessed forever? No contracted plans, no trifling thoughts, no low cares enter their bosoms; for they are already filled.

Who does not, more or less, feel the burden of sin? Make God the object of life, and you will not sin as you now do. The word of life is choked by cares; it is shut out by ambition; it is treated with scorn, when the soul presses on for present gratifications. The tempter never has so complete mastery over you, as when you fill the heart with this world, and live for its rewards. Not so when you live for your Maker. In vain he walked around the Redeemer, and heaped up his temptations; he found no place in him—not a spot where he could lodge a temptation. Do you never lament, at the close of the day, that you have fallen, here and there, during the day?—that your heart is frozen and fearful, when you attempt to pray?—that a dark cloud rolls in between you and the Sun of life? Fill the heart with good, and evil is shut out.

You need a principle which will lead you to be active for the welfare of men. Your reason and conscience may decide, that you ought to live for the good of your species; and, at times, you may rouse up; but the moving power is not uniform and steady You need a principle which will ever keep you alive to duty. You can act but a few days on earth. Between every rising and setting sun, multitudes drop into eternity. Your turn will come shortly. You will soon know whether you are forever to wear a crown, or be clothed with shame and everlasting contempt,—soon know how bright that crown is, or how deep that despair is. All the retributions of the eternal world will soon be rolled upon you, and you want a principle abiding within you, which will bear you on in duty, active, laborious, self-denying, widening your influence, and adding strength to your character and hopes through life; but this principle is to be obtained only by seeking His approbation from whom you receive every mercy that has ever visited your heart, every joy that has cheered you, and every hope for which the heart longs.

You love to see the results of your exertions in any cause; but you cannot, in all cases in which you plan, and fill up your plans. You may determine to be rich, and yet die a poor man. You may long for distinction, and yet never have it. You may sigh for pleasure, and yet every cup may be dashed, and every hope flee from you. All things around you may forsake you and elude your grasp. Not so if you live for God. Lay up wealth in heaven,—and you may increase it daily,—and it cannot fail you. Try to subdue that temper, so irritable, so unholy, and you will find that, if you do it for the purpose of honoring God, he will give you strength. Try to conquer that covetousness which is idolatry, and you can do it effectually and thoroughly by subduing the heart for the sake of living entirely to God. You offer a prayer for men;—it shall not be lost upon the wind. You send a copy of the Scriptures to the destitute;—it shall not be lost by the way-side. The messenger of mercy, whom you aid in sending abroad, will find the hungry, who will receive the bread of life. And when, at last, you come to be gathered to the home of prophets and apostles, and the spirits of just men made perfect, then will you still more clearly see the results of a life whose aim was to honor God. Then will the poor whom you fed, the sick whom you visited, the stranger whom you sheltered, the distressed whom you relieved, gather around you, and hail you a benefactor.

You ought to act upon principles which conscience

will, at all times and in all cases, approve. Do you know what it is to sit down to meditate, at the close of the day, and have something hang upon the soul like lead,—to have a cloud between you and the throne of prayer? Do you know what it is to lie down at night, and look back upon the day, and the days that are passing, and find no bright spot upon which the memory lingers with pleasure? Do you know what it is to lie on your pillow and feel the smitings of conscience, and have the heart ache, while the clock slowly measures off the hours of night? This is because conscience is at her post, calling the soul to account. She lashes, she heaves up the waves of guilt, till the soul feels like being buried under them. Do you not thus commune with your heart, at times? But if you will live for God—wholly for God—conscience will soothe you, comfort you, and bring hope to your soul, even in your darkest hour. No friend can be found to supply the place of a peaceful conscience. Men will give their property, their time, do penance, give their lives—any thing to appease conscience. Let them live for God and his service, and she will not chide; she will guide to the paths of peace and blessedness. The world will honor the man who lives for God. At times, men will shun the face of the pious, and profess to be disgusted with piety; but they will garnish the sepulchres of prophets, while the bones of the wicked lie forgotten.

The name of Howard will never perish; nor will the name of Martyn, or Mills, Brainerd, or Hannah More; while thousands of wicked men, with equal or more influence while living, die, and are forever gone from remembrance. But the approbation of men is of no consequence. You wish the approbation of Heaven. Though they are ten thousand times ten thousand, and their voices are without number, and though they enjoy the perfection of knowledge, the perfection of holiness, and the perfection of bliss, yet they are all witnesses—a great cloud—of your race. They bend over your pathway, as you run towards the New Jerusalem. Who would not be cheered, could he have the entire approbation of all his friends and acquaintances? But, though you cannot expect this, you can have what is far better. You can have the approbation of all the redeemed, of all the angels in heaven, and of the eternal God himself; and this, not for an hour, a day, or a week, for a fleeting year, but forever! The heavens shall depart as a scroll, and all things shall pass away, except the approbation of God. That shall never pass away. It would be worth your life to have his approbation a single hour when you come to die; but you will have him your Father, Friend, and Glory forever. Have you any doubt in your mind where wisdom would now lead you? "My first convictions on the subject of religion were confirmed from observing that really religious persons had some solid happiness among them, which I had felt that the vanities of the world could not give. I shall never forget standing by the bed of my sick mother.

"'Are you not afraid to die?'

"'No.'

"'No! Why does the uncertainty of another state give you no concern?'

"'Because God has said to me, *Fear not; when thou passest through the waters, I will be with thee; and through the rivers, they shall not overflow thee!*'

"The remembrance of this scene has oftentimes since drawn an ardent prayer from me, that I might die the death of the righteous."

It is a solemn season with a man who acts from conscience, when he comes to close his book, and bid his reader adieu. His motives may be good, yet it is human to err. He knows that he may have made impressions which may give a wrong bias to some, from which they will never recover. He may have wasted his strength, and his reader's time, upon some point of comparatively no importance, while that which was really of great importance may have been omitted. He may have disgusted where he hoped to instruct; he may have offended where he intended to impress. At any rate, he is about to send a book out into the world, which, whatever may be its fate, has given him the opportunity of doing good; and under that re sponsibility the writer must continue. If I mistake not, a sense of this responsibility is now felt by the author of these pages. I have addressed a class of my fellow-men who will yield to none in point of respectability, prospective influence, and importance. I have tried to throw before them such hints as my own wants and limited experience have suggested; and I am now about to take my leave of them till I meet them, face to face, at the last great day of assembling, where we shall all meet. I am speaking to you, reader, in your own behalf, and in behalf of a world which needs your influence, and your highest, holiest efforts. Others may talk of philanthropy and benevolence, but who give their hearts and their energies for the salvation of the world, except those whose minds have been enlightened, and whose hearts have been impressed by the truths of Christianity? Who built the first hospital known on earth? A Christian. Who conceived the idea of free schools for the whole community? A Christian. Who are the men who have pushed civilization among the barbarous, who have broken the fetters both from body and mind, and created civil liberty for man? Who ever made efforts, vigorous, systematic, untiring, to spread free inquiry, to instruct the ignorant, to invigorate the mind, and raise the intellectual and moral character of mankind? They are the enlightened men who act under the influence of the Bible The only effort which is now making, on the face of the whole earth, for the good of mankind, is making by the church of the living God. Upon this, and upon this alone, all our hopes for the salvation of the world from darkness, ignorance and sin, rest. To the youth of our nation—to those whose minds are now in a process of cultivation and discipline, we now look for the spirits who are soon to go abroad over the face of the earth, scattered, like the Levites, among all the tribes, for the good of all. Upon these young soldiers of the cross do we look, as God's appointed instruments for doing a great and a glorious work. If the mind of man shall ever be raised from its brutishness and debasement—if knowledge, human and divine, are to go abroad—if liberty is to wave her banner where tyranny now sits—if the female is ever to occupy the station for which she was created—*if* domestic happiness is to be known and enjoyed through the world,—the youth in our schools, who have been baptized by the Holy Ghost, have a great work to do.

Never did young men approach the stage of action under circumstances more intensely interesting—circumstances which demand a regenerated, purified heart, a balanced, disciplined mind, a burning zeal and eloquence, and a love for doing good which many waters cannot quench, nor floods drown. You tread upon ground bought with hardships, tears and prayers; enfranchised by toil and blood; amid institutions founded by the most devoted piety and anxious solicitude of our fathers. It is the land of the Pilgrims,—where the bones of more worthies sleep than were ever before buried in the same length of time. You enter among men in a country in its infancy. The nation is young —has all the joyous elasticity of the young giant—full of enterprise, growing in wealth, in population—increasing in daring experiments and hazardous enterprise. An experiment in regard to civil freedom, and the destiny of a nation let loose, with nothing to check or hold it but the intelligence and the religion which are diffused,—a nation let loose, and many centuries in advance of all other nations in the science of government, at least, and yet having the offals of all other Christian nations constantly floating to it,—is now making. You are to live and act among those who will give permanency to our institutions, or who will begin the work of undermining. You are coming forward at a time when mind seems to be exhausting itself, and Genius to be leaving poetry, that he may aid in subduing matter, so that a score of miles may be reduced to nothing, and time and space so annihilated, that a journey through the length and breadth of a continent is only a delightful excursion. Nature seems to bend to the torturing; and winds and tides, mountains and valleys, make no pretensions to being considered obstacles in the way of men. You are to act in a day when public opinion is omnipotent. A standing army retires before it, and marshals only in the shade of the thrones of tyrants. Every thing is controlled by it, and yet every one may do his part to mould that public opinion according to his pleasure. Every man has the best possible opportunity to do good or hurt. You may pen a sentence or a paragraph, and it will travel through the nation, into tens of thousands of families, and, in a few weeks, pass through Europe, and influence millions of immortal beings. You are coming forward at a time, and in a nation, where a good education is a sure passport to respectability, to influence, to office. No difficulties stand in your way. The teeming, busy millions of this land invite you to mingle your destiny with theirs, and aid them to rise in virtue, in knowledge, and in religion, as they roll on towards the judgment-day. You have friends to cheer you on in every worthy enterprise, who will uphold your hands when they fall, encourage you when the spirits fail, share your burdens, and rejoice in your success. You come forward with the history, the experience of all other nations before you; and at your feet lie pictures of men whose example it will be honor, and glory, and immortality to follow, as well as of men whose example is death. You have the Bible, too,—that mightiest of all weapons,—under whose broad and powerful aid, individual and national character soon ripens into greatness, and one which is, of all others, the grand instrument of blessing the world. Tens of thousands, breathing the spirit of that book, are already in the field at work, trying to bless and save the earth. Some fall—strong ones, too—"too much for piety to spare;" but the plan is the plan of God, and the removal of this or that agent does not a moment retard his great plans. Under the full, the pure, the purifying light of the gospel, you are called to live and act. If you live for God, fulfil the high destiny which is before you, you have thousands all around you to cheer you onward, to strike hands with you, and go forward as agents of a benevolence whose aim is, to bring many sons and daughters to glory. Above you are the pious dead, watching around your steps, and ready to minister to your wants. And there, high above all principalities and powers, sits the everlasting Redeemer, holding a crown which shall shortly be yours, if you are faithful to him. He will be near you. You shall never faint. Every sin you conquer shall give you new strength; every temptation you resist will make you more and more free in the Lord; every tear you shed will be noticed by your great High Priest; every sigh you raise will reach his ear. Up, then, my dear young friends! up, and gird on the armor of God. Enlist under the banner of Jesus Christ, and let your powers, your faculties, your energies, your heart, all, all be his. Bright and glorious is the day before you; white and full are the fields that wait for you; girded and strong are the companions who will go with you; beautiful upon the mountains shall be your feet, wherever they carry tidings of mercy. The state of the world is such, and so much depends on action, that every thing seems to say loudly, to every man, "Do something"—"do it!"—"do it!" Keep your heart with all diligence; break away from every sin; repent of every sin; live unto God; and your reward shall be what "ear hath not heard, eye hath not seen, neither hath it entered into the heart of man to conceive."

NOTES.

NOTE A.

JAMES FERGUSON, one of the most remarkable of self-educated men, was born in the year 1716, in the village of Keith, in Scotland. It was the practice of his father, who was a day-laborer, to teach his children himself to read and write, as they successively reached what he deemed the proper age; but James was too impatient to wait till his turn came. While his father was teaching one of his elder brothers, James was secretly occupied in listening to what was going on; and as soon as he was left alone used to get hold of the book and work hard in endeavoring to master the lesson which he had just heard. In this way, with the assistance of an old woman, he actually learned to read tolerably well before his father had any suspicion that he knew his letters. Being feeble in health, he spent some of his early years as a keeper of sheep in the service of a farmer in his native place, and while his flock were feeding around him he used to busy himself in making models of mills, spinning-wheels, &c., and in studying the stars at night. After the labors of the day he used to go at night into the fields with a blanket and a lighted candle. "I used," says he, "a thread with small beads upon it, at arms' length between my eye and the stars, sliding the beads upon it till it hid such and such stars from my eye, in order to take their apparent distances from one another, and then, laying down the thread on a paper, I marked the stars thereon by the beads." Being compelled to work for his daily subsistence, he was sometimes reduced almost to destitution. At one time he relates that a little oatmeal and water was all that was allowed him. At another, being out of service, and in a weak state from an injury received in his arm, he could not be idle, but, as he says, "In order to amuse myself in this low state, I made a wooden clock, and it kept time pretty well." The bell on which the hammer struck the hours was the neck of a broken bottle. He had accidentally seen a watch and a clock, and immediately made one of each in wood. In 1744 he came to London, and, in consequence of his astronomical rotula to show the new moon and eclipses, he was introduced to the learned and ingenious, and made fellow of the Royal Society. He was a man of inoffensive manners, mild and benevolent in his character

George III., at his accession, granted him a pension of fifty pounds a year, and occasionally took great delight in his conversation. He died in 1776. He wrote Select Mechanical Exercises, 1773; Introduction to Electricity, 1770—to Astronomy, 1772; Treatise on Perspective, 1775, and Astronomy Explained on Newton's principles, edited for the fourth time, 1770; Lectures on Mechanics, Hydrostatics, Hydraulics, Pneumatics, edited the fifth time, 1776, &c.

Note B.

Christopher Clavius, a Jesuit and mathematician, born at Bamberg, Germany, 1537. He was considered the Euclid of his age, and was employed by Gregory XIII. in the reformation of the calendar, which he ably defended against Joseph Scaliger. His works were printed in 5 vols. folio He died at Rome, 1612.

Note C.

Edmund Waller, an English poet, born March 3d, 1625, at Coleshill, in Herts, near Amersham. He was educated at Eton and King's College, Cambridge, and was chosen, when scarce seventeen, member for Amersham in the last Parliament of James I. In his parliamentary conduct he warmly opposed the measures of the court, and in the impeachment of Judge Crawley he spoke with such eloquence that twenty thousand copies of his speech were sold in one day. He was, in 1642, one of the commissioners who proposed conditions of peace from the Parliament to the king at Oxford; but, in the following year, he, with several other members of Parliament, was condemned to death on an accusation of a conspiracy to reduce the city of London and the Tower to the service of the monarch. He purchased his liberty, after a year's confinement, by a fine of ten thousand pounds. He retired for a while to France; but such was his address that he was the favorite of Cromwell, Charles II., and James II. He died at Beaconsfield, Oct. 1, 1687, and was buried there. As he was the first poet who showed us that our language had beauty and numbers, he is called the parent of English verse.

Note D.

Patrick Henry, Governor of Virginia, was born May 29th, 1736, in Hanover county of that State. His education was obtained at a common school. After spending some time as a farmer and merchant, he studied law and soon rose to eminence, rather by his resistless eloquence than the extent of his legal knowledge. In 1765 he was elected a member of the House of Burgesses, and, by some resolutions he introduced in reference to the Stamp Act, obtained the honor of being the first in commencing the opposition to the measures of the British government which terminated in the revolution. In 1774 he was elected a member of the Continental Congress, and here distinguished himself by his eloquence and zeal in the cause of liberty. On the retreat of Lord Dunmore, in 1776, he was chosen the first republican Governor of Virginia, and was afterwards repeatedly reëlected to the office. In 1788 he was chosen a member of the Convention of Virginia, appointed to consider the Constitution of the United States, and exerted himself strenuously to prevent its being accepted. In 1795 he was nominated, by Washington, Secretary of State, and by Adams, in 1799, Envoy to France; but he declined the appointments. He died June 6, 1799, at the age of 63, highly respected by his fellow-countrymen. The Virginians boast of him as an orator of nature. His appearance and manners were those of a plain farmer. In this character he always entered on the exordium of an oration. His unassuming looks and expressions of humility induced his hearers to listen to him as they would to an honest neighbor. After he had thus disarmed prejudice, the inspiration of his eloquence, when little expected, would pour on his audience with the authority of a prophet.

In private life he was as amiable and virtuous as he was conspicuous in his public career. He was temperate and never known to utter a profane expression. There is, however, some doubt as to the purity of his religious principles. He appeared too fond of his money, and remarked to a friend, just before his death, who found him reading the Bible, "Here is a book worth more than all the other books which ever were printed, yet it is my misfortune never to have, till lately, found time to read it with proper attention and feeling."

Note E.

Alexander Hamilton, first Secretary of the Treasury of the United States, was born in the island of St. Croix, in 1757. At the age of sixteen he accompanied his mother, who was an American, to New York, and entered King's College. While a student he gave proofs of his extraordinary talents, by the publication of several papers, vindicating the rights of the colonies, which exhibited such strength and sagacity that they were ascribed to the pen of Mr. Jay. He entered the American army, at the age of eighteen, as an officer of artillery, and soon attracted the notice of Washington, who, in 1777, selected him as an aid, with the rank of Lieutenant-Colonel. In the campaign of 1781 he commanded a battalion, and at the taking of Yorktown led the American detachment which stormed and took the British works. After the capture of Cornwallis, he studied the profession of law, and soon rose to distinction in New York. In 1787 he was appointed a member from New York of the federal Congress which formed the Constitution of the United States, and in 1789, when the government was organized, was placed by Washington at the head of the Treasury where he rendered most important services to his country. He had charge of the troops employed in 1794 to suppress the insurrection in Pennsylvania. After being at the head of the Treasury six years, he retired from public life to make a more ample provision for his family by his profession. In 1798, when the provisional army was raised, at the instance of Washington he was appointed second in command. He was challenged by Col. Burr, Vice-President of the United States, and, though in principle opposed to duelling, he accepted the challenge, and, on the eleventh of July, 1804, he fell on the same spot where, a few years before, his son had fallen a victim to the same miscalled principle of "honor," and in a similar violation of the law of God. On the following day he expired, universally lamented, second to none of his survivors in energy of understanding, extent of legal and political knowledge, lofty eloquence, integrity and promise of usefulness to his country.

NOTE F.

Roger Sherman, Senator of the United States, was born at Newton, Mass., April 19, 1724, and rose by the force of his superior genius to his distinction as a lawyer and statesman, without the advantage of a college education. In 1754 he began the practice of law in New Milford, Ct. In 1761 he removed to New Haven, and four years after became Judge of the County Court. In 1776 he was advanced to a seat on the bench of the Superior Court. In 1774 he was elected a member of Congress. He was one of the committee appointed to draw up the Declaration of Independence. He was a conspicuous member of the Convention which formed the Constitution of the United States. In 1791 he was chosen a Senator, which office he filled till his death, in 1793, in his seventy-third year. He received an honorary diploma of Master of Arts from Yale College, and was for many years treasurer of that institution. He was a profound and sagacious statesman, an able and an upright judge, an exemplary Christian. President Jefferson remarked of him, "He never said a foolish thing in his life."

NOTE G.

Oliver Ellsworth, LL. D., Chief Justice of the United States, was born at Windsor, Ct., April 29, 1745, and graduated at New Jersey College in 1766. In 1777 he was elected a delegate to the Continental Congress, and in 1784 appointed a Judge of the Superior Court of Connecticut. In 1787 he was chosen a member of the Convention which framed the federal Constitution. On the organization of the government, in 1789, he was elected a member of the Senate, and continued in this office till he was appointed, in 1796, Chief Justice of the Supreme Court, as the successor of Mr. Jay. In 1799 he was appointed Envoy Extraordinary to

France. His health failing, he resigned this office towards the close of the year 1800. He died in the year 1807. He was unassuming, economical in his own dress, equipage and mode of living, but liberal in promoting useful and benevolent designs. Meetings for social worship were countenanced by his presence, and in the cause of missions he was greatly interested. He made a profession of religion in his youth, and in all his intercourse with the polite and learned world he was not ashamed of the gospel of Christ.

Note H.

Hugo Grotius, or de Groot, was the son of John De Groot, a respectable burgomaster of Delft. He was born April 10, 1583 and very early showed a strong mind and retentive memory. In 1598 he accompanied an embassy to France, and was presented by Henry IV. with his picture and a gold chain. The University of Paris granted him a doctor's degree before his return to Delft, where he pleaded his first cause, and, though scarce seventeen, gained great applause. Though he wrote poetry, which was translated into Greek and French, he published in the same year the Phenomena of Aratus. In 1603 he was appointed Historiographer to the States of Holland. Next he was appointed Advocate-general for the fisc of Holland and Zealand, with an increased salary. For his treatise "De Antiquitate Republicæ Batavæ," to assert the independence of his country from the Roman yoke and the modern usurpations of Spain, he received the unanimous thanks of the States. In 1613 he was elected pensionary of Rotterdam. In consequence of the condemnation of the five articles of the Arminians by the Synod of Dort, Nov. 15, 1618, Grotius, who had been an able defender of this sect, was condemned to perpetual imprisonment. After a captivity of nearly two years, on pretence of removing books which she declared proved injurious to her husband's health, his wife was permitted to send away a small chest of drawers, of the length of three feet and a half, in which he was confined. Thus carried by two soldiers from the fortress of Louvestein, the chest was removed to Gorcum on horseback, and at the house of a friend the illustrious prisoner was liberated and immediately escaped, disguised as a mason with a rule and trowel, to Antwerp. From this city he wrote an apology, declaring his conduct was actuated by the love of his country; but it was received with such indignation that all persons were forbidden to read it upon pain of death, and the author was to be seized wherever found. Near Boulogne, in 1623, he began his great work on "The Rights of Peace and War." In 1631 he made a short visit to Holland, but was threatened with persecution, and retired from his ungrateful country. He went to Sweden, was appointed Counsellor to the Queen, and for eight years, till 1644, he was Swedish Ambassador to France. Weary of political cabals, he embarked for Lubec, Aug. 12, 1645. The vessel was driven by a storm into Pomerania, and after a journey of sixty miles to Rostock, exposed to the rain, he died of a fever, Aug. 28, 1645. He was buried at Delft. His monument bears this inscription, written by himself: —"Grotius hic Hugo est Batavûm captivus et exul, Legatus regni, Suecia magna, tui."

Note I.

George Louis le Clerc Count de Buffon was born at Montbard, in Burgundy, Sept. 7, 1707. His father intended him for the profession of law, but, after travelling in Italy and England, he returned home and began his career of fame by devoting fourteen hours every day to his studies in Natural History. At the death of his mother, he inherited a fortune of about twelve thousand pounds per annum; but he still continued his researches. He translated Newton's Fluxions and Hale's Statics, but his great and immortal work is his "Histoire Naturelle," 35 vols. 4to, or 62, 12mo, 1749—1765. In his private character he was a libertine, occasionally vain and puerile. "The works of men of genius," he would exclaim, "are few, only those of Newton, Montesquieu, Leibnitz, and my own." He died April 16, 1788. His funeral was attended by the learned and the great; and twenty thousand spectators are said to have assembled to see his remains borne to the vault of Montbard, where he wished to be placed near his wife.

Note J.

Daniel Wyttenbach, a learned philologist, of the Dutch school, was born in Berne, 1746. His father being appointed professor at Marburg, he was admitted a student to that university. He afterwards went to Gottingen to study under Heyne, with whose assistance he published, 1769, "Epistola Critica, ad Ruhnkerium." This learned work procured him the friendship of Ruhnker, whom he visited at Leyden, and who obtained for him the professorship of philosophy and literature in the College of the Remonstrants, in Amsterdam. He subsequently devoted his talents to the illustration of the works of *Plutarch*, and, in 1772, printed at Leyden the treatise of that writer, "De Sera Numinis Vindicata," with a learned commentary. In 1779, the magistrates of Amsterdam created a philosophical professorship at an institution called the "Illustrious Athenæum," to which Wyttenbach was presented, and in 1799 he was appointed Professor of Rhetoric at Leyden, where he died in 1819. The result of his researches relative to Plutarch, appeared in his excellent critical edition of the moral works of Plutarch, published at Oxford, 1795, 1810, 7 vols. 4to.

Prof. Wyttenbach was the author of "Præcepta Philosophiæ logicæ." Amsterdam, 4to, 1781. "Selecta Principum Græciæ

Historicorum," with notes, 1793, 1807. "Vita Ruhnkerii," 1800, 8vo, and some other works. His "Opuscula" appeared at Leyden in 1821, and there is a Life of him by Mahne. Ghent, 1823. — *Convers. Lexicon.*

NOTE K.

Alexander M. Fisher, Professor of Mathematics and Natural Philosophy in Yale College, was born in Franklin, Mass., in 1794. He was graduated at Yale in the year 1813, and in 1815 was appointed Tutor. In 1817 he was promoted to the professorship of Mathematics and Natural Philosophy. He early discovered very uncommon talents for the acquisition and communication of knowledge, and excited the highest expectations of his usefulness and distinction. His power of attention, quickness and clearness of apprehension, rapid discernment of the relations of objects, accuracy of judgment, and independence, caution and originality in investigation, are rarely equalled, and constituted a genius of the highest order for the department of science to which he devoted his attention; and his attainments were as extraordinary as his endowments. After having once delivered his course of lectures, he undertook a voyage to Europe, to improve himself in his professional studies, and perished in the wreck of the packet Albion, on the coast of Ireland, on the 22d of April, 1822, at the age of twenty-eight. He possessed great amiableness, modesty and delicacy of taste, and his conduct was marked by an uncommon regard to religious obligation. Several of his scientific papers may be seen in Silliman's Journal of Science and the Arts, among which is a very remarkable one on Music.

NOTE L.

Edward Daniel Clarke, LL.D., Professor of Mineralogy in the University of Cambridge, England, was educated in Jesus College, Cambridge, where he took the degree of Master of Arts in 1794. In 1799 he commenced a tour through the north of Europe, a part of Tartary, Circassia, Asia Minor, Greece and Turkey, of which he afterwards published a very copious narrative. He died April 9, 1822.

NOTE M.

Richard Baxter, a non-conformist, was born at Rowton, Shropshire, Nov. 12, 1615. He compensated for the deficiencies of a neglected education by unusual application, and, when only twenty-three years of age, was appointed head master of the endowed school at Dudley. In 1638 he was ordained by the Bishop of Winchester, and two years afterwards settled as minister at Kidderminster. On the breaking out of the war between Charles I and the Parliament, he accepted the office of Chaplain in the parliamentary army; but he opposed the usurpation of Cromwell, and had the boldness to defend monarchy in his presence. At the Restoration he was appointed one of the chaplains to Charles II., and was offered the bishopric of Hereford, which he declined. In 1685 he was tried before the infamous Lord Jefferies, for some passages in his paraphrase of the New Testament, and imprisoned for a short time. During this period, and while suffering from illness at the house of a friend, he was led to meditate on the "everlasting rest."

"It was a very narrow stream
Between his heavenly rest and him,
For he had lived beside its brim."

Within six months he wrote the "Saints' Everlasting Rest," with no books but a Bible and Concordance. Though he was a great sufferer he continued writing and preaching till his death, 1691. His writings amount in all to forty-five treatises, including his "Call to the Unconverted," in which, as well as in his "Saints' Rest," being dead, he will speak as long as the world endures.

Note N.

Dr. Herman Boerhaave was born Dec. 31, 1668, at Veerhout, a village two miles from Leyden. It is said that he was intended for the ministry, but that in his twelfth year, when suffering excruciating pains from an ulcer in his left side, which baffled the skill of his surgeon, he cured himself by a fomentation of salt and wine. This decided his profession. As his father was a clergyman, and died when Dr. Boerhaave was in his sixteenth year, leaving him the oldest of nine children, his studies were continued under many discouragements. His education was obtained at the University of Leyden, in which he was after Professor of Botany, Chemistry and Medicine. He was an honorary member of the Royal Society of London, and the Academy of Sciences at Paris. Several European princes committed pupils to his care, and when Peter the Great went to Holland, in 1715, to perfect himself in maritime affairs, he attended the lectures of Boerhaave. So well was he known in Asia and Europe, that a letter to him from a mandarin in China, inscribed "To the illustrious Boerhaave, Physician in Europe," came to him without mistake or delay. His property, at the time of his death, amounted to nearly a million of dollars, yet he was benevolent to poor patients. "These," he would say, "are the best patients, for God is their paymaster."

The charity and benevolence so conspicuous in his whole life were derived from a supreme regard to religion. He used to say that "it was his morning hour of meditation and of prayer that gave him spirit and vigor in the business of the day." He died on the 25th of Sept., 1738, in the seventieth year of his age, much honored, beloved and lamented. His funeral oration was spoken in Latin, in the University at Leyden, before a very numerous audience; and his works were afterwards published in five large quarto volumes. The city of Leyden erected a monument to his memory.

NOTE O.

Sir William Jones was born in London, 1748. He has given to the world an example of wonderful attainments, while engaged in the duties of a most laborious profession. In conformity to his rule of never neglecting an opportunity of improvement, while making surprising exertions in the study of the classic and oriental languages at Oxford, he took advantage of the vacations to learn riding and fencing, and to acquire a knowledge of the Italian, French, Spanish and Portuguese languages; thus, to use his own expression, "with the fortune of a peasant, giving himself the education of a prince." Being appointed to a judgeship in India, immediately on his arrival he exerted himself to form a society in Calcutta on the model of the Royal Society of London, and officiated as its president as long as he lived. Almost his only time for study was during the vacation of the law courts. He says, "In the morning, after writing one letter, he read ten chapters of the Bible, and then studied Sanscrit Grammar and Hindoo Law." His afternoons he devoted to the geography of India and Roman History, closing the day with a few games of chess or a little Italian. His hour of rising was between three and four. Writing from Cristhma, his vacation residence in 1787, he says, "Though these three months are called a vacation, yet I have no vacant hours."

NOTE P.

Bishop Launcelot Andrews was born at London in 1555. While a student at the University at Cambridge he received a scholarship, and gained great reputation for his eloquence as a lecturer in theology. After the accession of James I., who greatly admired his pulpit eloquence and respected his piety, his promotion was rapid and wonderful. He was appointed Lord Almoner, Privy Councillor of England and Scotland; Dean of the Chapel Royal, Bishop of Chichester, Ely, and finally of Winchester. He was distinguished for great learning, industry and humility. Though bountiful and even elegant in his hospitality, he "rejoiced to release the prisoner in his cell, and to send clothing, food or medicine to the sufferer, preferring to do it so secretly that they might not discover whence the benefaction came." To Mr. Mulcaster, the instructor of his boyhood, he continued through life to manifest the most respectful regard, and caused his portrait to be placed over the door of his study. A teacher of his earlier childhood having died, he sought out his son and bestowed upon him a valuable rectory. He delighted to search the universities for young men of promise and piety, that he might promote them. He possessed a knowledge of fifteen languages, and in the conference at Hampton Court, his name stands first of those to whom the new translation of the Scriptures was committed. The portion executed by him was a share of the Pentateuch and the books from Joshua to the first of Chronicles. His "*Private Devotions, and Manual for the Sick*," have passed through more numerous editions than any of his published writings. They were originally composed in Greek, he having a peculiar fondness for that language. This manuscript work which was not translated until after his death, he often used in his closet devotions. During his last illness it was almost constantly in his hands. "It was found worn thin by his fingers, and wet with his tears." He left in his will a bequest of several thousand pounds, the interest of which was to be divided, four times in a year, among widows, orphans, prisoners and "aged poor men, especially seafaring men." His filial affection suggested the last, for his father was a mariner. At the close of life his lips moved in prayer even while he seemed to slumber, till at last the uplifting of his eyes alone told the prayer of his heart. He died at the age of seventy-one, Sept. 27, 1626. — ***Mrs. Sigourney's Examples of Life and Death.***

CPSIA information can be obtained
at www.ICGtesting.com
Printed in the USA
LVHW101059140223
739388LV00003B/195

9 783382 105914